An Invitation from a Crab

panpanya

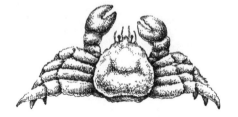

DENPA

TABLE OF CONTENTS

An Invitation from a Crab

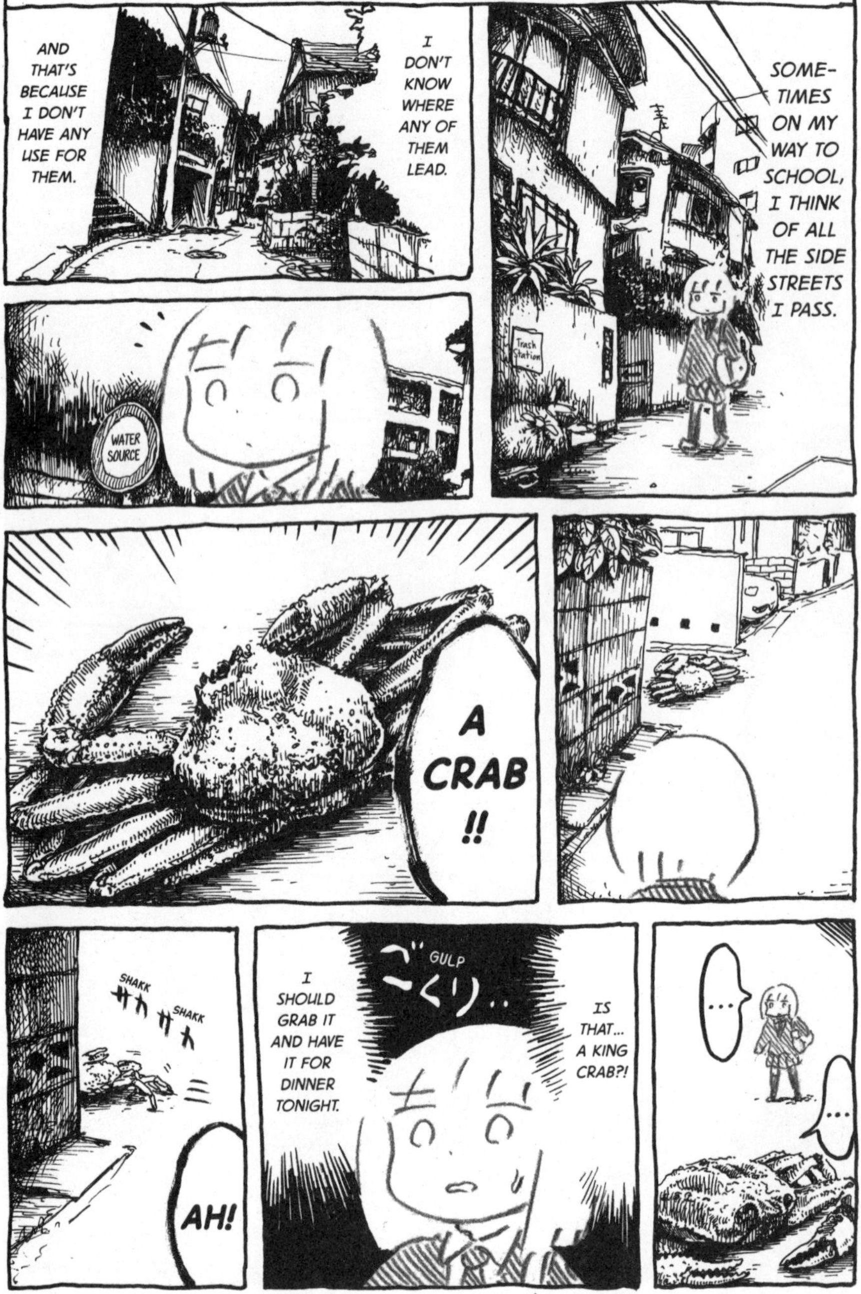
SOMETIMES ON MY WAY TO SCHOOL, I THINK OF ALL THE SIDE STREETS I PASS.
Trash Station
I DON'T KNOW WHERE ANY OF THEM LEAD.
AND THAT'S BECAUSE I DON'T HAVE ANY USE FOR THEM.
WATER SOURCE
A CRAB !!
...
...
IS THAT... A KING CRAB?!
GULP
ごくり..
I SHOULD GRAB IT AND HAVE IT FOR DINNER TONIGHT.
SHAKK
サカ
SHAKK
サカ
AH!

Note: It's a snow crab.

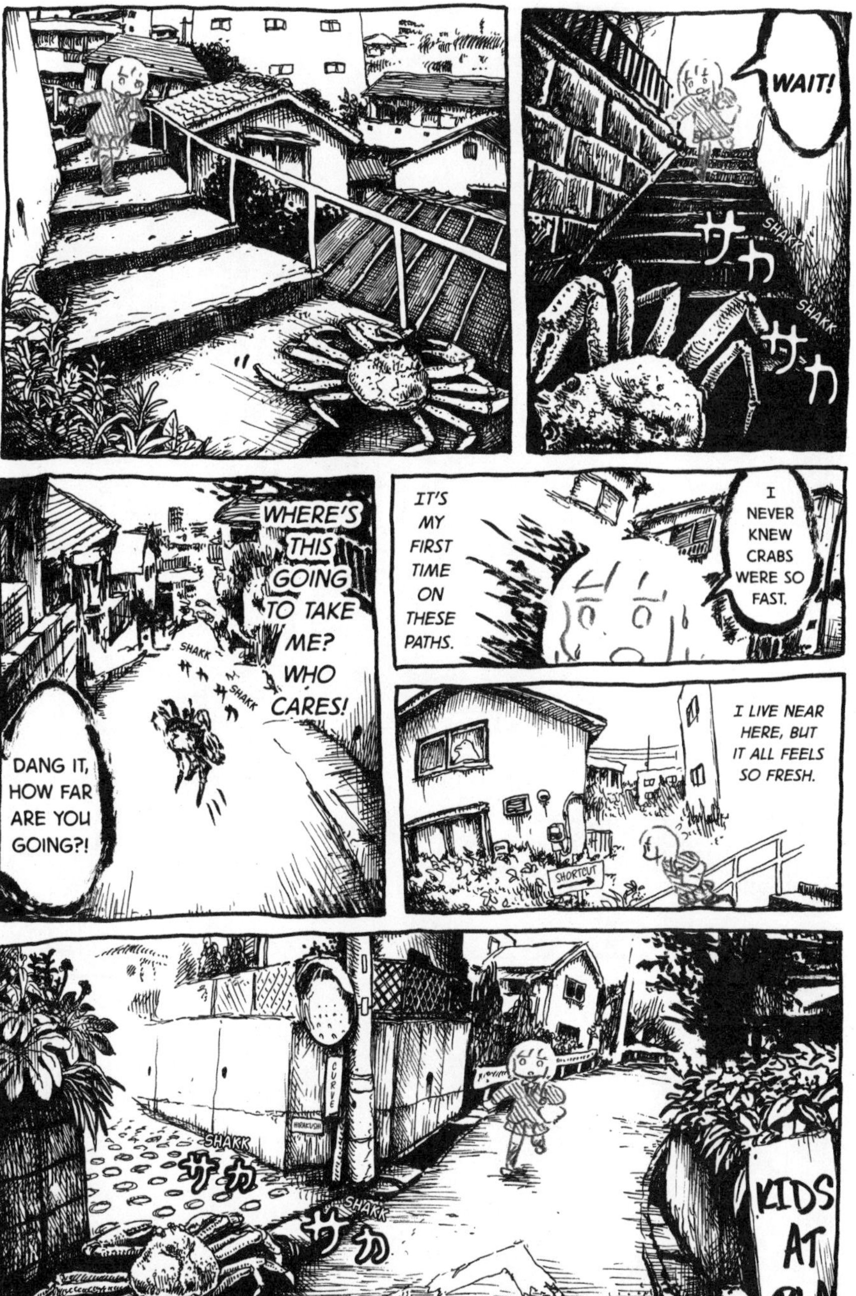
WAIT!
SHAKK
サカ
SHAKK
サカ
I NEVER KNEW CRABS WERE SO FAST.
IT'S MY FIRST TIME ON THESE PATHS.
I LIVE NEAR HERE, BUT IT ALL FEELS SO FRESH.
SHORTCUT
WHERE'S THIS GOING TO TAKE ME? WHO CARES!
SHAKK
サカ
SHAKK
サカ
DANG IT, HOW FAR ARE YOU GOING?!
KIDS AT PLA
CURVE
SHAKK
サカ
SHAKK
サカ

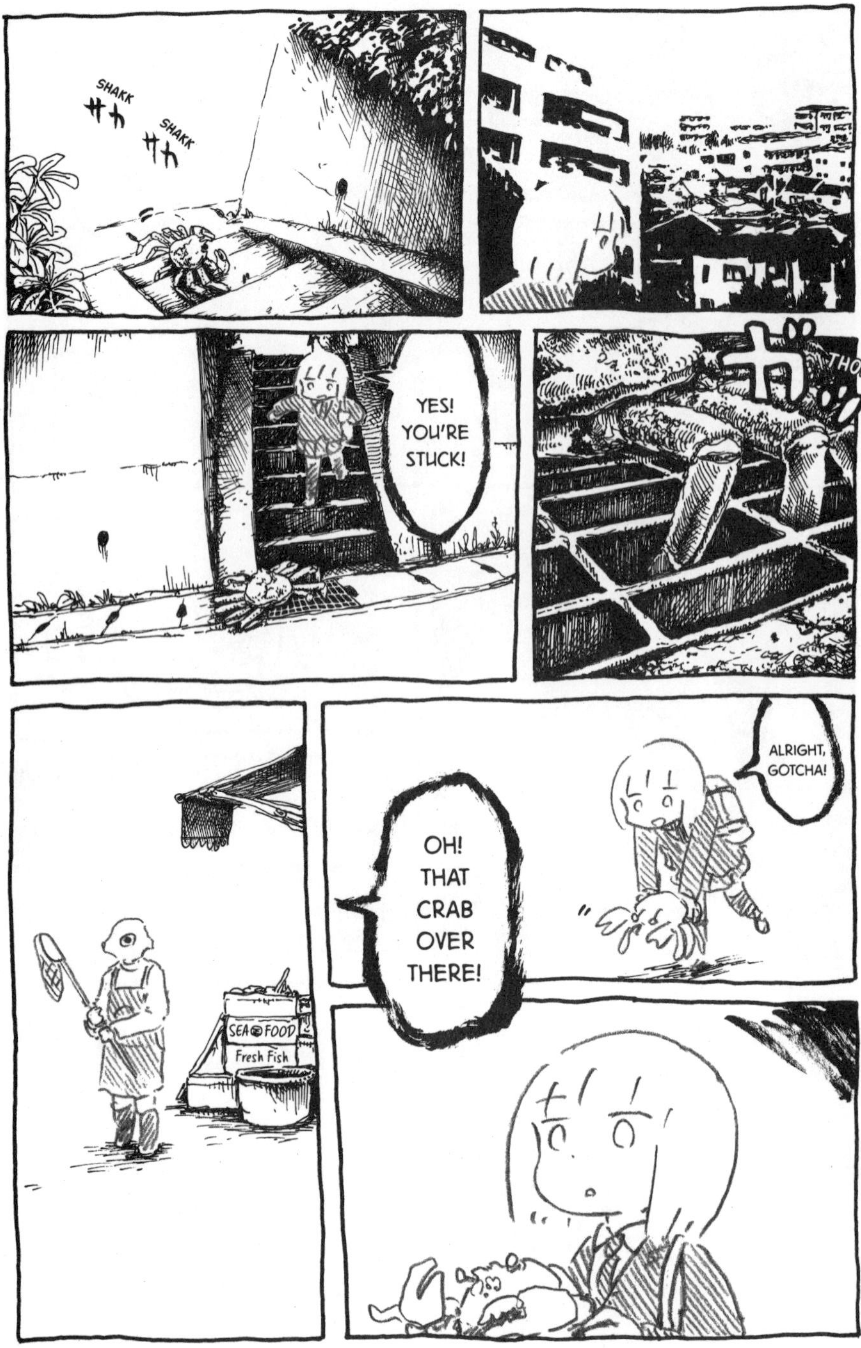
SHAKK
SHAKK
THOK
YES! YOU'RE STUCK!
ALRIGHT, GOTCHA!
OH! THAT CRAB OVER THERE!
SEA FOOD
Fresh Fish

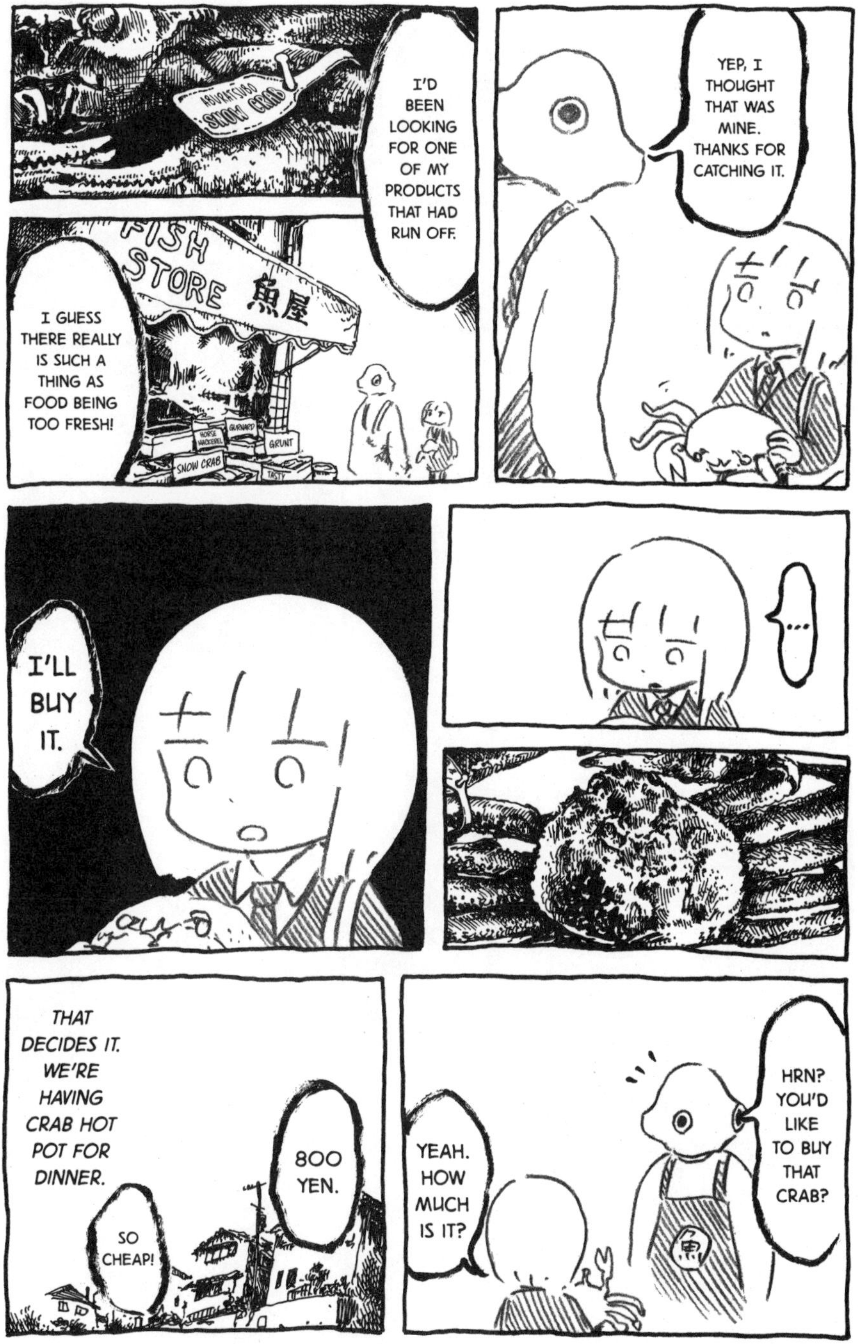
YEP, I THOUGHT THAT WAS MINE. THANKS FOR CATCHING IT.
ABURATSUBO
SNOW CRAB
I'D BEEN LOOKING FOR ONE OF MY PRODUCTS THAT HAD RUN OFF.
FISH STORE 魚屋
HORSE MACKEREL
GURNARD
GRUNT
SNOW CRAB
TASTY
I GUESS THERE REALLY IS SUCH A THING AS FOOD BEING TOO FRESH!
...
I'LL BUY IT.
HRN? YOU'D LIKE TO BUY THAT CRAB?
YEAH. HOW MUCH IS IT?
800 YEN.
SO CHEAP!
THAT DECIDES IT. WE'RE HAVING CRAB HOT POT FOR DINNER.

Feelings in the Air

I was watching something, I think it might have been an old news broadcast. An announcer was explaining what was going on as black-and-white images were shown on the screen. I thought about how the announcer's pronunciation sounded old-timey, but then I began to wonder where that old-timeyness came from.

When I watch the news now, the announcers speak in a flowing cadence that is crisp and clear. But when I listen to the way that newscasters in the black-and-white days spoke, they sound angular and stilted, with monotone, robotic voices that seem as though they're trying not to put too much emotion in their words. It's like they're speaking in a uniquely announcer-like way.

Newscasters always speak in a way that makes it easy for people to understand them. So, could that mean different eras have different ways of speaking that are better understood?

When I think of it that way, I begin to consider the role that technological advances play here. The quality of old recording equipment and home television audio was worse back then, so maybe they spoke in an excessively clear way so that they were even easier to understand. Everyone knows that sound quality will be good now, so there's no need to compensate for that by yourself any longer. That could be why they started to speak in a flowing way that's easier to naturally listen to.

In that case, maybe there was a transition period as broadcasting evolved where there were both distinctive announcers with laid-back, flowing speech, as well as slightly harsh announcers that used this old-timey way of talking. Or maybe there's something like a newscaster training school where people get taught the ways of speaking that correspond to whatever age they are in.

The overall feeling in the air during any era is created by the nature of its technology and its media. While we don't know what that feeling is while we're inside of it, we can find out the nature of the air we were once surrounded by after there are innovations in technology and media. We become capable of thinking that they're old-timey.

In some ways, the air we live in acts as a benchmark. We use the current moment as a standard to look at the air that once surrounded us. What were those old standards like?

August 8, 2013

Incomprehensible Memories

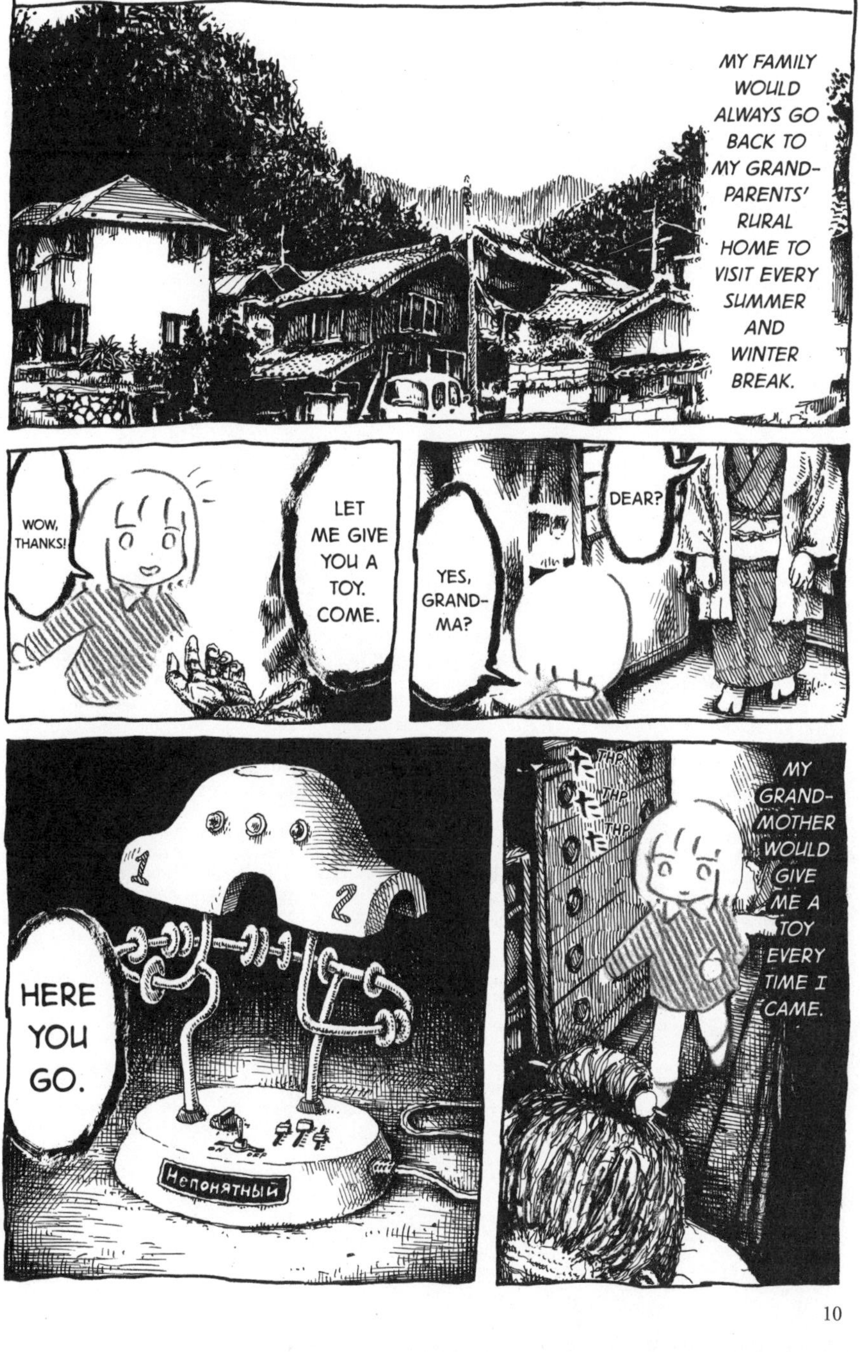

MY FAMILY WOULD ALWAYS GO BACK TO MY GRAND-PARENTS' RURAL HOME TO VISIT EVERY SUMMER AND WINTER BREAK.
DEAR?
YES, GRAND-MA?
LET ME GIVE YOU A TOY. COME.
WOW, THANKS!
たたた
THP THP THP
MY GRAND-MOTHER WOULD GIVE ME A TOY EVERY TIME I CAME.
HERE YOU GO.
1
2
Непонятный

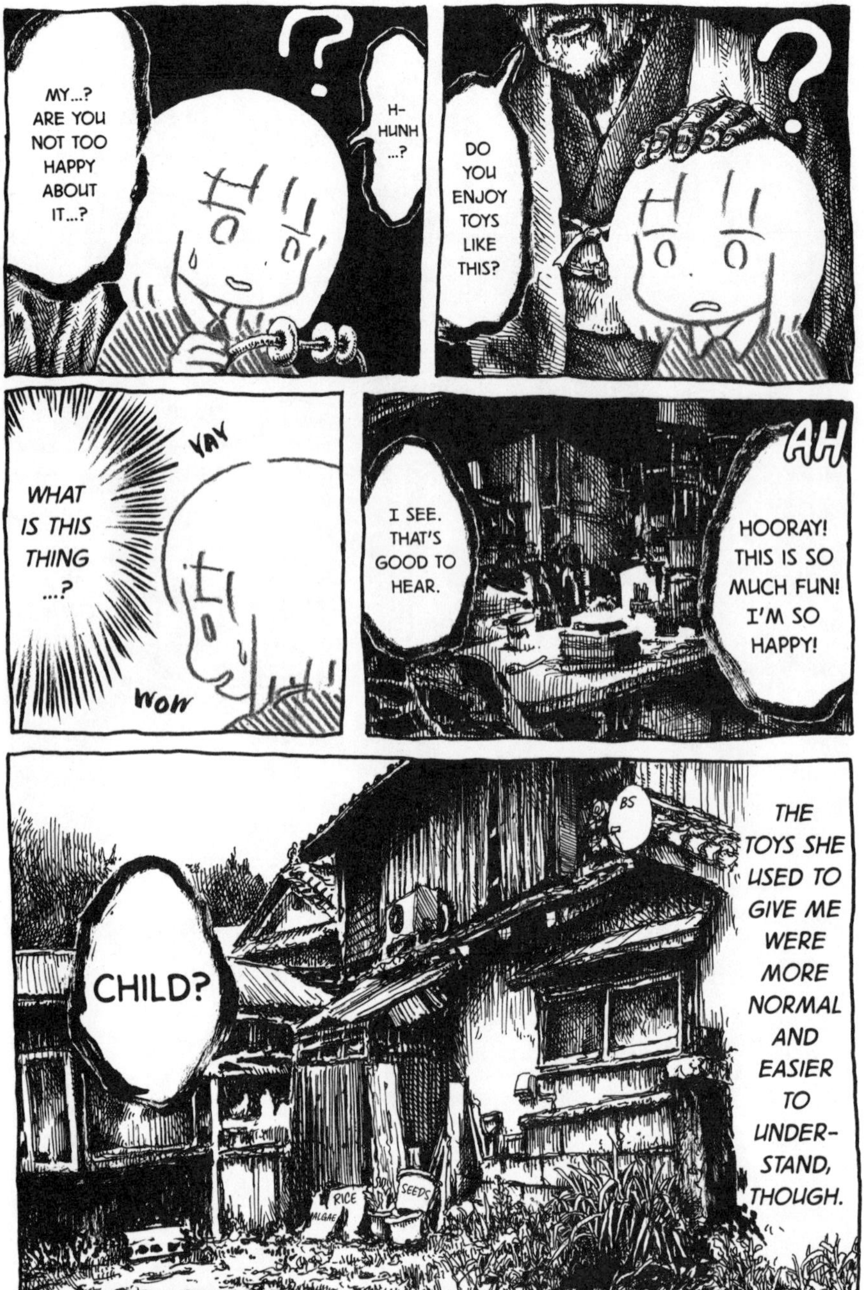
?
DO YOU ENJOY TOYS LIKE THIS?
?
H-HUNH...?
MY...? ARE YOU NOT TOO HAPPY ABOUT IT...?
AH
HOORAY! THIS IS SO MUCH FUN! I'M SO HAPPY!
I SEE. THAT'S GOOD TO HEAR.
YAY
WHAT IS THIS THING ...?
WOW
THE TOYS SHE USED TO GIVE ME WERE MORE NORMAL AND EASIER TO UNDER-STAND, THOUGH.
BS
CHILD?
SEEDS
RICE
ALGAE

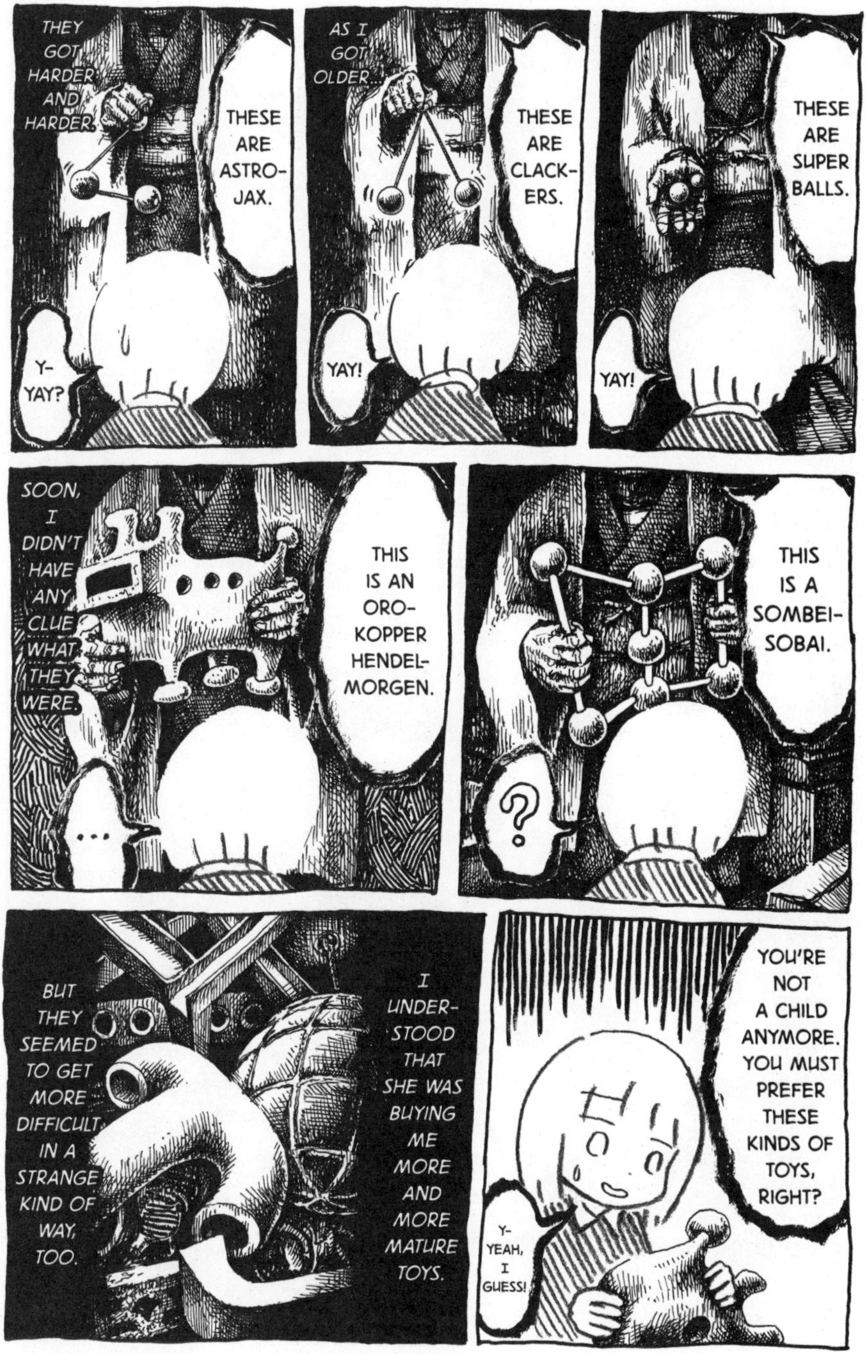
THESE ARE SUPER BALLS.
YAY!
AS I GOT OLDER...
THESE ARE CLACK-ERS.
YAY!
THEY GOT HARDER AND HARDER.
THESE ARE ASTRO-JAX.
Y- YAY?
THIS IS A SOMBEI-SOBAI.
?
SOON, I DIDN'T HAVE ANY CLUE WHAT THEY WERE.
THIS IS AN ORO-KOPPER HENDEL-MORGEN.
...
YOU'RE NOT A CHILD ANYMORE. YOU MUST PREFER THESE KINDS OF TOYS, RIGHT?
Y- YEAH, I GUESS!
I UNDER-STOOD THAT SHE WAS BUYING ME MORE AND MORE MATURE TOYS.
BUT THEY SEEMED TO GET MORE DIFFICULT IN A STRANGE KIND OF WAY, TOO.

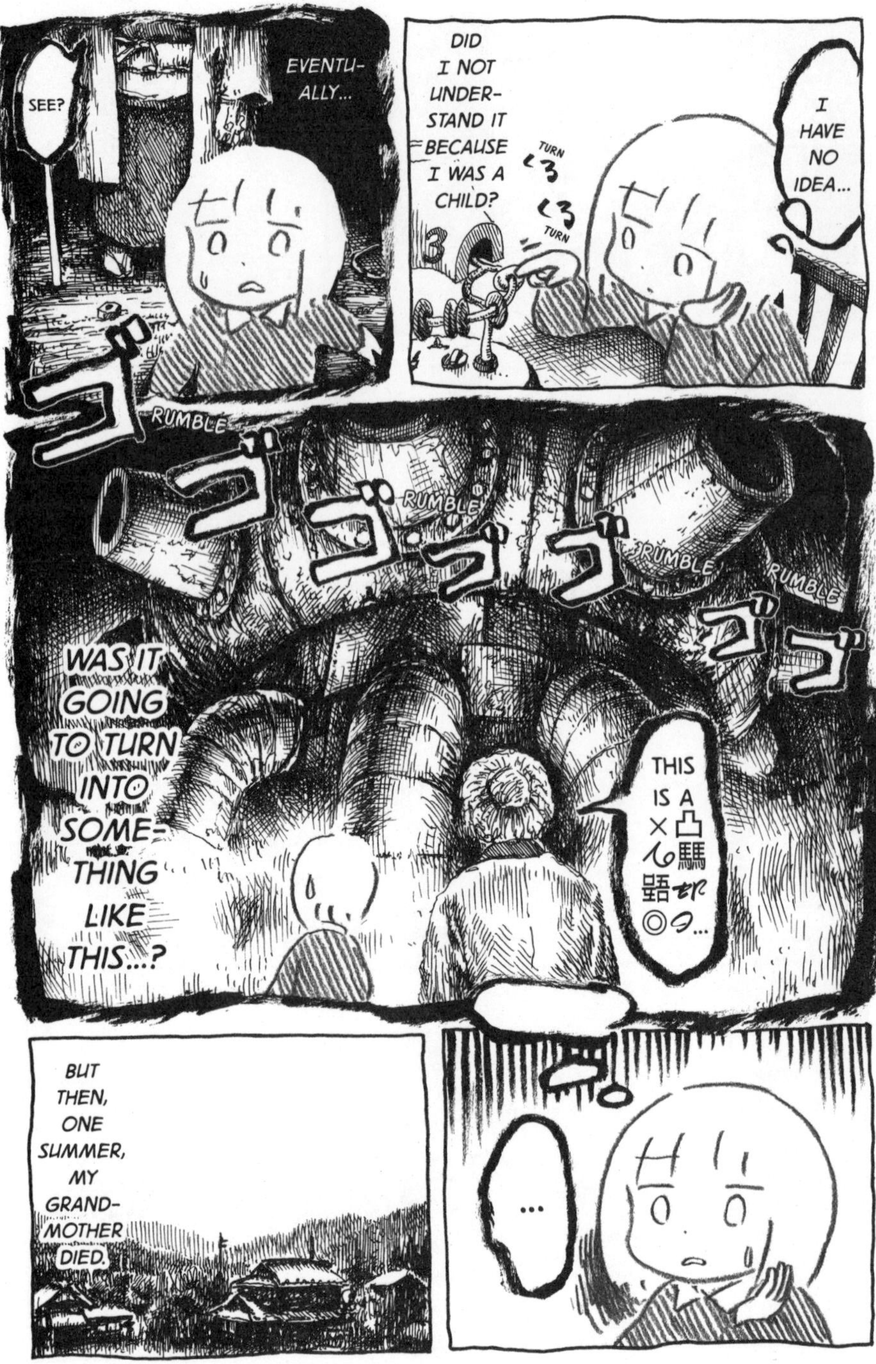
DID I NOT UNDERSTAND IT BECAUSE I WAS A CHILD?
TURN くる
くる TURN
I HAVE NO IDEA...
EVENTUALLY...
SEE?
ゴ RUMBLE
ゴ
ゴ RUMBLE
ゴ
ゴ RUMBLE
ゴ RUMBLE
ゴ
ゴ
THIS IS A
WAS IT GOING TO TURN INTO SOMETHING LIKE THIS...?
...
BUT THEN, ONE SUMMER, MY GRANDMOTHER DIED.

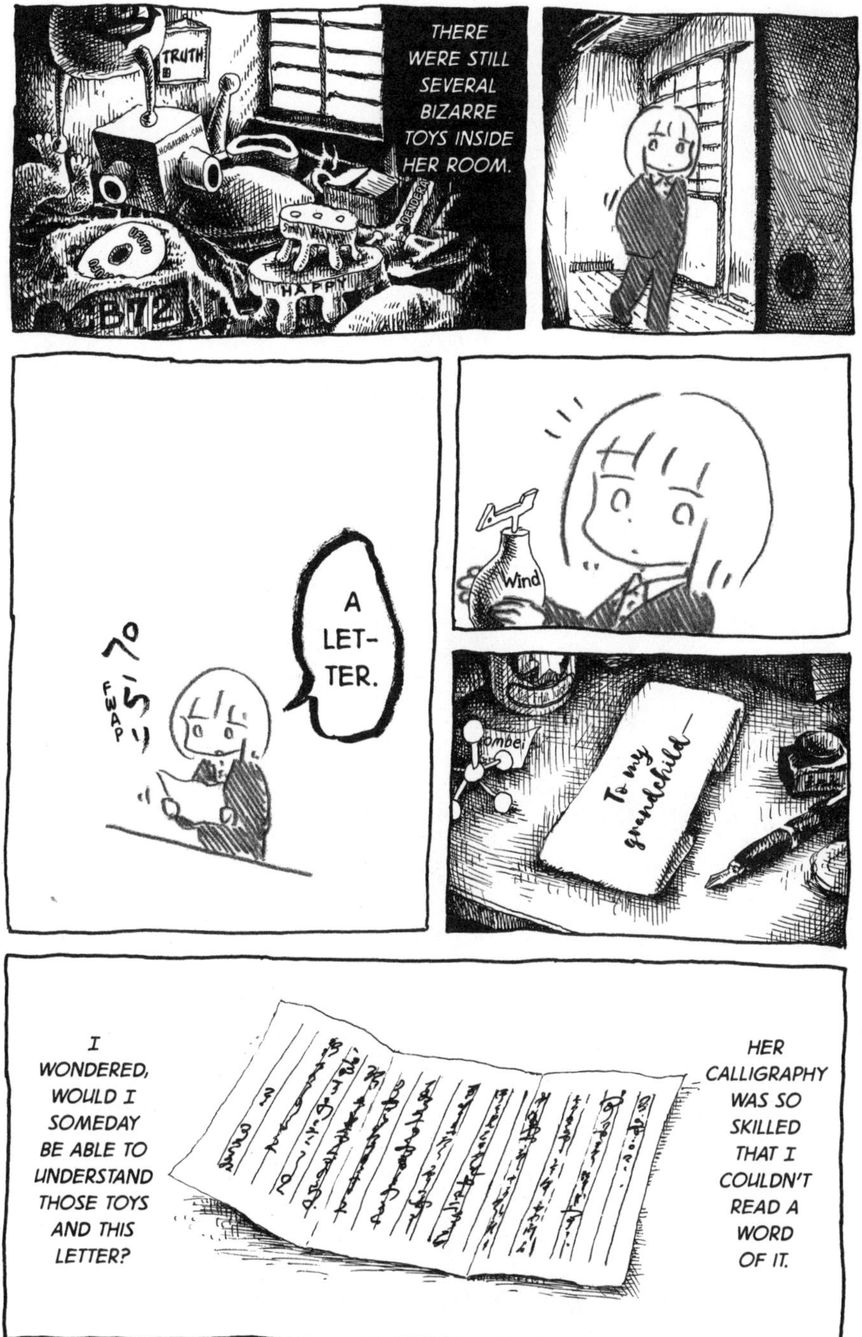
TRUTH
HAPPY
THERE WERE STILL SEVERAL BIZARRE TOYS INSIDE HER ROOM.
Wind
To my grandchild—
FWAP
A LETTER.
HER CALLIGRAPHY WAS SO SKILLED THAT I COULDN'T READ A WORD OF IT.
I WONDERED, WOULD I SOMEDAY BE ABLE TO UNDERSTAND THOSE TOYS AND THIS LETTER?

Disconnect

I went out one night to throw out my burnable garbage. I do this at night because I tend to oversleep or forget to do it in the mornings. It's also about two hundred meters from my doorstep to the waste collection point.

The stars were out, and I watched them as I walked. Just then, an airplane flew by, blinking. A strange feeling came over me when I thought about how it must have been carrying people inside. Airplanes fly at a height of about ten thousand meters. That meant it was ten kilometers away. It was nothing more than a distant vehicle, but the sense of disconnect I felt between me and it was stronger because it was in the sky. I doubted I could have been seen from the airplane, but could they at least see the street lights? Would they get distracted and look away? I didn't know, of course.

It reminded me of driving a car down the highway. There's a special feeling of disconnect that I get when I look at the world from a highway with no side roads. As you pass by rural areas at night, you often see dots of light coming from homes on the opposite side of rice fields or on the foothills of a mountain. So, it feels strange when I think about how there's a human living there within every single bright dot. It made me think that maybe airline pilots get a similar feeling when they see a neighborhood's street lights. Maybe they can imagine that there could be someone down there taking out their trash.

There could be people reading these words who live in homes you can see from the highway, and I think about the distance between myself and those people as well. Do people who live near highways watch cars passing by there as they take out the trash and feel the same way I feel when looking up at airplanes from the ground?

We don't know their names or their faces, but we're aware that someone is there moving.

June 3, 2013

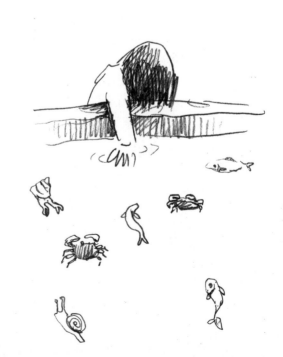

A Story About Fish

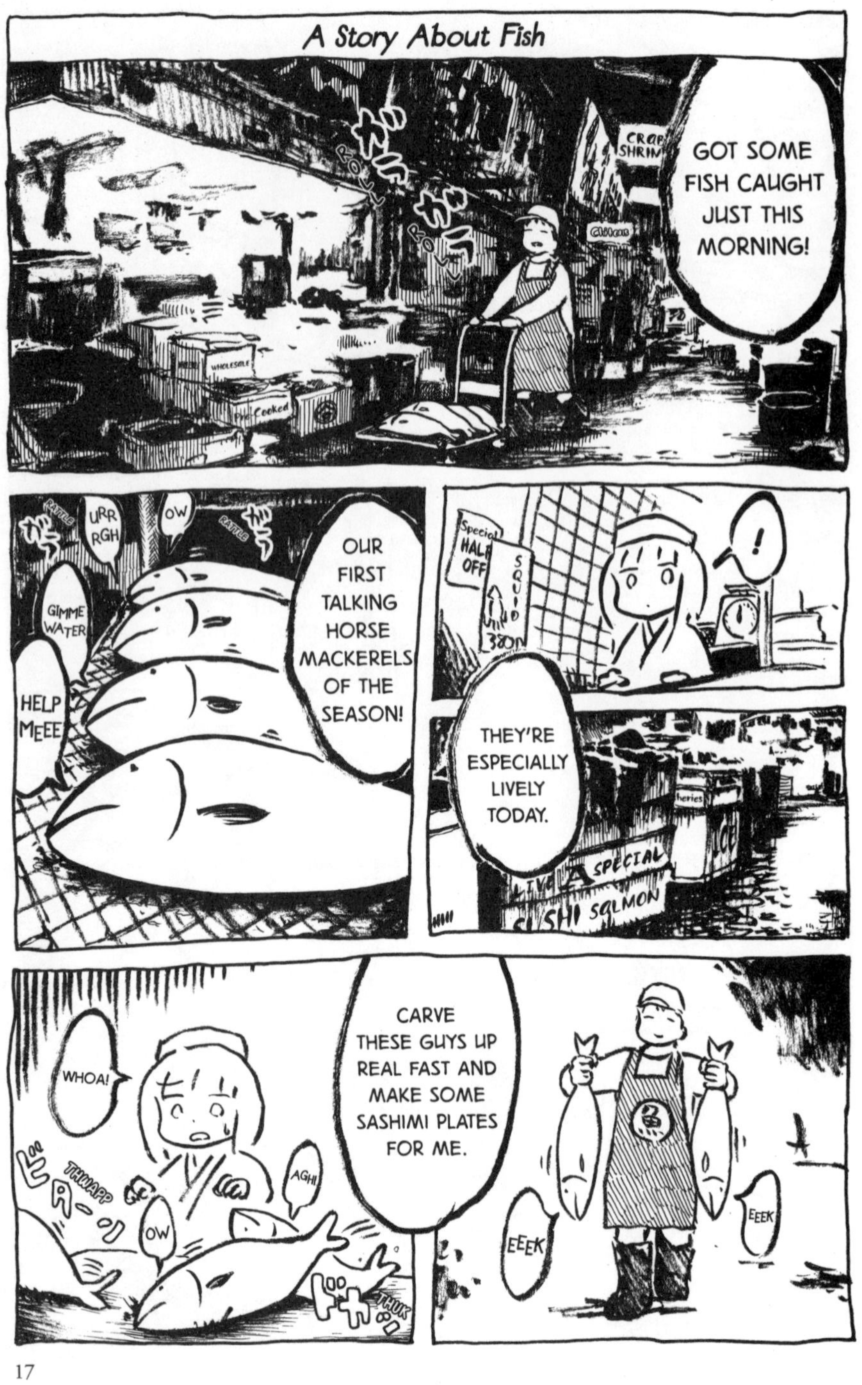
ROLL
ROLL
GOT SOME FISH CAUGHT JUST THIS MORNING!
WHOLESALE
Pre-cooked
!
Special HALF OFF
SQUID
380円
THEY'RE ESPECIALLY LIVELY TODAY.
SPECIAL
salmon
OUR FIRST TALKING HORSE MACKERELS OF THE SEASON!
RATTLE
OW
URR RGH
RATTLE
GIMME WATER
HELP MEEE
CARVE THESE GUYS UP REAL FAST AND MAKE SOME SASHIMI PLATES FOR ME.
EEEK
EEEK
WHOA!
AGH!
THWAPP
OW
THUK

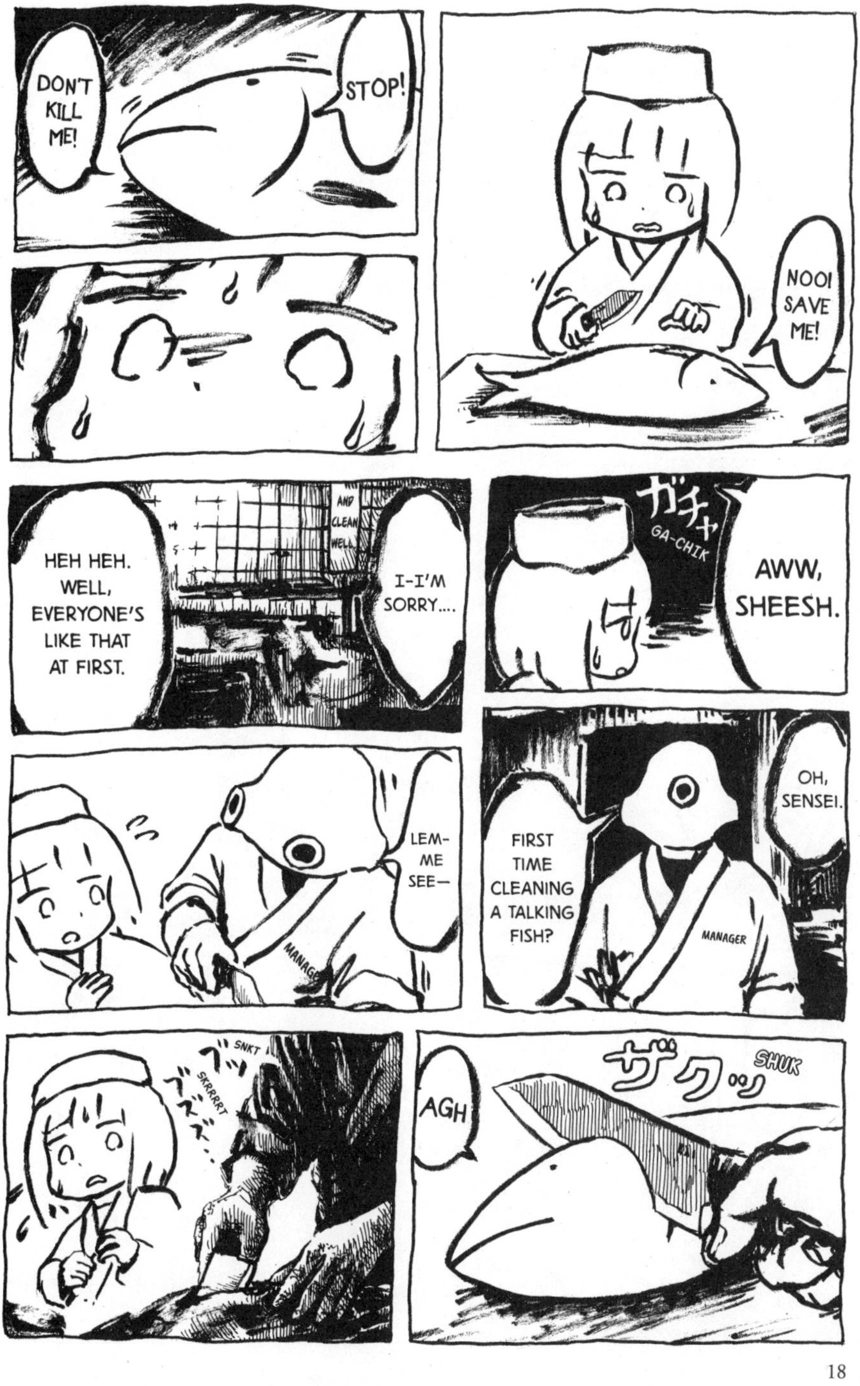
NOO! SAVE ME!
STOP!
DON'T KILL ME!
ガチャ
GA-CHIK
AWW, SHEESH.
I-I'M SORRY....
AND CLEAN WELL
HEH HEH. WELL, EVERYONE'S LIKE THAT AT FIRST.
OH, SENSEI.
FIRST TIME CLEANING A TALKING FISH?
MANAGER
LEM-ME SEE—
ザクッ
SHUK
AGH
SNKT
SKRRRRT

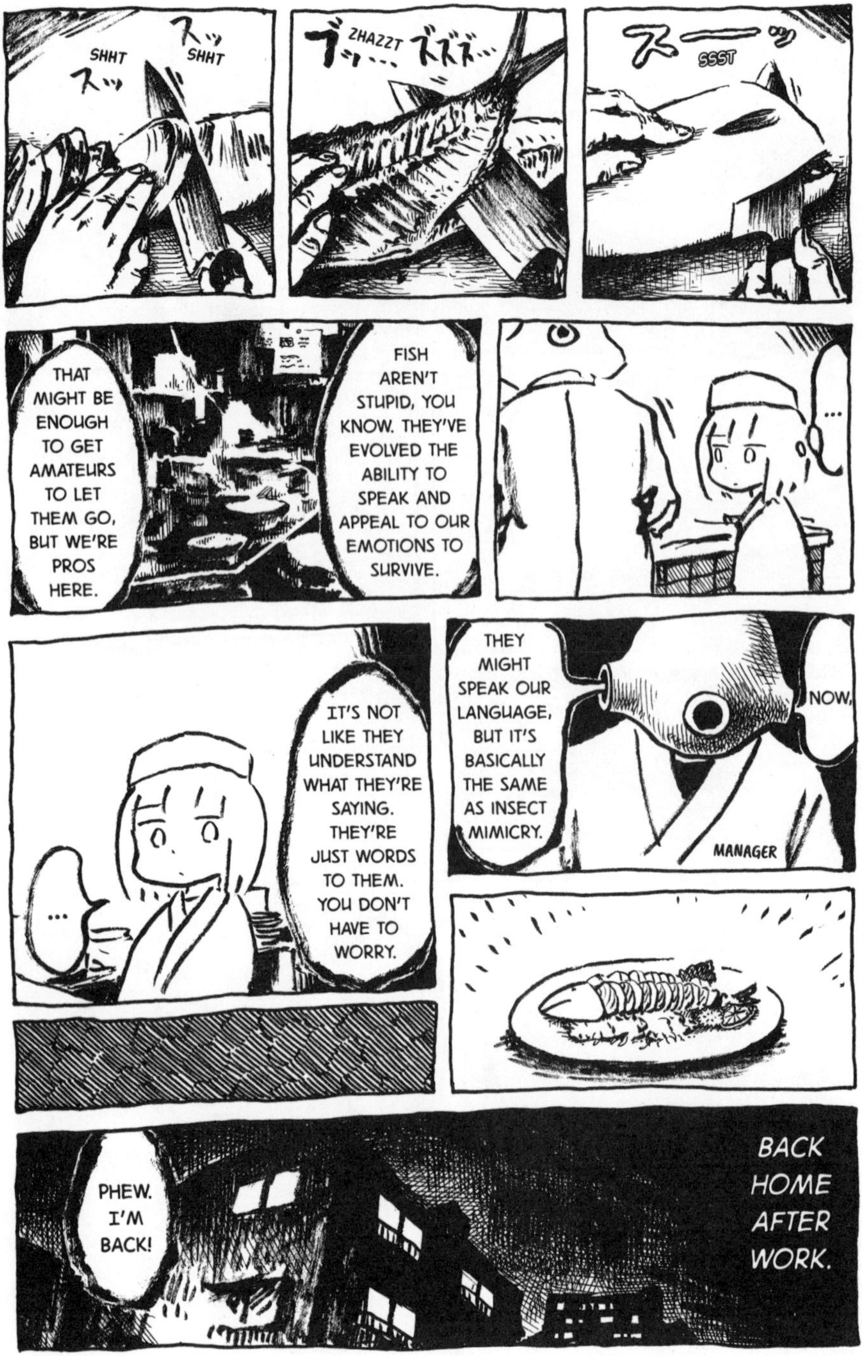

スーッ
SSST
ブッ…
ZHAZZT
ズズズ…
スッ
SHHT
スッ
SHHT
...
FISH AREN'T STUPID, YOU KNOW. THEY'VE EVOLVED THE ABILITY TO SPEAK AND APPEAL TO OUR EMOTIONS TO SURVIVE.
THAT MIGHT BE ENOUGH TO GET AMATEURS TO LET THEM GO, BUT WE'RE PROS HERE.
NOW,
THEY MIGHT SPEAK OUR LANGUAGE, BUT IT'S BASICALLY THE SAME AS INSECT MIMICRY.
MANAGER
IT'S NOT LIKE THEY UNDERSTAND WHAT THEY'RE SAYING. THEY'RE JUST WORDS TO THEM. YOU DON'T HAVE TO WORRY.
...
BACK HOME AFTER WORK.
PHEW. I'M BACK!

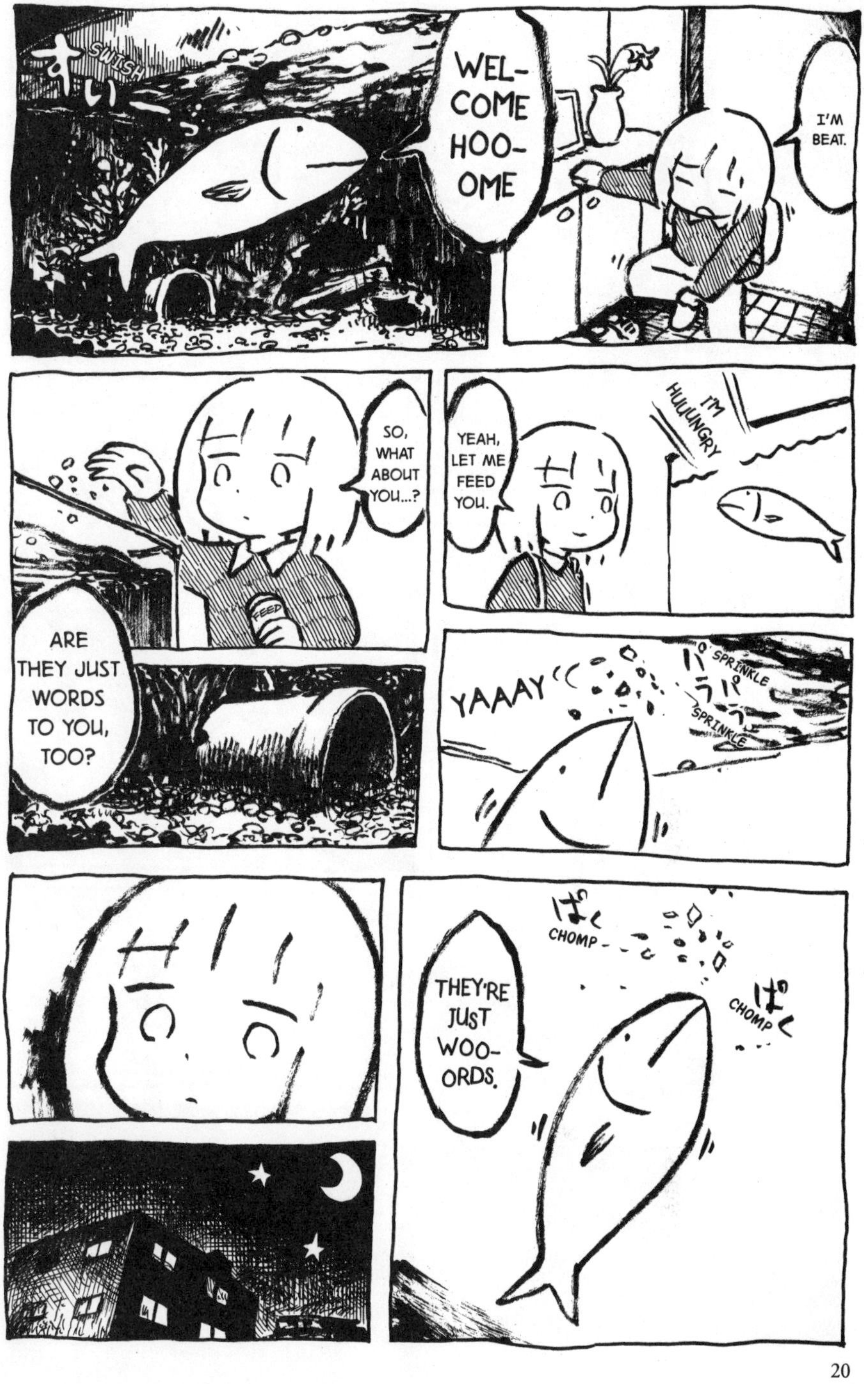
I'M BEAT.
WEL-COME HOO-OME
すいー
SWISH
I'M HUUUNGRY
YEAH, LET ME FEED YOU.
パラパラ
SPRINKLE
SPRINKLE
YAAAY
SO, WHAT ABOUT YOU...?
FEED
ARE THEY JUST WORDS TO YOU, TOO?
ぱく
CHOMP
ぱく
CHOMP
THEY'RE JUST WOOORDS.

innovation

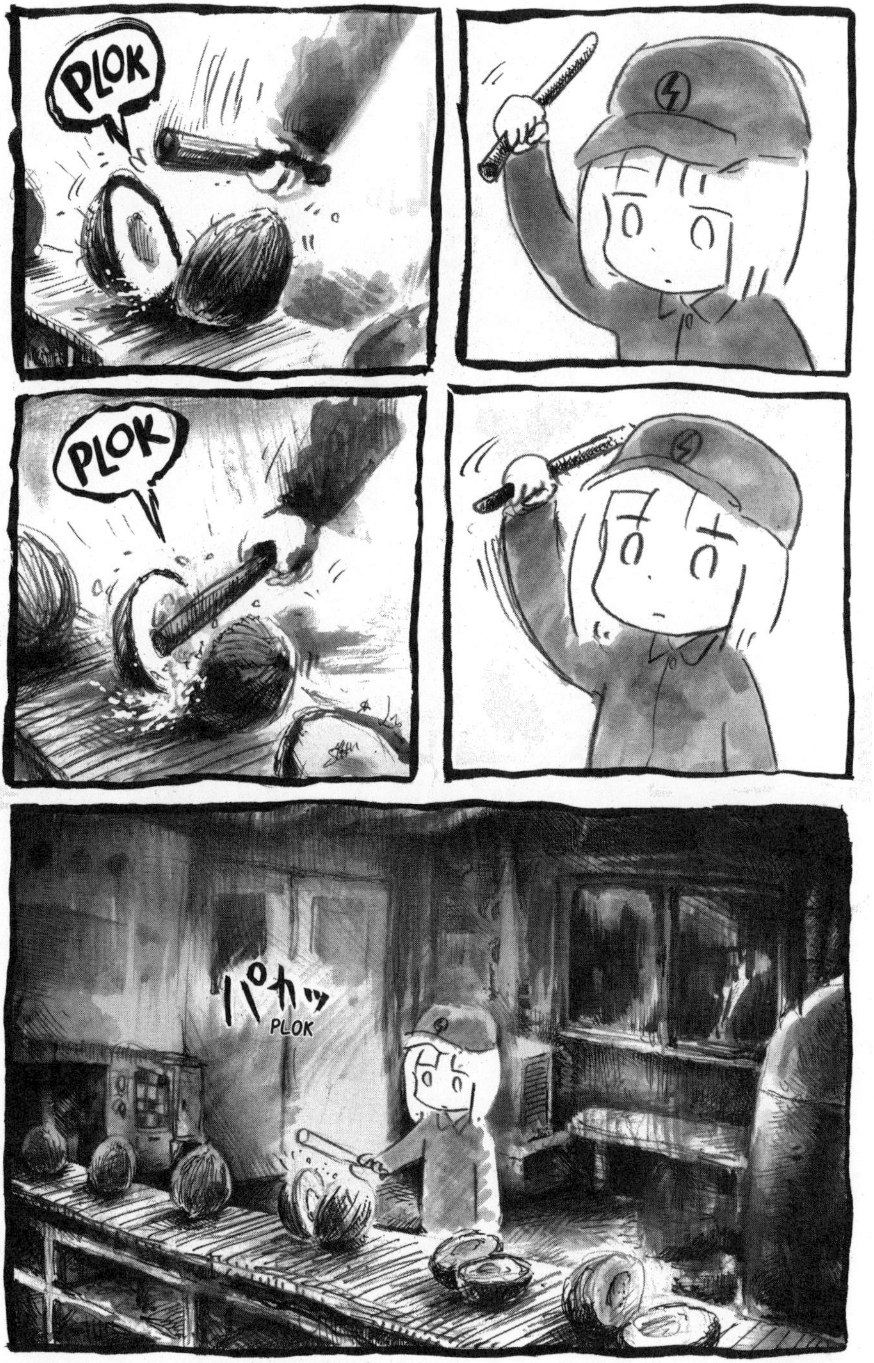
PLOK
PLOK
パカッ
PLOK

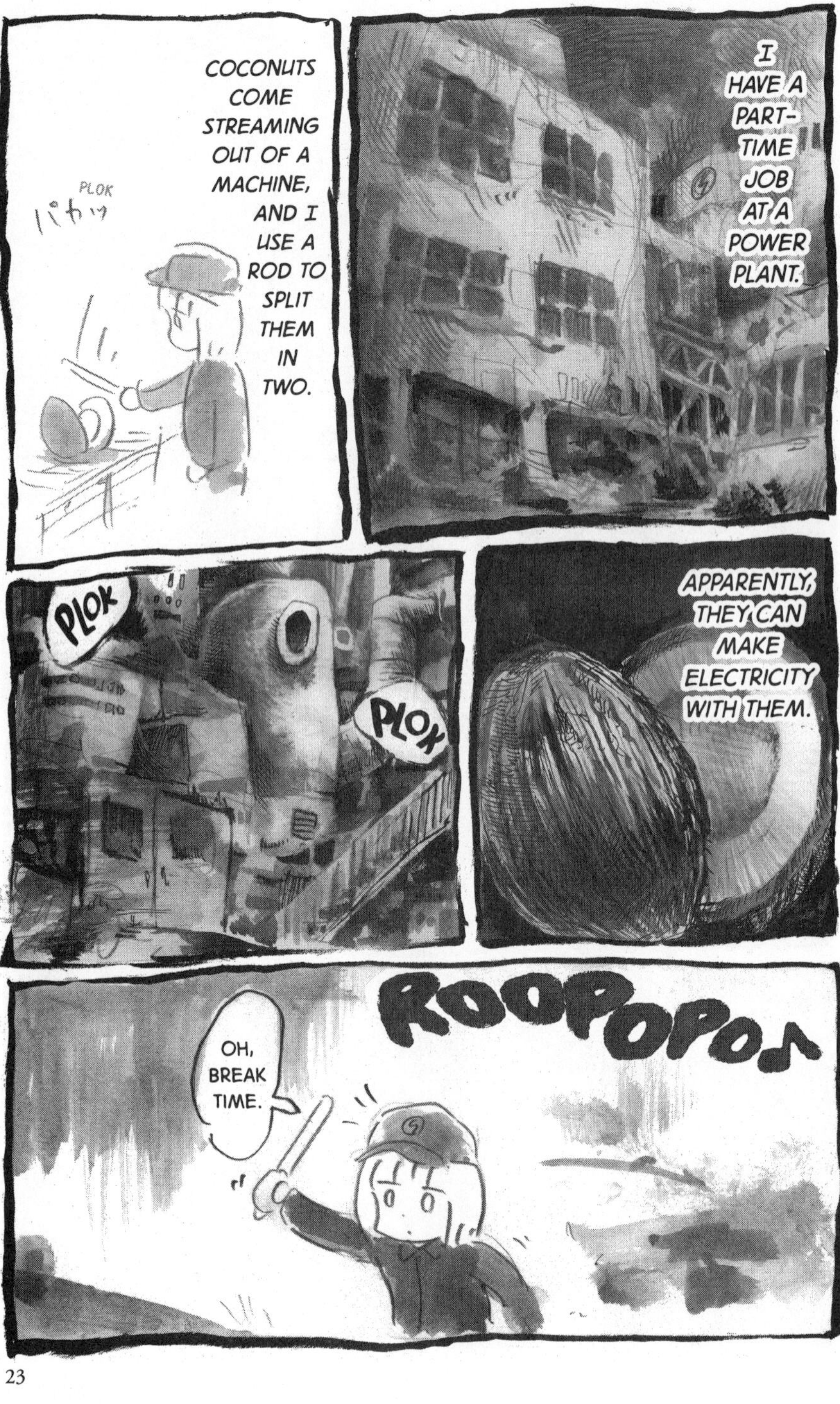
I HAVE A PART-TIME JOB AT A POWER PLANT.
COCONUTS COME STREAMING OUT OF A MACHINE, AND I USE A ROD TO SPLIT THEM IN TWO.
PLOK
パカッ
APPARENTLY, THEY CAN MAKE ELECTRICITY WITH THEM.
PLOK
PLOK
ROOPOPO♪
OH, BREAK TIME.

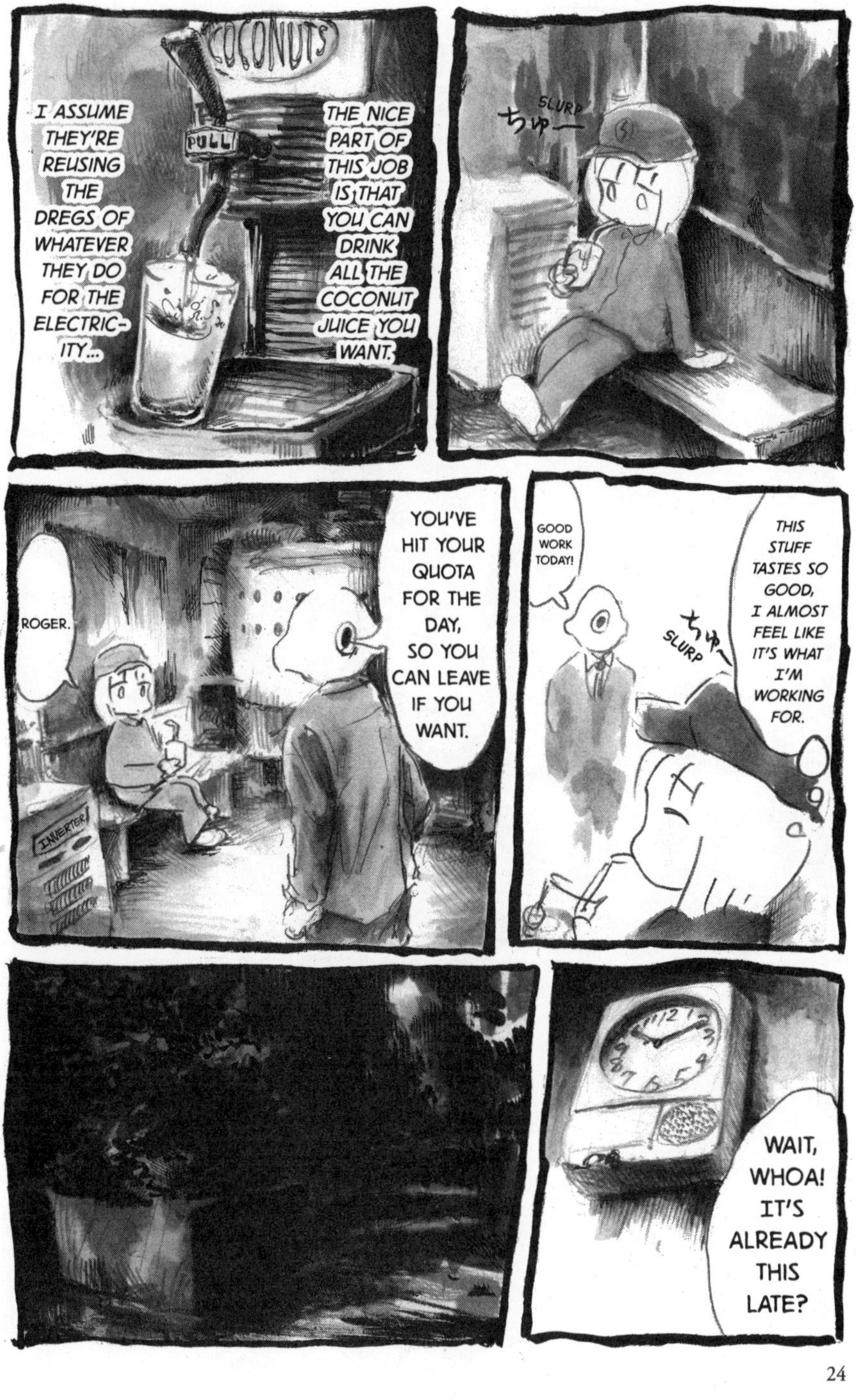
SLURP
ちゅー
COCONUTS
PULL
THE NICE PART OF THIS JOB IS THAT YOU CAN DRINK ALL THE COCONUT JUICE YOU WANT.
I ASSUME THEY'RE REUSING THE DREGS OF WHATEVER THEY DO FOR THE ELECTRIC-ITY...
THIS STUFF TASTES SO GOOD, I ALMOST FEEL LIKE IT'S WHAT I'M WORKING FOR.
ちゅー
SLURP
GOOD WORK TODAY!
YOU'VE HIT YOUR QUOTA FOR THE DAY, SO YOU CAN LEAVE IF YOU WANT.
ROGER.
INVERTER
WAIT, WHOA! IT'S ALREADY THIS LATE?

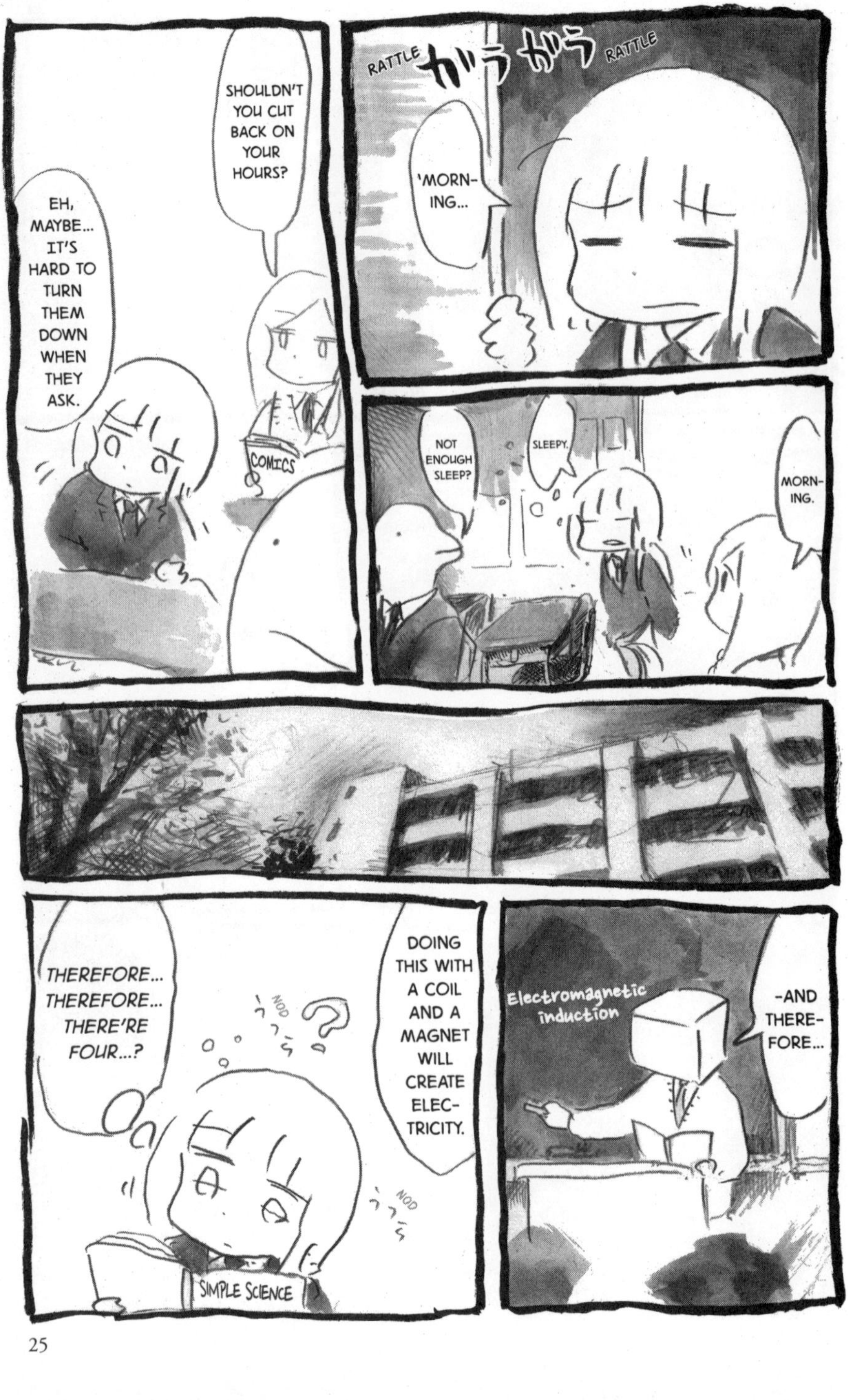

RATTLE がらがら RATTLE
'MORNING...
MORNING.
SLEEPY.
NOT ENOUGH SLEEP?
SHOULDN'T YOU CUT BACK ON YOUR HOURS?
EH, MAYBE... IT'S HARD TO TURN THEM DOWN WHEN THEY ASK.
COMICS
-AND THEREFORE...
Electromagnetic induction
DOING THIS WITH A COIL AND A MAGNET WILL CREATE ELECTRICITY.
NOD
THEREFORE... THEREFORE... THERE'RE FOUR...?
NOD
SIMPLE SCIENCE

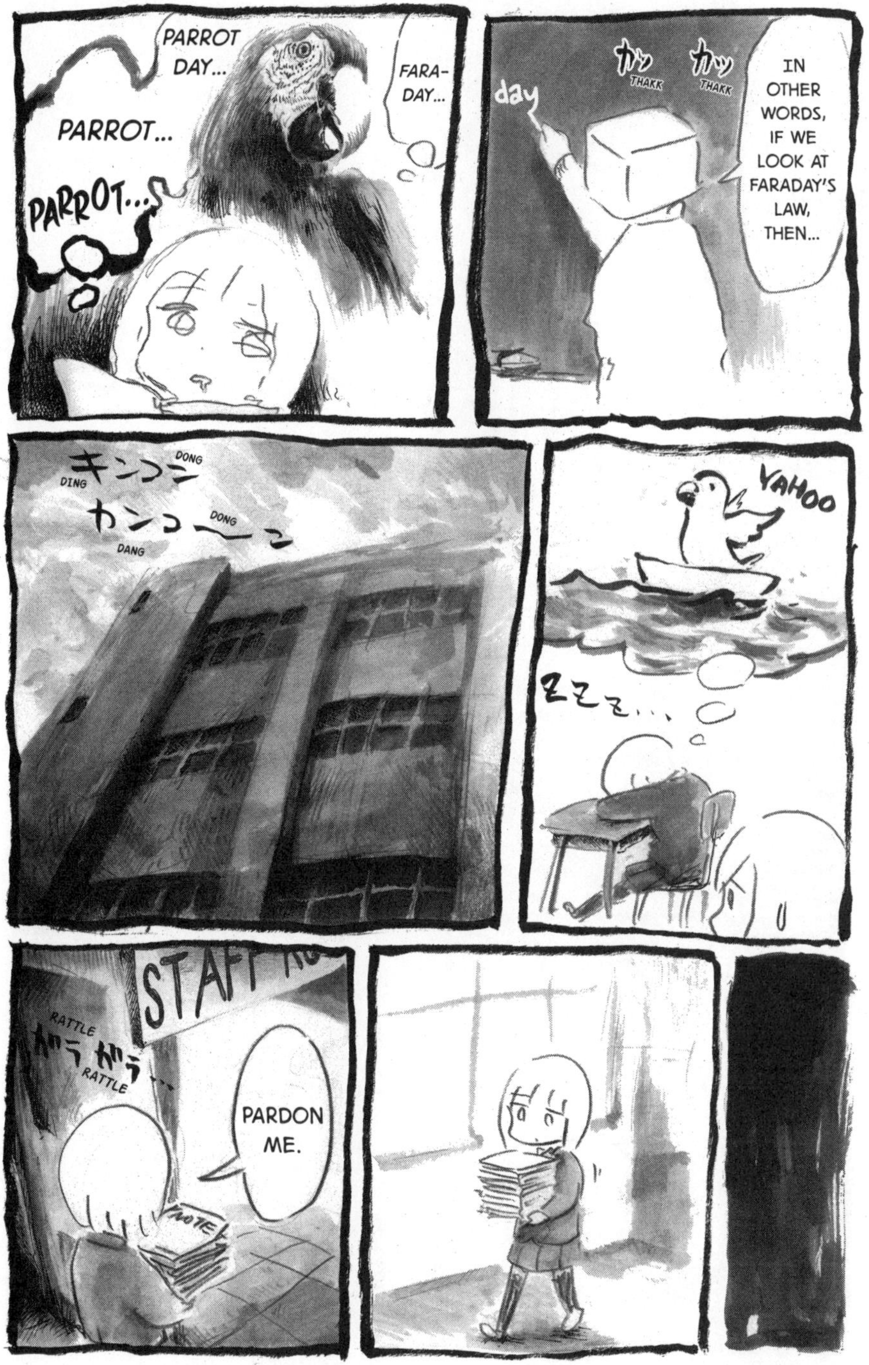
カッ
THAKK
カッ
THAKK
IN OTHER WORDS, IF WE LOOK AT FARADAY'S LAW, THEN...
day
FARA-DAY...
PARROT DAY...
PARROT...
PARROT...
YAHOO
ZZZ...
DONG
DING
DONG
DANG
STAFF
RATTLE
ガラガラ
RATTLE
PARDON ME.
NOTE

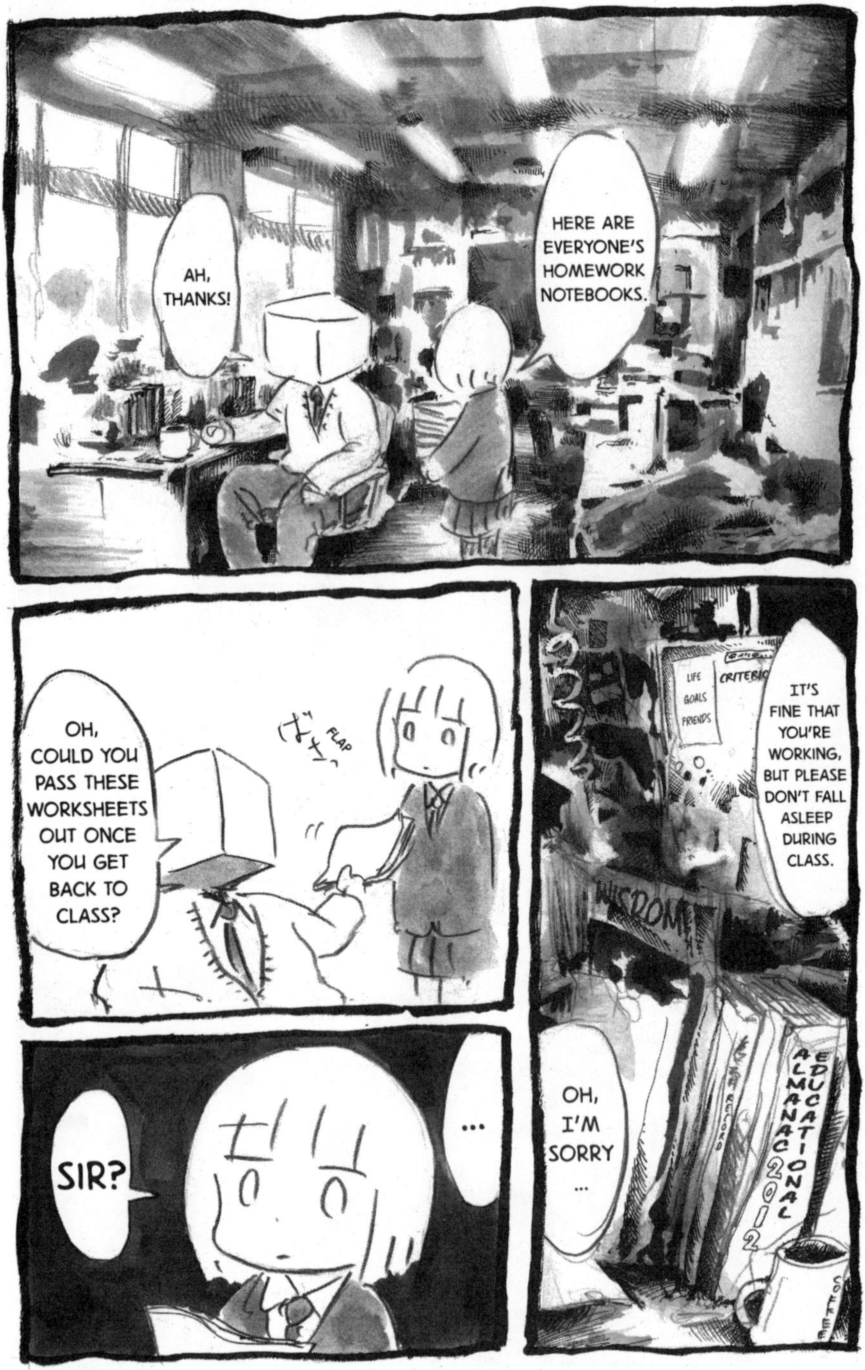
HERE ARE EVERYONE'S HOMEWORK NOTEBOOKS.
AH, THANKS!
IT'S FINE THAT YOU'RE WORKING, BUT PLEASE DON'T FALL ASLEEP DURING CLASS.
LIFE
GOALS
FRIENDS
CRITERIO
WISDOM
OH, I'M SORRY ...
EDUCATIONAL ALMANAC 2012
FLAP
OH, COULD YOU PASS THESE WORKSHEETS OUT ONCE YOU GET BACK TO CLASS?
...
SIR?

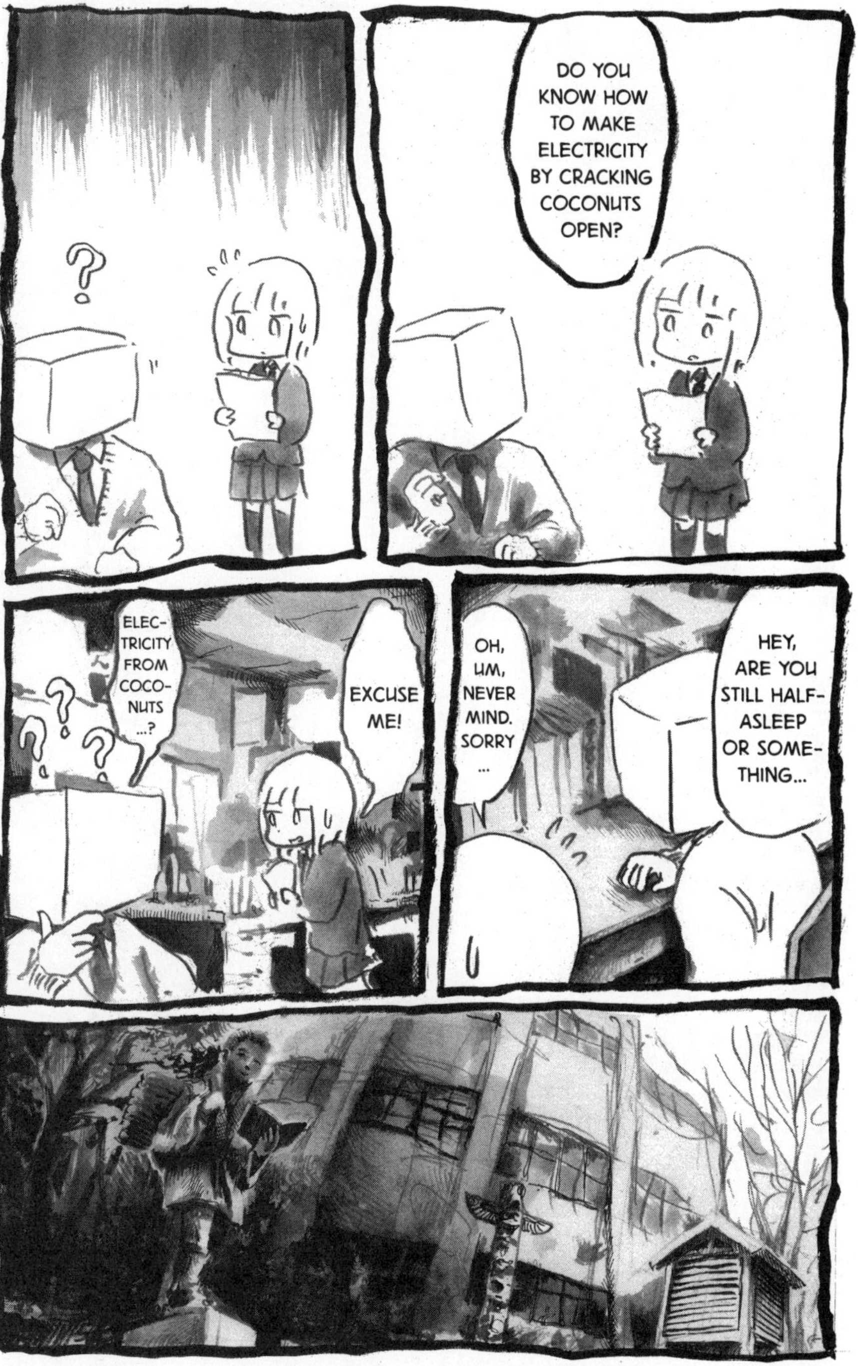
DO YOU KNOW HOW TO MAKE ELECTRICITY BY CRACKING COCONUTS OPEN?
HEY, ARE YOU STILL HALF-ASLEEP OR SOMETHING...
OH, UM, NEVER MIND. SORRY ...
EXCUSE ME!
ELECTRICITY FROM COCONUTS ...?

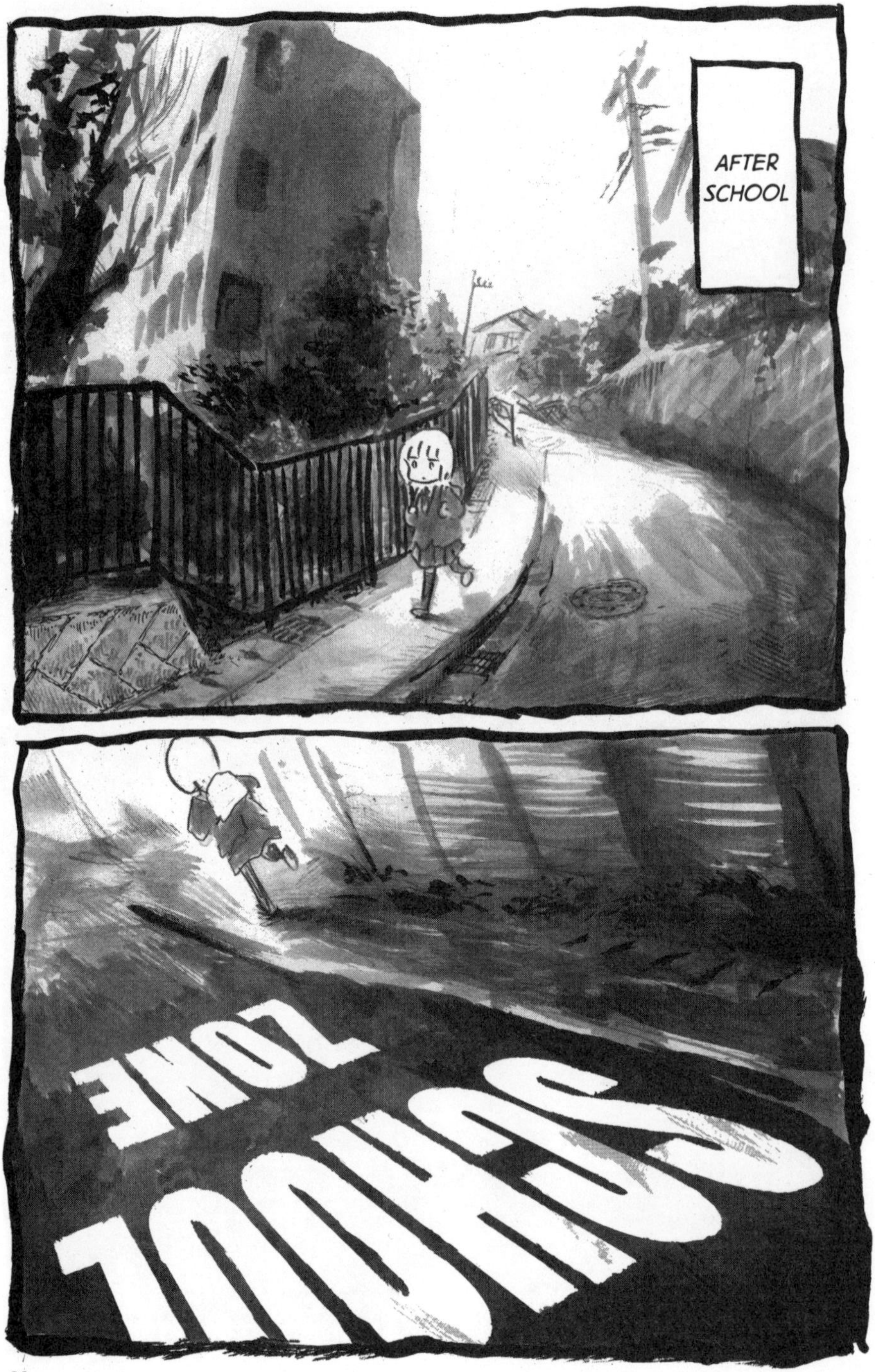
AFTER SCHOOL
SCHOOL ZONE

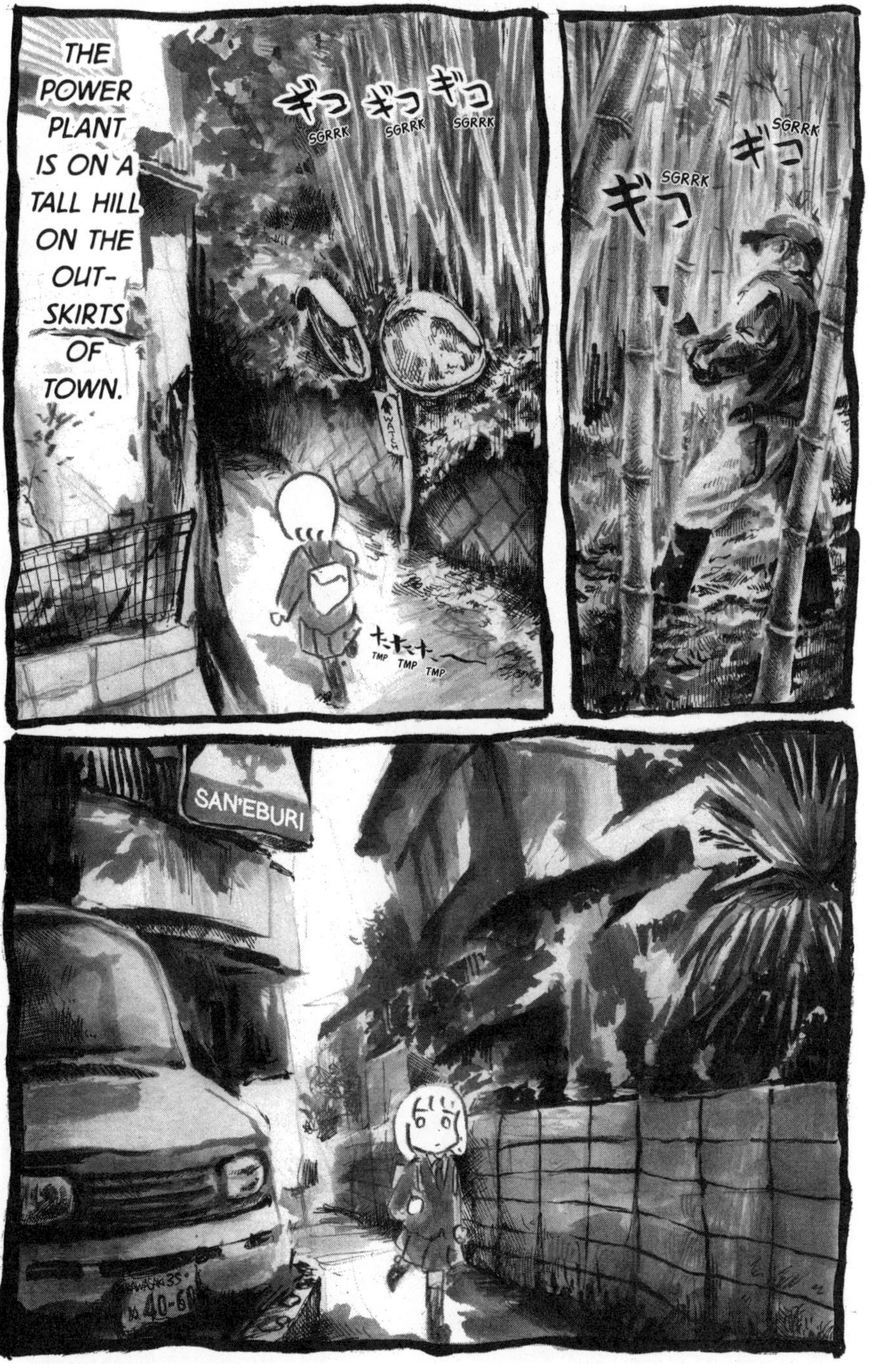
SGRRK
ギコ
SGRRK
ギコ
THE POWER PLANT IS ON A TALL HILL ON THE OUT-SKIRTS OF TOWN.
ギコギコギコ
SGRRK SGRRK SGRRK
WATCH
たたた～
TMP TMP TMP
SAN'EBURI

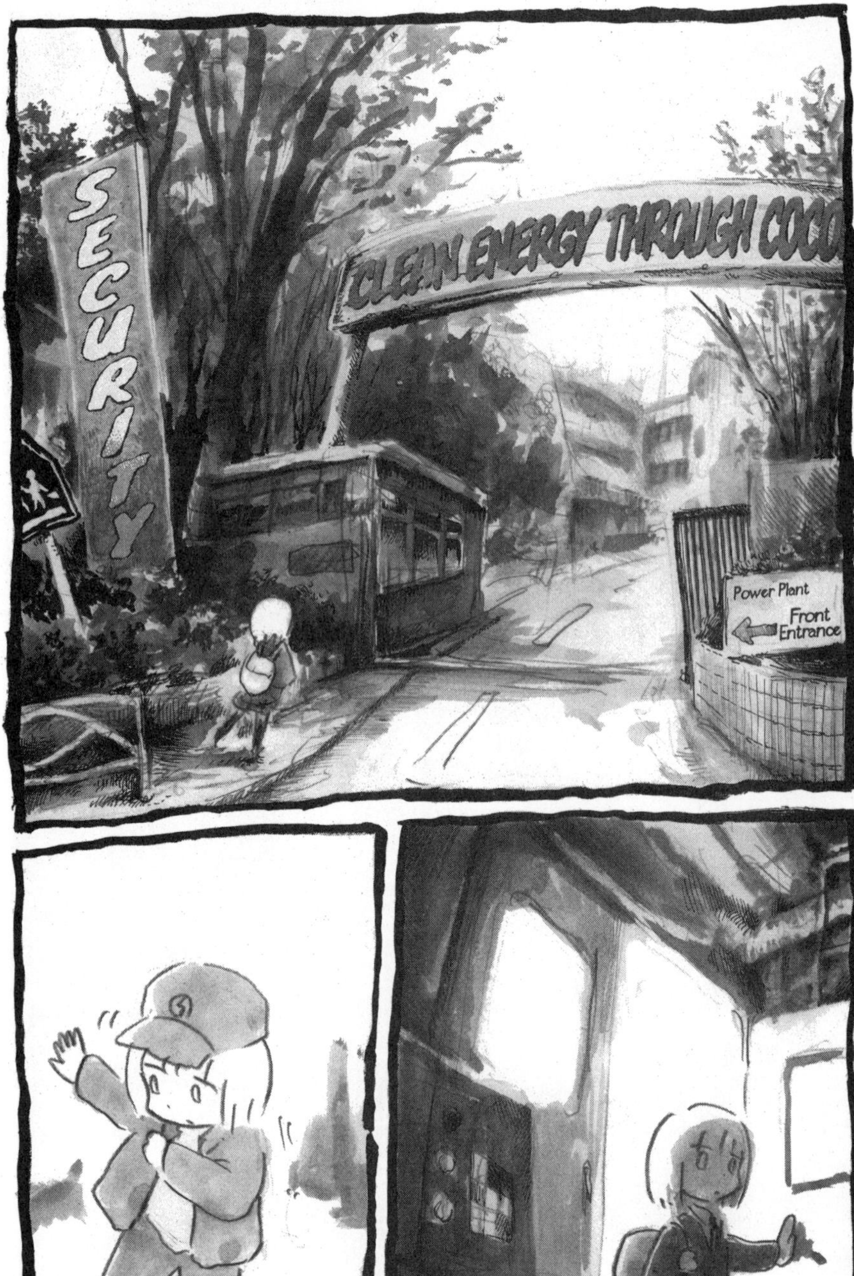
SECURITY
CLEAN ENERGY THROUGH COCO
Power Plant
Front Entrance

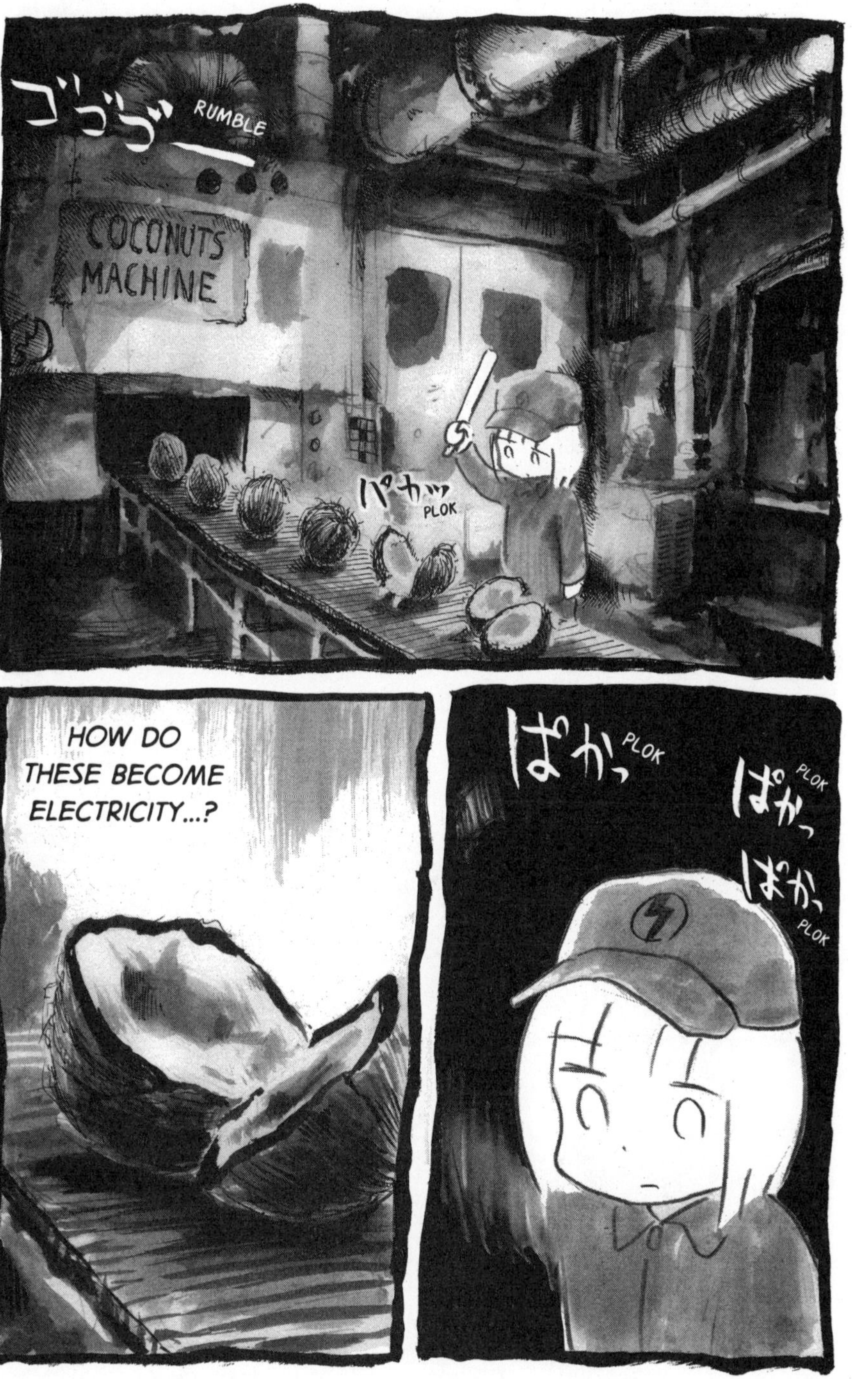
ゴゴゴゴー
RUMBLE
COCONUTS MACHINE
パカッ
PLOK
ぱかっ
PLOK
ぱかっ
PLOK
ぱかっ
PLOK
HOW DO THESE BECOME ELECTRICITY...?

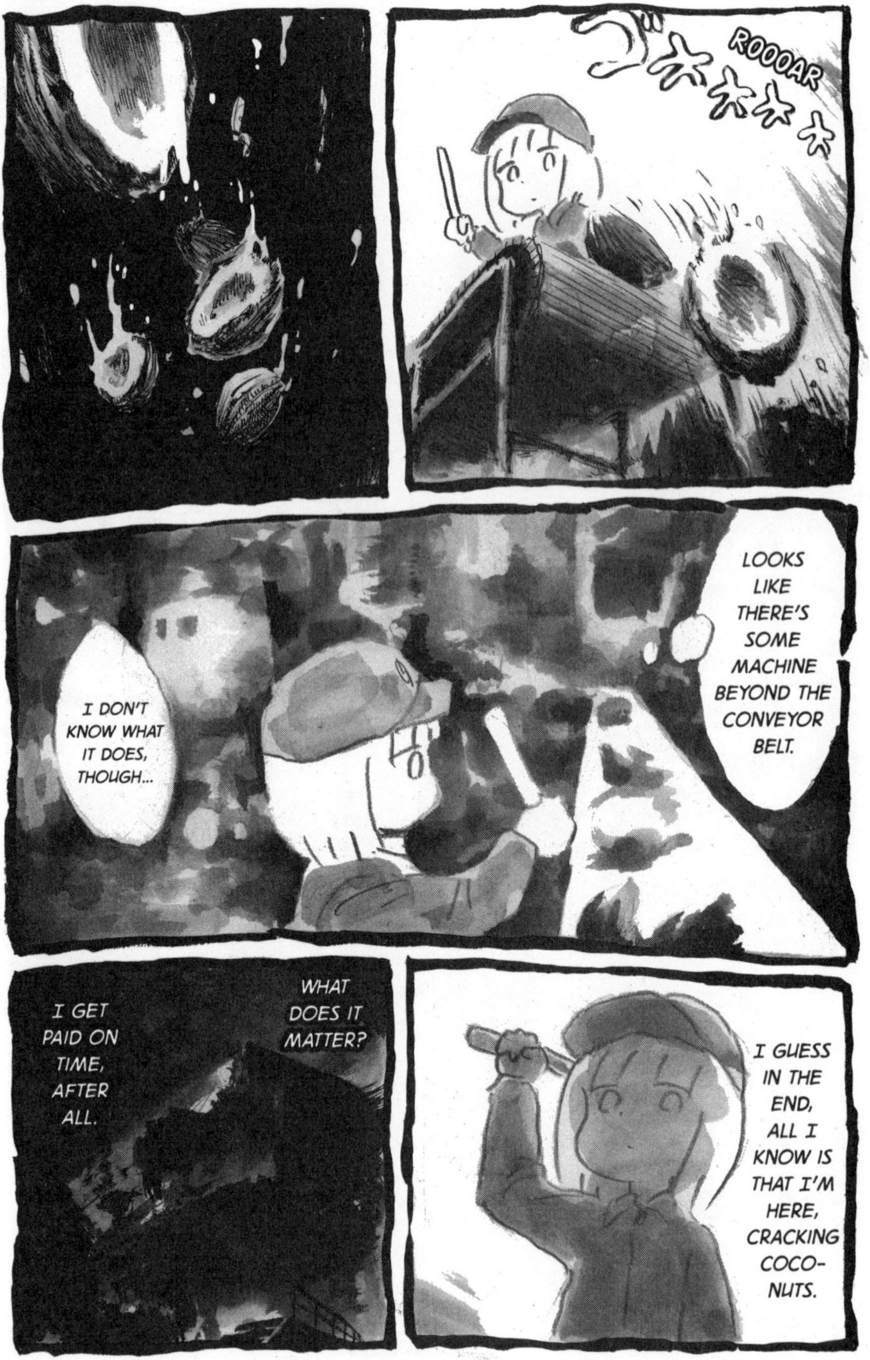
ROOOAR
LOOKS LIKE THERE'S SOME MACHINE BEYOND THE CONVEYOR BELT.
I DON'T KNOW WHAT IT DOES, THOUGH...
I GUESS IN THE END, ALL I KNOW IS THAT I'M HERE, CRACKING COCO-NUTS.
WHAT DOES IT MATTER?
I GET PAID ON TIME, AFTER ALL.

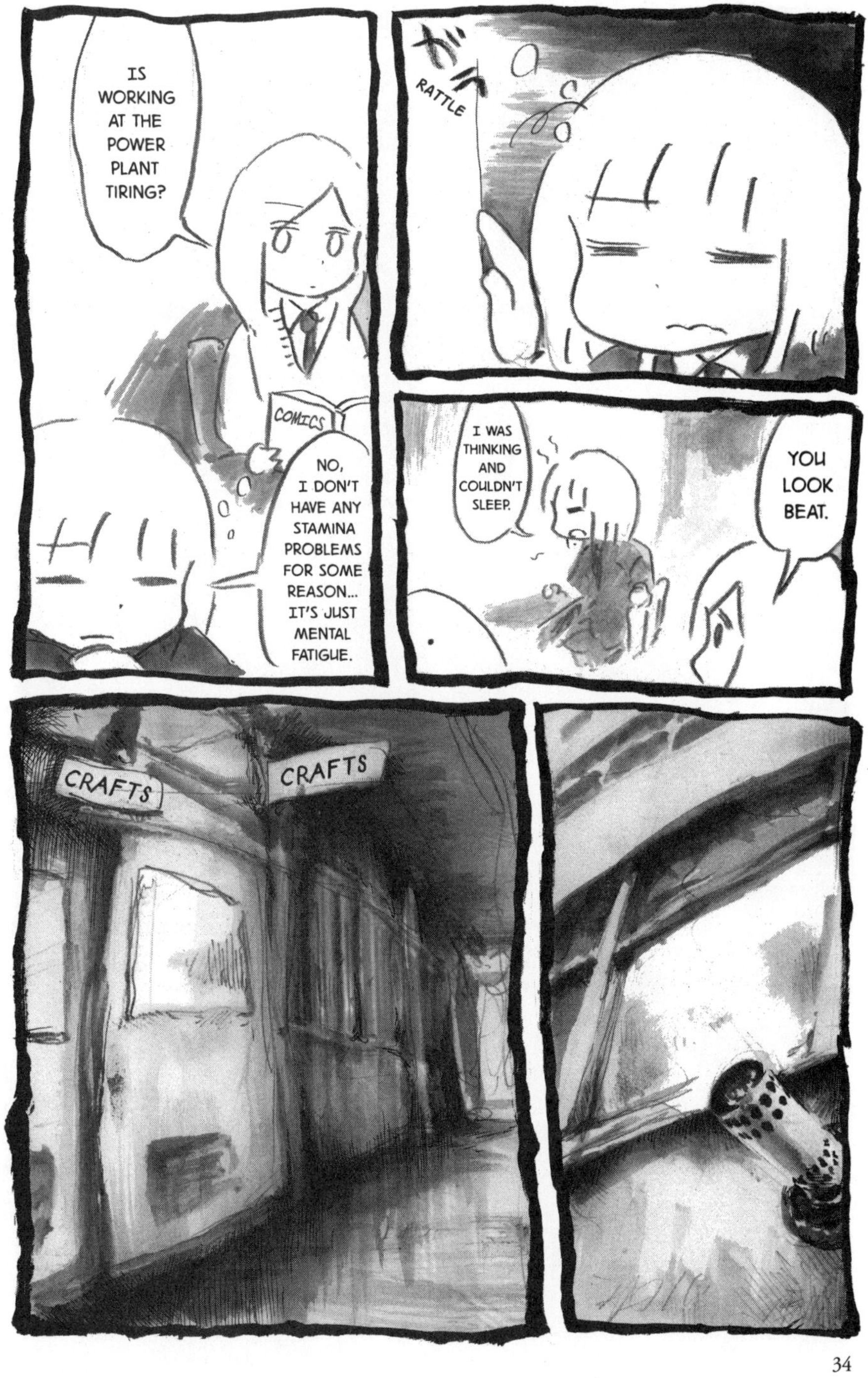
RATTLE
YOU LOOK BEAT.
I WAS THINKING AND COULDN'T SLEEP.
IS WORKING AT THE POWER PLANT TIRING?
COMICS
NO, I DON'T HAVE ANY STAMINA PROBLEMS FOR SOME REASON... IT'S JUST MENTAL FATIGUE.
CRAFTS
CRAFTS

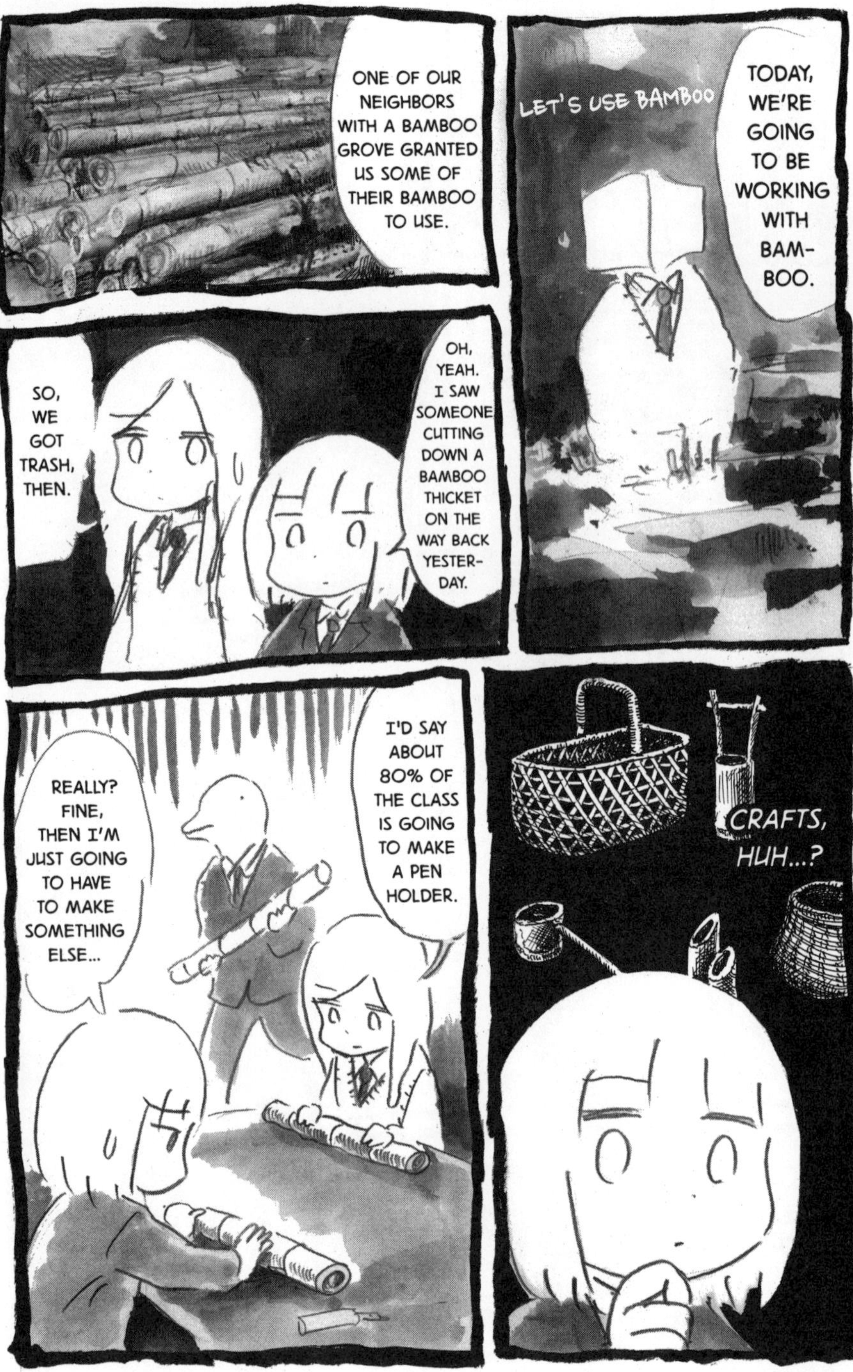
TODAY, WE'RE GOING TO BE WORKING WITH BAM-BOO.
LET'S USE BAMBOO
ONE OF OUR NEIGHBORS WITH A BAMBOO GROVE GRANTED US SOME OF THEIR BAMBOO TO USE.
OH, YEAH. I SAW SOMEONE CUTTING DOWN A BAMBOO THICKET ON THE WAY BACK YESTER-DAY.
SO, WE GOT TRASH, THEN.
CRAFTS, HUH...?
I'D SAY ABOUT 80% OF THE CLASS IS GOING TO MAKE A PEN HOLDER.
REALLY? FINE, THEN I'M JUST GOING TO HAVE TO MAKE SOMETHING ELSE...

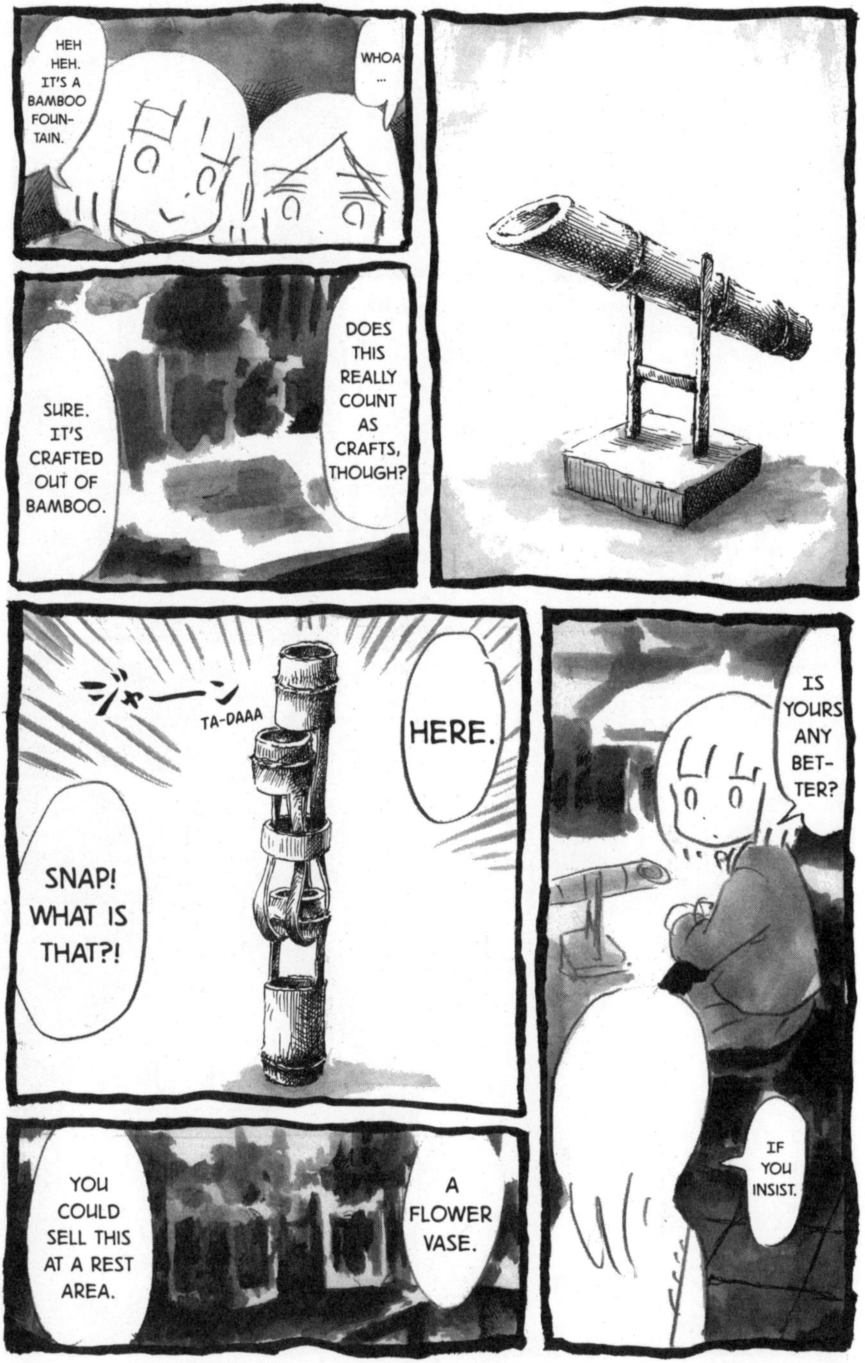
WHOA ...
HEH HEH. IT'S A BAMBOO FOUN-TAIN.
DOES THIS REALLY COUNT AS CRAFTS, THOUGH?
SURE. IT'S CRAFTED OUT OF BAMBOO.
IS YOURS ANY BET-TER?
IF YOU INSIST.
HERE.
ジャーン
TA-DAAA
SNAP! WHAT IS THAT?!
A FLOWER VASE.
YOU COULD SELL THIS AT A REST AREA.

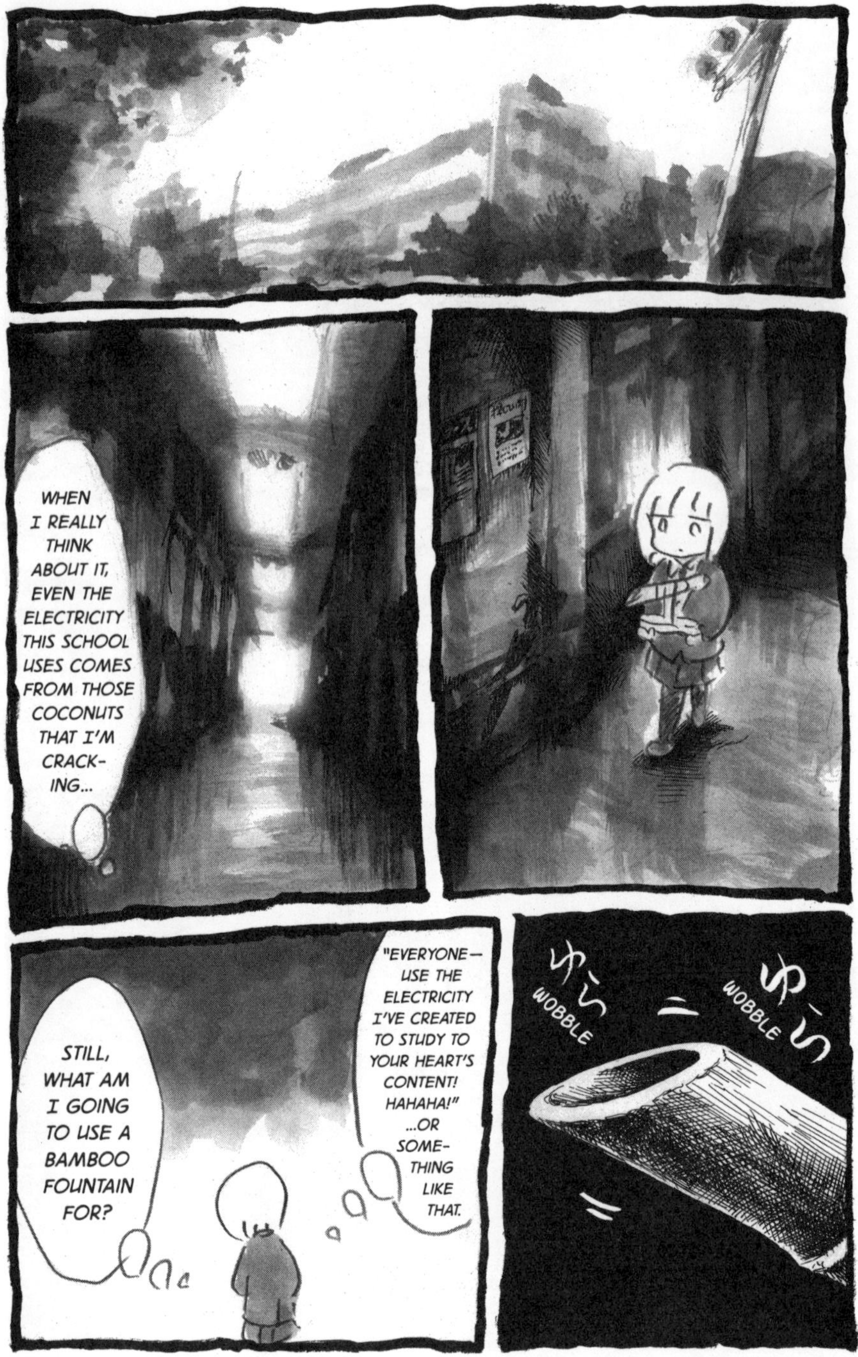
WHEN I REALLY THINK ABOUT IT, EVEN THE ELECTRICITY THIS SCHOOL USES COMES FROM THOSE COCONUTS THAT I'M CRACK-ING...
ゆら
WOBBLE
ゆら
WOBBLE
"EVERYONE—USE THE ELECTRICITY I'VE CREATED TO STUDY TO YOUR HEART'S CONTENT! HAHAHA!" ...OR SOME-THING LIKE THAT.
STILL, WHAT AM I GOING TO USE A BAMBOO FOUNTAIN FOR?

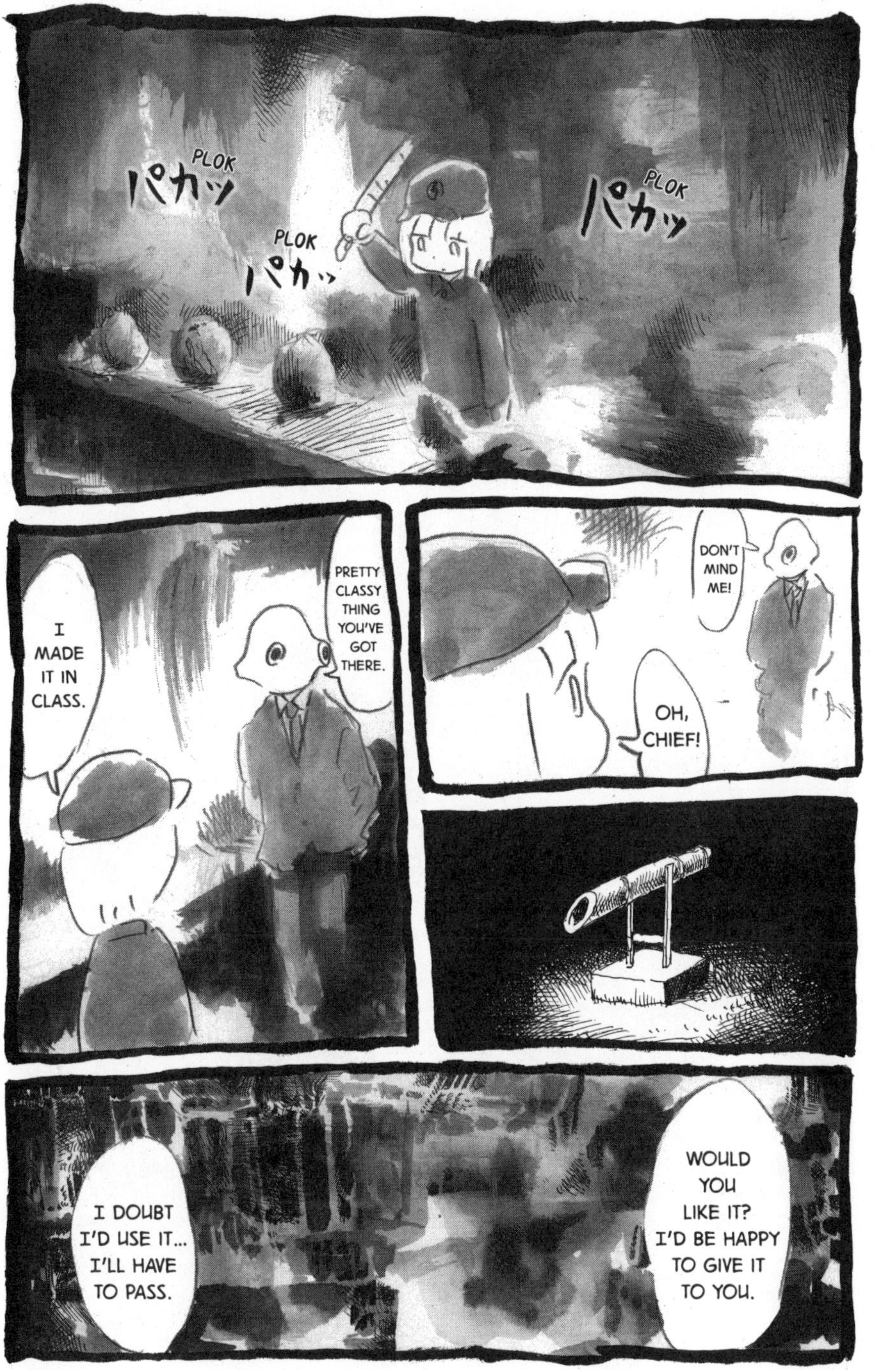
パカッ
PLOK
PLOK
パカッ
PLOK
パカッ
DON'T MIND ME!
OH, CHIEF!
PRETTY CLASSY THING YOU'VE GOT THERE.
I MADE IT IN CLASS.
WOULD YOU LIKE IT? I'D BE HAPPY TO GIVE IT TO YOU.
I DOUBT I'D USE IT... I'LL HAVE TO PASS.

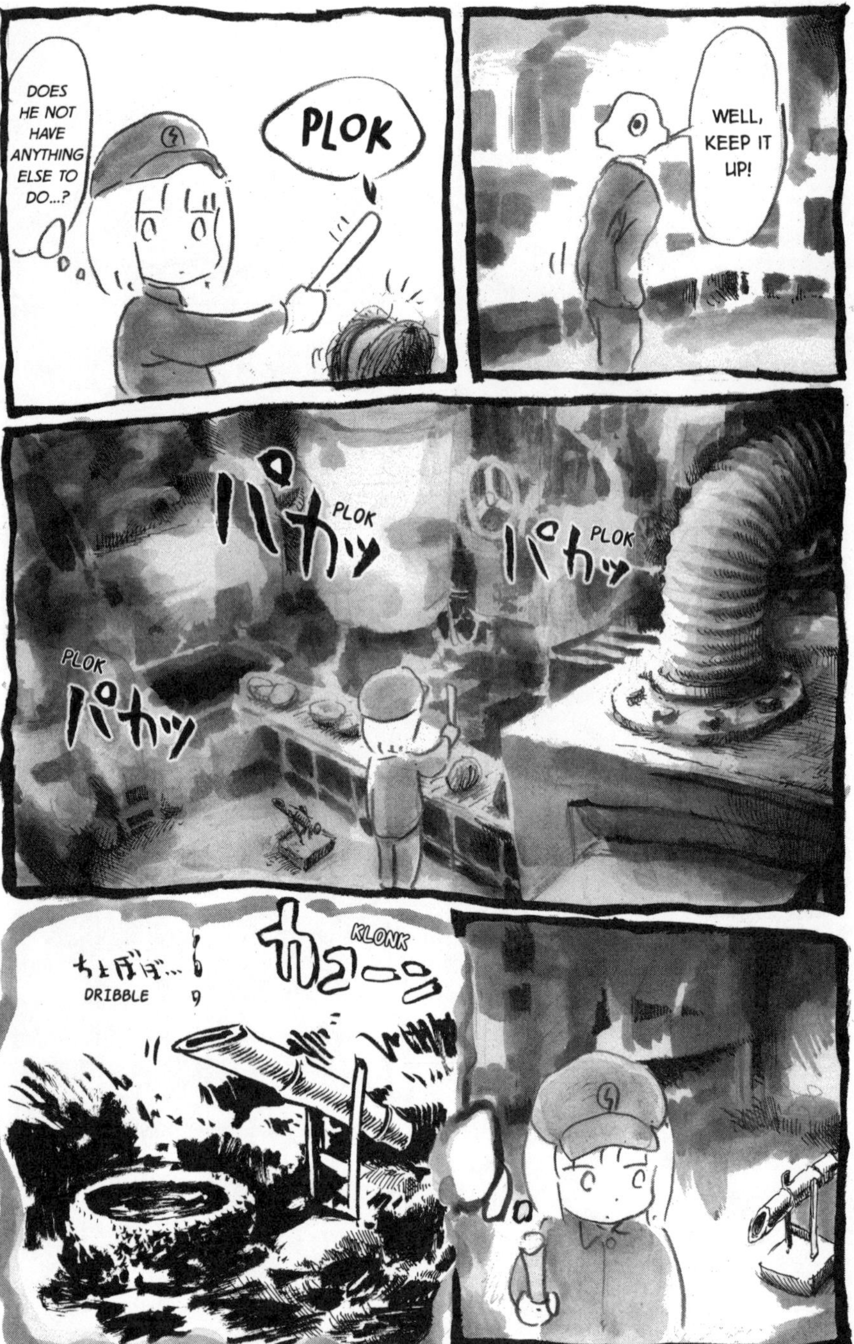
WELL, KEEP IT UP!
PLOK
DOES HE NOT HAVE ANYTHING ELSE TO DO...?
パカッ
PLOK
パカッ
PLOK
PLOK
パカッ
カコーン
KLONK
ちょぼぼ...
DRIBBLE

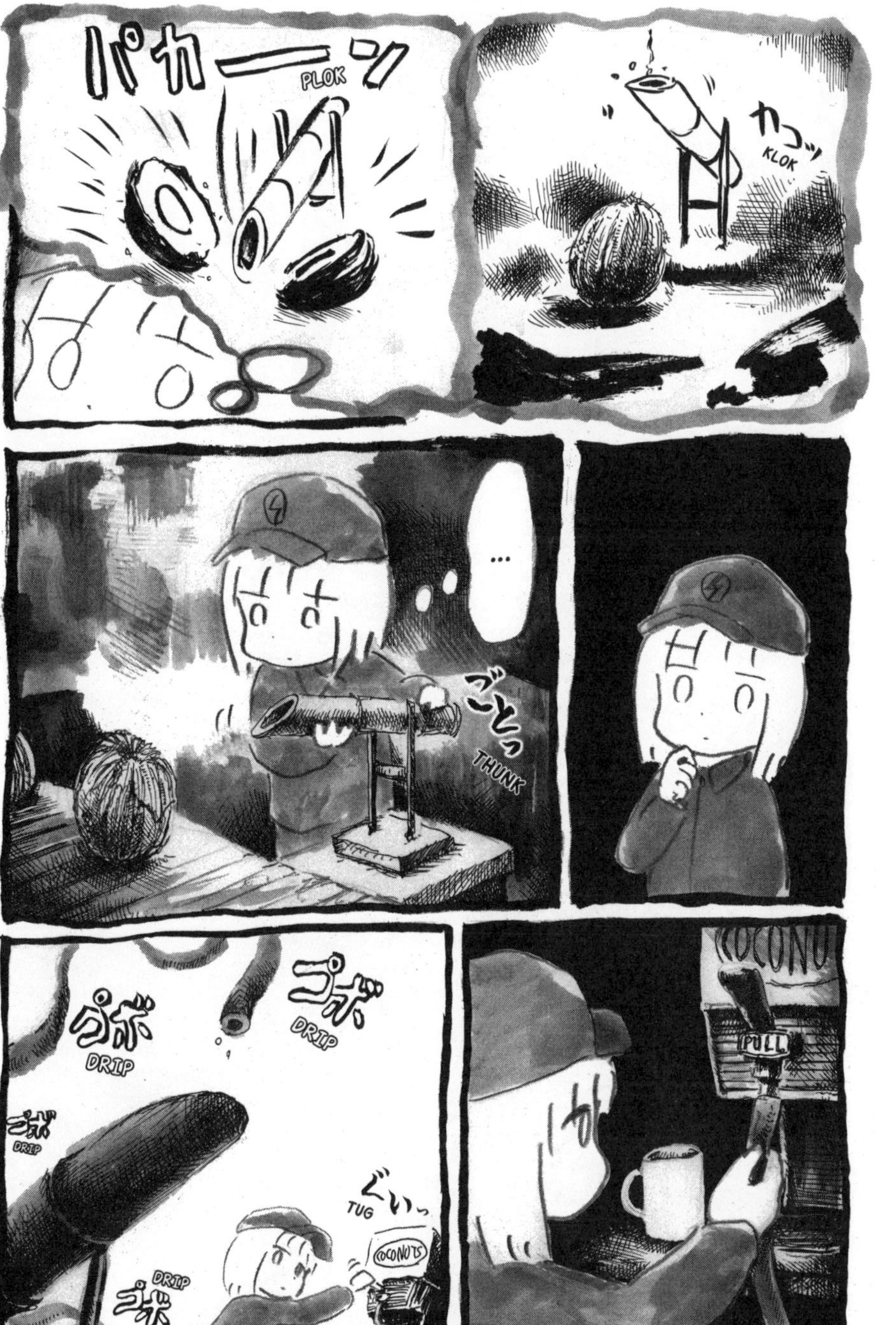
カッ
KLOK
パカーッ
PLOK
...
ごとっ
THUNK
COCONU
PULL
ごぽ
DRIP
ぷぽ
DRIP
ごぽ
DRIP
ぐいっ
TUG
COCONUTS
ごぽ
DRIP

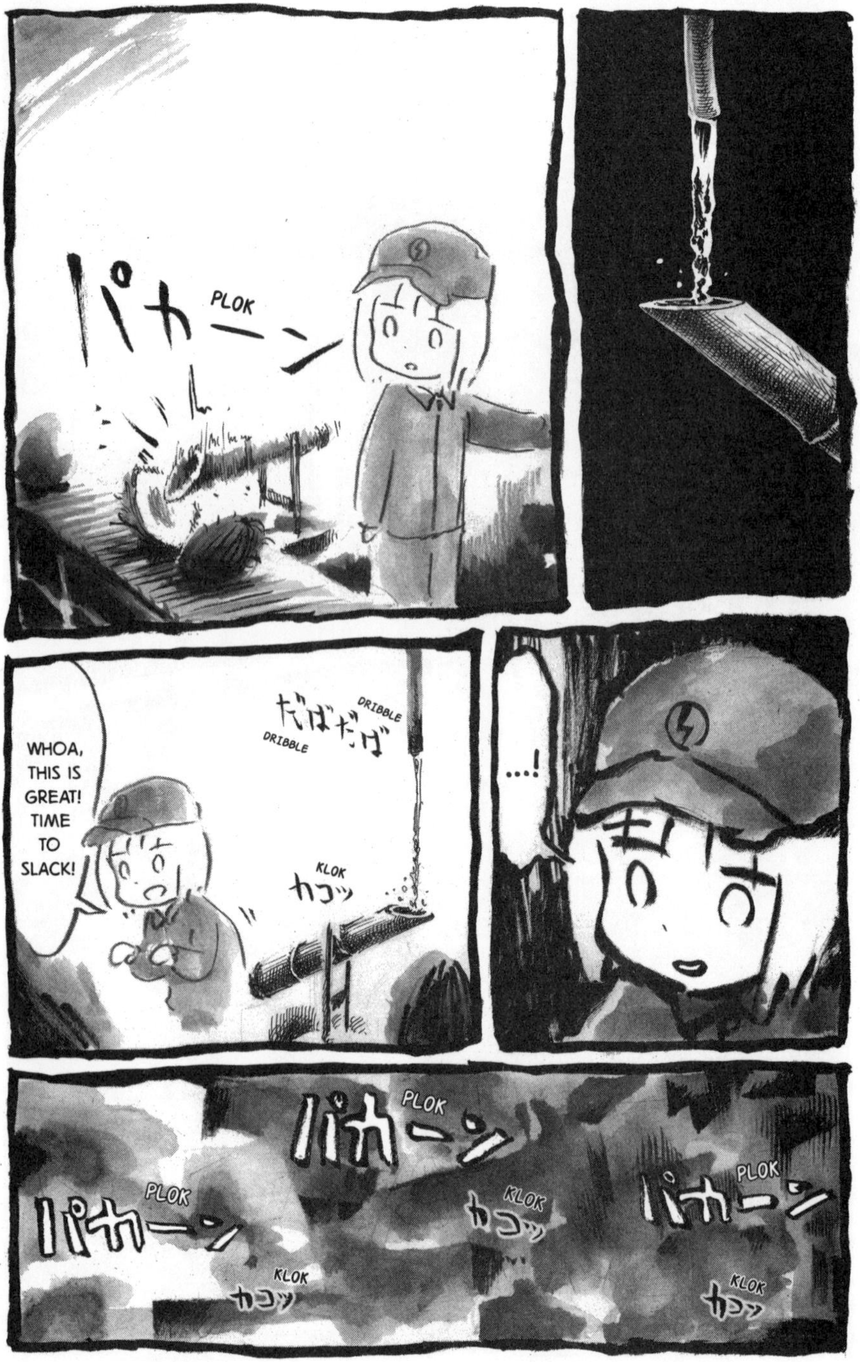

パカーン
PLOK
...!
だばだば
DRIBBLE
DRIBBLE
WHOA, THIS IS GREAT! TIME TO SLACK!
カコッ
KLOK
パカーン
PLOK
PLOK
パカーン
KLOK
カコッ
PLOK
パカーン
KLOK
カコッ
KLOK
カコッ

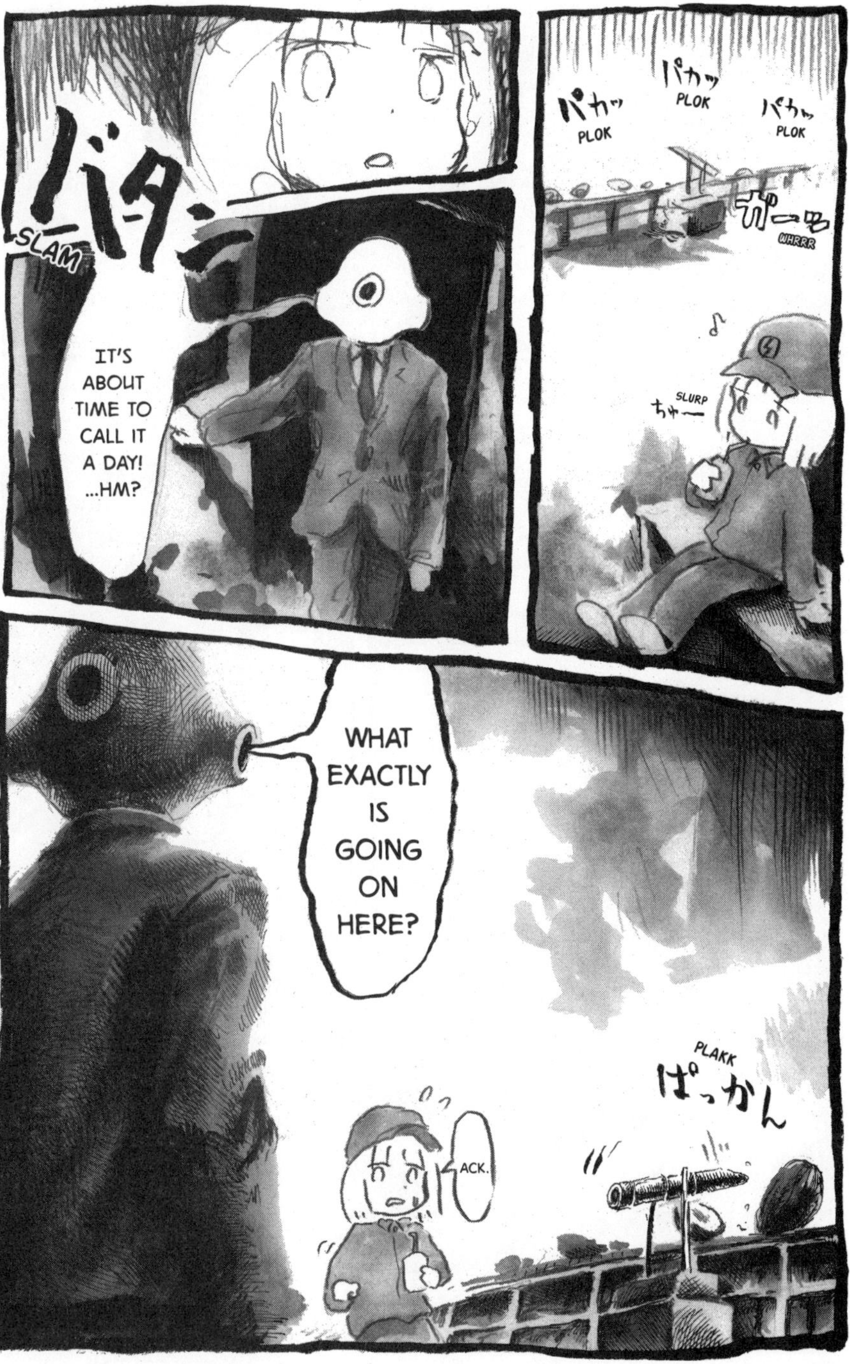

パカッ PLOK
パカッ PLOK
パカッ PLOK
WHRRR
♪
ちゃー SLURP
バタン SLAM
IT'S ABOUT TIME TO CALL IT A DAY! ...HM?
WHAT EXACTLY IS GOING ON HERE?
ぱっかん PLAKK
ACK.

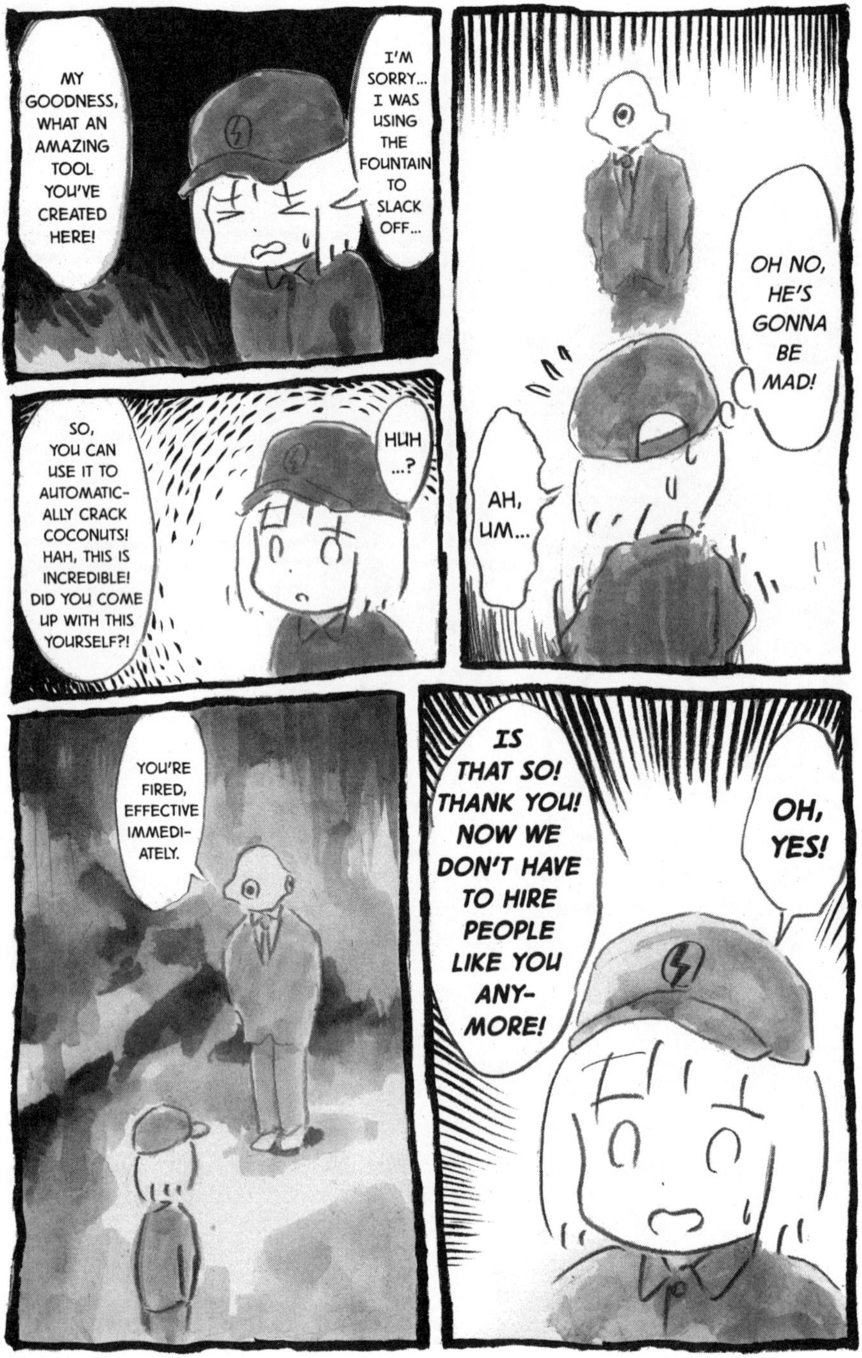
OH NO, HE'S GONNA BE MAD!
AH, UM...
I'M SORRY... I WAS USING THE FOUNTAIN TO SLACK OFF...
MY GOODNESS, WHAT AN AMAZING TOOL YOU'VE CREATED HERE!
HUH ...?
SO, YOU CAN USE IT TO AUTOMATIC-ALLY CRACK COCONUTS! HAH, THIS IS INCREDIBLE! DID YOU COME UP WITH THIS YOURSELF?!
OH, YES!
IS THAT SO! THANK YOU! NOW WE DON'T HAVE TO HIRE PEOPLE LIKE YOU ANY-MORE!
YOU'RE FIRED, EFFECTIVE IMMEDI-ATELY.

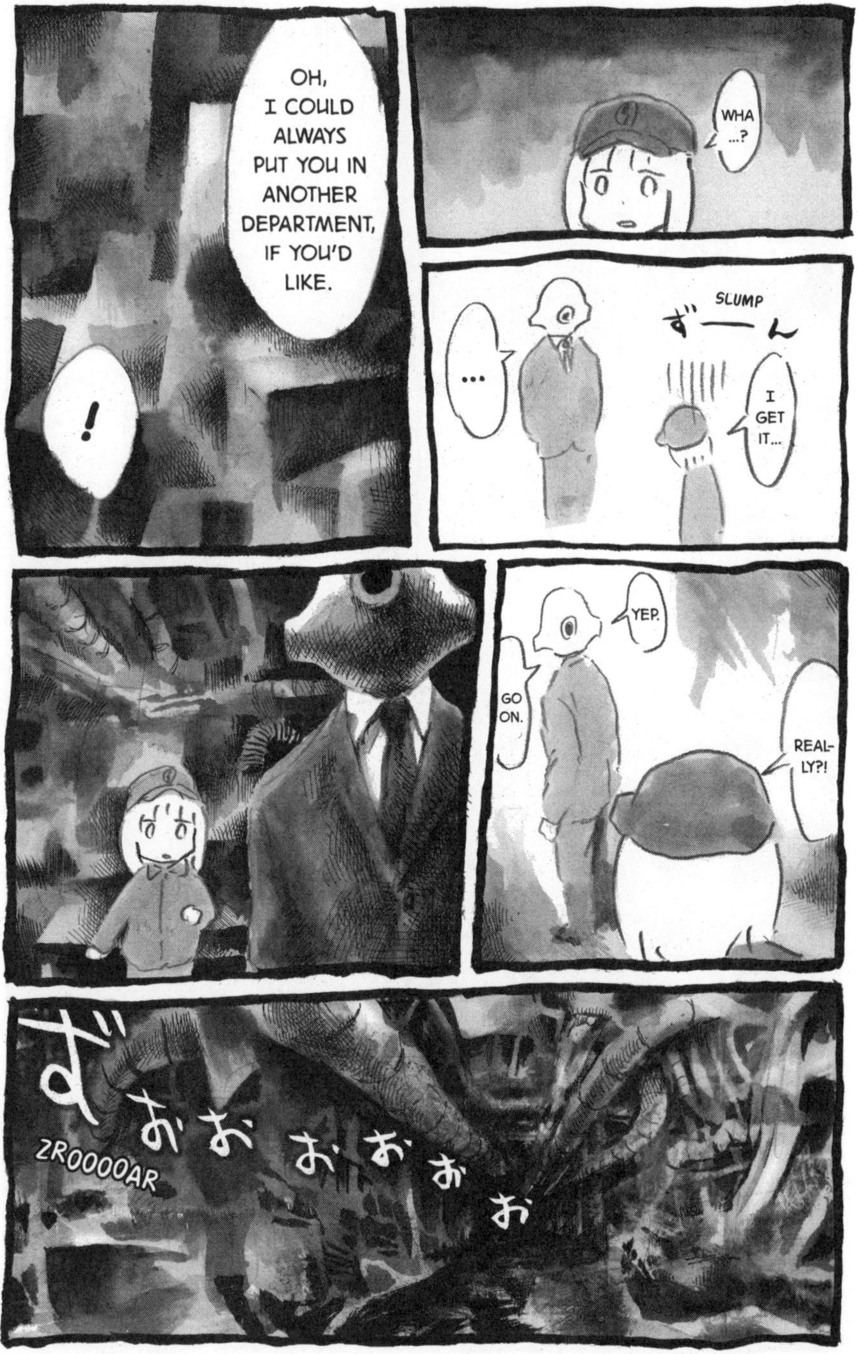
WHA ...?
SLUMP
ずーん
I GET IT...
...
OH, I COULD ALWAYS PUT YOU IN ANOTHER DEPARTMENT, IF YOU'D LIKE.
!
YEP.
REAL-LY?!
GO ON.
ずおおおおおお
ZROOOOAR

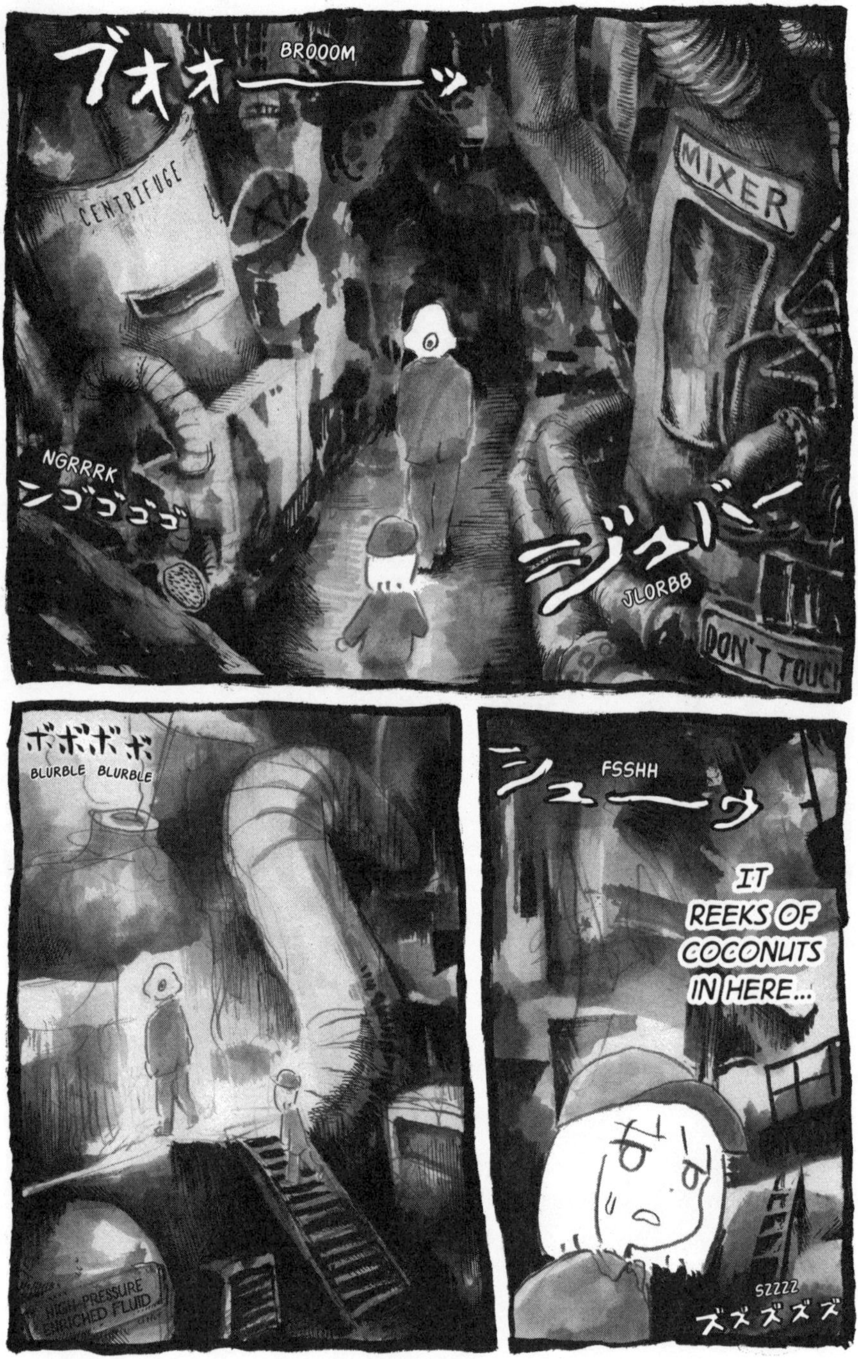
MIXER
ブオオーーッ
BROOOM
CENTRIFUGE
ジュバー
JLORBB
DON'T TOUCH
NGRRRK
ゴゴゴゴ
シューーゥ
FSSHH
IT REEKS OF COCONUTS IN HERE...
SZZZZ
ズズズズズ
ボボボボ
BLURBLE BLURBLE
HIGH-PRESSURE ENRICHED FLUID

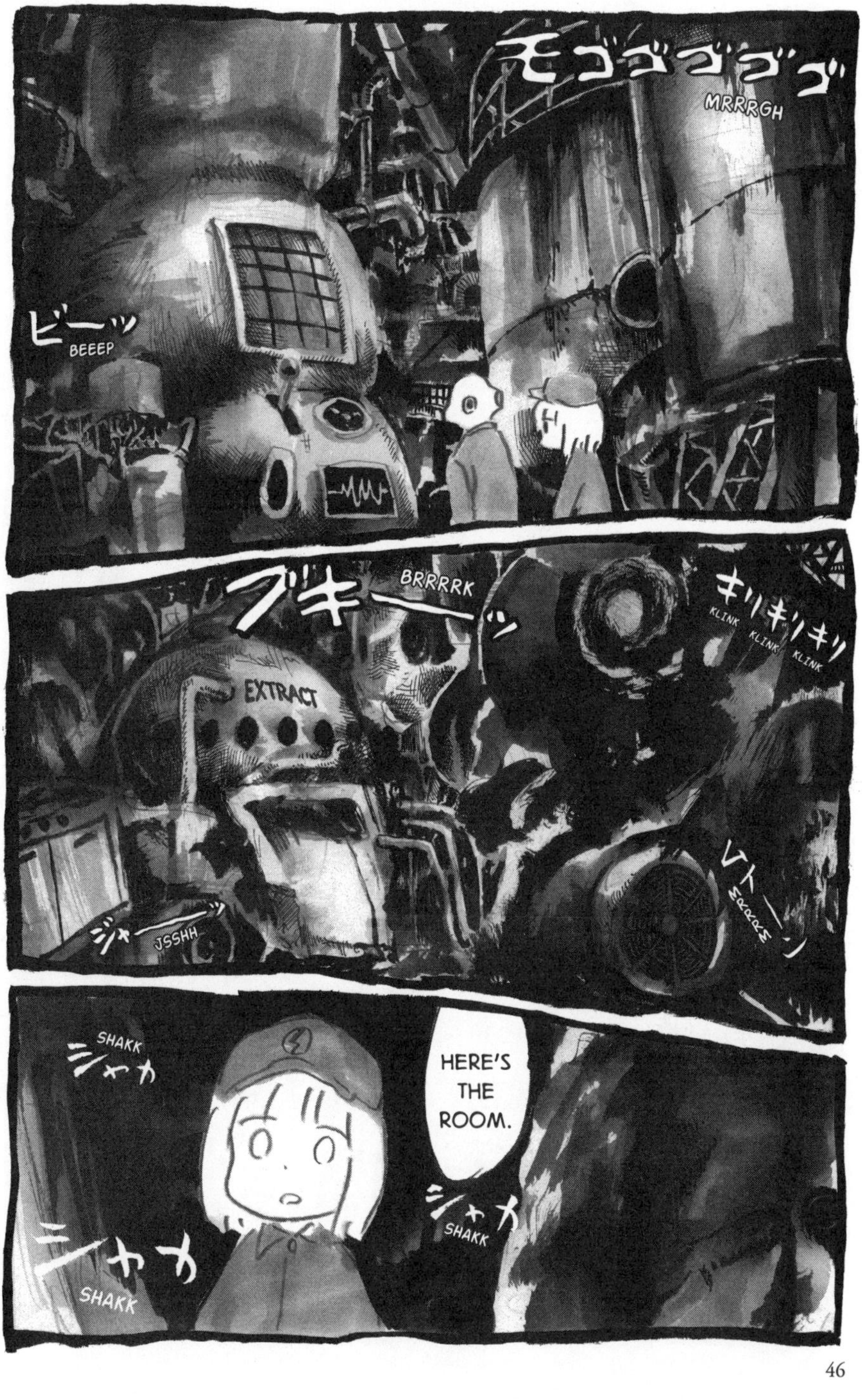
MRRRGH
BEEEP
KLINK KLINK KLINK
BRRRRK
EXTRACT
JSSHH
HERE'S THE ROOM.
SHAKK
SHAKK
SHAKK

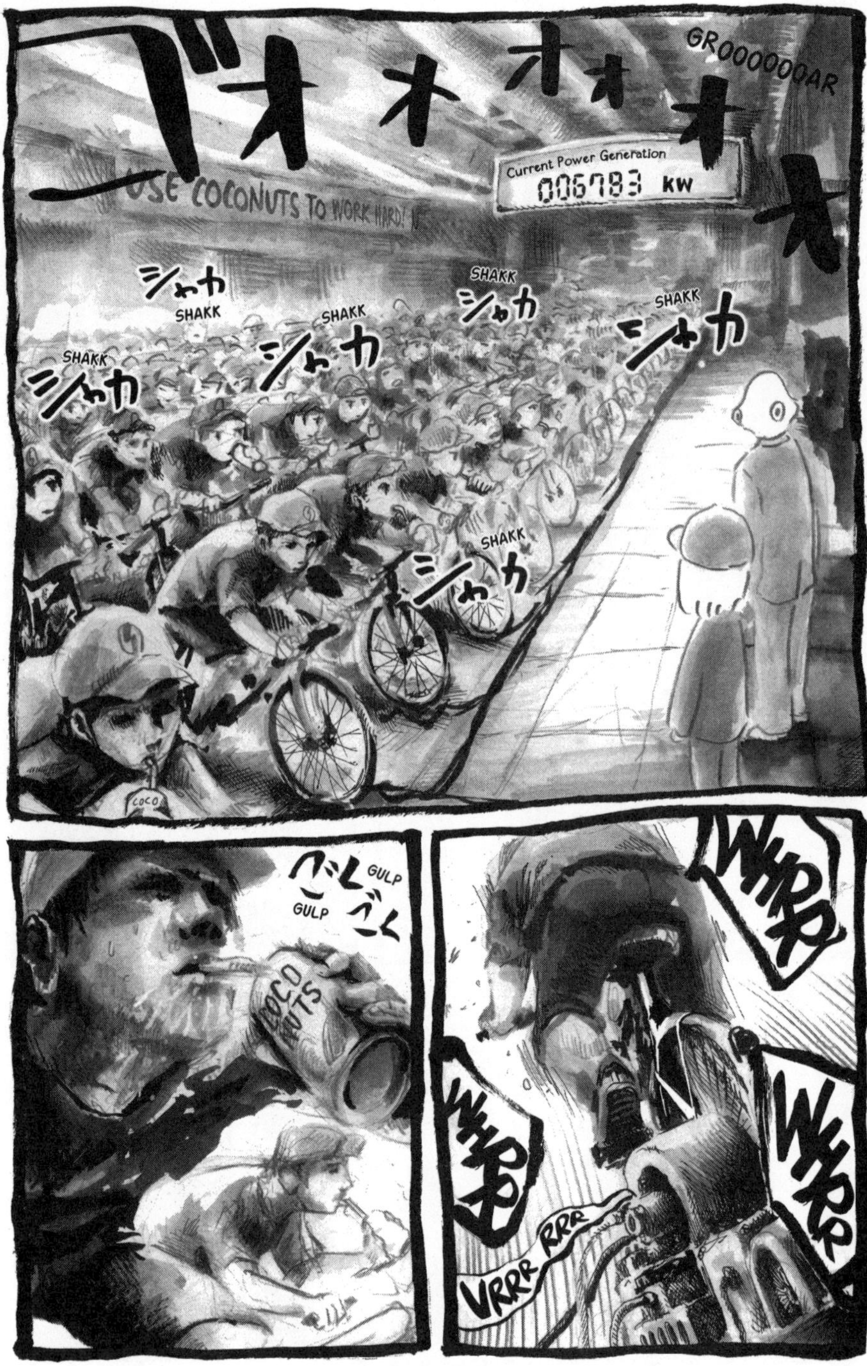
ゴオオオオオオ
GROOOOOOOAR
Current Power Generation
006783 kw
USE COCONUTS TO WORK HARD!
シャカ
SHAKK
シャカ
SHAKK
シャカ
SHAKK
シャカ
SHAKK
シャカ
SHAKK
シャカ
SHAKK
COCO
WHRR
WHRR
WHRR
VRRR RRR
ごく
GULP
ごく
GULP
COCONUTS

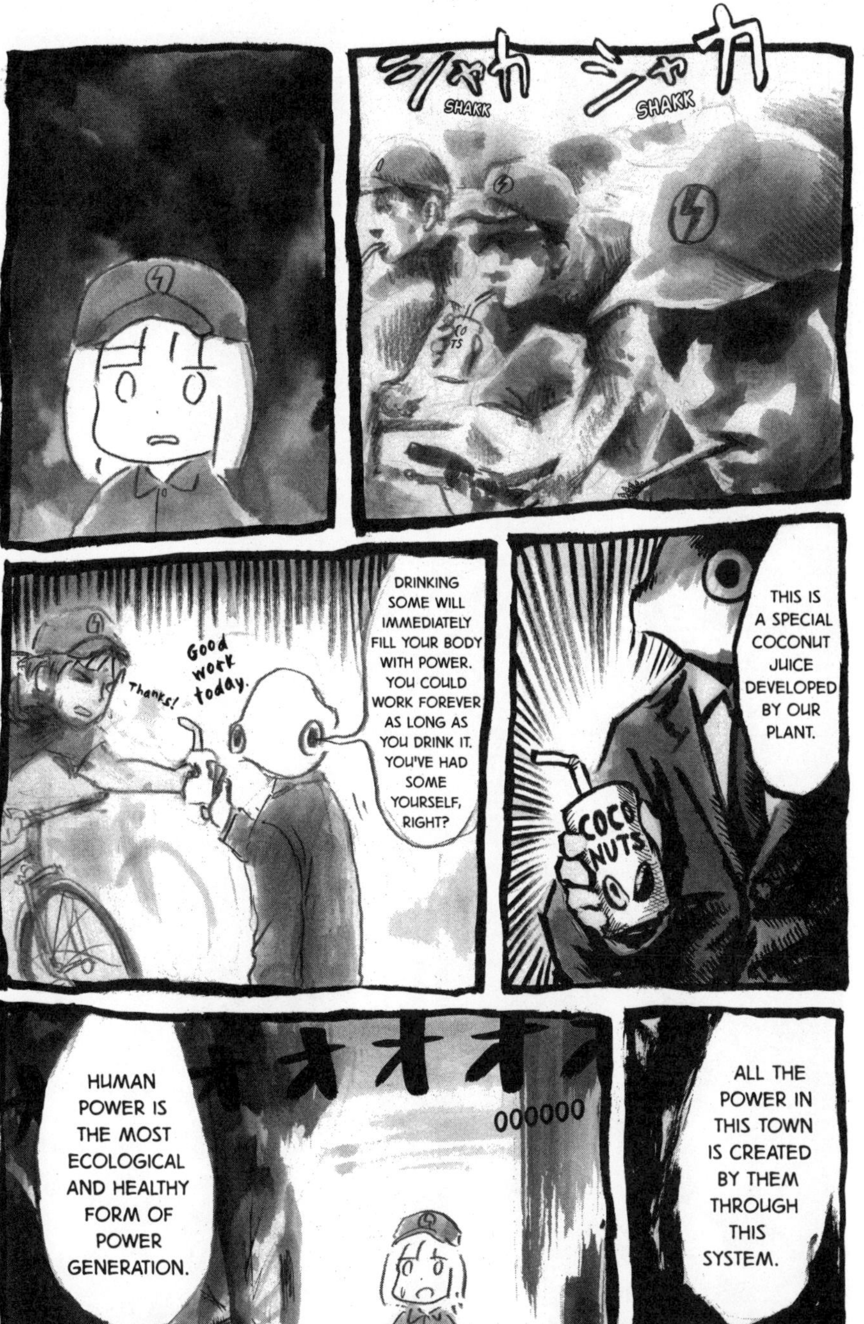
シャカ シャカ
SHAKK
SHAKK
THIS IS A SPECIAL COCONUT JUICE DEVELOPED BY OUR PLANT.
COCO NUTS
DRINKING SOME WILL IMMEDIATELY FILL YOUR BODY WITH POWER. YOU COULD WORK FOREVER AS LONG AS YOU DRINK IT. YOU'VE HAD SOME YOURSELF, RIGHT?
Good work today.
Thanks!
ALL THE POWER IN THIS TOWN IS CREATED BY THEM THROUGH THIS SYSTEM.
OOOOOO
HUMAN POWER IS THE MOST ECOLOGICAL AND HEALTHY FORM OF POWER GENERATION.

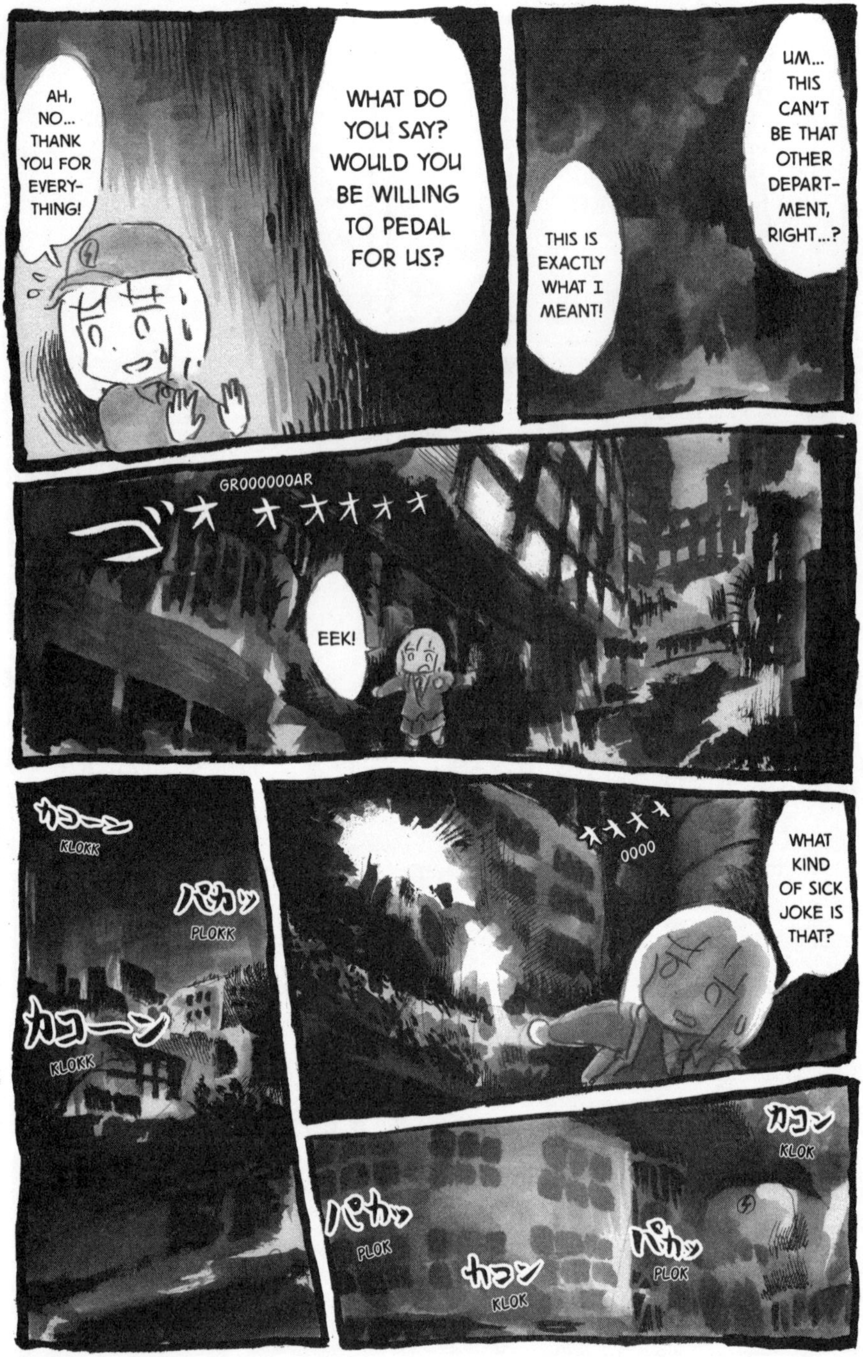
UM... THIS CAN'T BE THAT OTHER DEPART-MENT, RIGHT...?
THIS IS EXACTLY WHAT I MEANT!
WHAT DO YOU SAY? WOULD YOU BE WILLING TO PEDAL FOR US?
AH, NO... THANK YOU FOR EVERY-THING!
ゴオオオオオオ
GROOOOOOAR
EEK!
オオオオ
OOOO
WHAT KIND OF SICK JOKE IS THAT?
カコン
KLOK
パカッ
PLOK
カコン
KLOK
パカッ
PLOK
カコーン
KLOKK
パカッ
PLOKK
カコーン
KLOKK

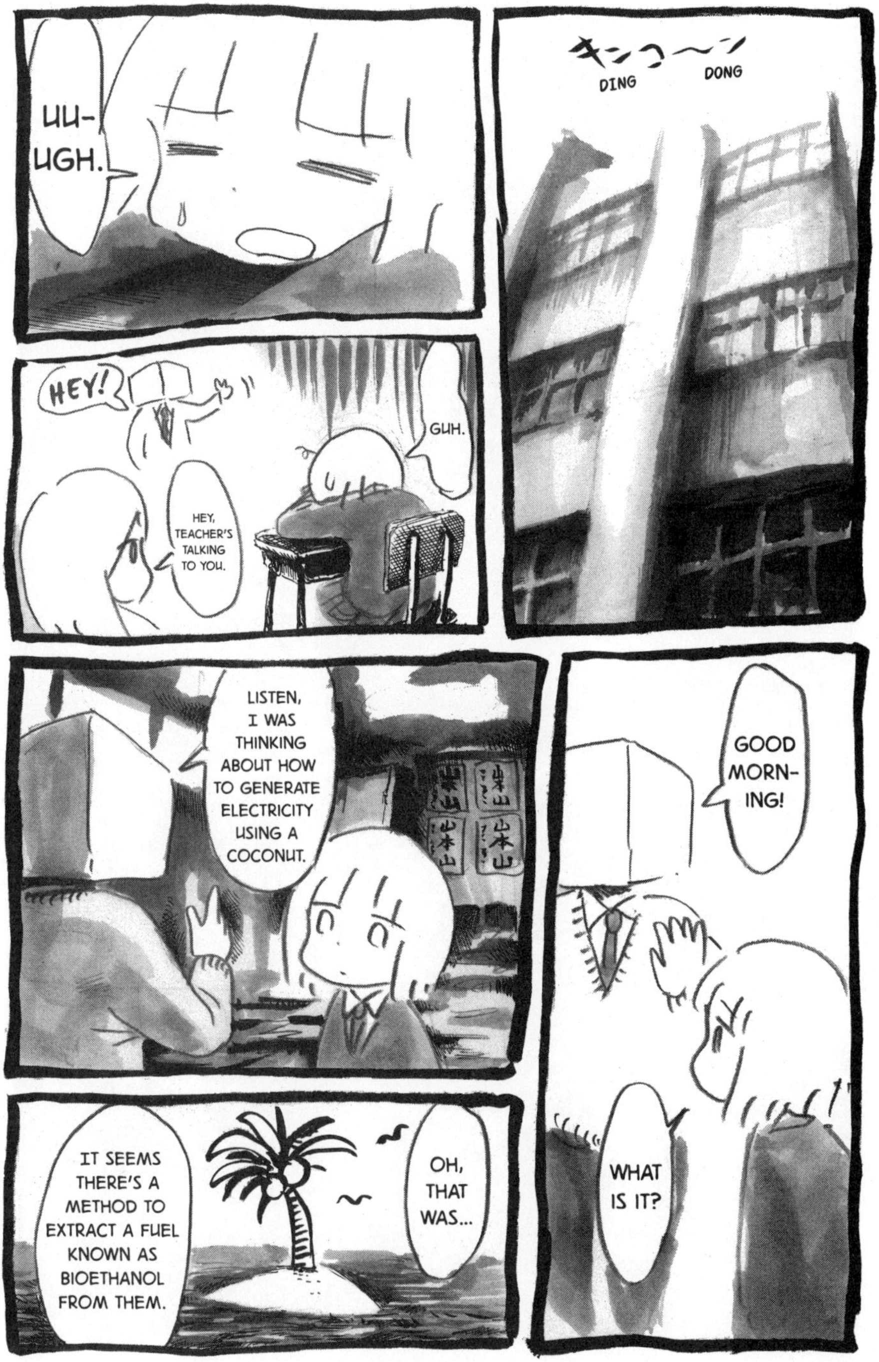

キンコ〜ン
DING DONG
UU-UGH.
GUH.
HEY!
HEY, TEACHER'S TALKING TO YOU.
GOOD MORNING!
WHAT IS IT?
LISTEN, I WAS THINKING ABOUT HOW TO GENERATE ELECTRICITY USING A COCONUT.
OH, THAT WAS...
IT SEEMS THERE'S A METHOD TO EXTRACT A FUEL KNOWN AS BIOETHANOL FROM THEM.

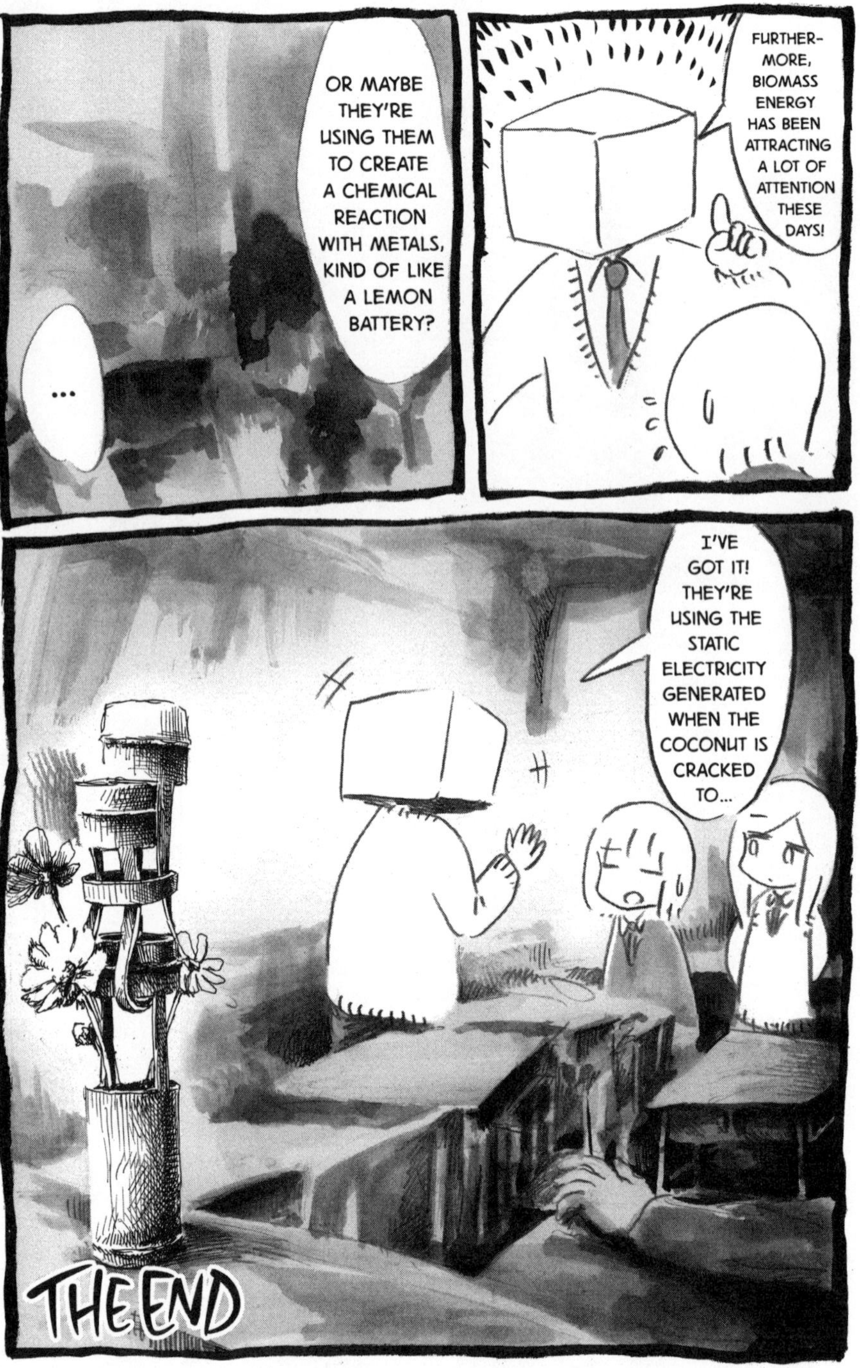
FURTHER-MORE, BIOMASS ENERGY HAS BEEN ATTRACTING A LOT OF ATTENTION THESE DAYS!
OR MAYBE THEY'RE USING THEM TO CREATE A CHEMICAL REACTION WITH METALS, KIND OF LIKE A LEMON BATTERY?
...
I'VE GOT IT! THEY'RE USING THE STATIC ELECTRICITY GENERATED WHEN THE COCONUT IS CRACKED TO...
THE END

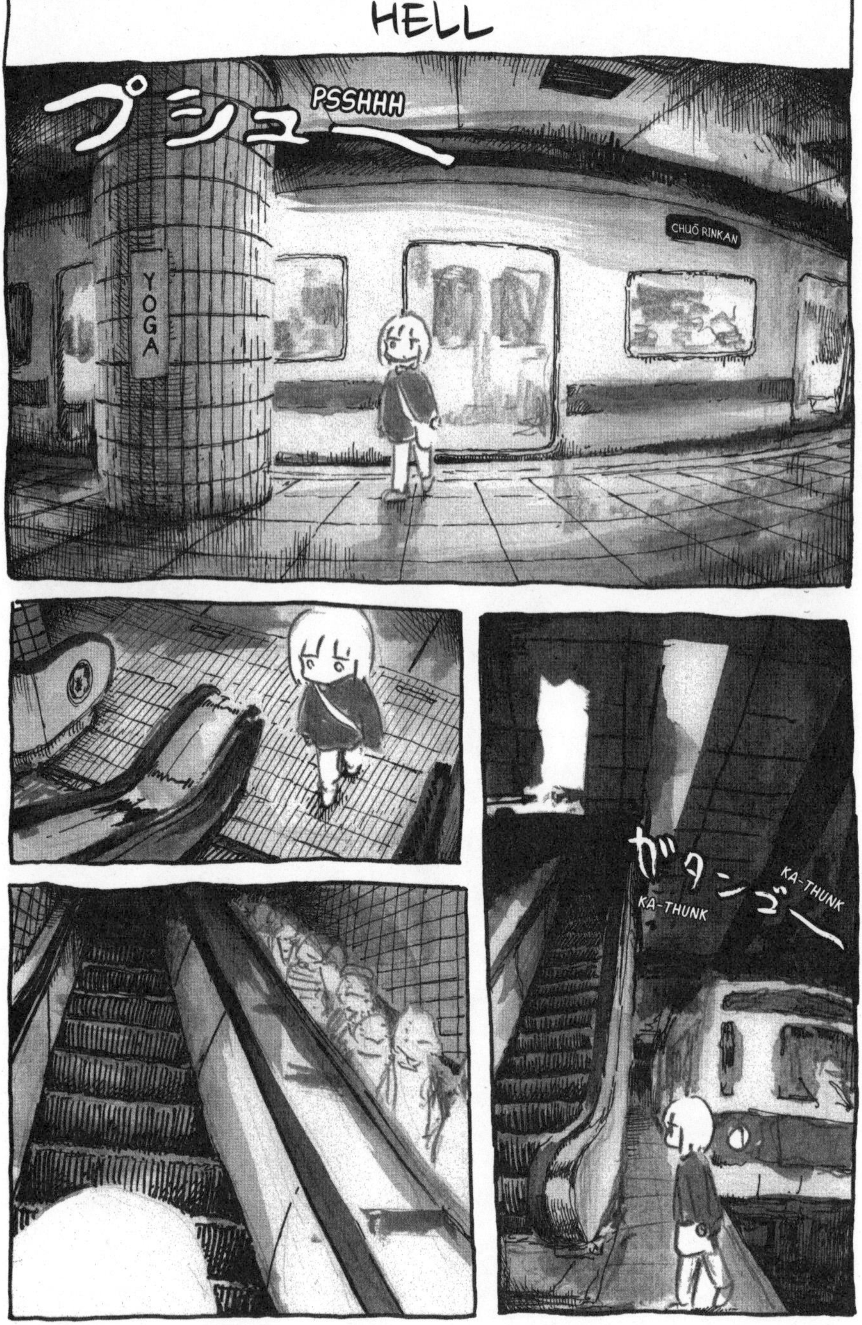
HELL
プシュー
PSSHHH
CHUŌ RINKAN
YOGA
ガタンゴー
KA-THUNK
KA-THUNK

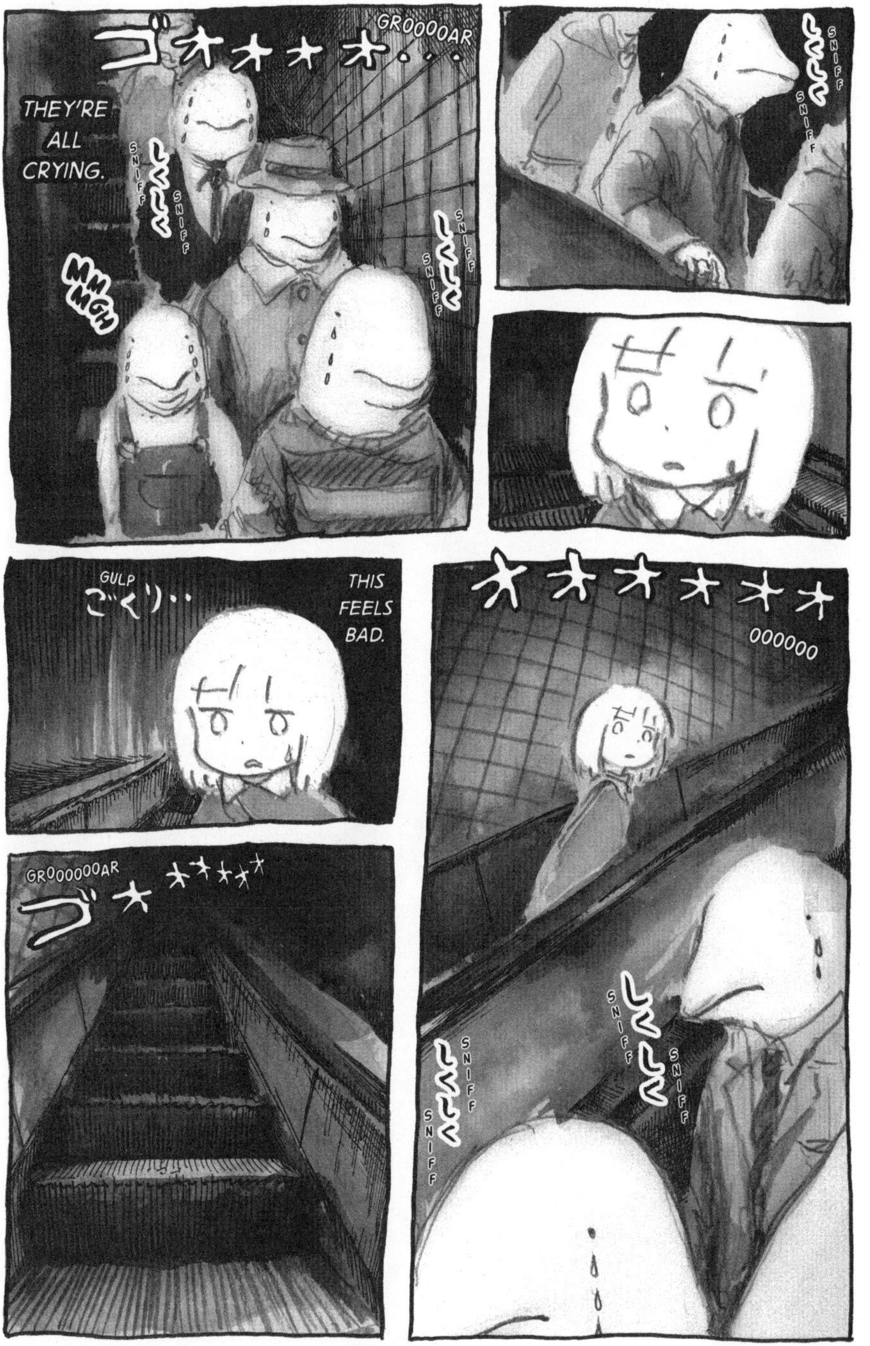
しくしく
SNIFF SNIFF
GROOOOAR
ゴオオオオ・・・
THEY'RE ALL CRYING.
しくしく
SNIFF SNIFF
MMMGH
しくしく
SNIFF SNIFF
オオオオオオ
OOOOOO
しくしく
SNIFF SNIFF
しくしく
SNIFF SNIFF
THIS FEELS BAD.
GULP
ごくり・・
GROOOOOOAR

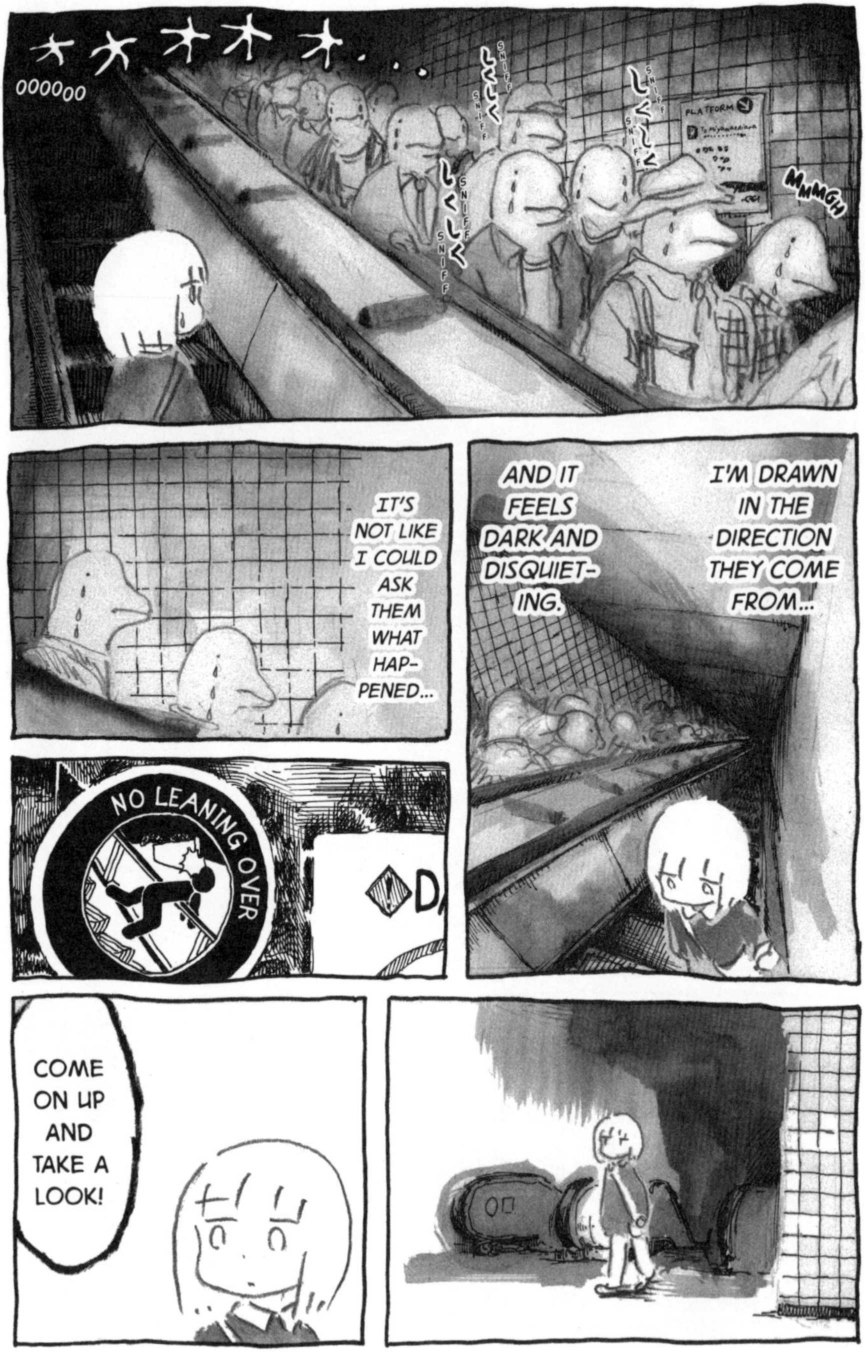
オオオオオ・・・
OOOOOO
しくしく
SNIFF SNIFF
しくしく
SNIFF SNIFF
しくしく
SNIFF SNIFF
MMMGH
I'M DRAWN IN THE DIRECTION THEY COME FROM...
AND IT FEELS DARK AND DISQUIET-ING.
IT'S NOT LIKE I COULD ASK THEM WHAT HAP-PENED...
NO LEANING OVER
COME ON UP AND TAKE A LOOK!

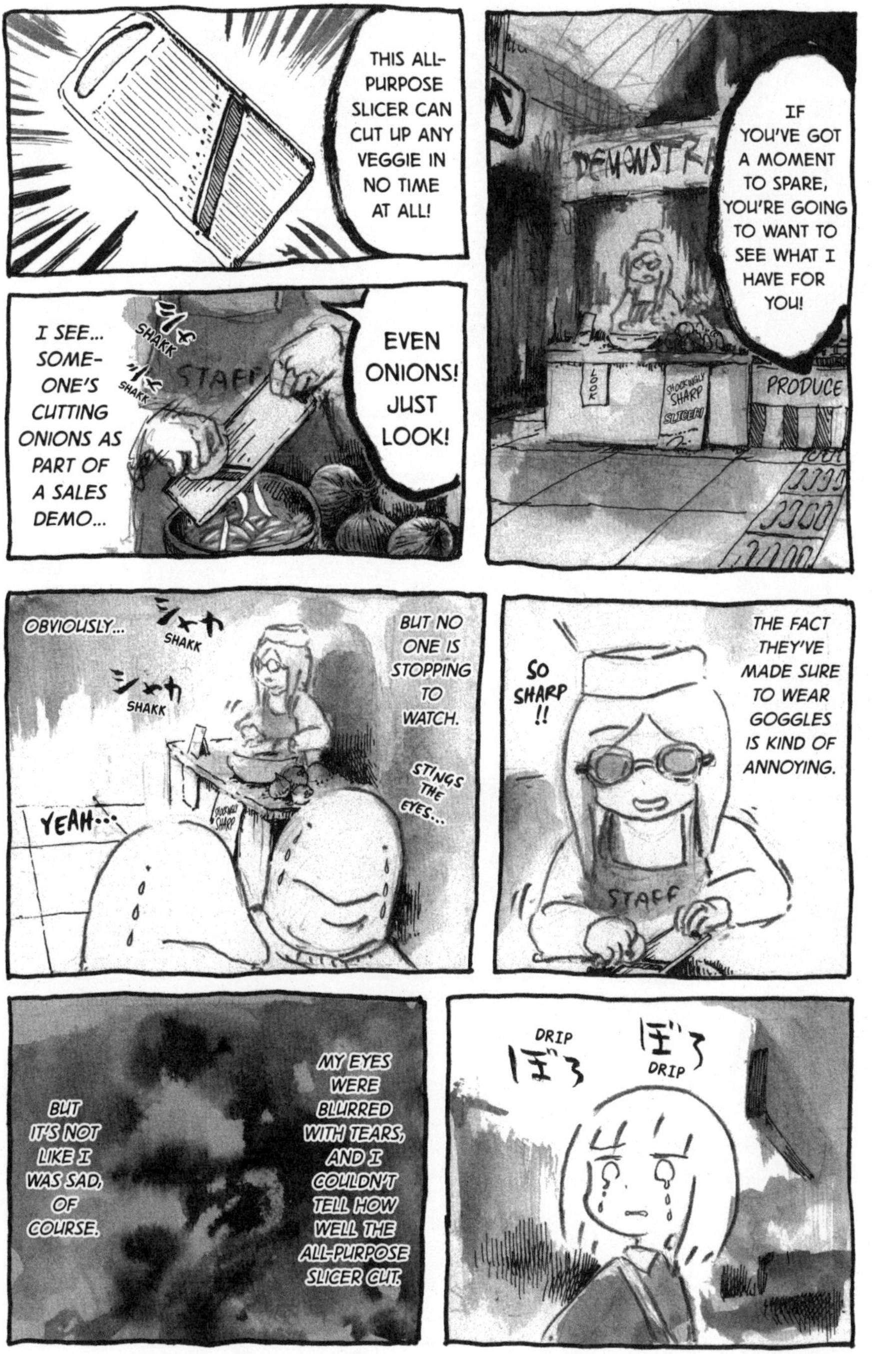
IF YOU'VE GOT A MOMENT TO SPARE, YOU'RE GOING TO WANT TO SEE WHAT I HAVE FOR YOU!
LOOK
SHOCKINGLY SHARP SLICER!
PRODUCE
THIS ALL-PURPOSE SLICER CAN CUT UP ANY VEGGIE IN NO TIME AT ALL!
EVEN ONIONS! JUST LOOK!
STAFF
SHAKK
SHAKK
I SEE... SOME-ONE'S CUTTING ONIONS AS PART OF A SALES DEMO...
THE FACT THEY'VE MADE SURE TO WEAR GOGGLES IS KIND OF ANNOYING.
SO SHARP !!
STAFF
BUT NO ONE IS STOPPING TO WATCH.
STINGS THE EYES...
SHAKK
OBVIOUSLY...
SHAKK
YEAH...
DRIP
DRIP
MY EYES WERE BLURRED WITH TEARS, AND I COULDN'T TELL HOW WELL THE ALL-PURPOSE SLICER CUT.
BUT IT'S NOT LIKE I WAS SAD, OF COURSE.

Fluctuation

As I was waiting for the light to change at a T-shaped intersection, I saw a tree about four meters tall growing from what looked like a field diagonally in front of me. It swayed back and forth in an unnatural way. It wasn't as if there was any wind blowing, and it didn't sway like it would from a gust, anyway.

When I looked at it carefully, I saw a stepladder at the bottom of the tree and realized that someone was climbing it. Then, from behind the leaves, I got a glance at what looked like a human's jacket. Maybe a child was climbing the tree causing it to swing back and forth. But bringing a stepladder seemed too circumspect for a child.

I kept on observing, and the way it swung was just so mechanical. But just as I thought I was figuring it out, the light turned green.

The moment I passed the tree, I realized someone was on top of it, sawing off its branches. So, the tree was swaying from the saw's rhythmical, severing movements. I thought I'd looked at it for a while, but perhaps not much time had passed at all. Or maybe he was trying to cut off an especially thick branch. And for the whole time I watched, not a single branch fell to the ground.

November 30, 2013

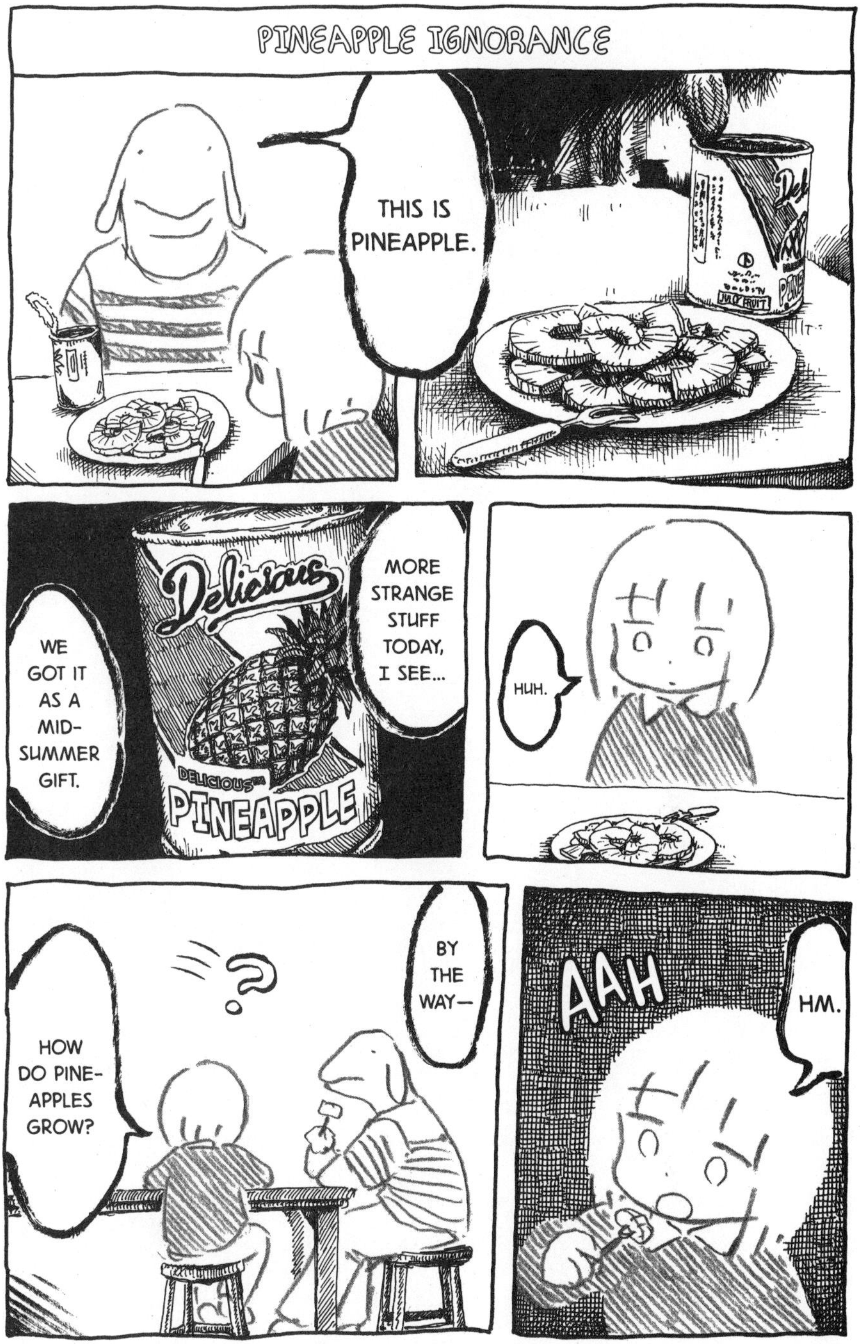
PINEAPPLE IGNORANCE
THIS IS PINEAPPLE.
HUH.
MORE STRANGE STUFF TODAY, I SEE...
Delicious
DELICIOUS™
PINEAPPLE
WE GOT IT AS A MID-SUMMER GIFT.
HM.
AAH
BY THE WAY—
HOW DO PINE-APPLES GROW?

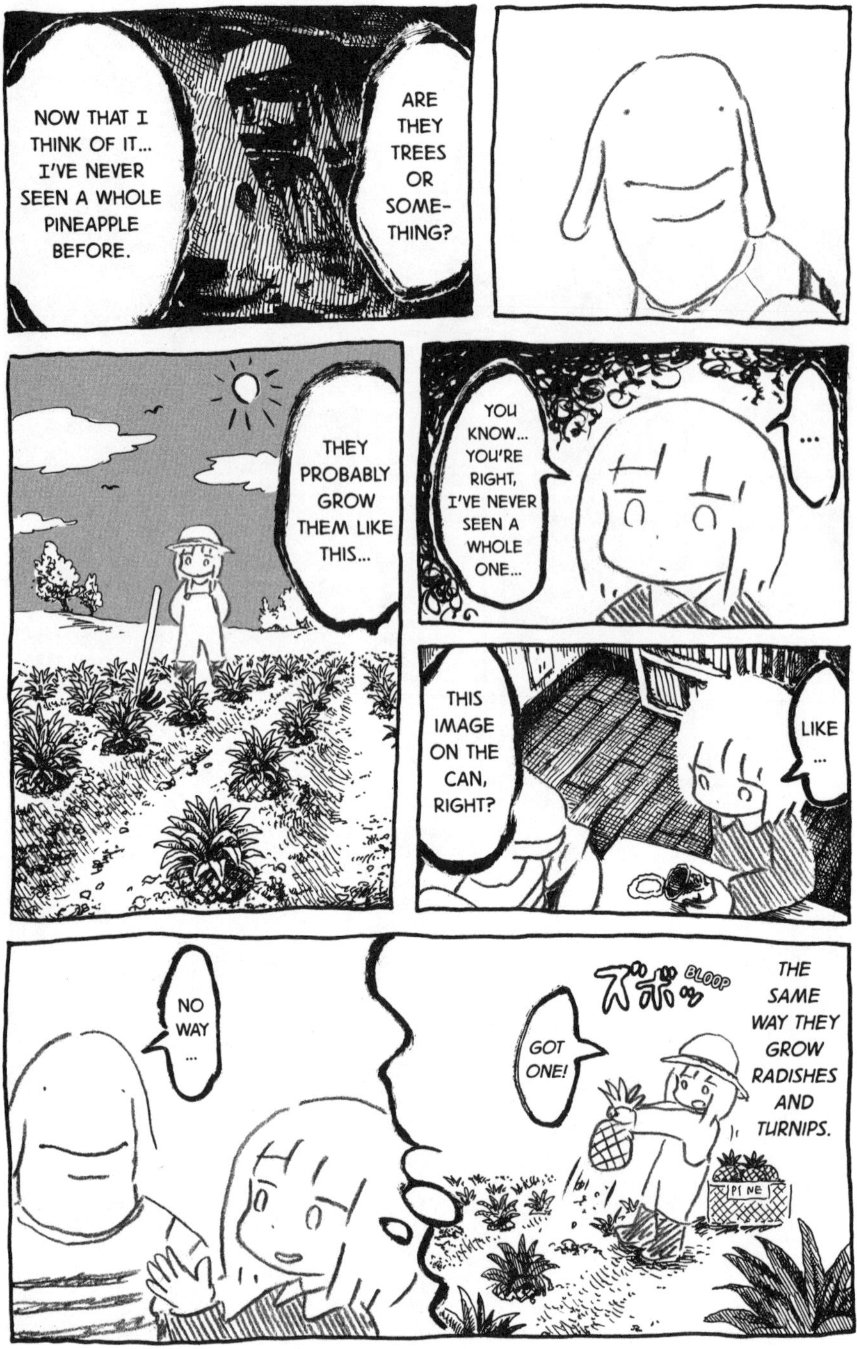
ARE THEY TREES OR SOME-THING?
NOW THAT I THINK OF IT... I'VE NEVER SEEN A WHOLE PINEAPPLE BEFORE.
...
YOU KNOW... YOU'RE RIGHT, I'VE NEVER SEEN A WHOLE ONE...
LIKE ...
THIS IMAGE ON THE CAN, RIGHT?
THEY PROBABLY GROW THEM LIKE THIS...
THE SAME WAY THEY GROW RADISHES AND TURNIPS.
ズボッ BLOOP
GOT ONE!
PINE
NO WAY ...

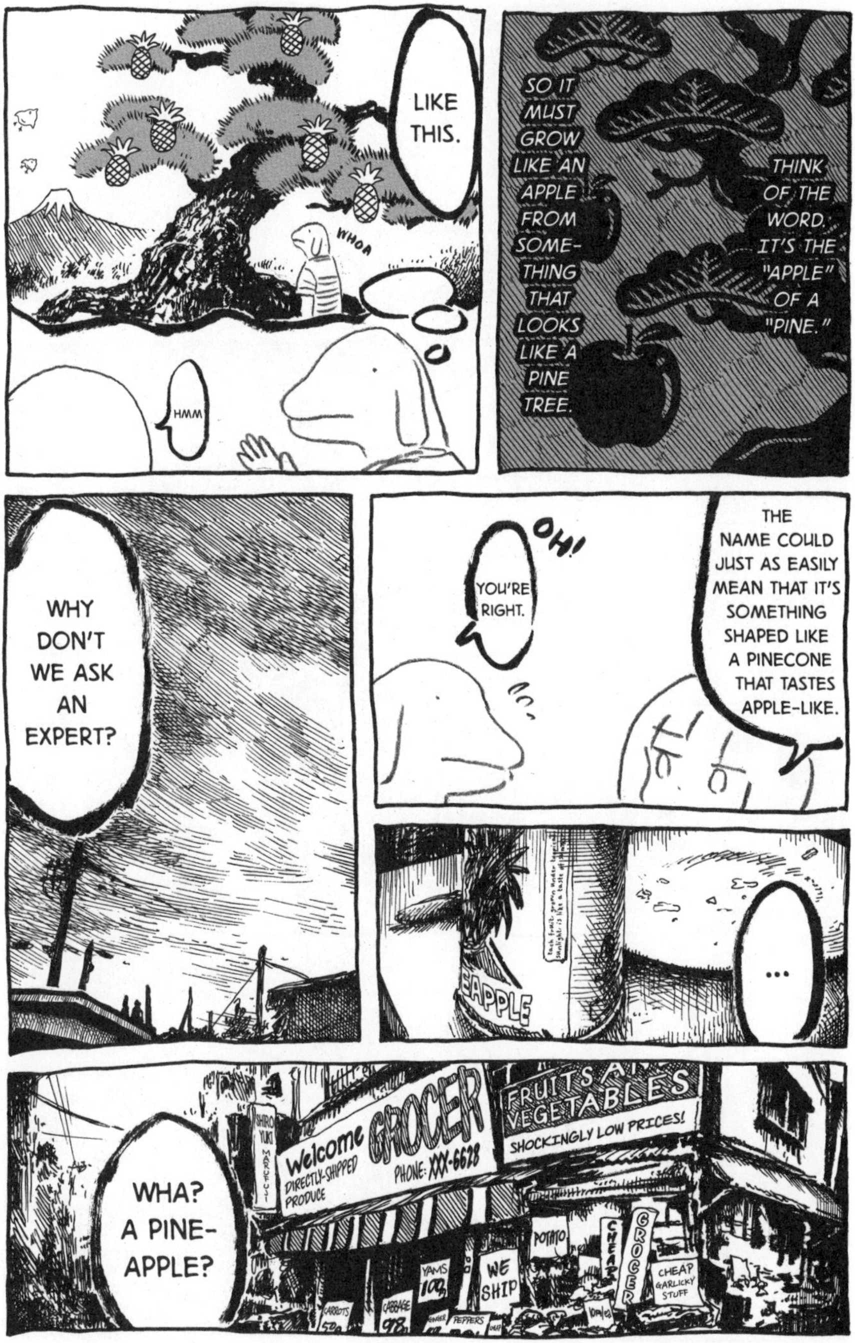
THINK OF THE WORD. IT'S THE "APPLE" OF A "PINE."
SO IT MUST GROW LIKE AN APPLE FROM SOME-THING THAT LOOKS LIKE A PINE TREE.
LIKE THIS.
WHOA
HMM
THE NAME COULD JUST AS EASILY MEAN THAT IT'S SOMETHING SHAPED LIKE A PINECONE THAT TASTES APPLE-LIKE.
OH!
YOU'RE RIGHT.
...
EAPPLE
WHY DON'T WE ASK AN EXPERT?
FRUITS AN
VEGETABLES
SHOCKINGLY LOW PRICES!
GROCER
Welcome
DIRECTLY-SHIPPED PRODUCE
PHONE: XXX-6628
WHA? A PINE-APPLE?
POTATO
CHEAP
GROCER
WE SHIP
YAMS 100
CHEAP GARLICKY STUFF
CARROTS
CABBAGE
PEPPERS

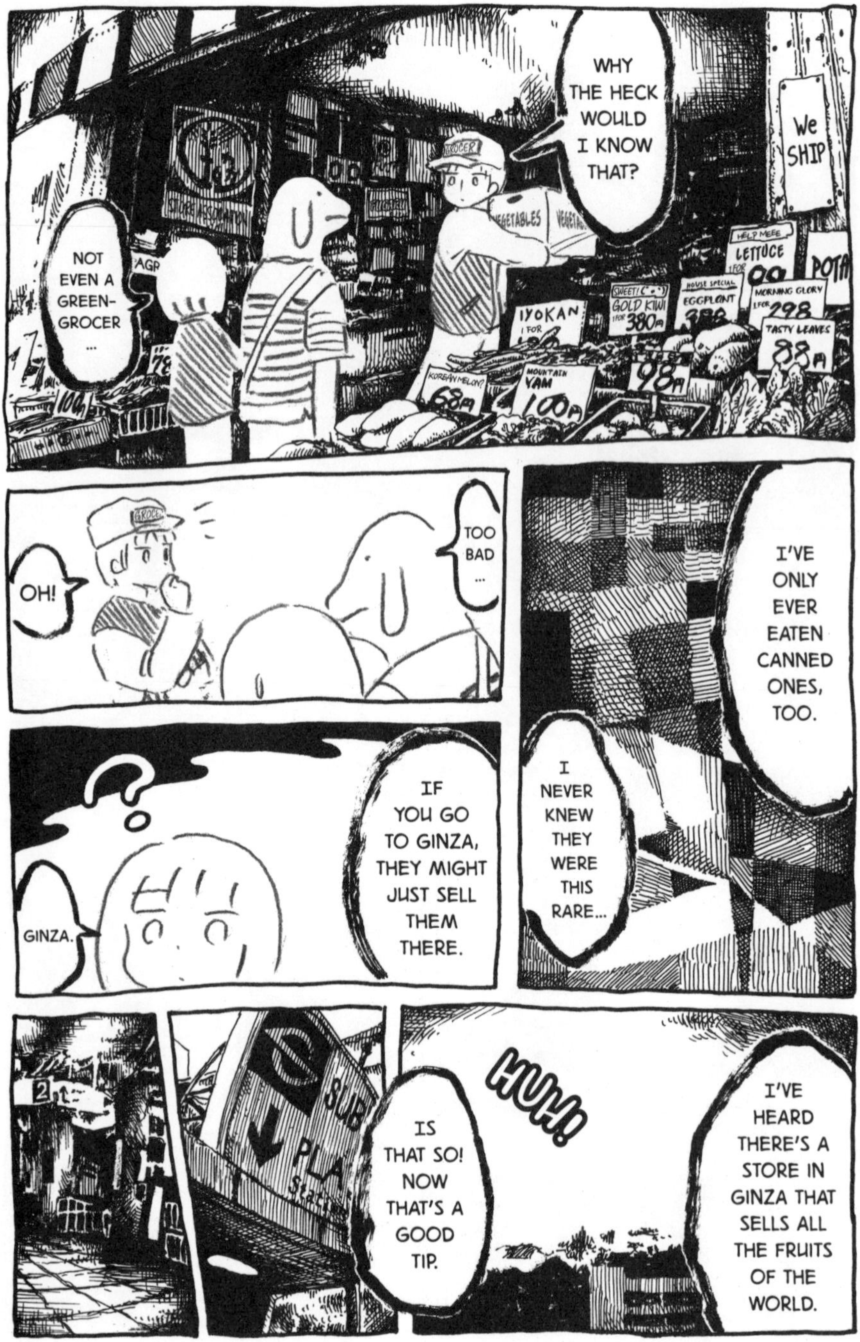
We SHIP
GROCER
WHY THE HECK WOULD I KNOW THAT?
VEGETABLES
HELP MEEE
LETTUCE
SWEET!
GOLD KIWI 1 FOR 380円
HOUSE SPECIAL EGGPLANT
MORNING GLORY 1 FOR 298
TASTY LEAVES 88円
98円
IYOKAN 1 FOR
MOUNTAIN YAM 100円
KOREAN MELON? 68円
STORE ASSOCIATION
NOT EVEN A GREEN-GROCER ...
I'VE ONLY EVER EATEN CANNED ONES, TOO.
I NEVER KNEW THEY WERE THIS RARE...
TOO BAD ...
OH!
IF YOU GO TO GINZA, THEY MIGHT JUST SELL THEM THERE.
GINZA.
I'VE HEARD THERE'S A STORE IN GINZA THAT SELLS ALL THE FRUITS OF THE WORLD.
HUH!
IS THAT SO! NOW THAT'S A GOOD TIP.

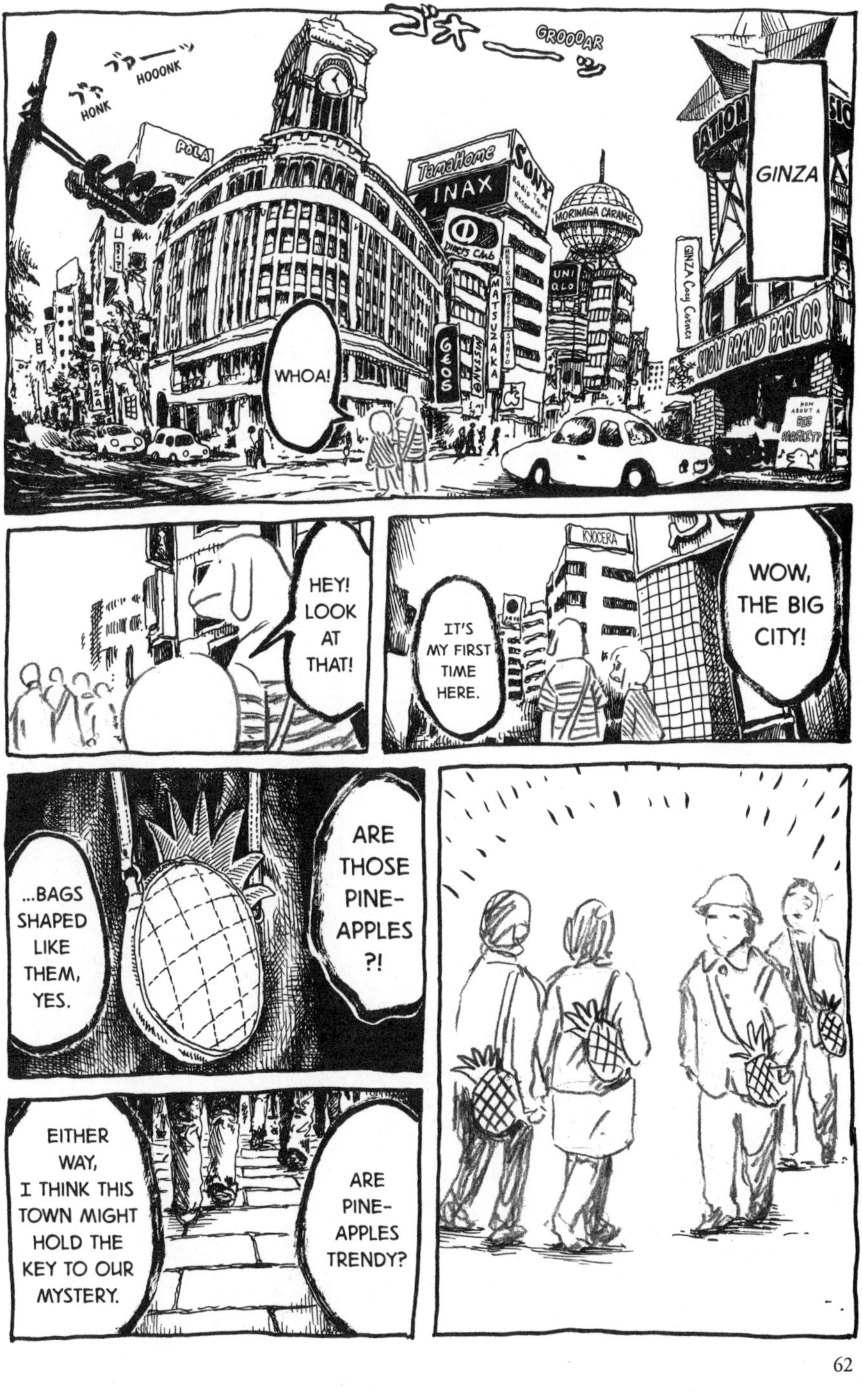
ゴオーーッ
GROOOAR
ブァーッ
HOOONK
ブァ
HONK
GINZA
POLA
TamaHome
INAX
SONY
MORINAGA CARAMEL
UNIQLO
GINZA Cozy Corner
SNOW BRAND PARLOR
HOW ABOUT A BIG PARFAIT?
GEOS
MATSUZAKA
WHOA!
KYOCERA
WOW, THE BIG CITY!
IT'S MY FIRST TIME HERE.
HEY! LOOK AT THAT!
ARE THOSE PINEAPPLES ?!
...BAGS SHAPED LIKE THEM, YES.
ARE PINEAPPLES TRENDY?
EITHER WAY, I THINK THIS TOWN MIGHT HOLD THE KEY TO OUR MYSTERY.

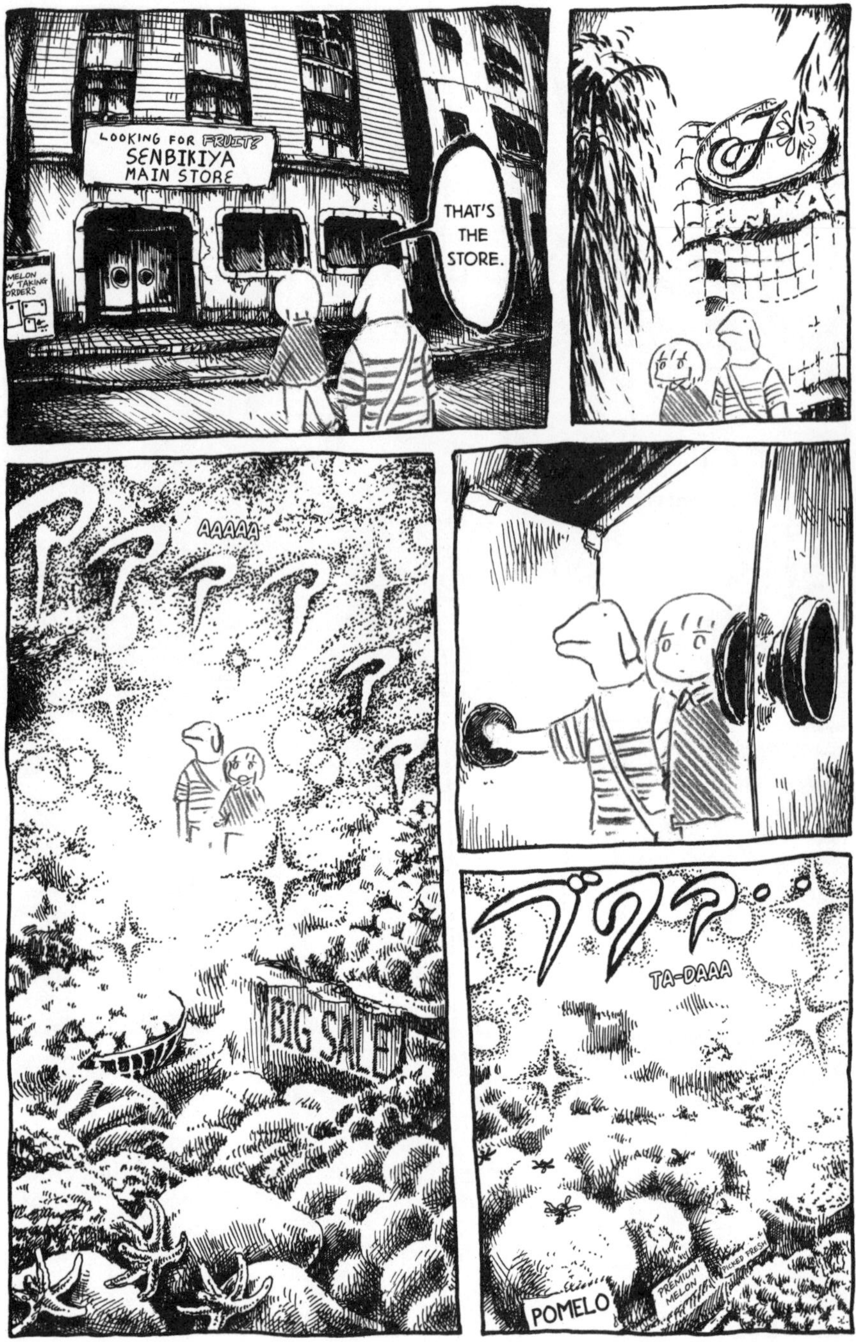

LOOKING FOR FRUIT?
SENBIKIYA
MAIN STORE
THAT'S THE STORE.
TA-DAAA
POMELO
PREMIUM MELON
PICKED FRESH
AAAAA
BIG SALE

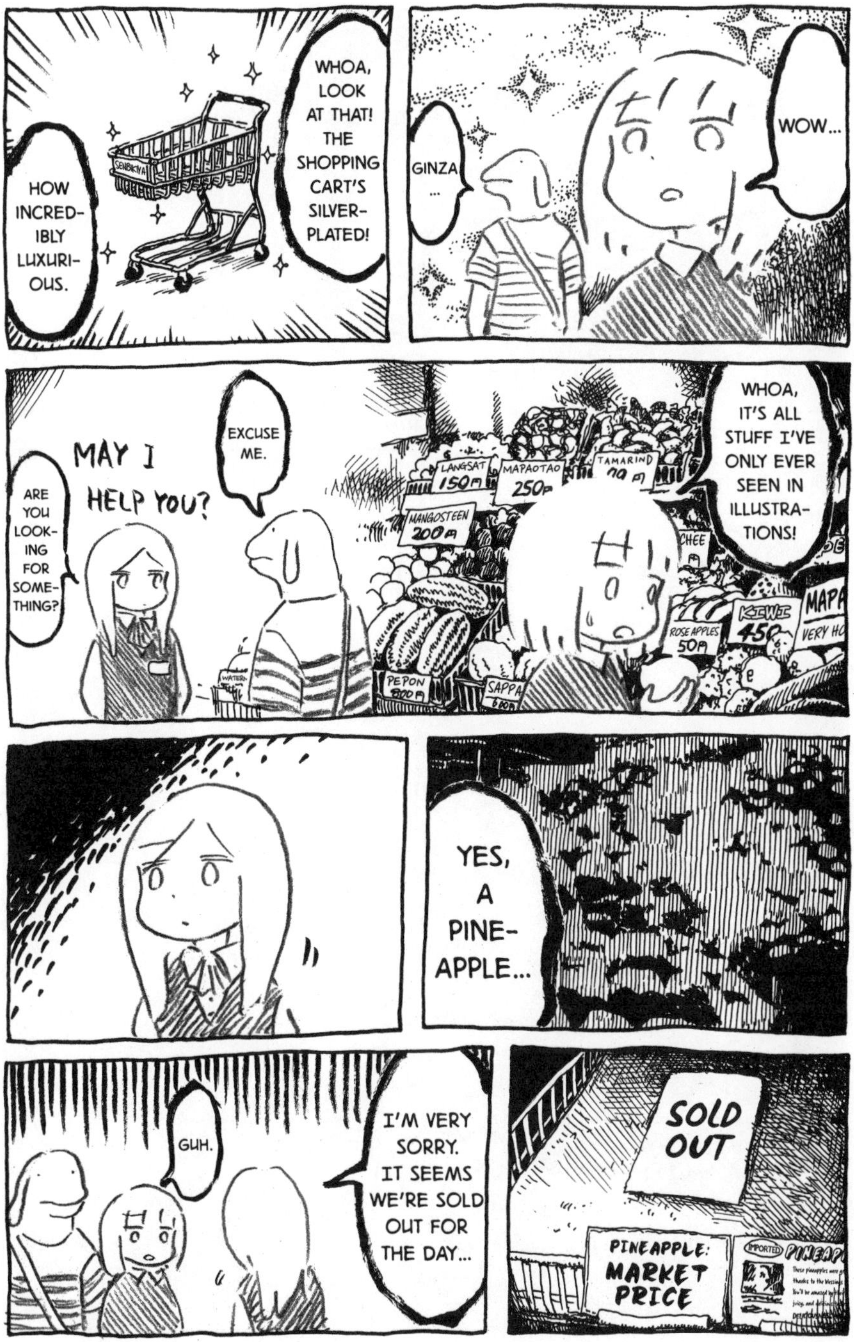
WOW...
GINZA...
WHOA, LOOK AT THAT! THE SHOPPING CART'S SILVER-PLATED!
HOW INCRED-IBLY LUXURI-OUS.
WHOA, IT'S ALL STUFF I'VE ONLY EVER SEEN IN ILLUSTRA-TIONS!
LANGSAT 150円
MAPAOTAO 250円
TAMARIND
MANGOSTEEN 200円
ROSE APPLES 50円
KIWI
PEPON
SAPPA
EXCUSE ME.
MAY I HELP YOU?
ARE YOU LOOK-ING FOR SOME-THING?
YES, A PINE-APPLE...
SOLD OUT
PINEAPPLE: MARKET PRICE
IMPORTED
I'M VERY SORRY. IT SEEMS WE'RE SOLD OUT FOR THE DAY...
GUH.

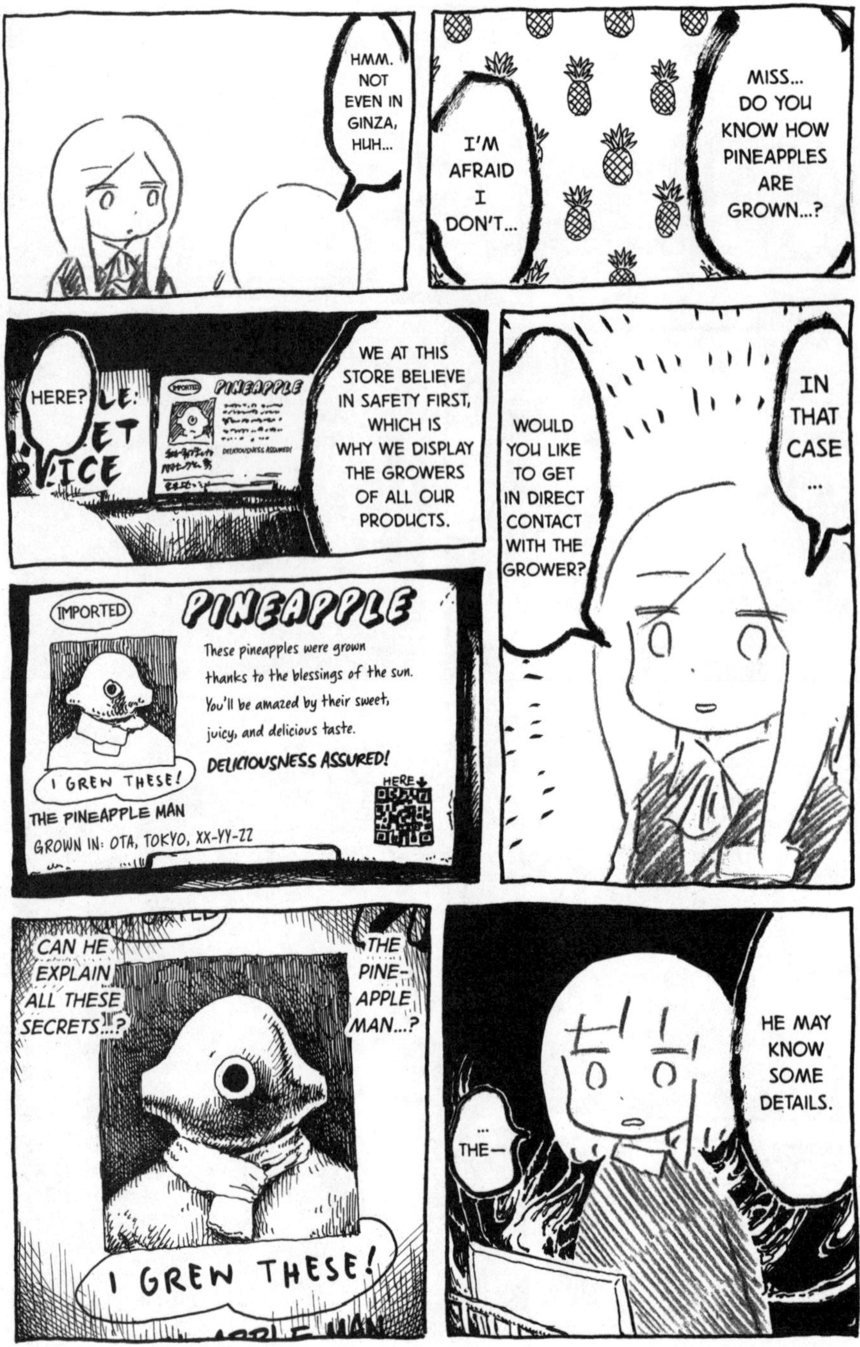
MISS... DO YOU KNOW HOW PINEAPPLES ARE GROWN...?
I'M AFRAID I DON'T...
HMM. NOT EVEN IN GINZA, HUH...
IN THAT CASE ...
WOULD YOU LIKE TO GET IN DIRECT CONTACT WITH THE GROWER?
WE AT THIS STORE BELIEVE IN SAFETY FIRST, WHICH IS WHY WE DISPLAY THE GROWERS OF ALL OUR PRODUCTS.
HERE?
IMPORTED
PINEAPPLE
These pineapples were grown thanks to the blessings of the sun. You'll be amazed by their sweet, juicy, and delicious taste.
DELICIOUSNESS ASSURED!
I GREW THESE!
THE PINEAPPLE MAN
GROWN IN: OTA, TOKYO, XX-YY-ZZ
HERE
HE MAY KNOW SOME DETAILS.
... THE—
THE PINE-APPLE MAN...?
CAN HE EXPLAIN ALL THESE SECRETS...?
I GREW THESE!

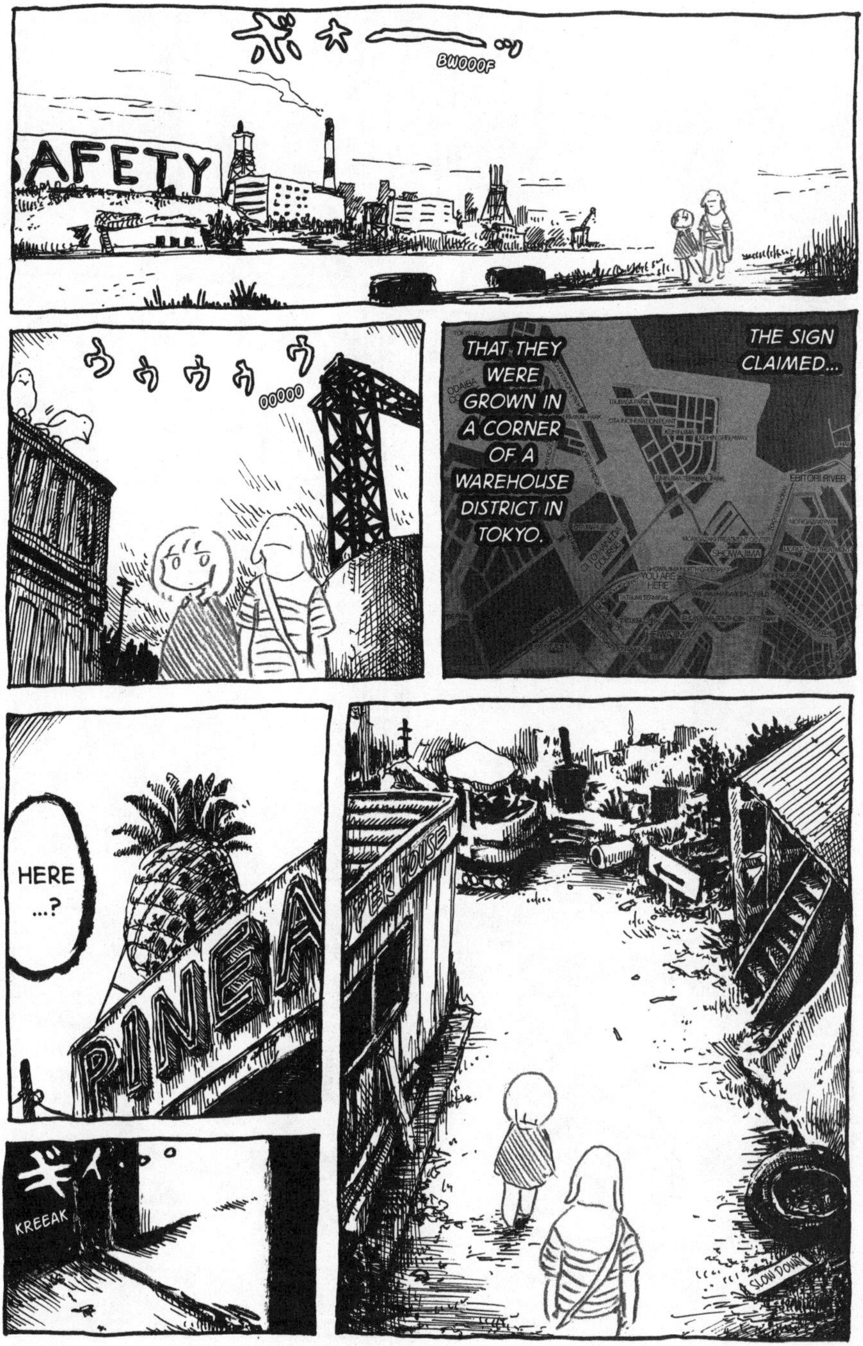

ボォーーーっ
BWOOOF
SAFETY
THE SIGN CLAIMED...
THAT THEY WERE GROWN IN A CORNER OF A WAREHOUSE DISTRICT IN TOKYO.
EBITORI RIVER
SHOWAJIMA
YOU ARE HERE
ぅゥウゥウ
OOOOO
SLOW DOWN
HERE ...?
PINEA
ギイ…
KREEAK

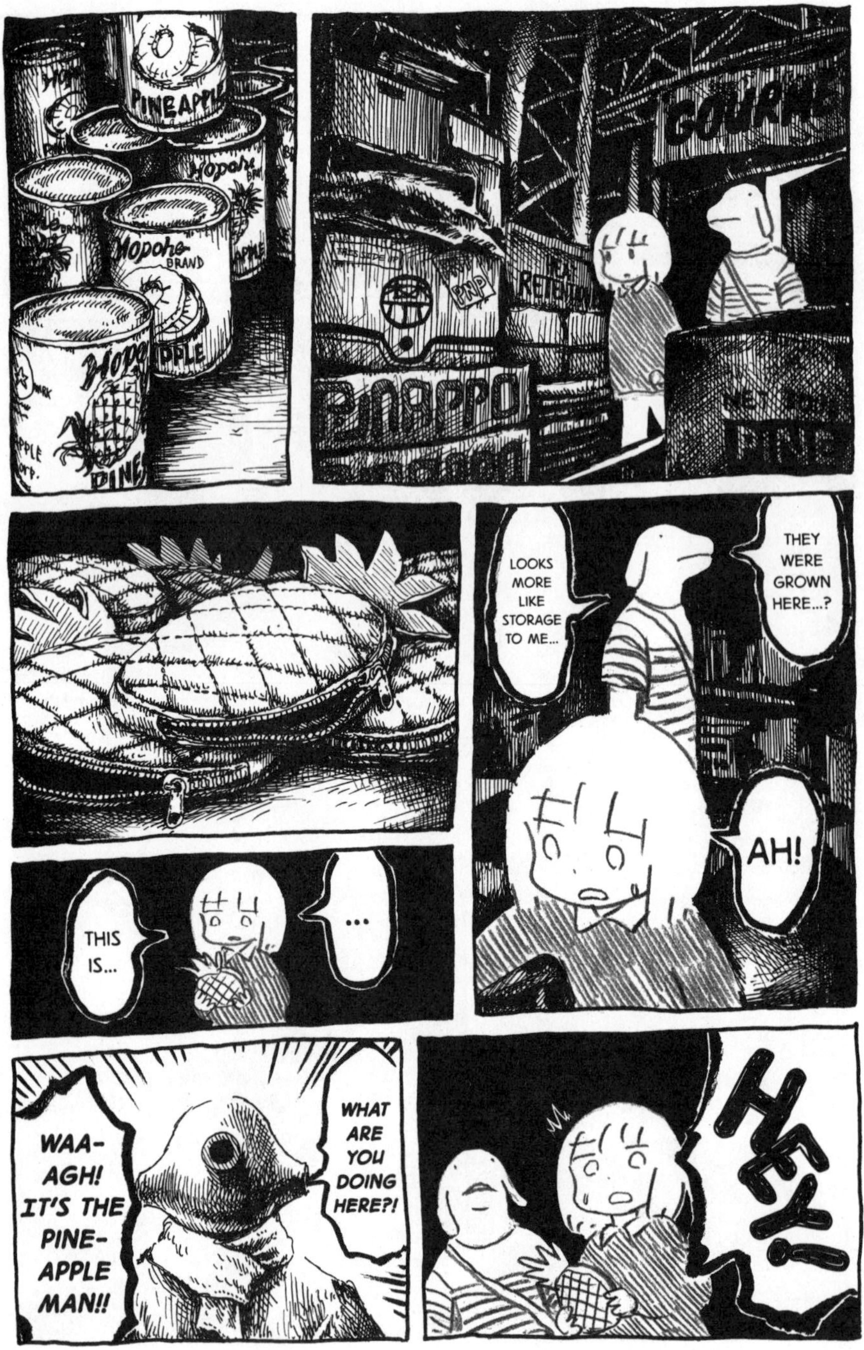
GOURME
PINEAPPLE
Hopohe BRAND
THEY WERE GROWN HERE...?
LOOKS MORE LIKE STORAGE TO ME...
AH!
...
THIS IS...
HEY!!
WHAT ARE YOU DOING HERE?!
WAA-AGH! IT'S THE PINE-APPLE MAN!!

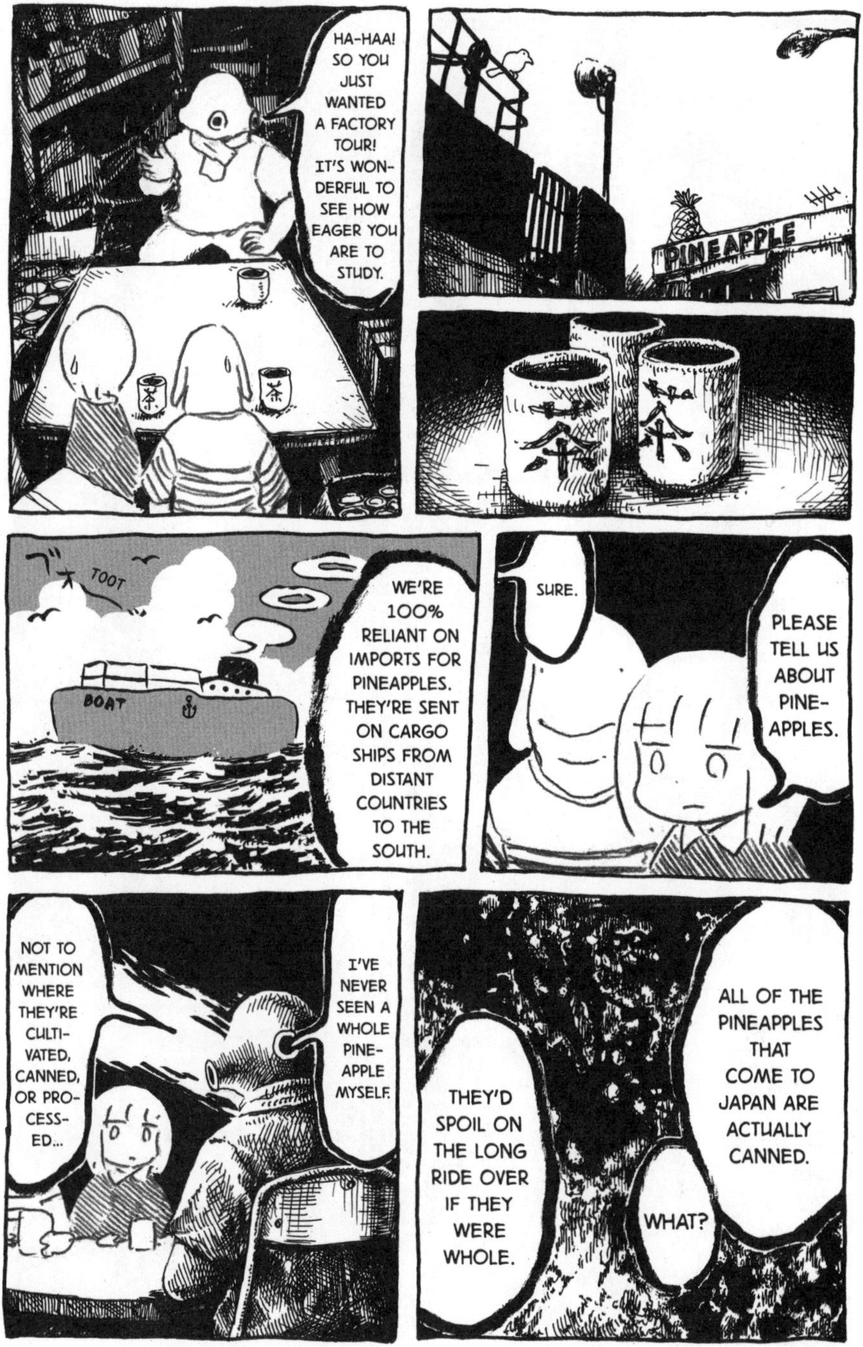
PINEAPPLE
HA-HAA! SO YOU JUST WANTED A FACTORY TOUR! IT'S WONDERFUL TO SEE HOW EAGER YOU ARE TO STUDY.
PLEASE TELL US ABOUT PINE-APPLES.
SURE.
TOOT
WE'RE 100% RELIANT ON IMPORTS FOR PINEAPPLES. THEY'RE SENT ON CARGO SHIPS FROM DISTANT COUNTRIES TO THE SOUTH.
BOAT
ALL OF THE PINEAPPLES THAT COME TO JAPAN ARE ACTUALLY CANNED.
WHAT?
THEY'D SPOIL ON THE LONG RIDE OVER IF THEY WERE WHOLE.
I'VE NEVER SEEN A WHOLE PINE-APPLE MYSELF.
NOT TO MENTION WHERE THEY'RE CULTI-VATED, CANNED, OR PROC-ESS-ED...

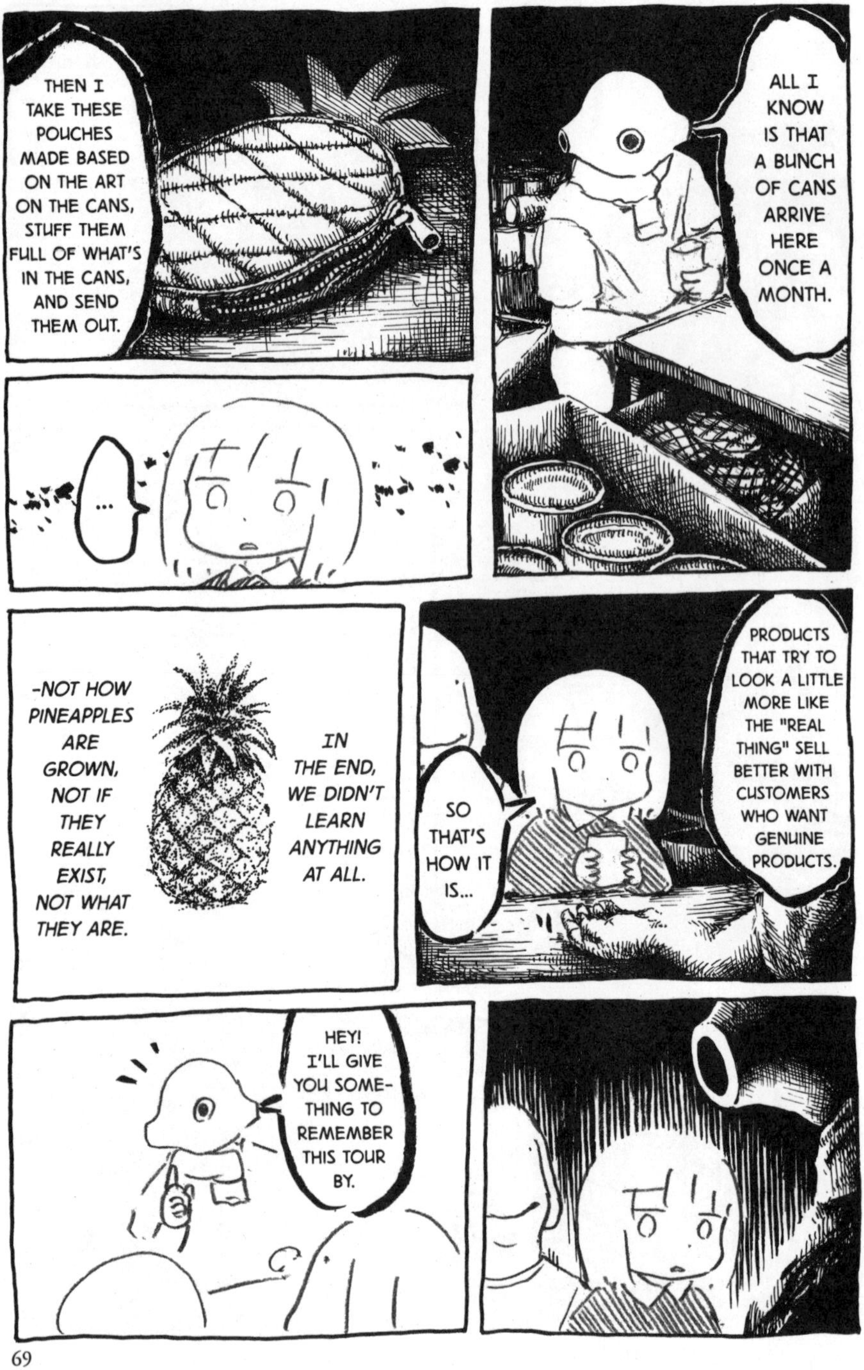
ALL I KNOW IS THAT A BUNCH OF CANS ARRIVE HERE ONCE A MONTH.
THEN I TAKE THESE POUCHES MADE BASED ON THE ART ON THE CANS, STUFF THEM FULL OF WHAT'S IN THE CANS, AND SEND THEM OUT.
...
PRODUCTS THAT TRY TO LOOK A LITTLE MORE LIKE THE "REAL THING" SELL BETTER WITH CUSTOMERS WHO WANT GENUINE PRODUCTS.
SO THAT'S HOW IT IS...
IN THE END, WE DIDN'T LEARN ANYTHING AT ALL.
-NOT HOW PINEAPPLES ARE GROWN, NOT IF THEY REALLY EXIST, NOT WHAT THEY ARE.
HEY! I'LL GIVE YOU SOME-THING TO REMEMBER THIS TOUR BY.

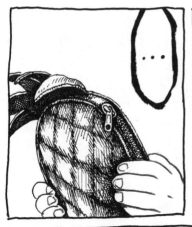

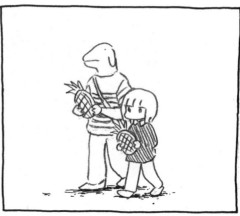

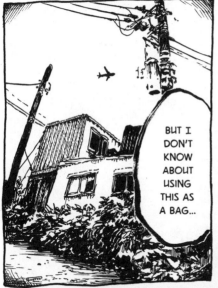

...
SOUNDS LIKE IT'S POPULAR TO REUSE IT AS A BAG ONCE YOU'RE DONE EATING WHAT'S INSIDE.
All trendy-like!
YEAH, IT DID SEEM TO BE POPULAR IN GINZA...
BUT I DON'T KNOW ABOUT USING THIS AS A BAG...
ROO-POPO
HOME.

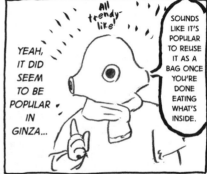

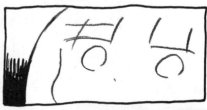

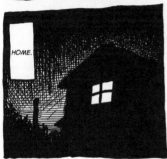

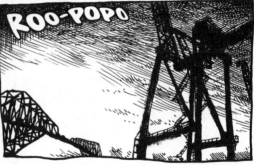

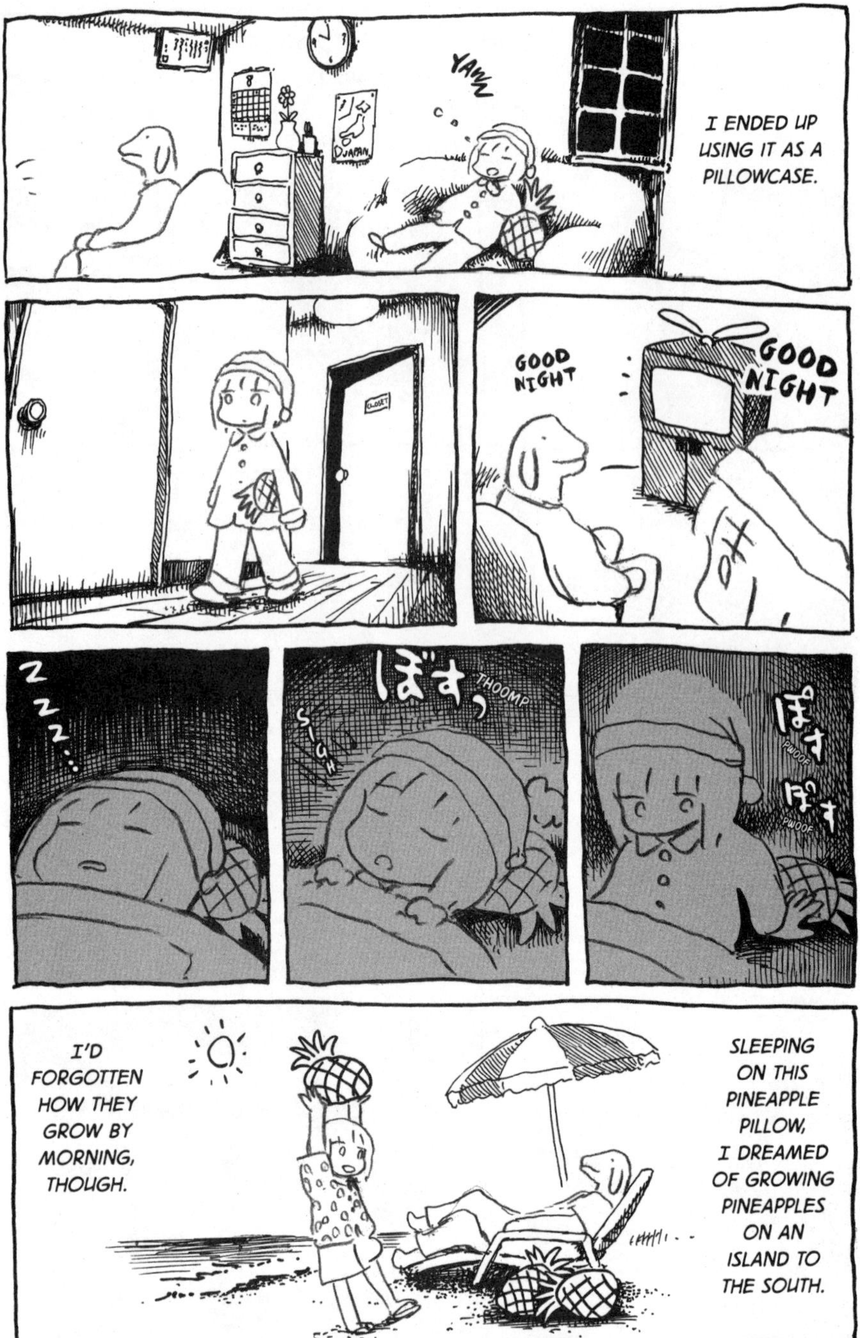
I ENDED UP USING IT AS A PILLOWCASE.
YAWN
JAPAN
GOOD NIGHT
GOOD NIGHT
CLOSET
ぽす
PWOOF
ぽす
PWOOF
ぼす,
THOOMP
SIGH
Z Z Z...
SLEEPING ON THIS PINEAPPLE PILLOW, I DREAMED OF GROWING PINEAPPLES ON AN ISLAND TO THE SOUTH.
I'D FORGOTTEN HOW THEY GROW BY MORNING, THOUGH.

The Pond that Appeared

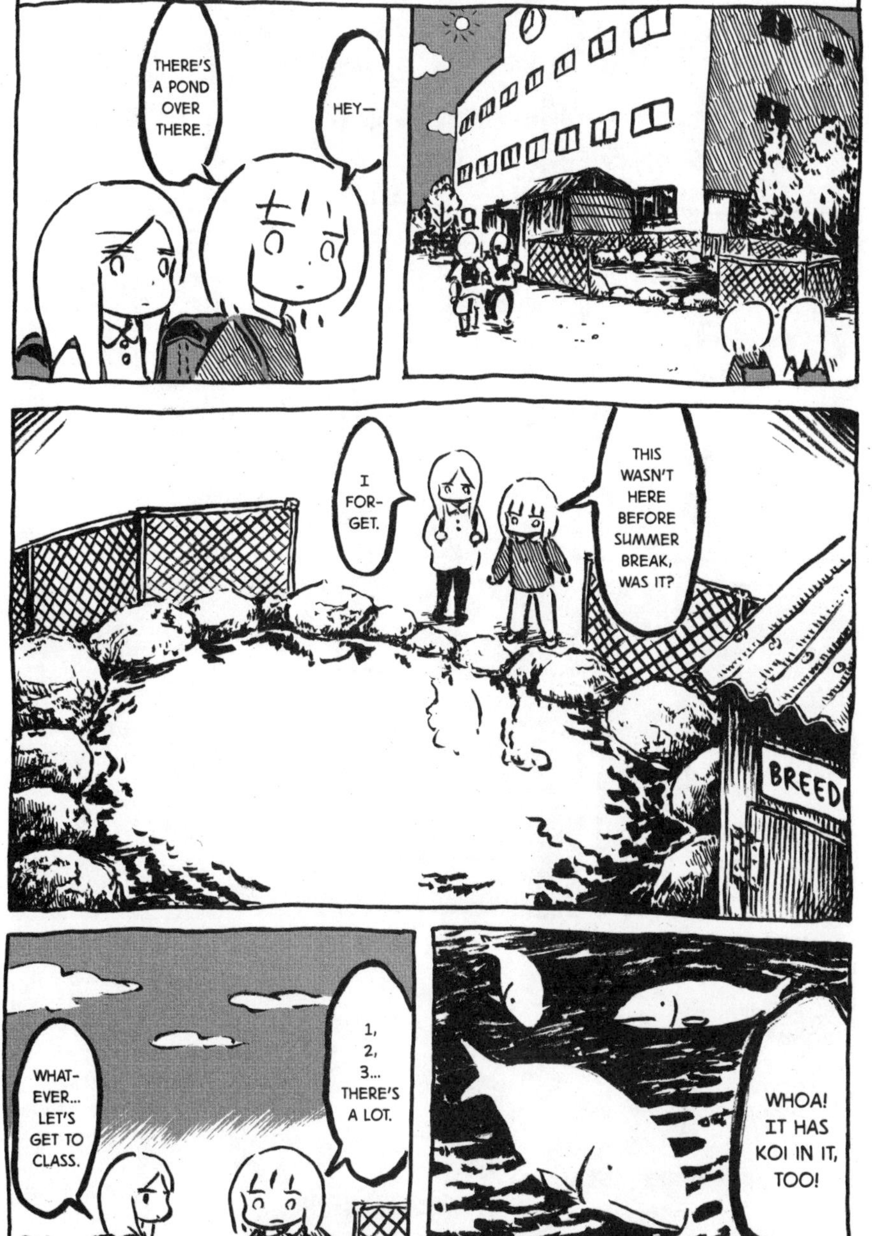
HEY—
THERE'S A POND OVER THERE.
THIS WASN'T HERE BEFORE SUMMER BREAK, WAS IT?
I FORGET.
BREED
WHOA! IT HAS KOI IN IT, TOO!
1, 2, 3... THERE'S A LOT.
WHAT-EVER... LET'S GET TO CLASS.

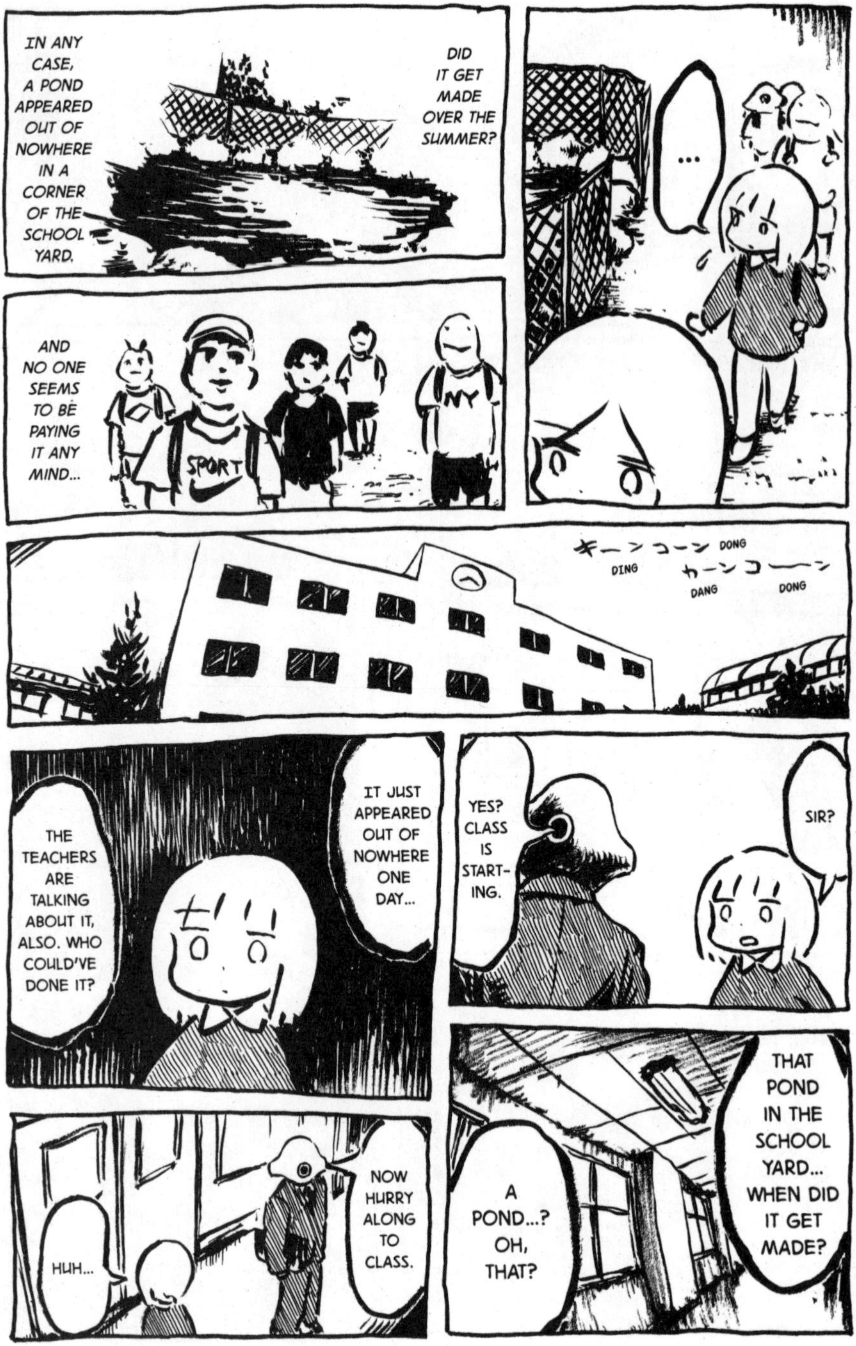
...
DID IT GET MADE OVER THE SUMMER?
IN ANY CASE, A POND APPEARED OUT OF NOWHERE IN A CORNER OF THE SCHOOL YARD.
AND NO ONE SEEMS TO BE PAYING IT ANY MIND...
SPORT
NY
キーンコーン DING DONG
カーンコーーン DANG DONG
SIR?
YES? CLASS IS STARTING.
THAT POND IN THE SCHOOL YARD... WHEN DID IT GET MADE?
A POND...? OH, THAT?
IT JUST APPEARED OUT OF NOWHERE ONE DAY...
THE TEACHERS ARE TALKING ABOUT IT, ALSO. WHO COULD'VE DONE IT?
NOW HURRY ALONG TO CLASS.
HUH...

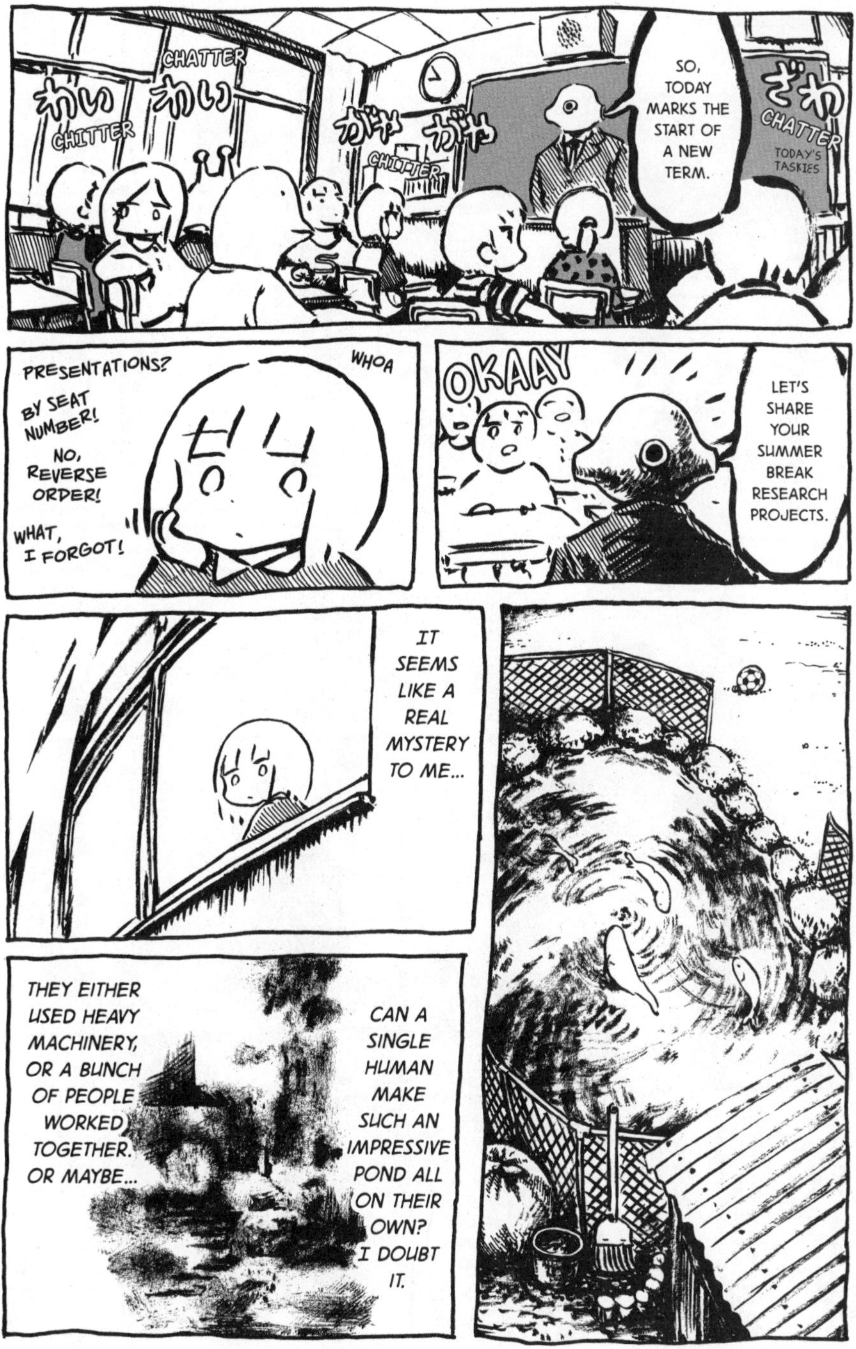
ざわ
CHATTER
TODAY'S TASKIES
SO, TODAY MARKS THE START OF A NEW TERM.
がや がや
CHITTER
わい わい
CHATTER
CHITTER
LET'S SHARE YOUR SUMMER BREAK RESEARCH PROJECTS.
OKAAY
WHOA
PRESENTATIONS?
BY SEAT NUMBER!
NO, REVERSE ORDER!
WHAT, I FORGOT!
IT SEEMS LIKE A REAL MYSTERY TO ME...
CAN A SINGLE HUMAN MAKE SUCH AN IMPRESSIVE POND ALL ON THEIR OWN? I DOUBT IT.
THEY EITHER USED HEAVY MACHINERY, OR A BUNCH OF PEOPLE WORKED TOGETHER. OR MAYBE...

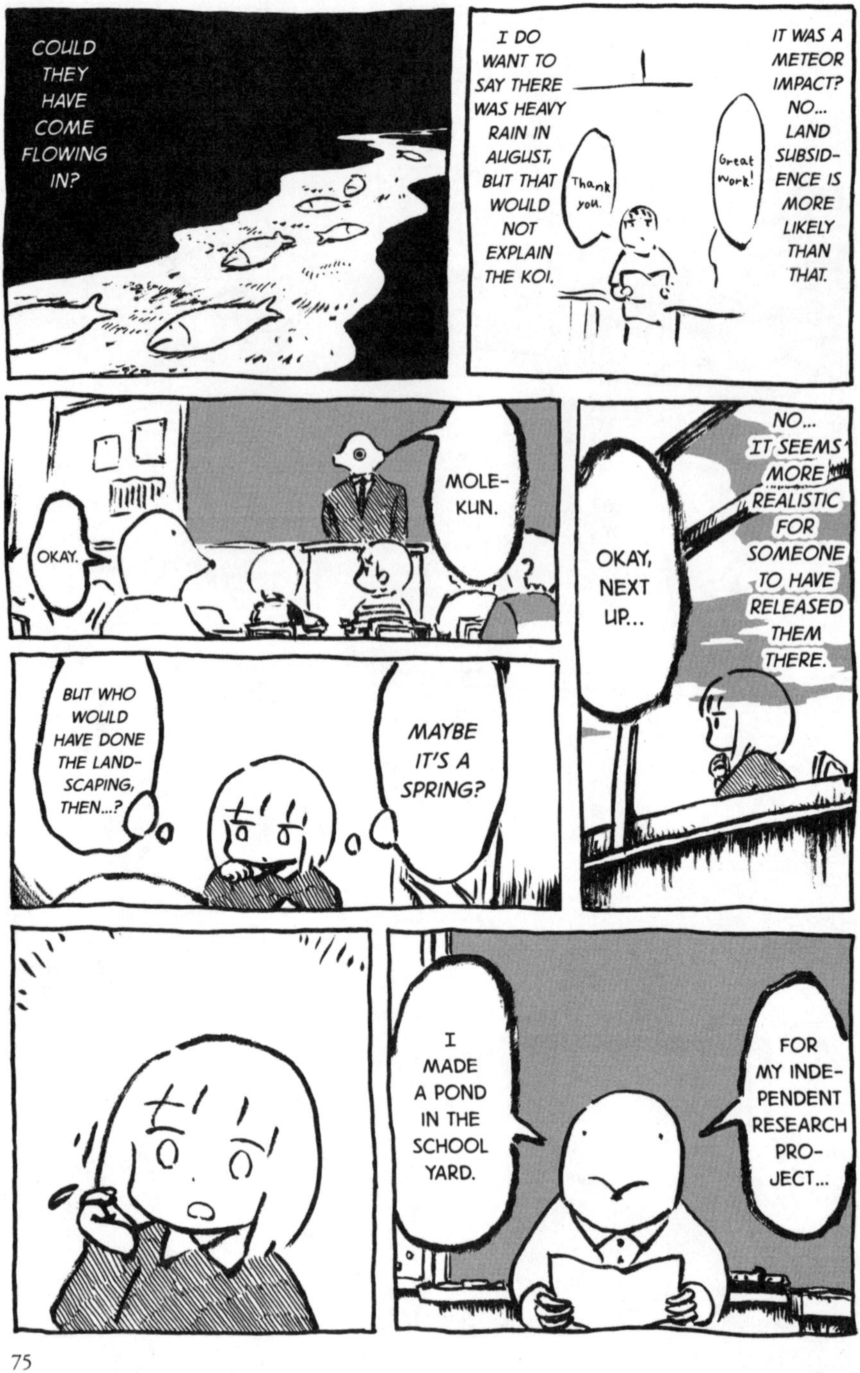
IT WAS A METEOR IMPACT? NO... LAND SUBSIDENCE IS MORE LIKELY THAN THAT.
Great work!
Thank you.
I DO WANT TO SAY THERE WAS HEAVY RAIN IN AUGUST, BUT THAT WOULD NOT EXPLAIN THE KOI.
COULD THEY HAVE COME FLOWING IN?
NO... IT SEEMS MORE REALISTIC FOR SOMEONE TO HAVE RELEASED THEM THERE.
OKAY, NEXT UP...
MOLE-KUN.
OKAY.
MAYBE IT'S A SPRING?
BUT WHO WOULD HAVE DONE THE LAND-SCAPING, THEN...?
FOR MY INDE-PENDENT RESEARCH PRO-JECT...
I MADE A POND IN THE SCHOOL YARD.

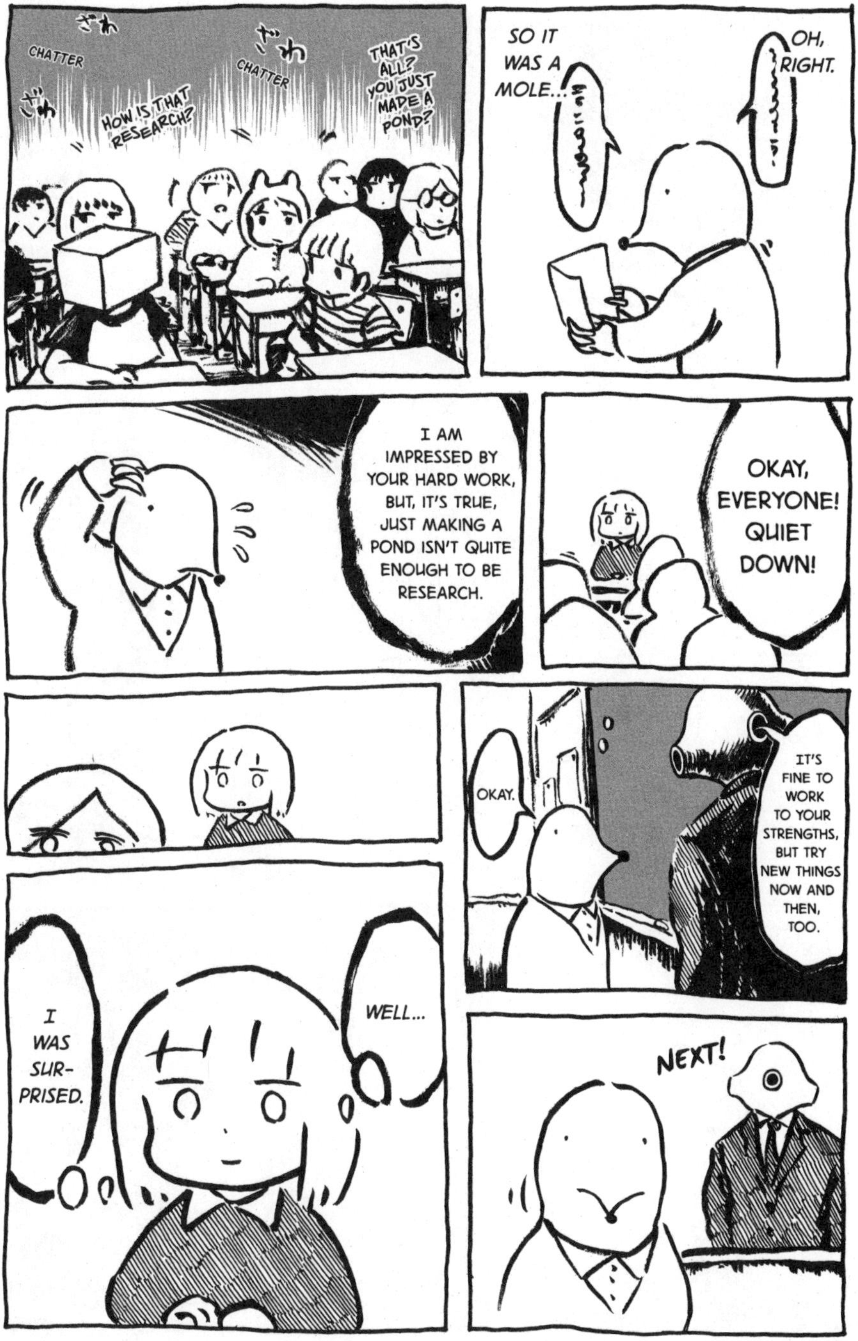
OH, RIGHT.
SO IT WAS A MOLE...
THAT'S ALL? YOU JUST MADE A POND?
ざわ
CHATTER
HOW IS THAT RESEARCH?
ざわ
CHATTER
ざわ
OKAY, EVERYONE! QUIET DOWN!
I AM IMPRESSED BY YOUR HARD WORK, BUT, IT'S TRUE, JUST MAKING A POND ISN'T QUITE ENOUGH TO BE RESEARCH.
IT'S FINE TO WORK TO YOUR STRENGTHS, BUT TRY NEW THINGS NOW AND THEN, TOO.
OKAY.
WELL...
I WAS SUR-PRISED.
NEXT!

Wandering, Wondering

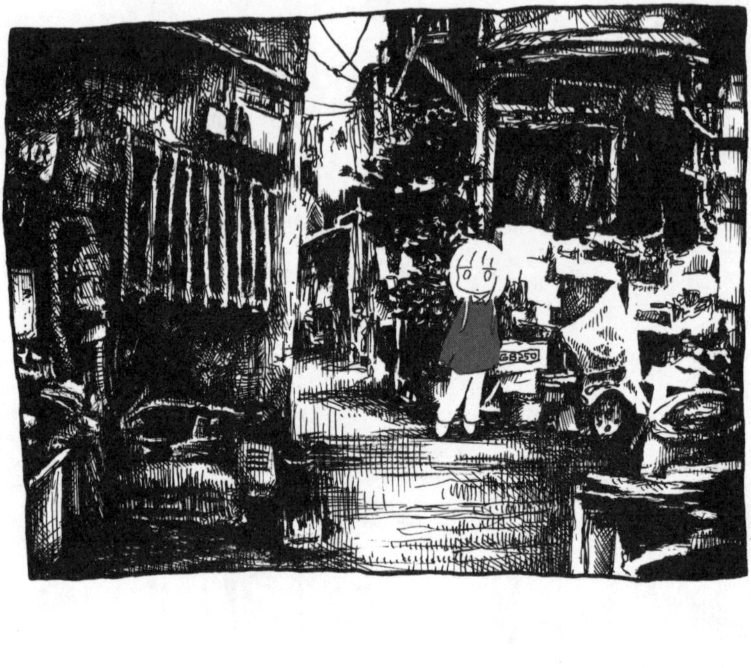
GB250

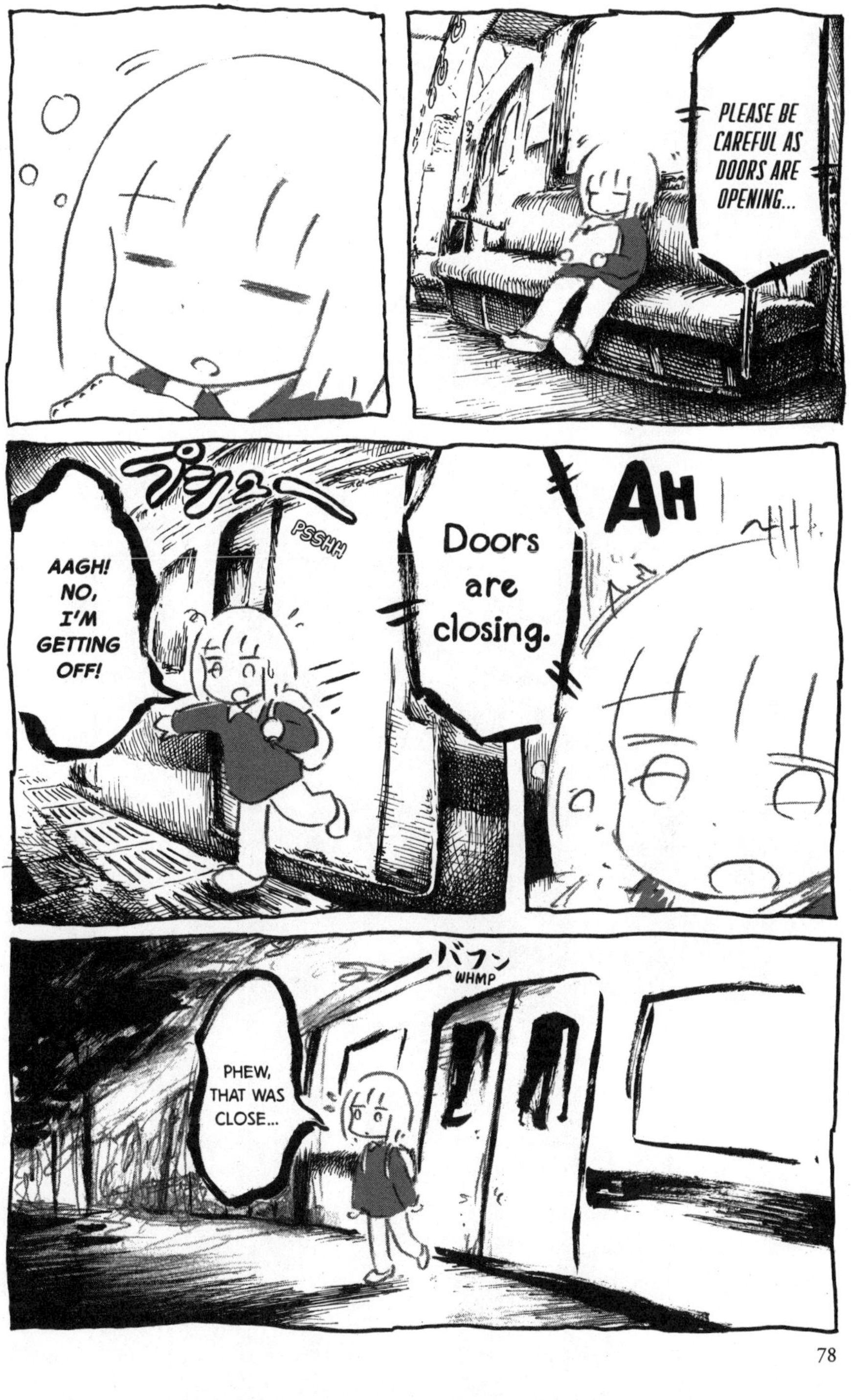
PLEASE BE CAREFUL AS DOORS ARE OPENING...
AH
Doors are closing.
プシュー
PSSHH
AAGH! NO, I'M GETTING OFF!
バフン
WHMP
PHEW, THAT WAS CLOSE...

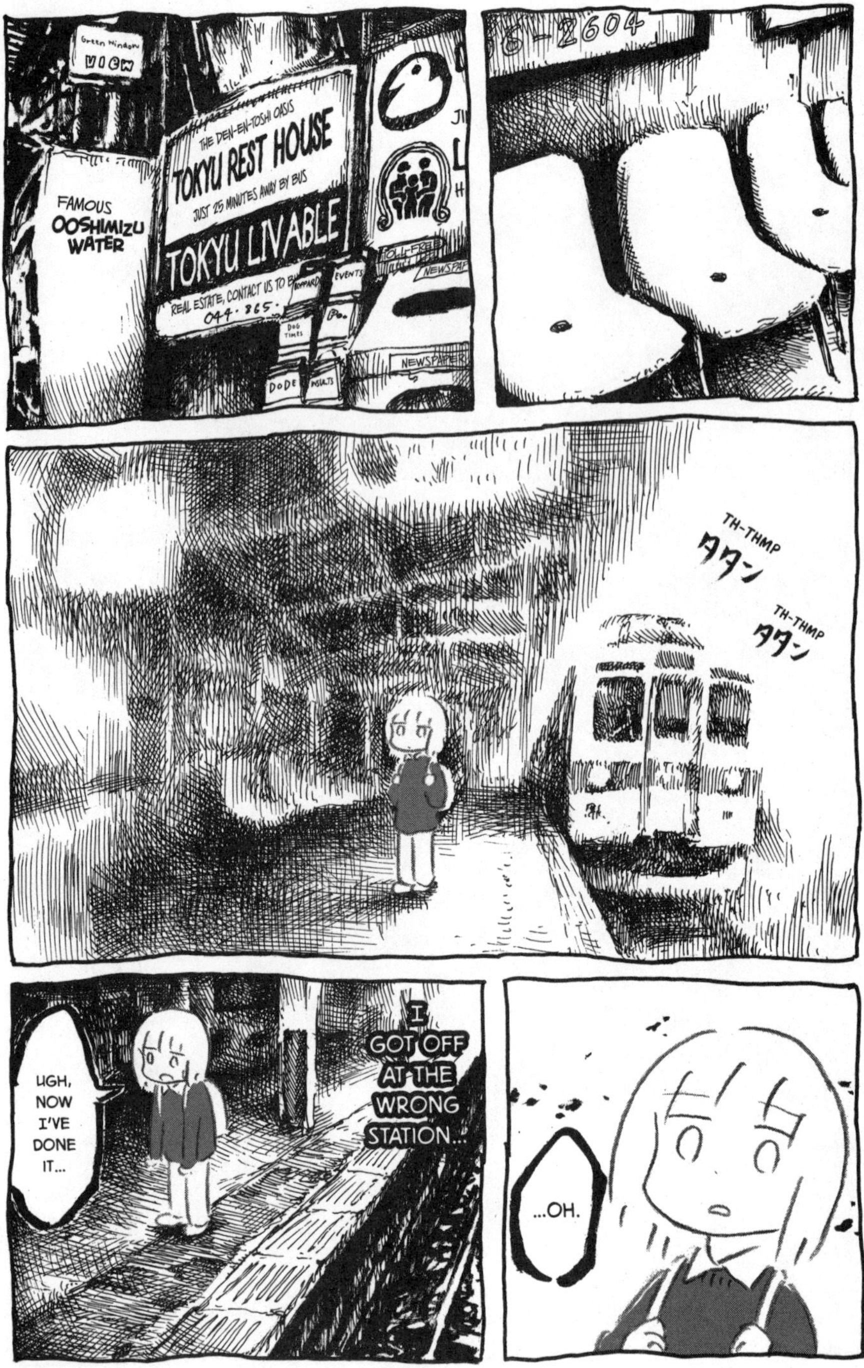
Green Window
VIEW
FAMOUS OOSHIMIZU WATER
THE DEN-EN-TOSHI OASIS
TOKYU REST HOUSE
JUST 25 MINUTES AWAY BY BUS
TOKYU LIVABLE
REAL ESTATE, CONTACT US TO B
044-865-
EVENTS
DOG TIMES
NEWSPAPER
TH-THMP
タタン
TH-THMP
タタン
...OH.
I GOT OFF AT THE WRONG STATION...
UGH, NOW I'VE DONE IT...

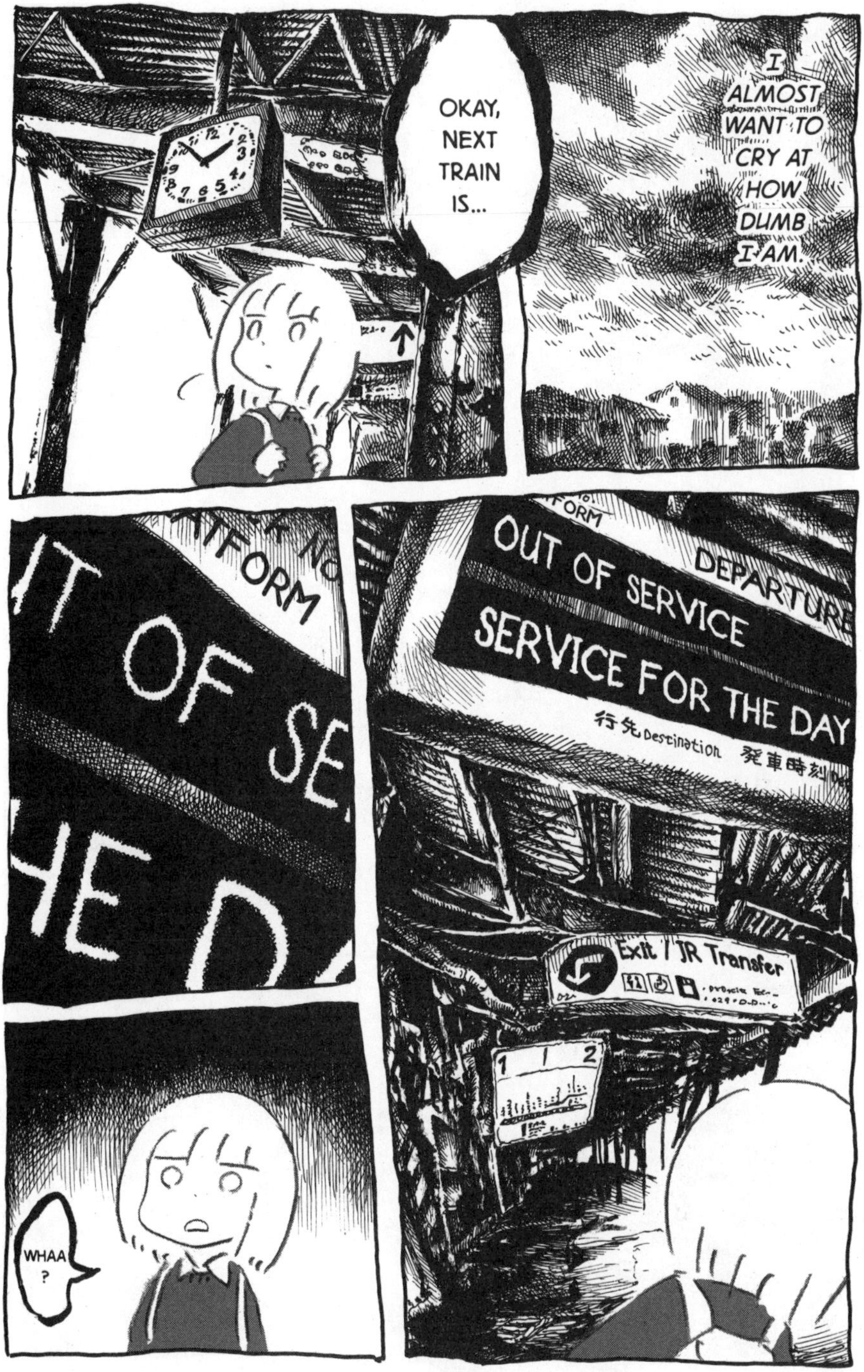
I ALMOST WANT TO CRY AT HOW DUMB I AM.
OKAY, NEXT TRAIN IS...
OUT OF SERVICE
DEPARTURE
SERVICE FOR THE DAY
行先Destination 発車時刻
Exit / JR Transfer
WHAA?

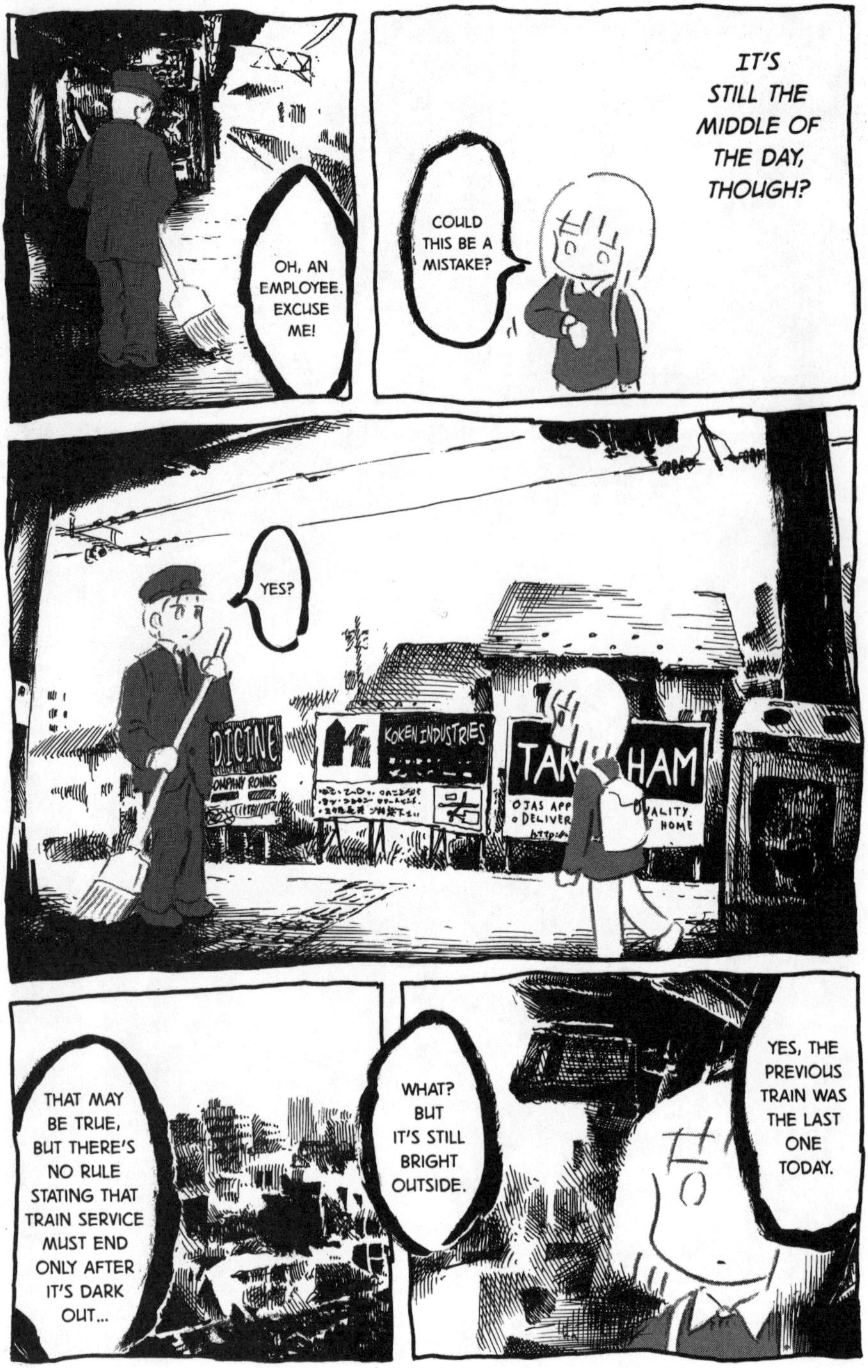
IT'S STILL THE MIDDLE OF THE DAY, THOUGH?
COULD THIS BE A MISTAKE?
OH, AN EMPLOYEE. EXCUSE ME!
YES?
KOKEN INDUSTRIES
YES, THE PREVIOUS TRAIN WAS THE LAST ONE TODAY.
WHAT? BUT IT'S STILL BRIGHT OUTSIDE.
THAT MAY BE TRUE, BUT THERE'S NO RULE STATING THAT TRAIN SERVICE MUST END ONLY AFTER IT'S DARK OUT...

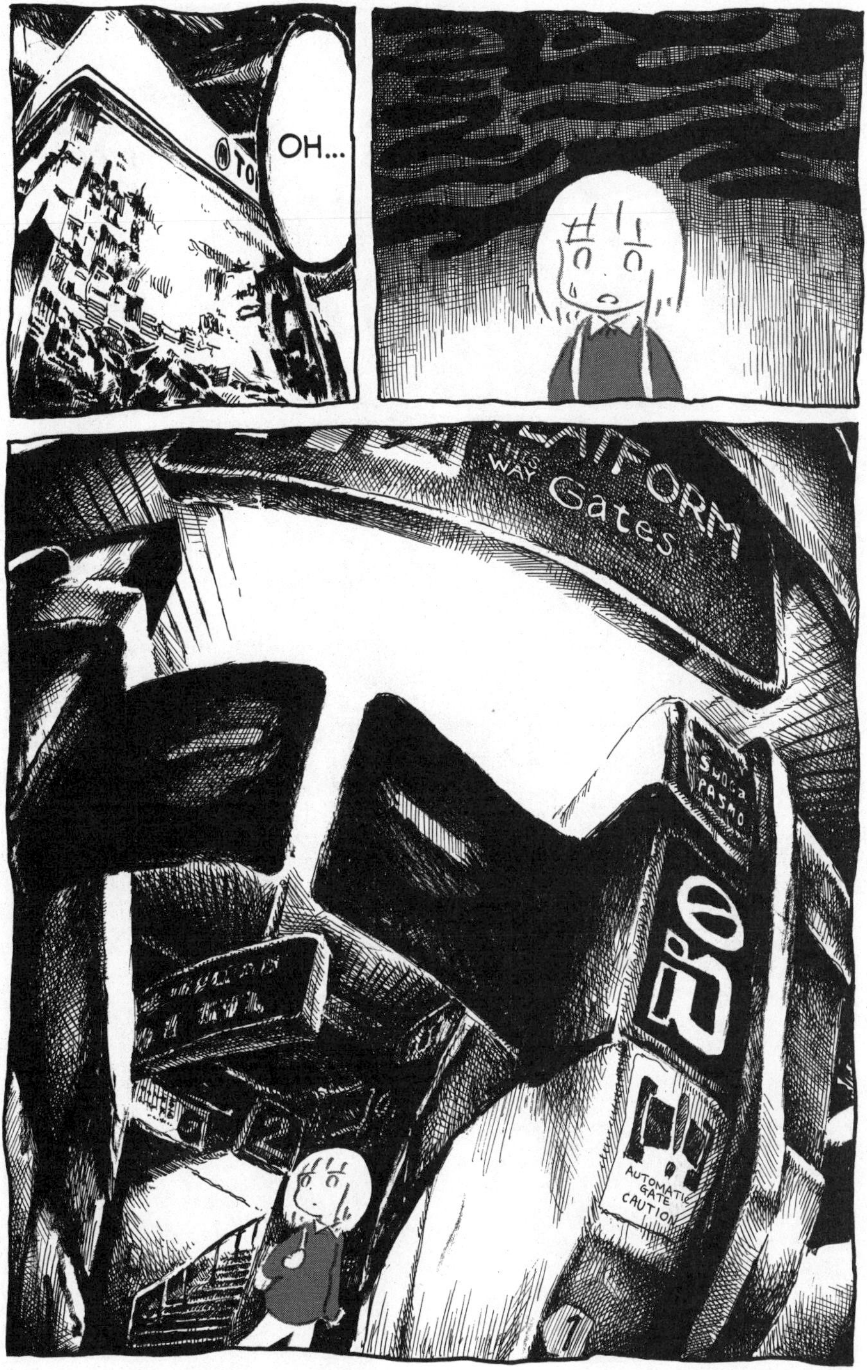
OH...
THIS WAY Gates
Suica PASMO
AUTOMATIC GATE CAUTION

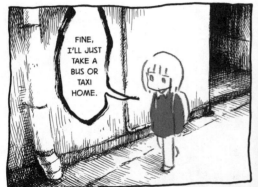

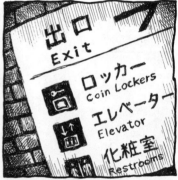

出口
Exit
ロッカー
Coin Lockers
エレベーター
Elevator
化粧室
Restrooms
FINE, I'LL JUST TAKE A BUS OR TAXI HOME.
駅前商店街駅
Station-Front Shopping Arcade Sta.
TOKYU DENTETSU
FRONT SHOPPING ARC
I GUESS THE STATION'S NAMED AFTER THIS SHOPPING ARCADE.
IT'S MY FIRST TIME GETTING OFF HERE...

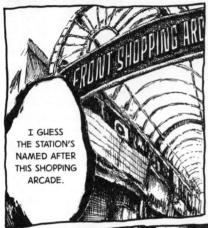

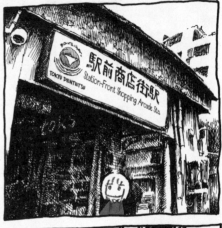

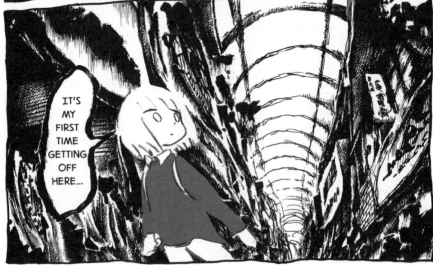

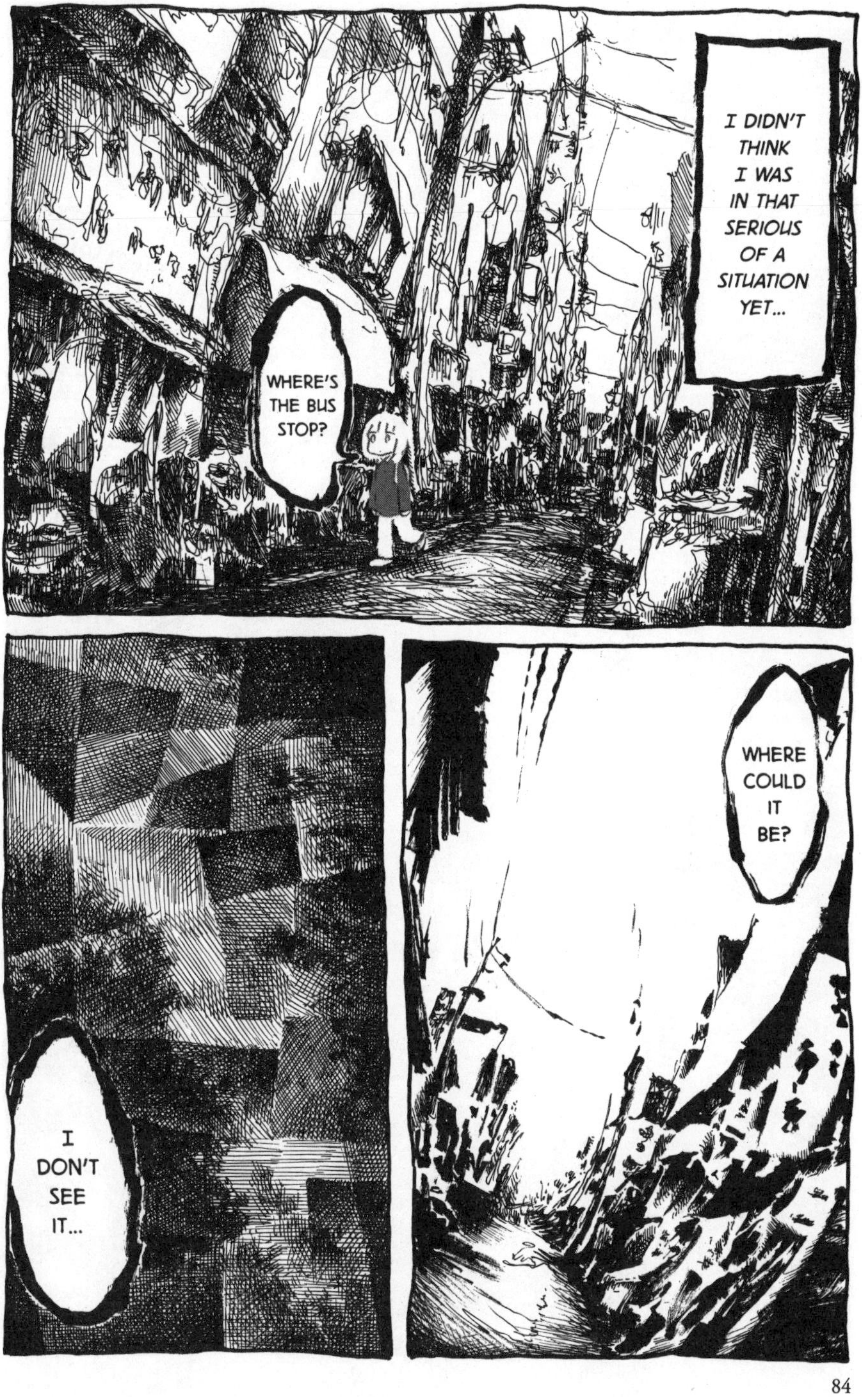
I DIDN'T THINK I WAS IN THAT SERIOUS OF A SITUATION YET...
WHERE'S THE BUS STOP?
WHERE COULD IT BE?
I DON'T SEE IT...

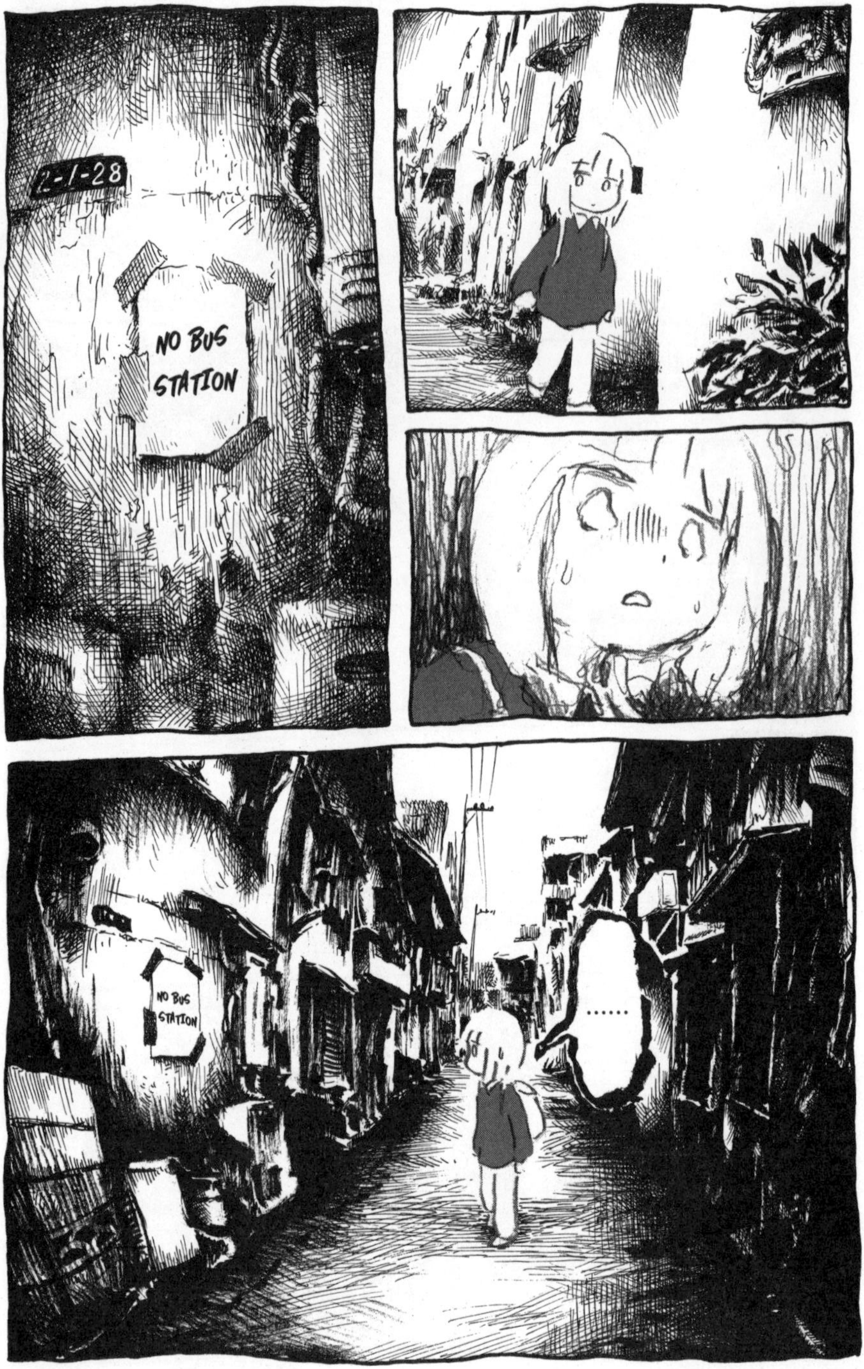
2-1-28
NO BUS STATION
……
NO BUS STATION

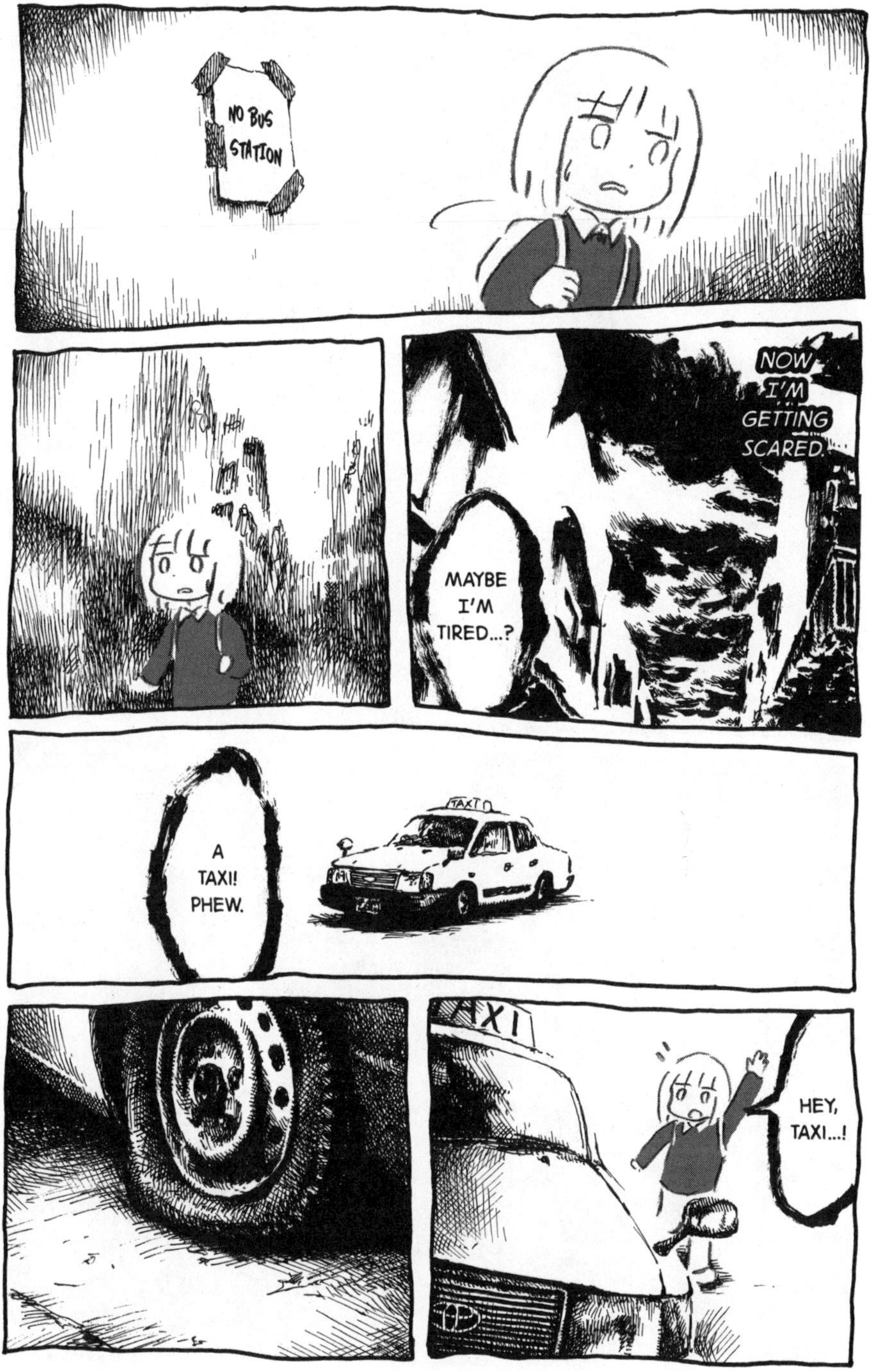
NO BUS STATION
NOW I'M GETTING SCARED.
MAYBE I'M TIRED...?
A TAXI! PHEW.
TAXI
HEY, TAXI...!

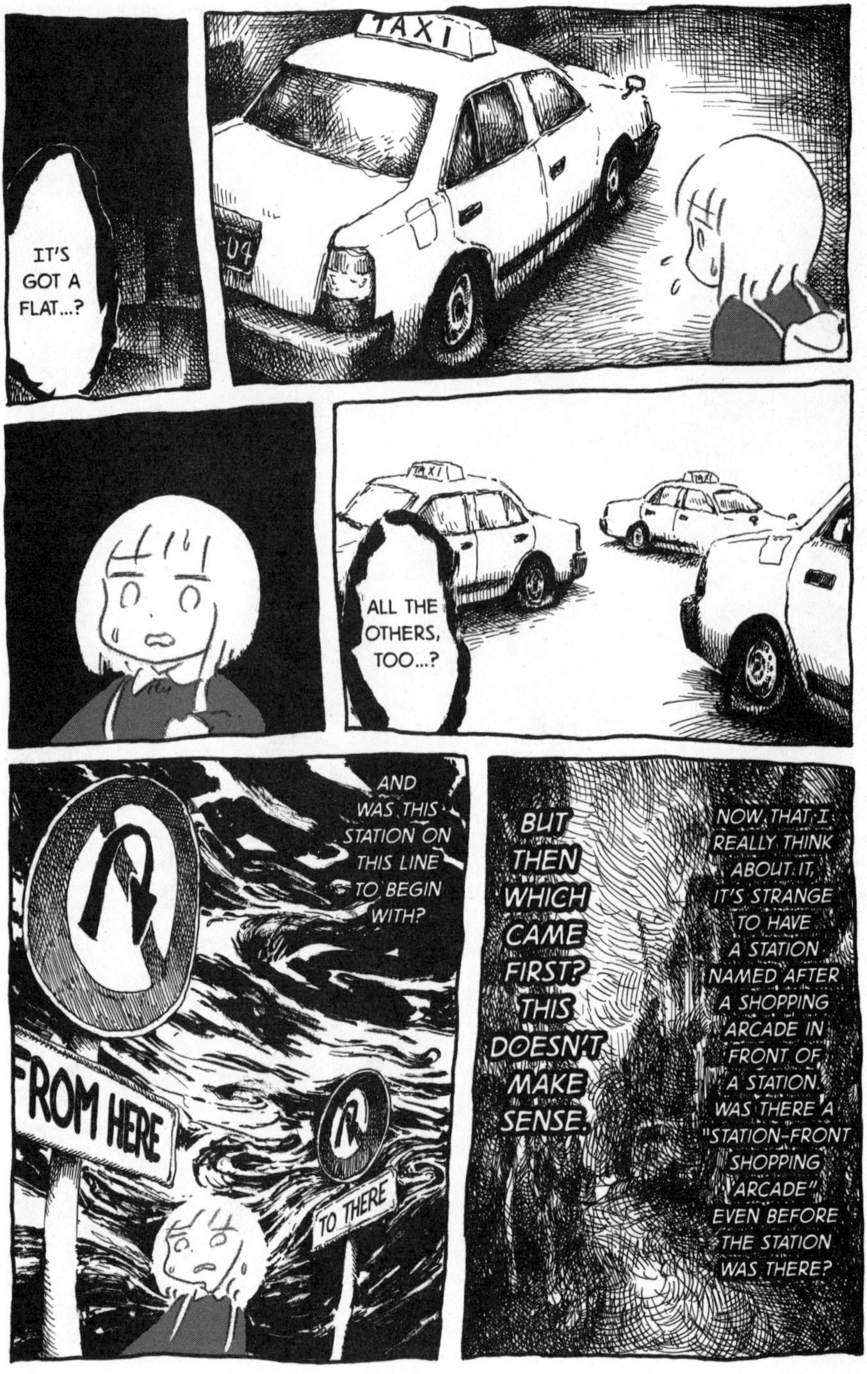
IT'S GOT A FLAT...?
ALL THE OTHERS, TOO...?
NOW THAT I REALLY THINK ABOUT IT, IT'S STRANGE TO HAVE A STATION NAMED AFTER A SHOPPING ARCADE IN FRONT OF A STATION. WAS THERE A "STATION-FRONT SHOPPING ARCADE" EVEN BEFORE THE STATION WAS THERE?
BUT THEN WHICH CAME FIRST? THIS DOESN'T MAKE SENSE.
AND WAS THIS STATION ON THIS LINE TO BEGIN WITH?
FROM HERE
TO THERE

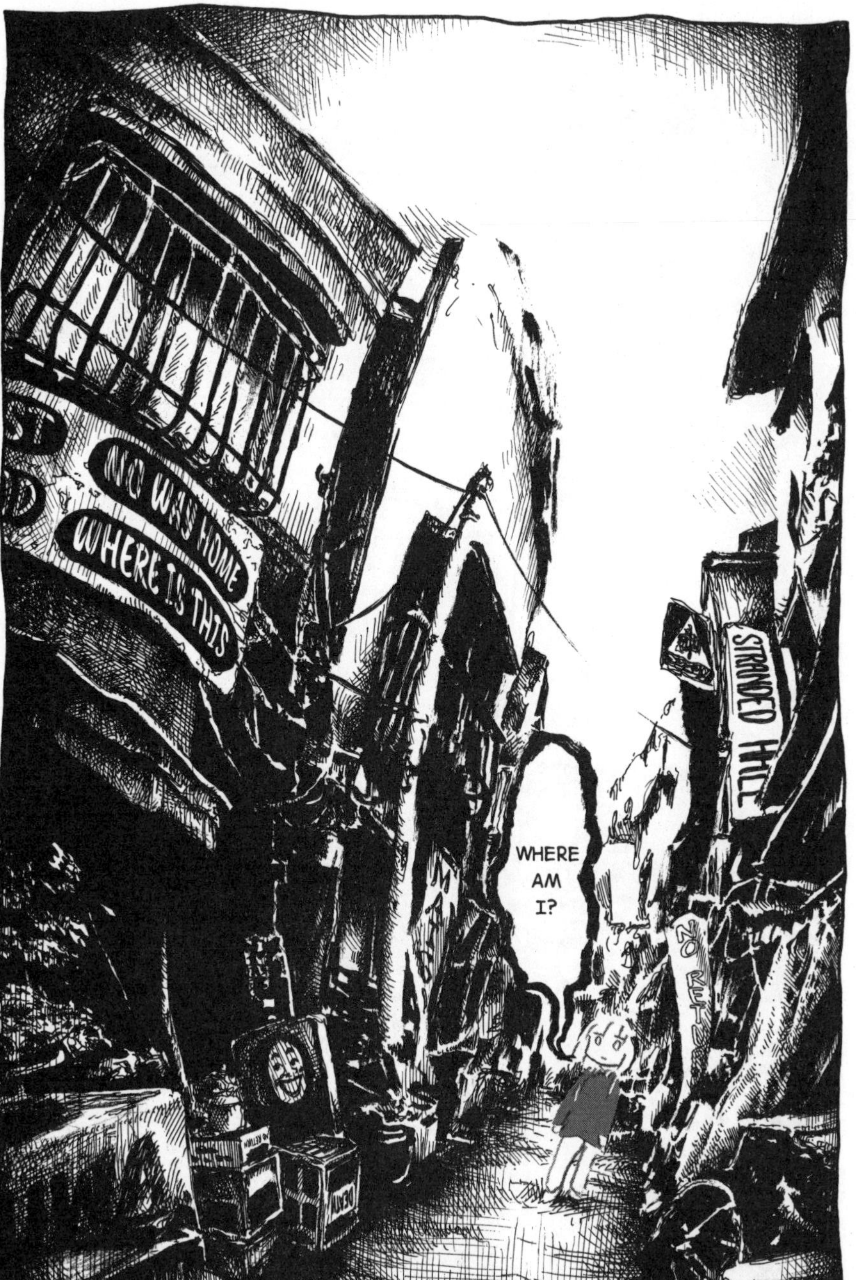
NO WAS HOME
WHERE IS THIS
STRANDED HALL
WHERE AM I?

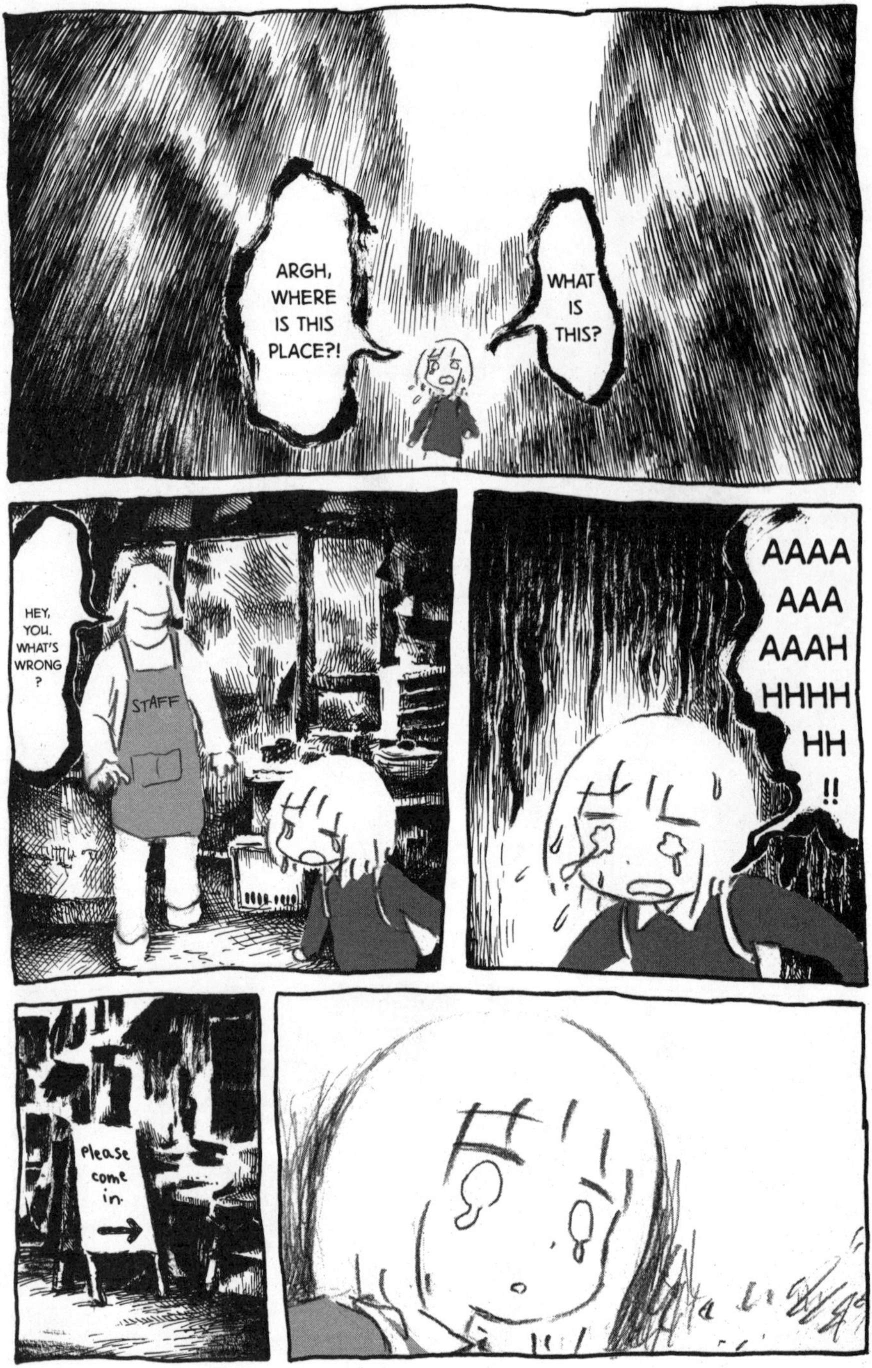
WHAT IS THIS?
ARGH, WHERE IS THIS PLACE?!
AAAAAAAAAAHHHHHHH!!
HEY, YOU. WHAT'S WRONG?
STAFF
Please come in.

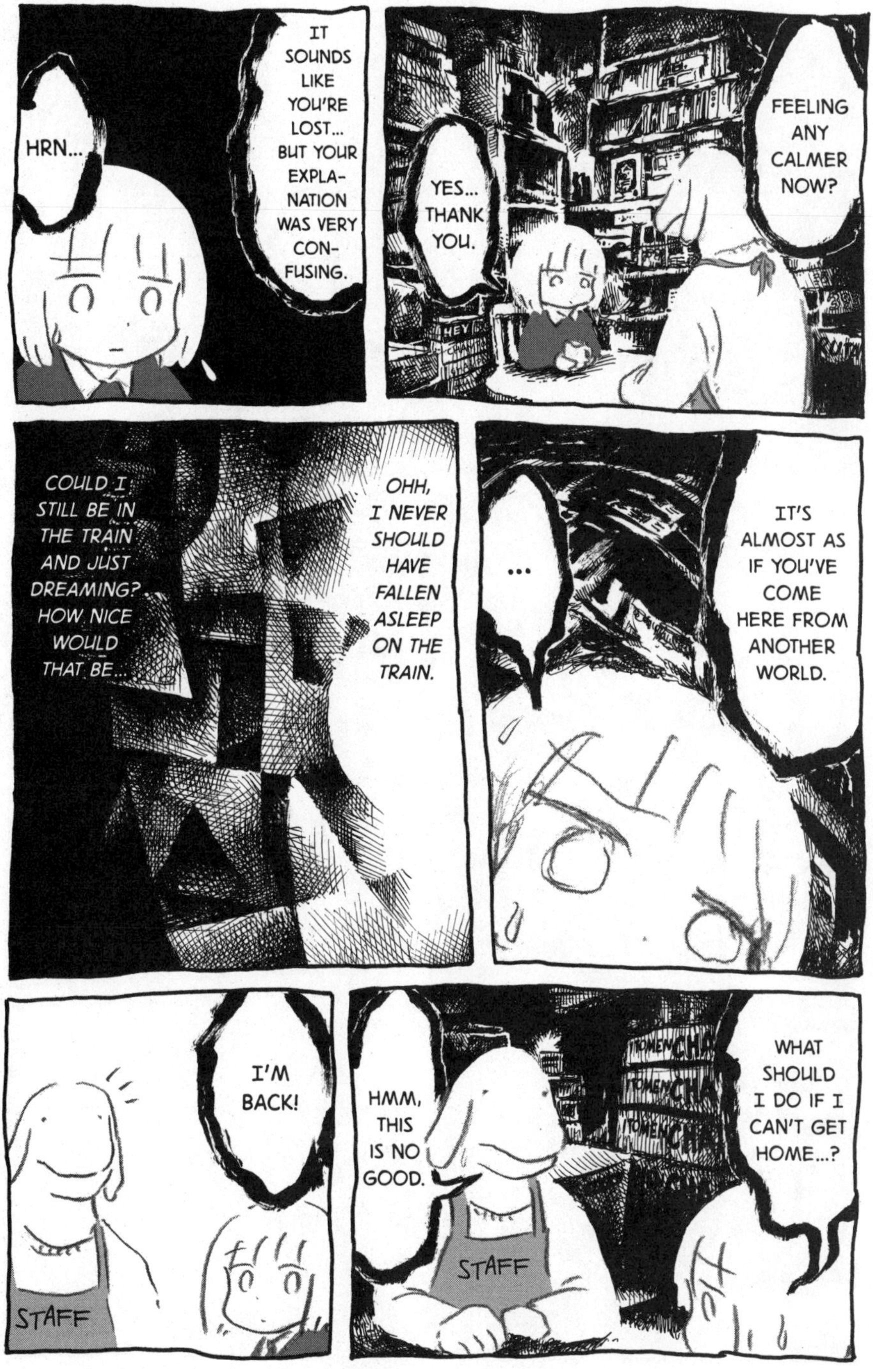
FEELING ANY CALMER NOW?
YES... THANK YOU.
IT SOUNDS LIKE YOU'RE LOST... BUT YOUR EXPLANATION WAS VERY CONFUSING.
HRN...
IT'S ALMOST AS IF YOU'VE COME HERE FROM ANOTHER WORLD.
...
OHH, I NEVER SHOULD HAVE FALLEN ASLEEP ON THE TRAIN.
COULD I STILL BE IN THE TRAIN AND JUST DREAMING? HOW NICE WOULD THAT BE...
WHAT SHOULD I DO IF I CAN'T GET HOME...?
HMM, THIS IS NO GOOD.
STAFF
I'M BACK!
STAFF

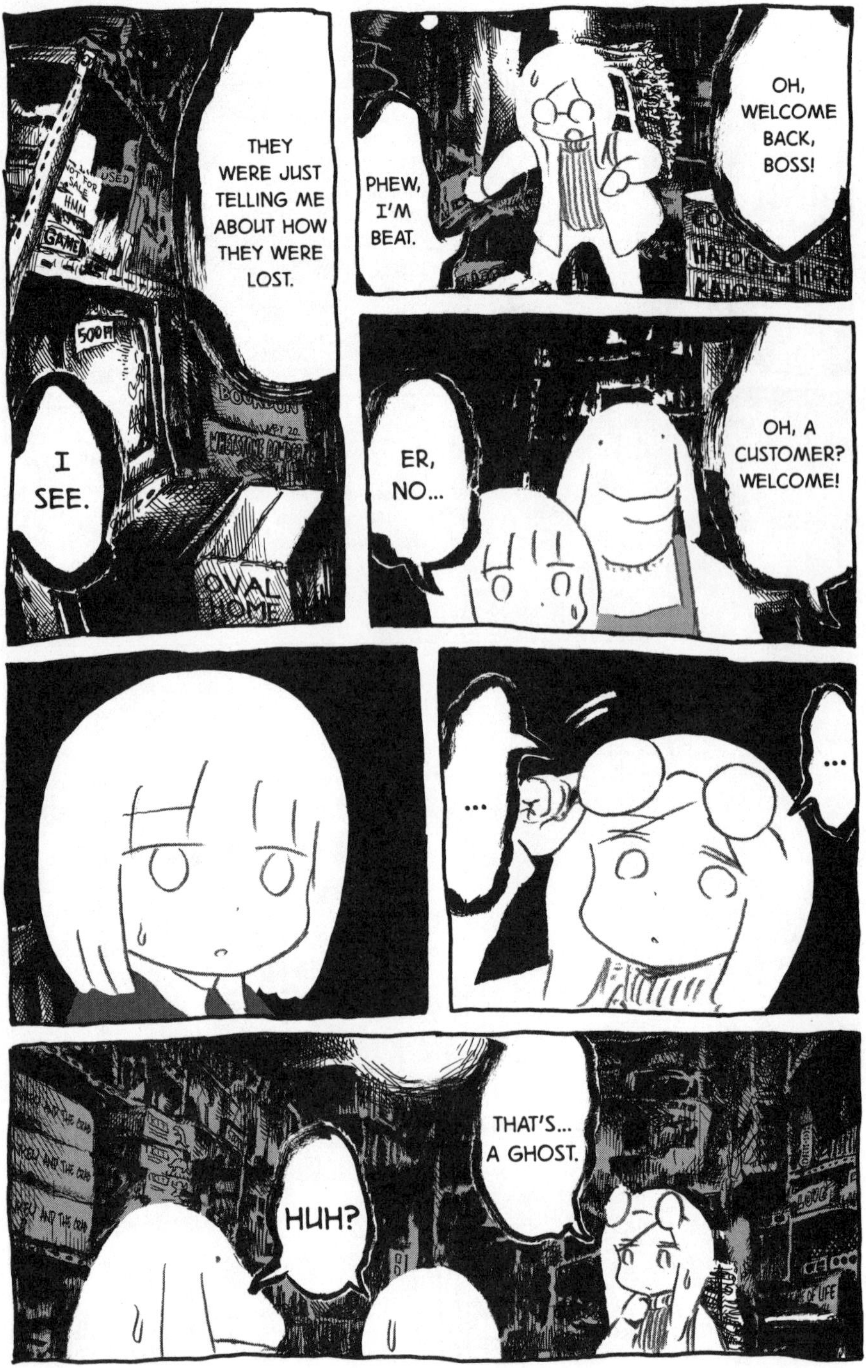
OH, WELCOME BACK, BOSS!
PHEW, I'M BEAT.
OH, A CUSTOMER? WELCOME!
ER, NO...
THEY WERE JUST TELLING ME ABOUT HOW THEY WERE LOST.
NOT FOR SALE
USED
GAME
I SEE.
OVAL HOME
...
...
THAT'S... A GHOST.
HUH?

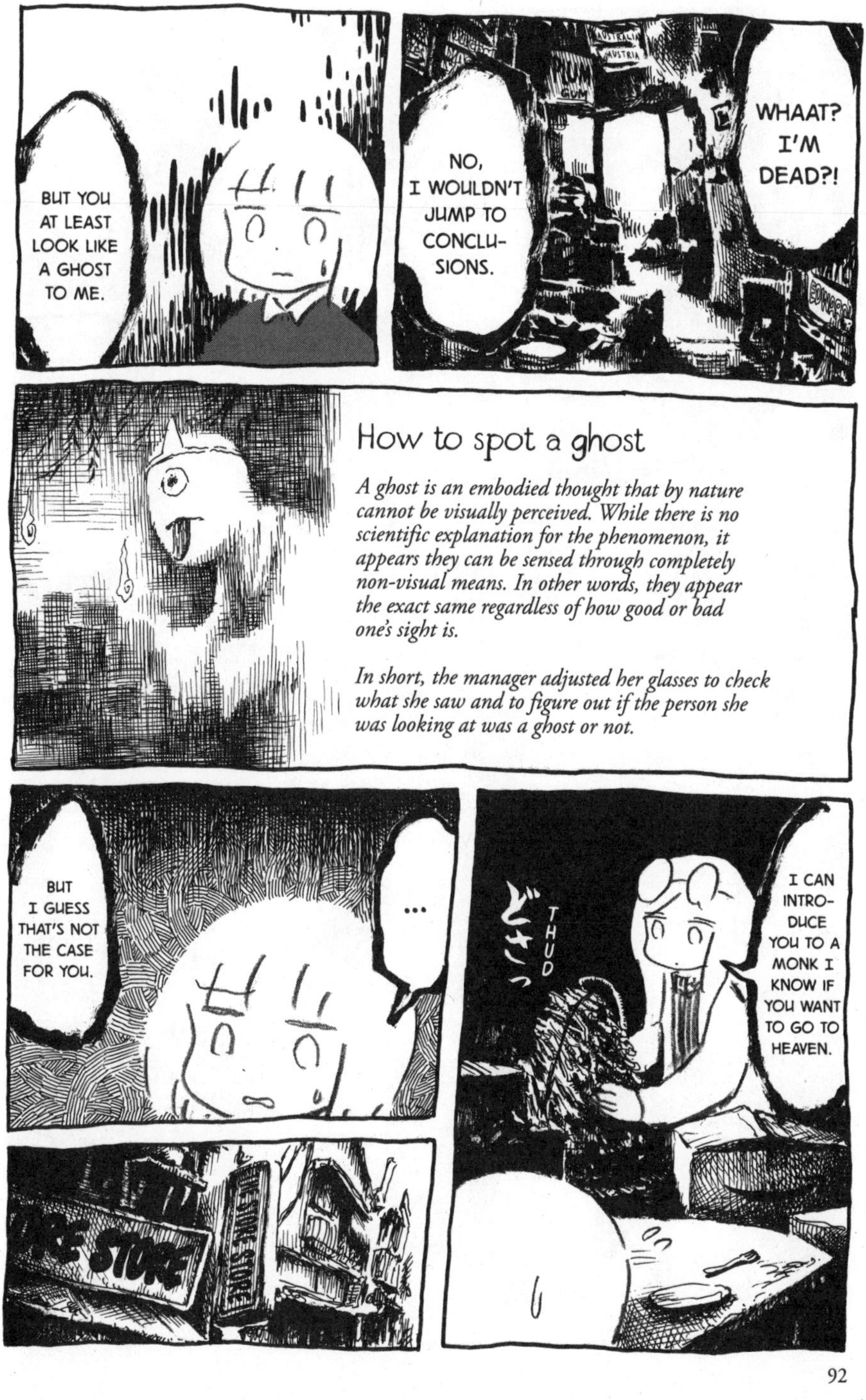
WHAAT? I'M DEAD?!
NO, I WOULDN'T JUMP TO CONCLUSIONS.
BUT YOU AT LEAST LOOK LIKE A GHOST TO ME.
How to spot a ghost
A ghost is an embodied thought that by nature cannot be visually perceived. While there is no scientific explanation for the phenomenon, it appears they can be sensed through completely non-visual means. In other words, they appear the exact same regardless of how good or bad one's sight is.
In short, the manager adjusted her glasses to check what she saw and to figure out if the person she was looking at was a ghost or not.
どさっ THUD
I CAN INTRODUCE YOU TO A MONK I KNOW IF YOU WANT TO GO TO HEAVEN.
...
BUT I GUESS THAT'S NOT THE CASE FOR YOU.

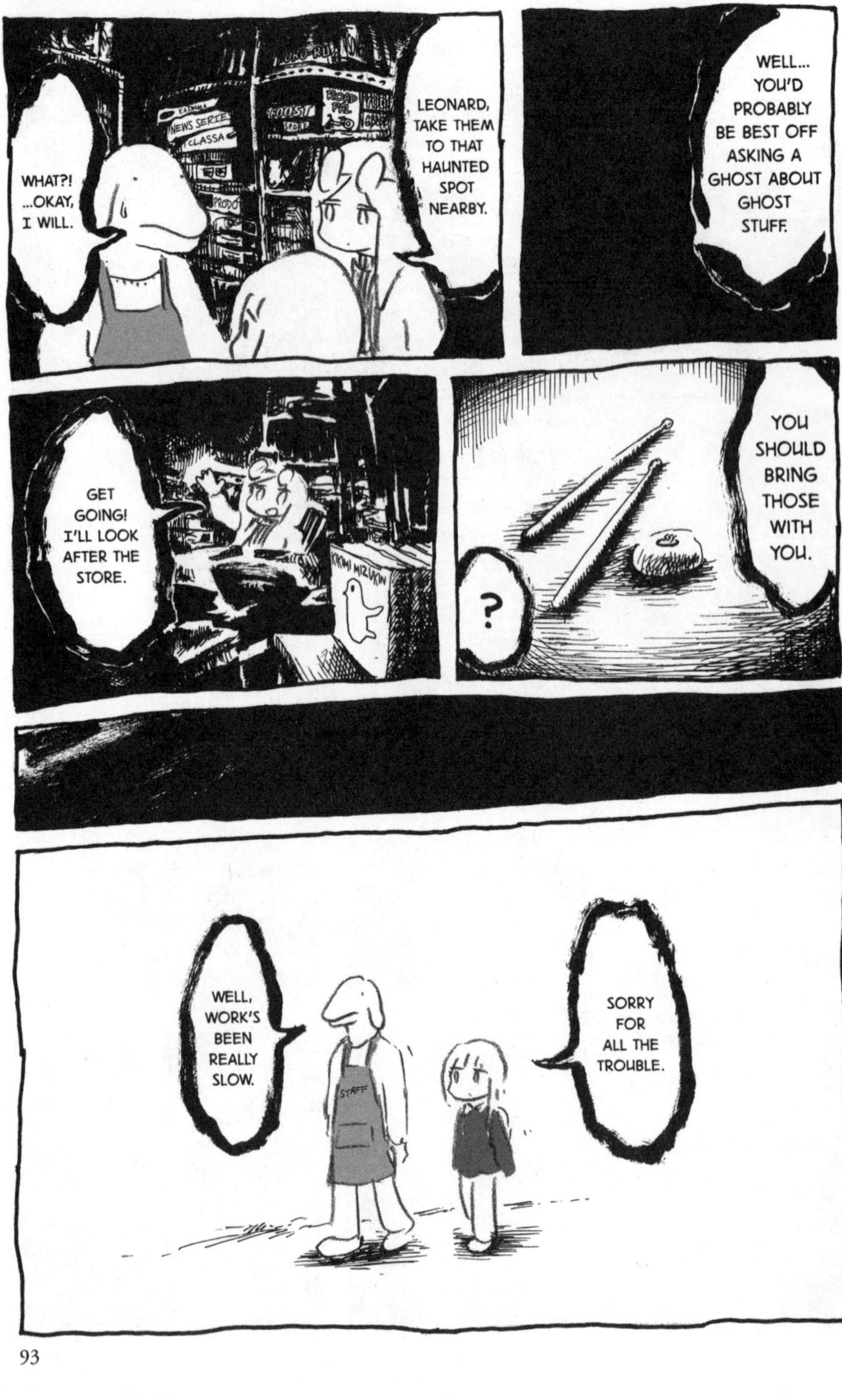
WELL... YOU'D PROBABLY BE BEST OFF ASKING A GHOST ABOUT GHOST STUFF.
LEONARD, TAKE THEM TO THAT HAUNTED SPOT NEARBY.
WHAT?! ...OKAY, I WILL.
YOU SHOULD BRING THOSE WITH YOU.
?
GET GOING! I'LL LOOK AFTER THE STORE.
SORRY FOR ALL THE TROUBLE.
WELL, WORK'S BEEN REALLY SLOW.
STAFF

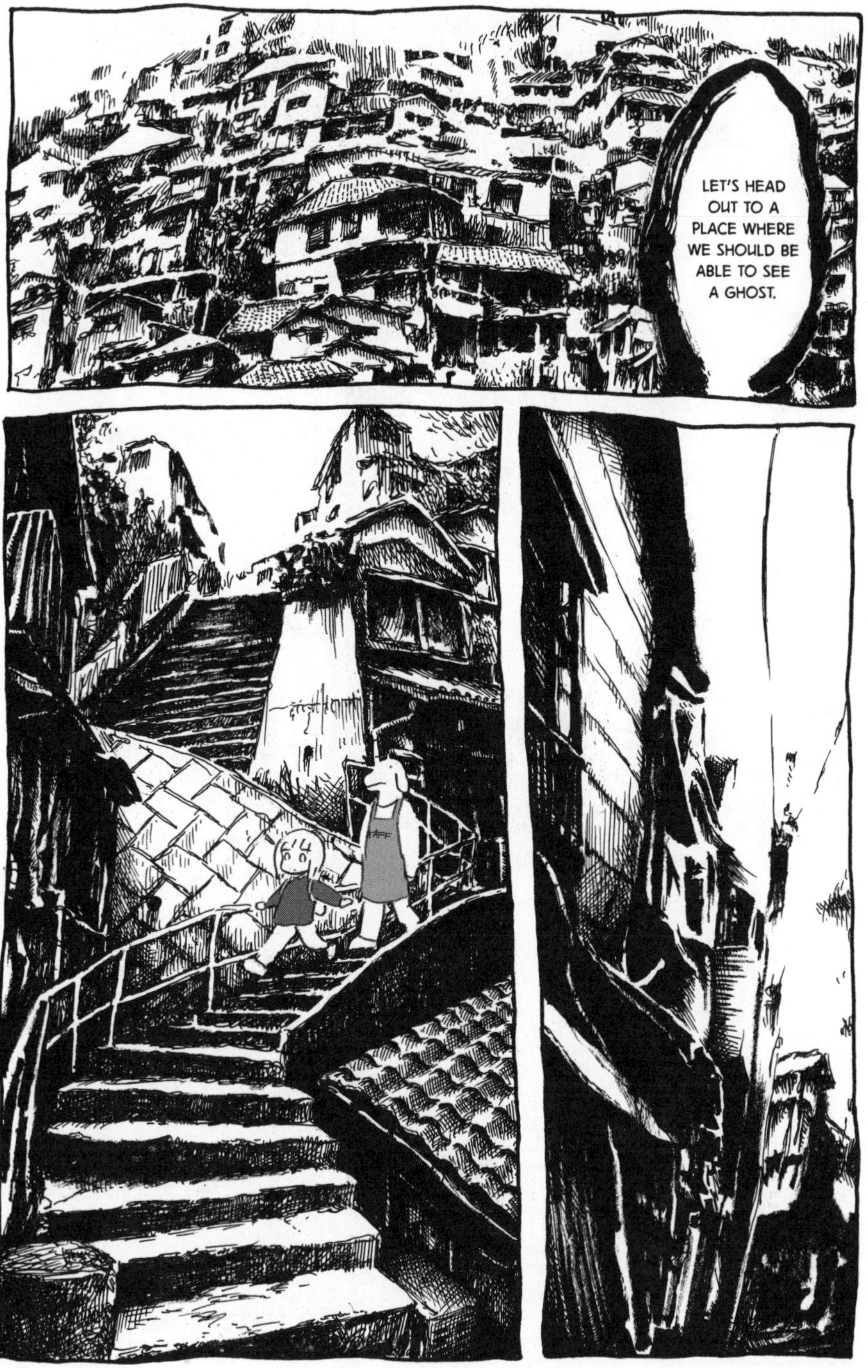
LET'S HEAD OUT TO A PLACE WHERE WE SHOULD BE ABLE TO SEE A GHOST.

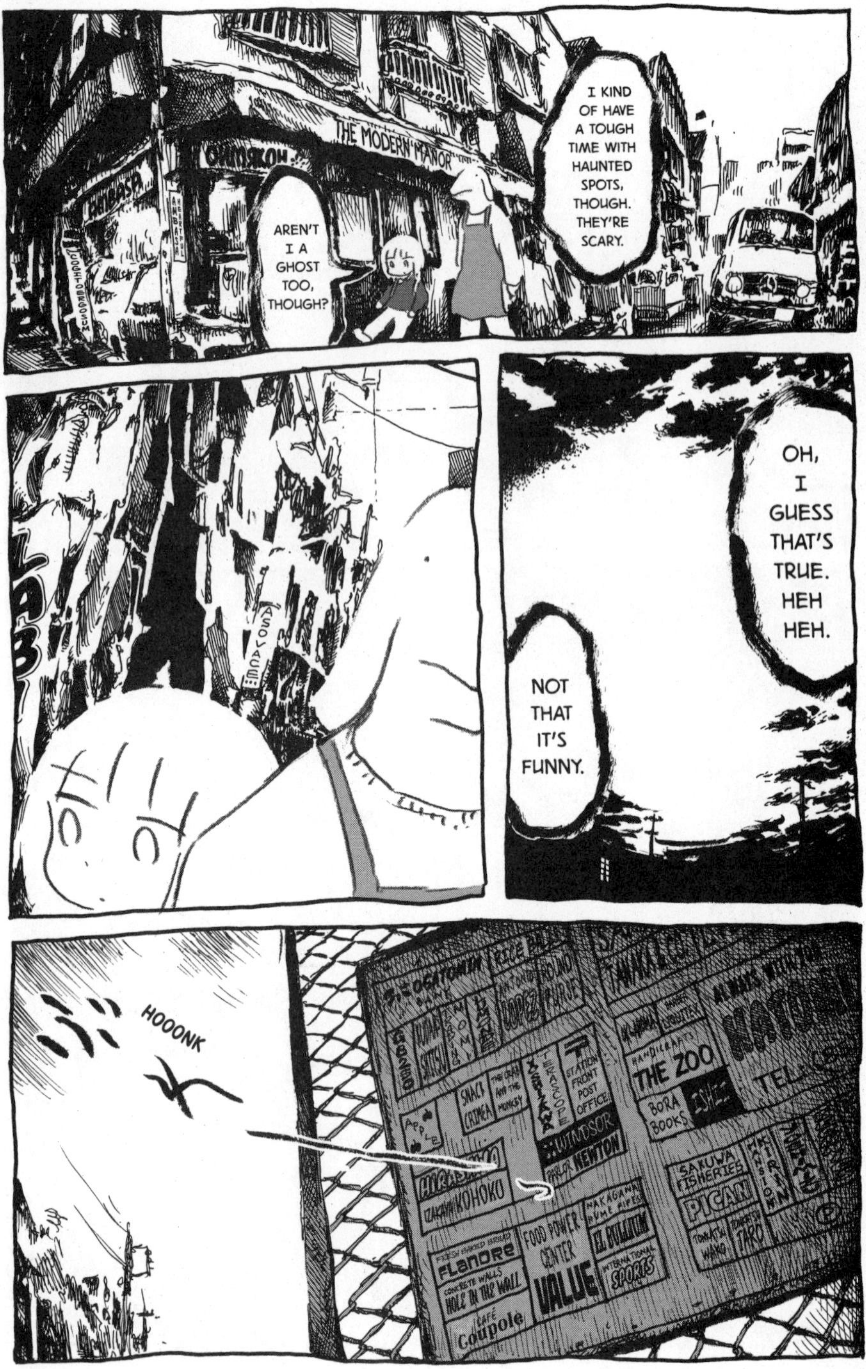
THE MODERN MANOR
I KIND OF HAVE A TOUGH TIME WITH HAUNTED SPOTS, THOUGH. THEY'RE SCARY.
AREN'T I A GHOST TOO, THOUGH?
OH, I GUESS THAT'S TRUE. HEH HEH.
NOT THAT IT'S FUNNY.
ASOVACE
THE ZOO
BORA BOOKS
STATION FRONT POST OFFICE
WINDSOR
NEWTON
SAKUWA FISHERIES
PICAN
FOOD POWER CENTER
VALUE
SPORTS
Flandre
HOLE IN THE WALL
Coupole
HOOONK

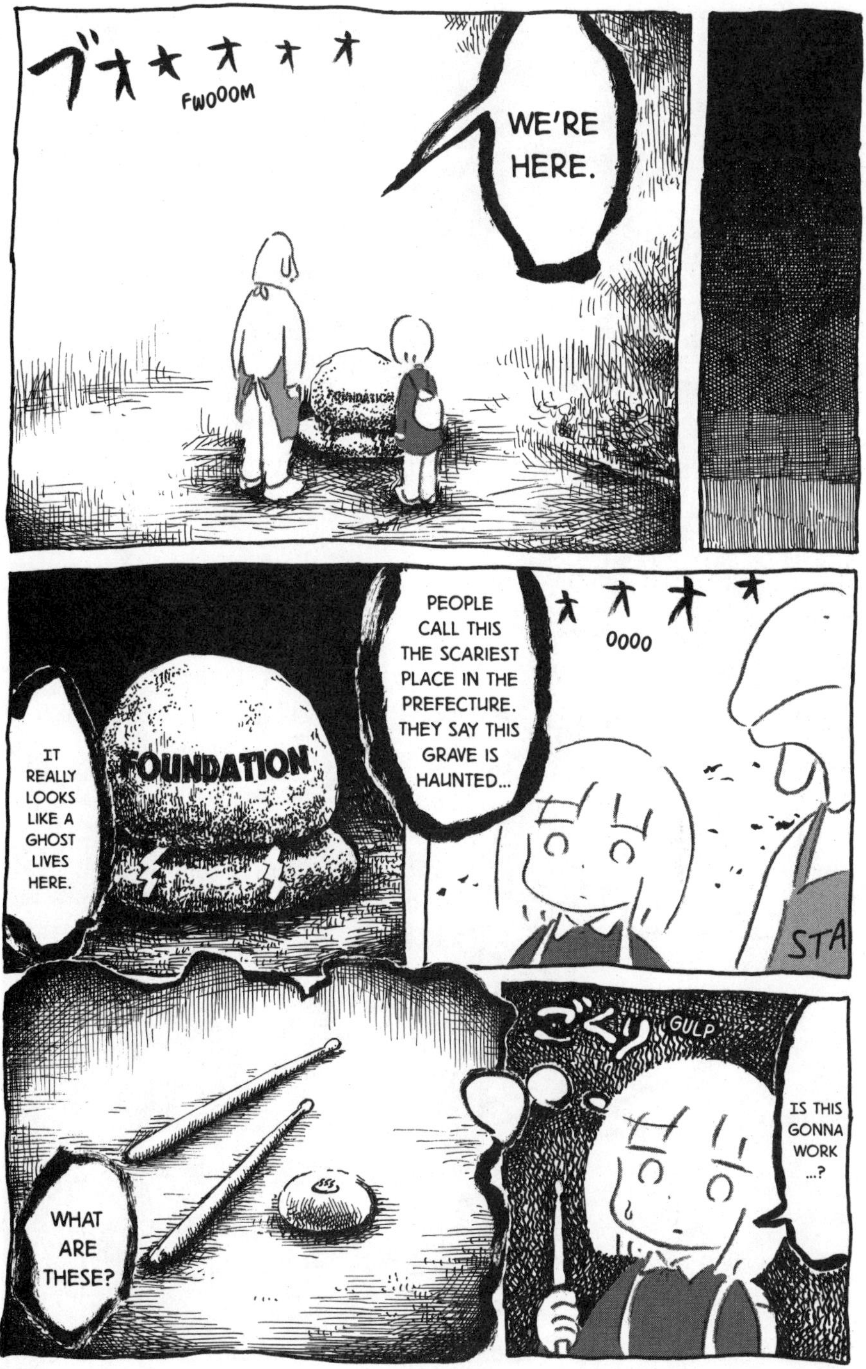
ブオォォォォ
FWOOOM
WE'RE HERE.
FOUNDATION
ォォォォ
OOOO
STA
PEOPLE CALL THIS THE SCARIEST PLACE IN THE PREFECTURE. THEY SAY THIS GRAVE IS HAUNTED...
FOUNDATION
IT REALLY LOOKS LIKE A GHOST LIVES HERE.
ごくり
GULP
IS THIS GONNA WORK ...?
WHAT ARE THESE?
...

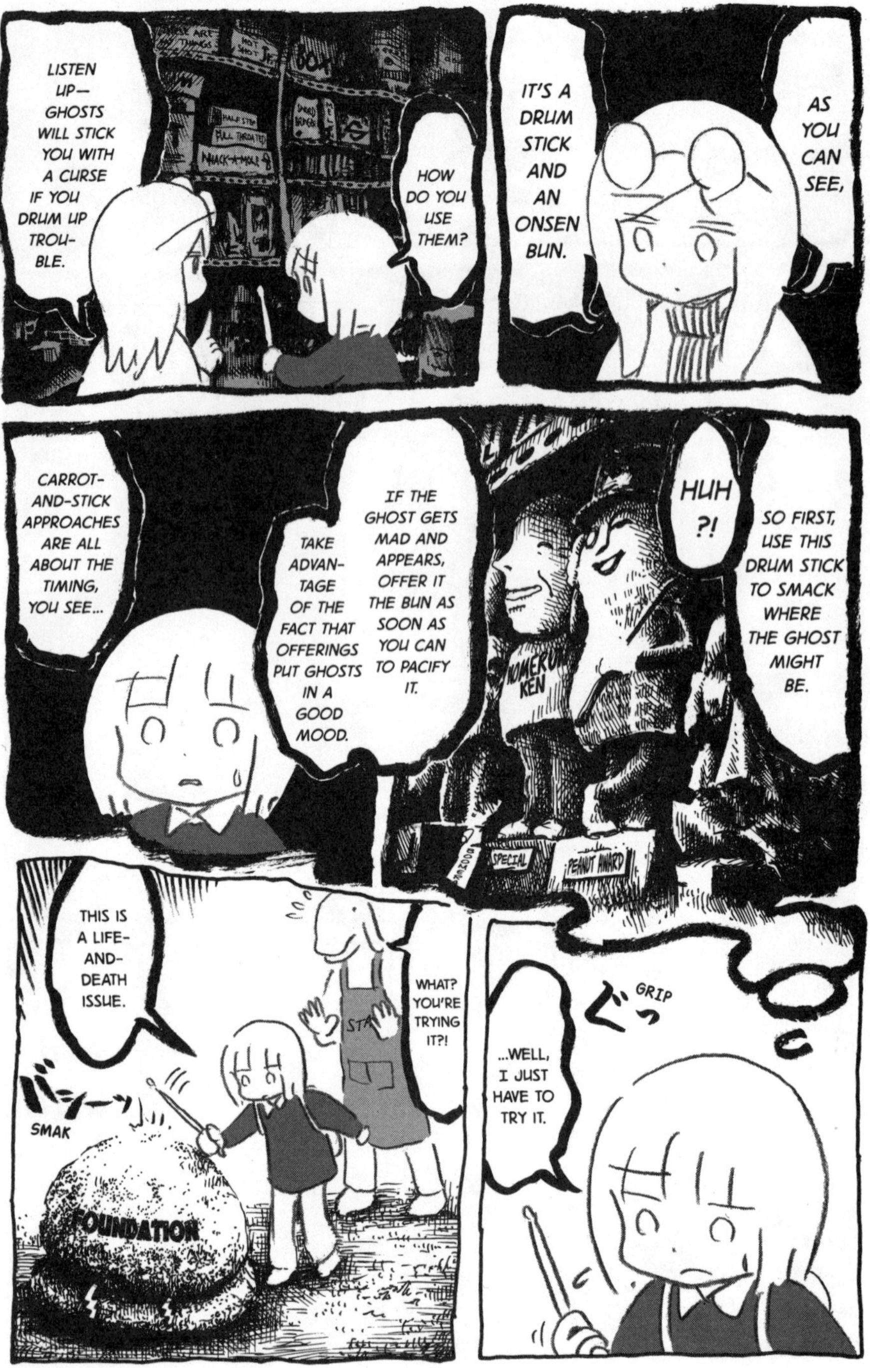
AS YOU CAN SEE,
IT'S A DRUM STICK AND AN ONSEN BUN.
HOW DO YOU USE THEM?
LISTEN UP—GHOSTS WILL STICK YOU WITH A CURSE IF YOU DRUM UP TROU-BLE.
SO FIRST, USE THIS DRUM STICK TO SMACK WHERE THE GHOST MIGHT BE.
HUH ?!
SPECIAL
PEANUT AWARD
IF THE GHOST GETS MAD AND APPEARS, OFFER IT THE BUN AS SOON AS YOU CAN TO PACIFY IT.
TAKE ADVAN-TAGE OF THE FACT THAT OFFERINGS PUT GHOSTS IN A GOOD MOOD.
CARROT-AND-STICK APPROACHES ARE ALL ABOUT THE TIMING, YOU SEE...
GRIP
...WELL, I JUST HAVE TO TRY IT.
WHAT? YOU'RE TRYING IT?!
THIS IS A LIFE-AND-DEATH ISSUE.
SMAK
FOUNDATION

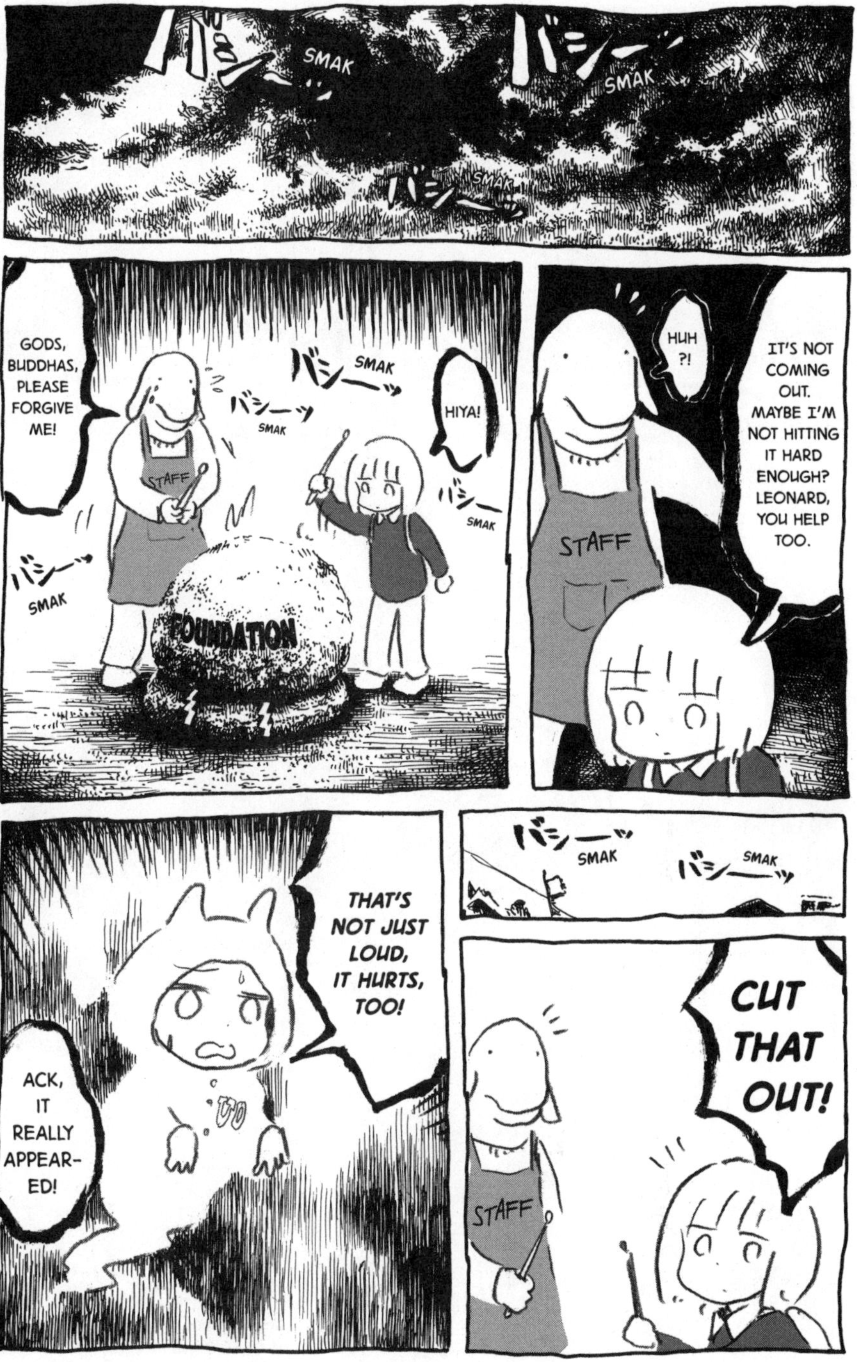
SMAK
SMAK
SMAK
HUH?!
IT'S NOT COMING OUT. MAYBE I'M NOT HITTING IT HARD ENOUGH? LEONARD, YOU HELP TOO.
SMAK
HIYA!
SMAK
SMAK
GODS, BUDDHAS, PLEASE FORGIVE ME!
FOUNDATION
SMAK
SMAK
SMAK
SMAK
CUT THAT OUT!
THAT'S NOT JUST LOUD, IT HURTS, TOO!
ACK, IT REALLY APPEAR-ED!

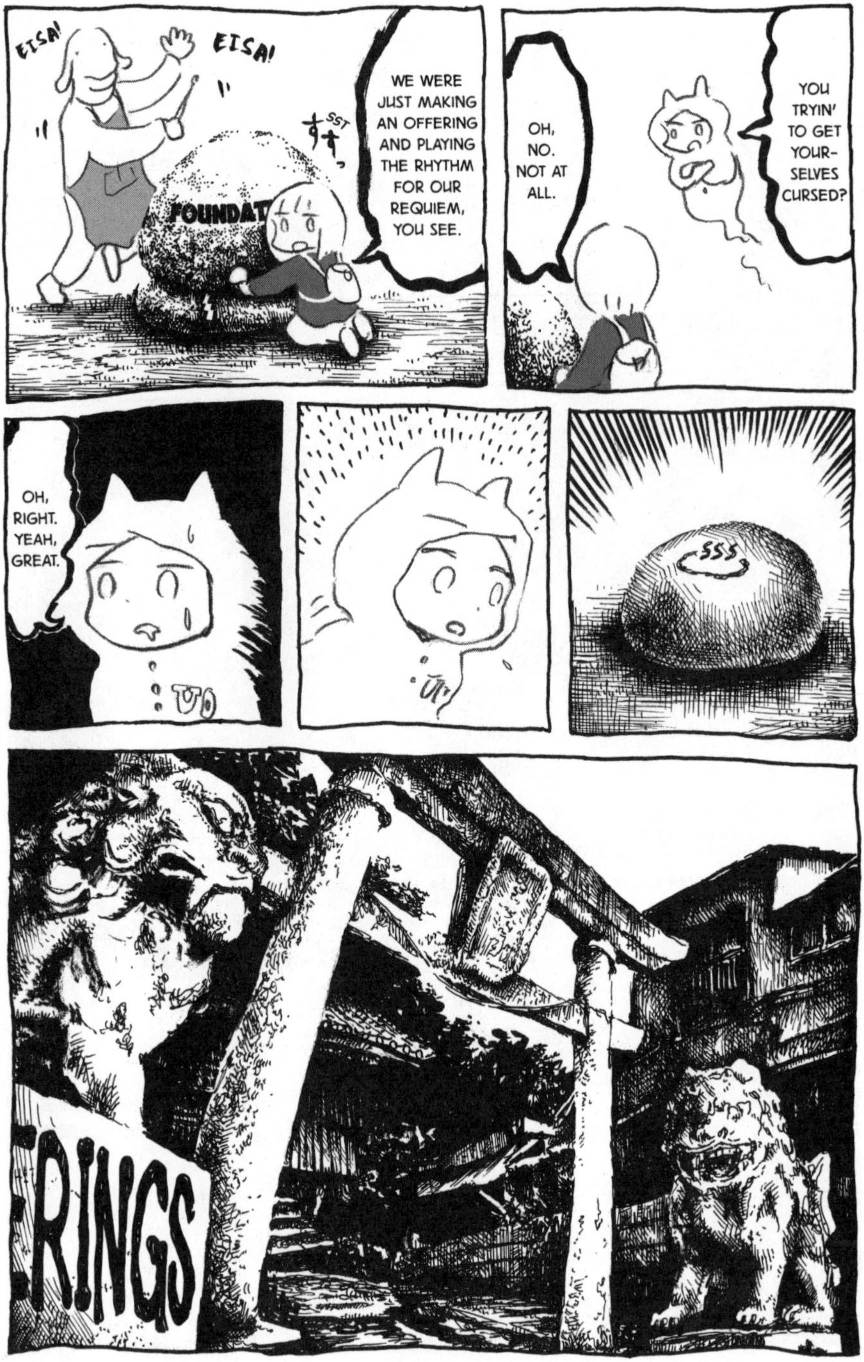
YOU TRYIN' TO GET YOUR-SELVES CURSED?
OH, NO. NOT AT ALL.
WE WERE JUST MAKING AN OFFERING AND PLAYING THE RHYTHM FOR OUR REQUIEM, YOU SEE.
SST
すす
EISA!
EISA!
FOUNDAT
SSS
OH, RIGHT. YEAH, GREAT.
RINGS

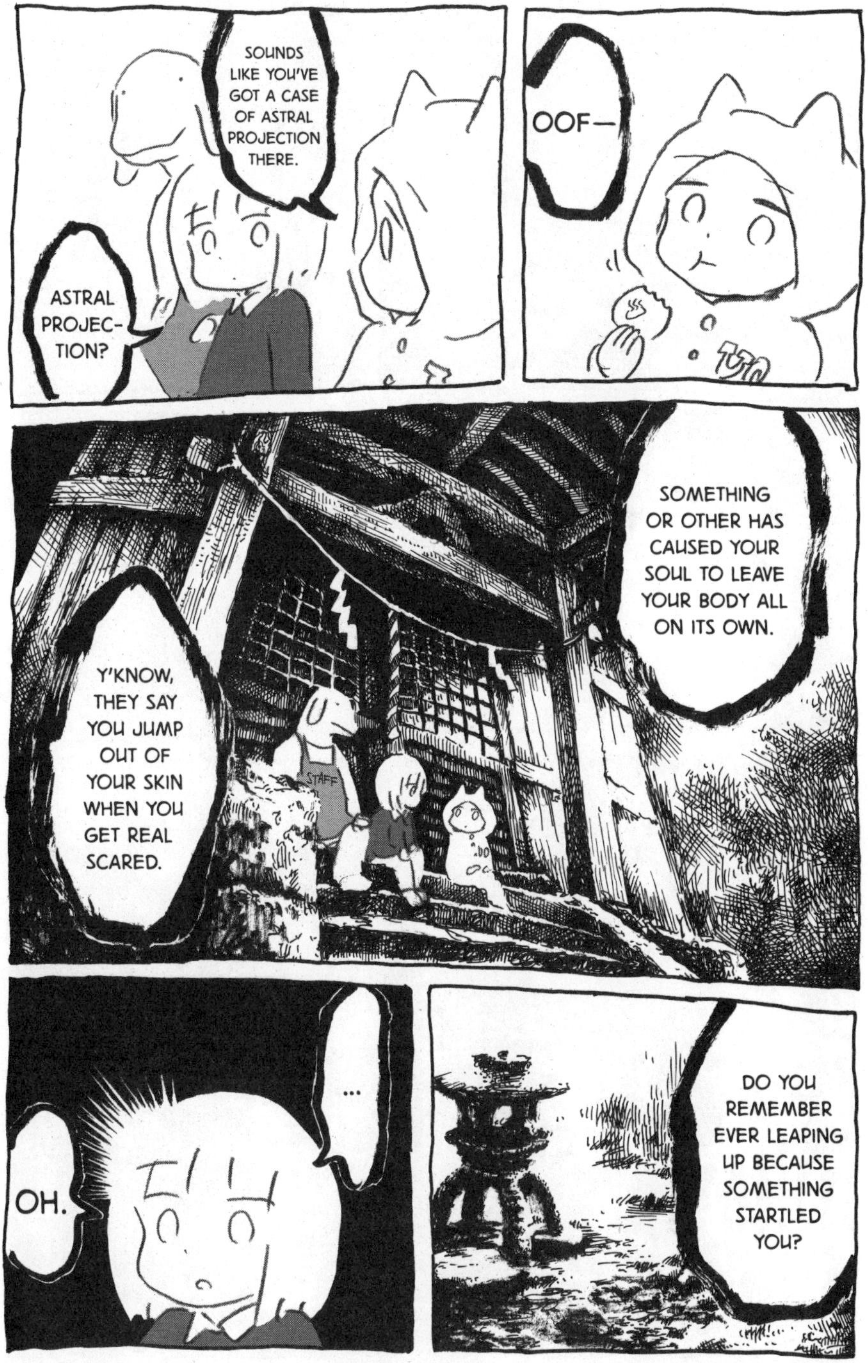
OOF—
SOUNDS LIKE YOU'VE GOT A CASE OF ASTRAL PROJECTION THERE.
ASTRAL PROJEC-TION?
SOMETHING OR OTHER HAS CAUSED YOUR SOUL TO LEAVE YOUR BODY ALL ON ITS OWN.
Y'KNOW, THEY SAY YOU JUMP OUT OF YOUR SKIN WHEN YOU GET REAL SCARED.
STAFF
DO YOU REMEMBER EVER LEAPING UP BECAUSE SOMETHING STARTLED YOU?
...
OH.

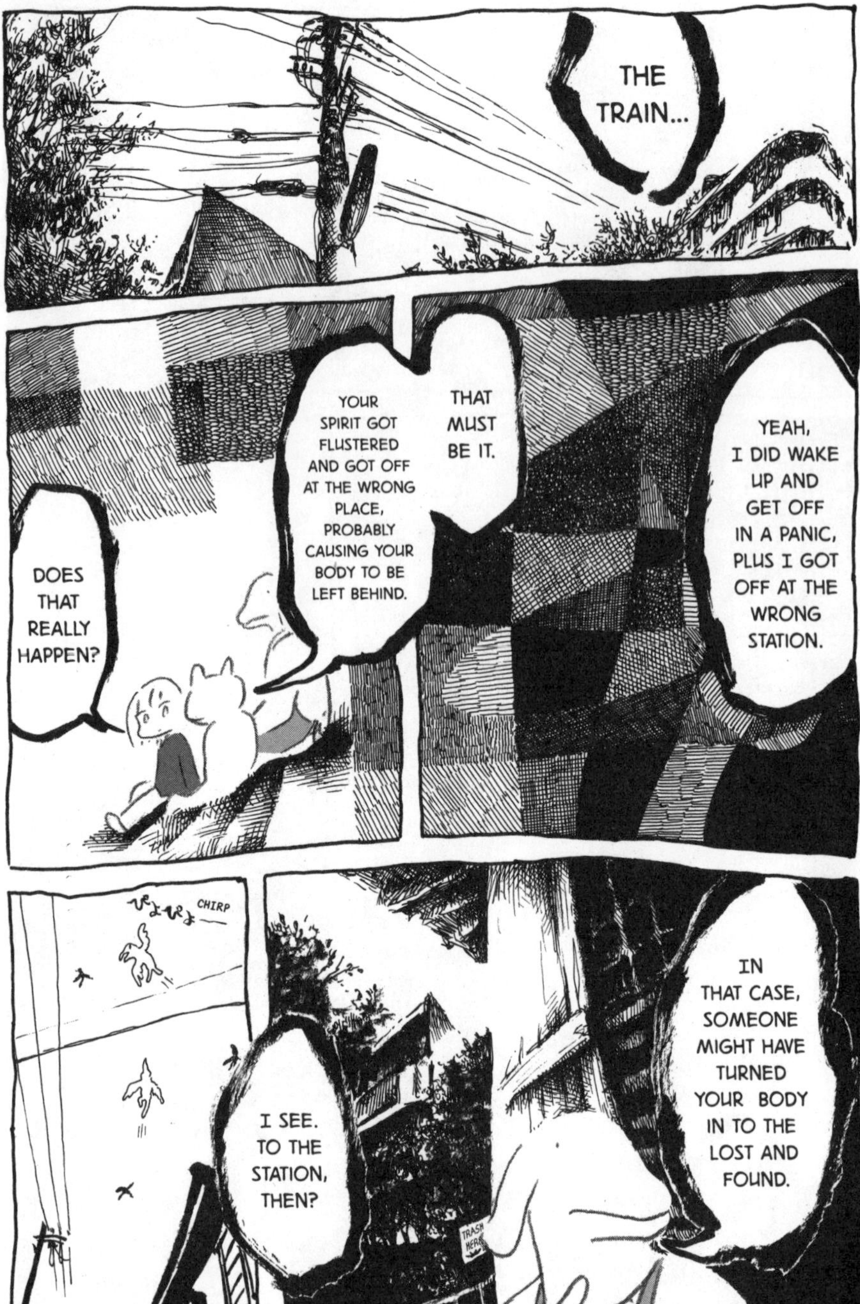
THE TRAIN...
YEAH, I DID WAKE UP AND GET OFF IN A PANIC, PLUS I GOT OFF AT THE WRONG STATION.
THAT MUST BE IT.
YOUR SPIRIT GOT FLUSTERED AND GOT OFF AT THE WRONG PLACE, PROBABLY CAUSING YOUR BODY TO BE LEFT BEHIND.
DOES THAT REALLY HAPPEN?
IN THAT CASE, SOMEONE MIGHT HAVE TURNED YOUR BODY IN TO THE LOST AND FOUND.
I SEE. TO THE STATION, THEN?
ぴよぴよ
CHIRP

THANKS A LOT.
SORRY ABOUT BEING SO ROUGH WHEN WE SUMMONED YOU.
IT'S FINE. THANKS FOR THE BUN.
FOUNDATION
STAFF
I WANT TO SAY THAT THE LOST AND FOUND WAS IN THE BACK OF THE FREIGHT TERMINAL.
HM.

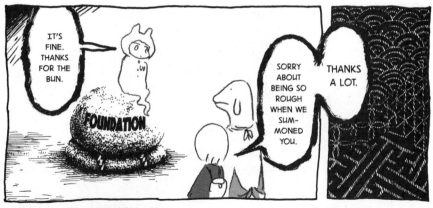

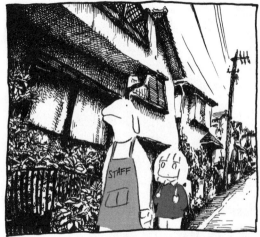

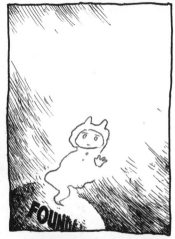

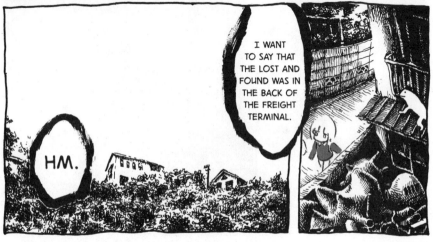

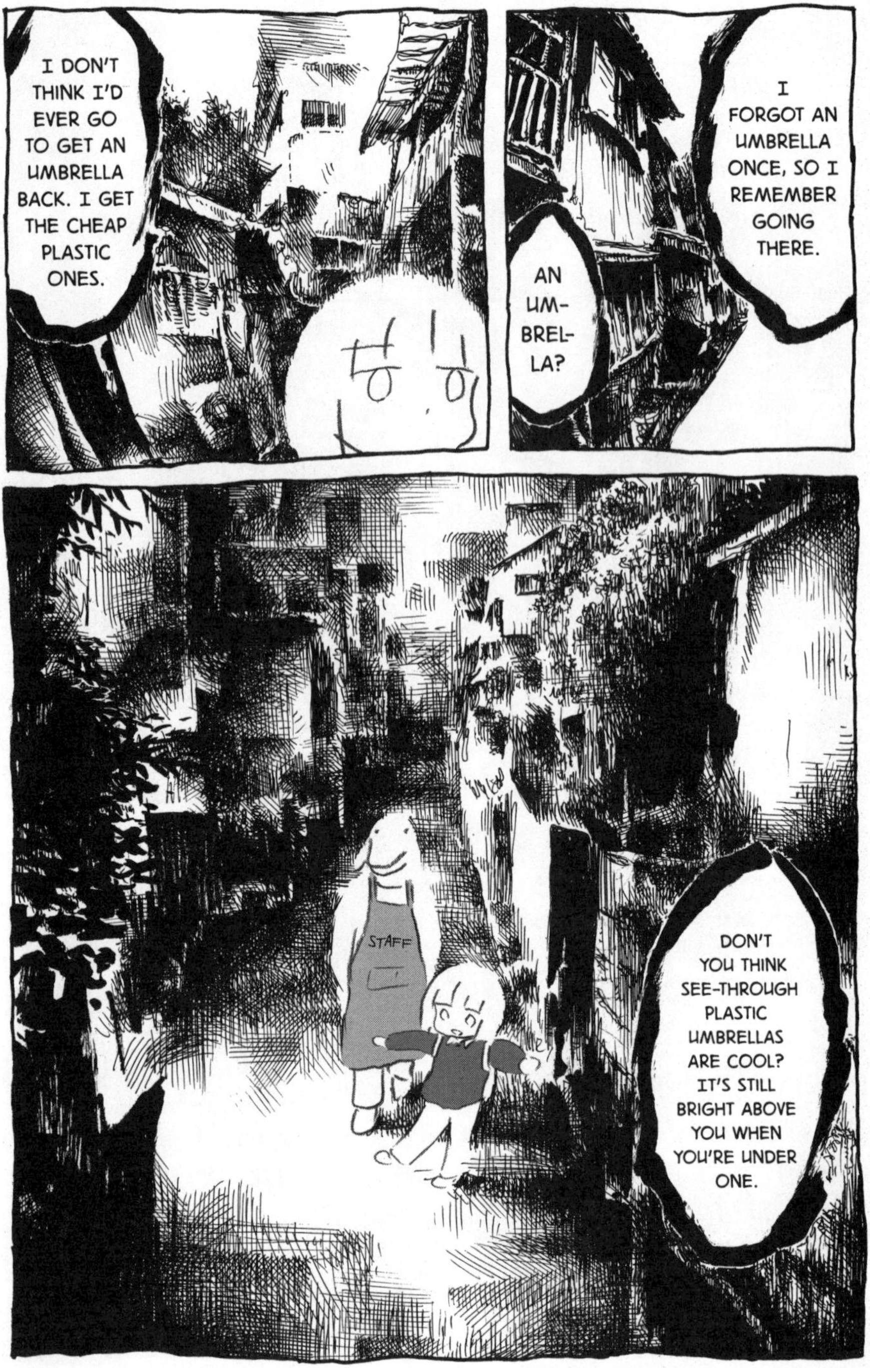
I FORGOT AN UMBRELLA ONCE, SO I REMEMBER GOING THERE.
AN UM-BREL-LA?
I DON'T THINK I'D EVER GO TO GET AN UMBRELLA BACK. I GET THE CHEAP PLASTIC ONES.
DON'T YOU THINK SEE-THROUGH PLASTIC UMBRELLAS ARE COOL? IT'S STILL BRIGHT ABOVE YOU WHEN YOU'RE UNDER ONE.
STAFF

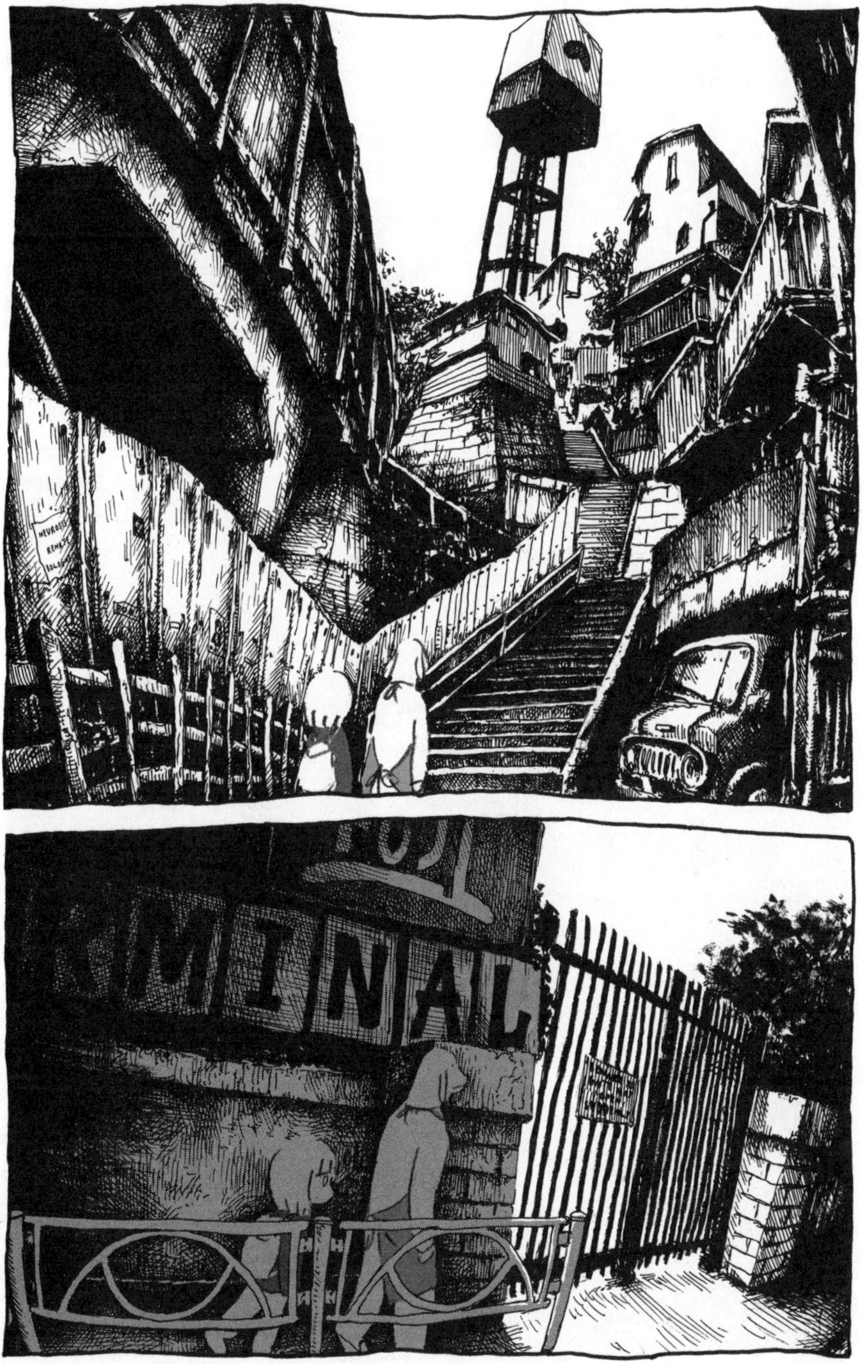
RMINAL

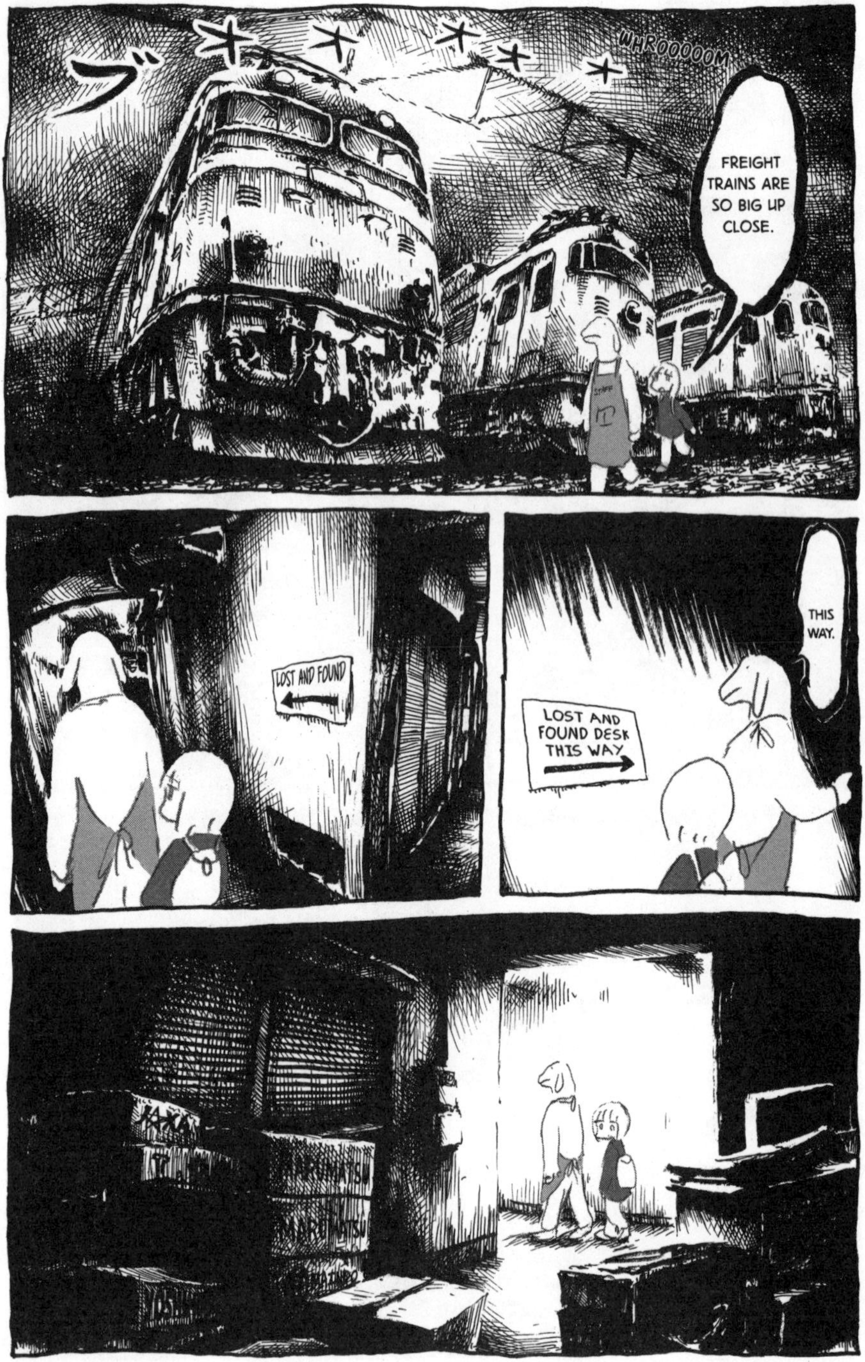
WHROOOOOM
FREIGHT TRAINS ARE SO BIG UP CLOSE.
THIS WAY.
LOST AND FOUND DESK THIS WAY
LOST AND FOUND

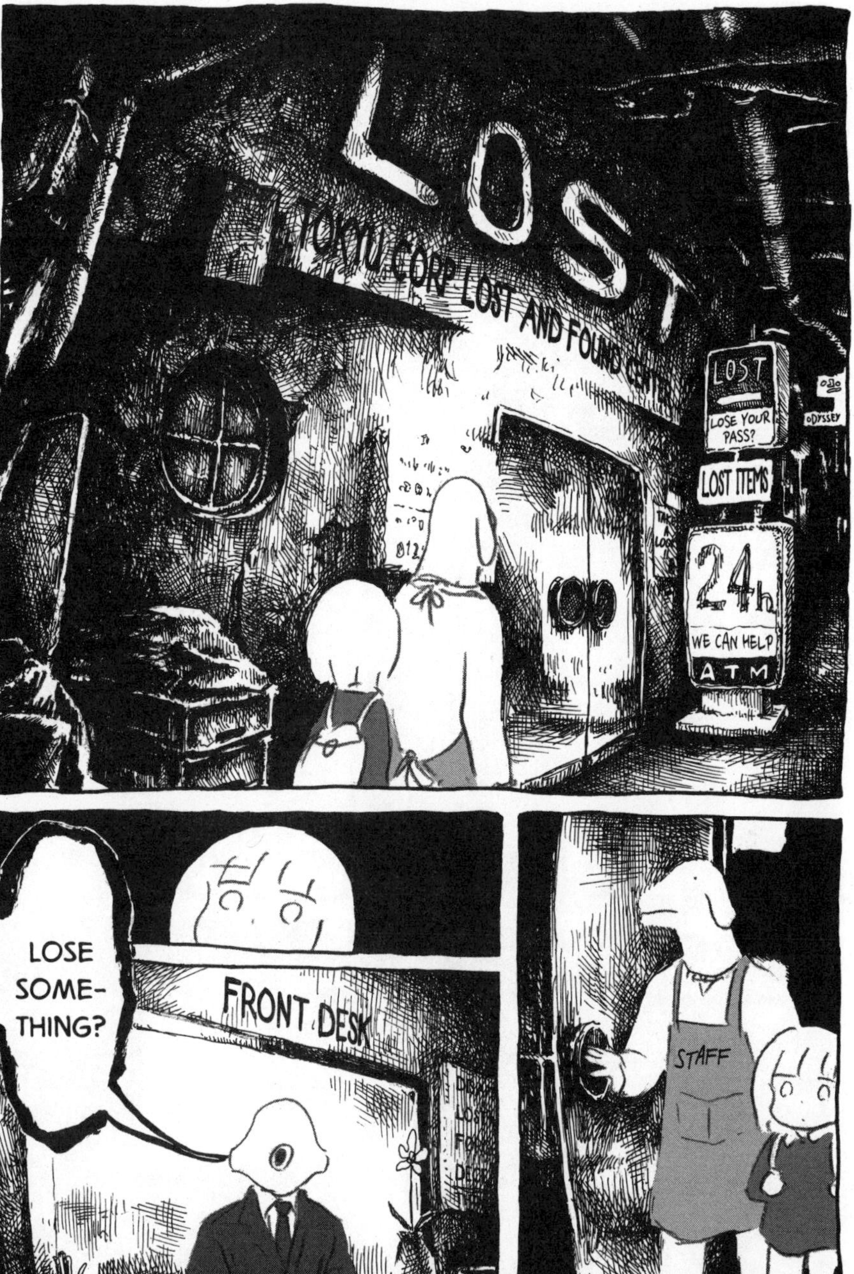
LOST
TOKYU CORP LOST AND FOUND
LOST
LOSE YOUR PASS?
ODYSSEY
LOST ITEMS
24h
WE CAN HELP
ATM
STAFF
LOSE SOMETHING?
FRONT DESK

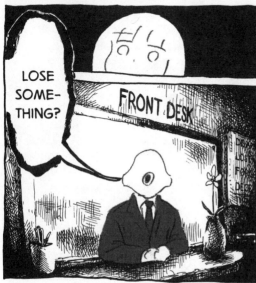

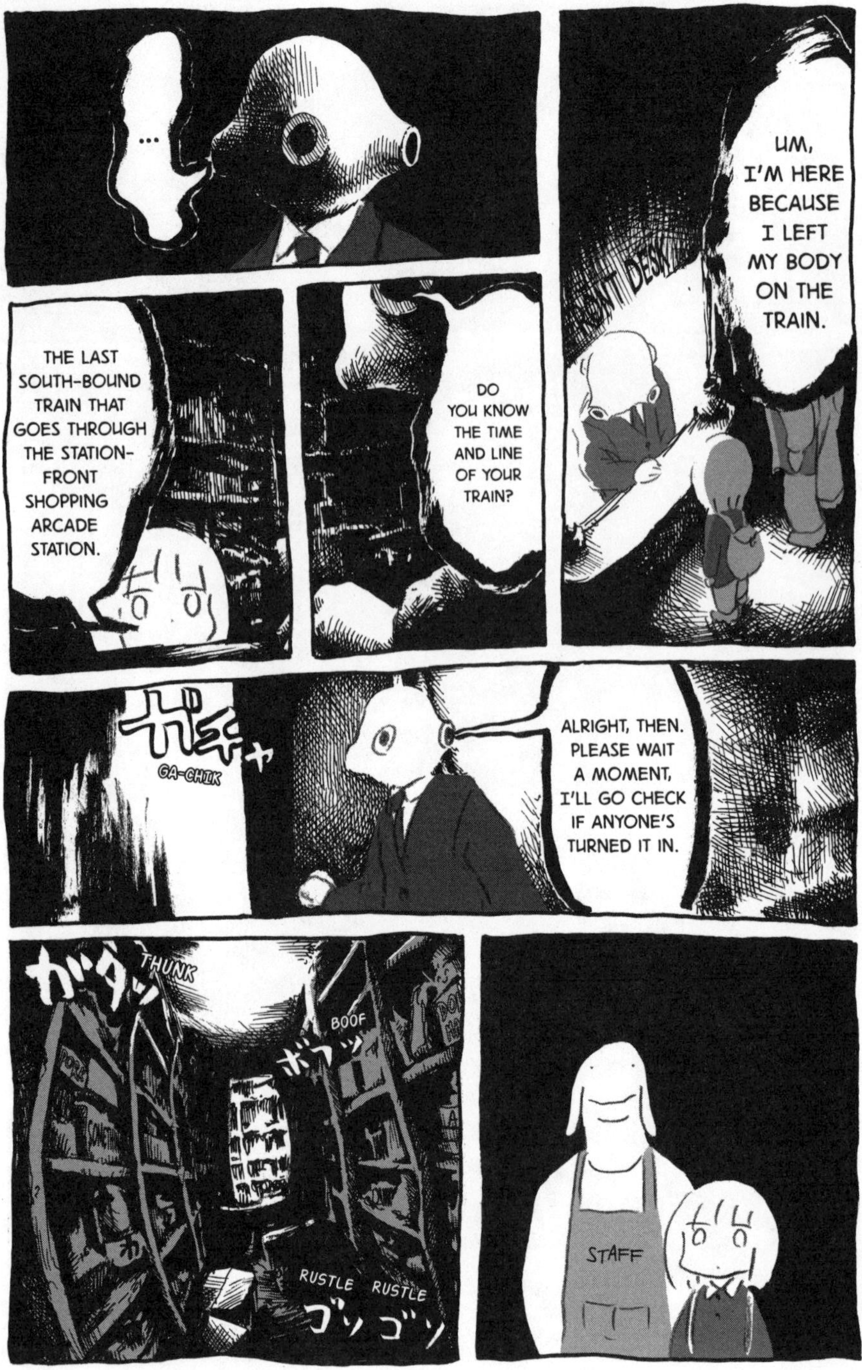
FRONT DESK
UM, I'M HERE BECAUSE I LEFT MY BODY ON THE TRAIN.
...
DO YOU KNOW THE TIME AND LINE OF YOUR TRAIN?
THE LAST SOUTH-BOUND TRAIN THAT GOES THROUGH THE STATION-FRONT SHOPPING ARCADE STATION.
ALRIGHT, THEN. PLEASE WAIT A MOMENT, I'LL GO CHECK IF ANYONE'S TURNED IT IN.
GA-CHIK
STAFF
THUNK
BOOF
RUSTLE RUSTLE

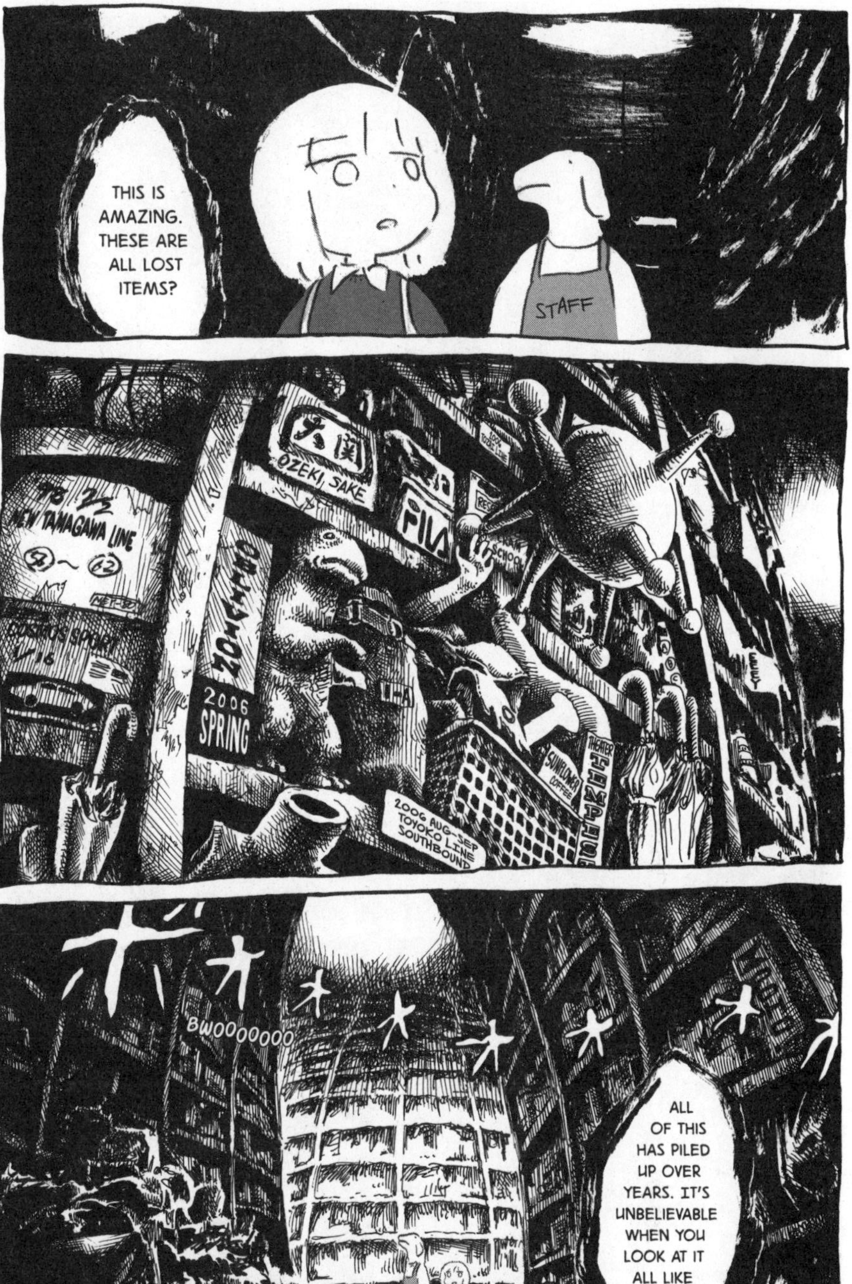

THIS IS AMAZING. THESE ARE ALL LOST ITEMS?
STAFF
OZEKI SAKE
NEW TAMAGAWA LINE
2006 SPRING
SCHOOL
THEATER
SUNFLOWER COFFEE
2006 AUG-SEP TOYOKO LINE SOUTHBOUND
BWOOOOOOOO
ALL OF THIS HAS PILED UP OVER YEARS. IT'S UNBELIEVABLE WHEN YOU LOOK AT IT ALL LIKE THIS.

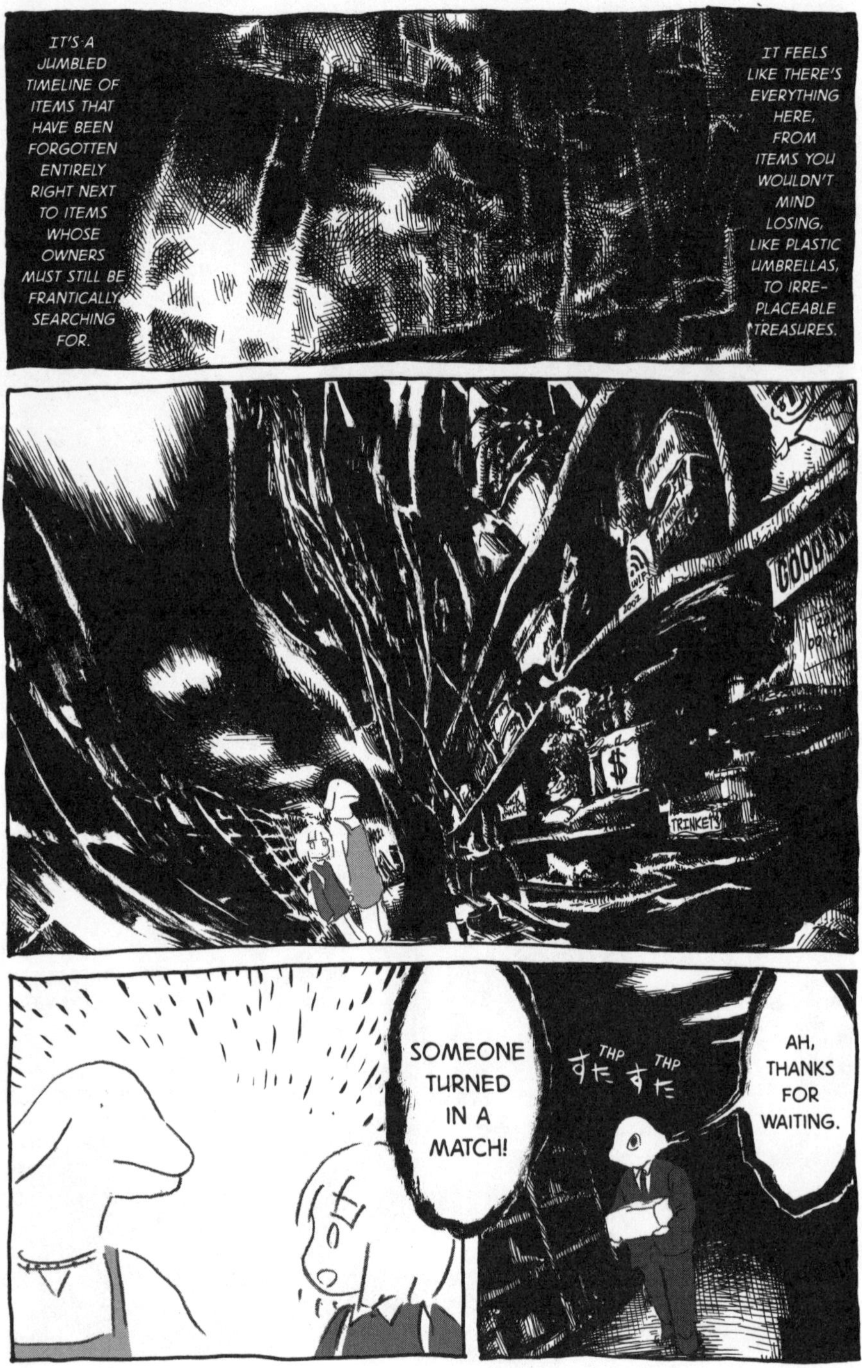
IT FEELS LIKE THERE'S EVERYTHING HERE, FROM ITEMS YOU WOULDN'T MIND LOSING, LIKE PLASTIC UMBRELLAS, TO IRRE-PLACEABLE TREASURES.
IT'S A JUMBLED TIMELINE OF ITEMS THAT HAVE BEEN FORGOTTEN ENTIRELY RIGHT NEXT TO ITEMS WHOSE OWNERS MUST STILL BE FRANTICALLY SEARCHING FOR.
WALKMAN
TRINKETS
AH, THANKS FOR WAITING.
すた すた THP THP
SOMEONE TURNED IN A MATCH!

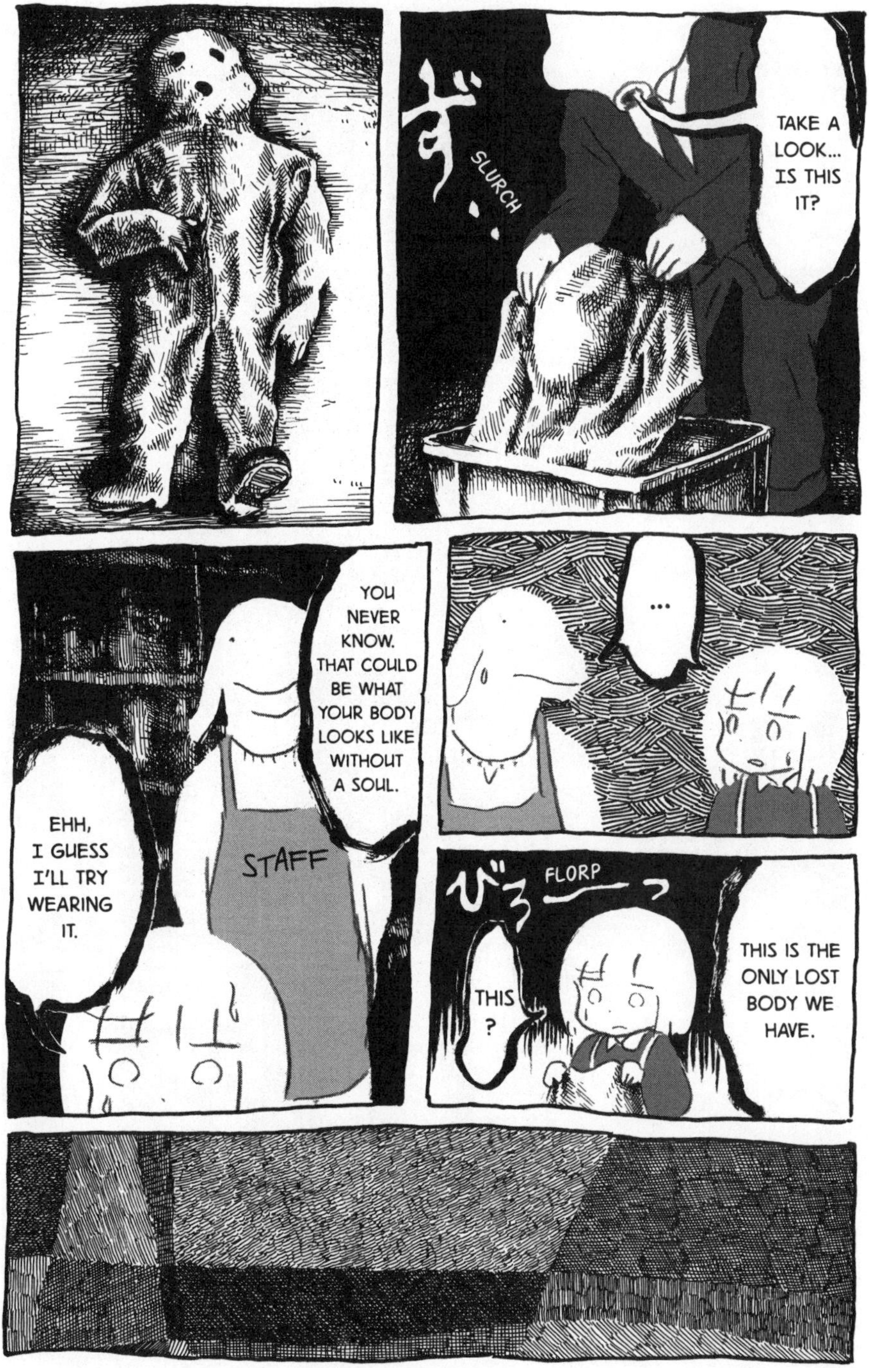
TAKE A LOOK... IS THIS IT?
ず
SLURCH
...
THIS IS THE ONLY LOST BODY WE HAVE.
びろ
FLORP
THIS ?
YOU NEVER KNOW. THAT COULD BE WHAT YOUR BODY LOOKS LIKE WITHOUT A SOUL.
STAFF
EHH, I GUESS I'LL TRY WEARING IT.

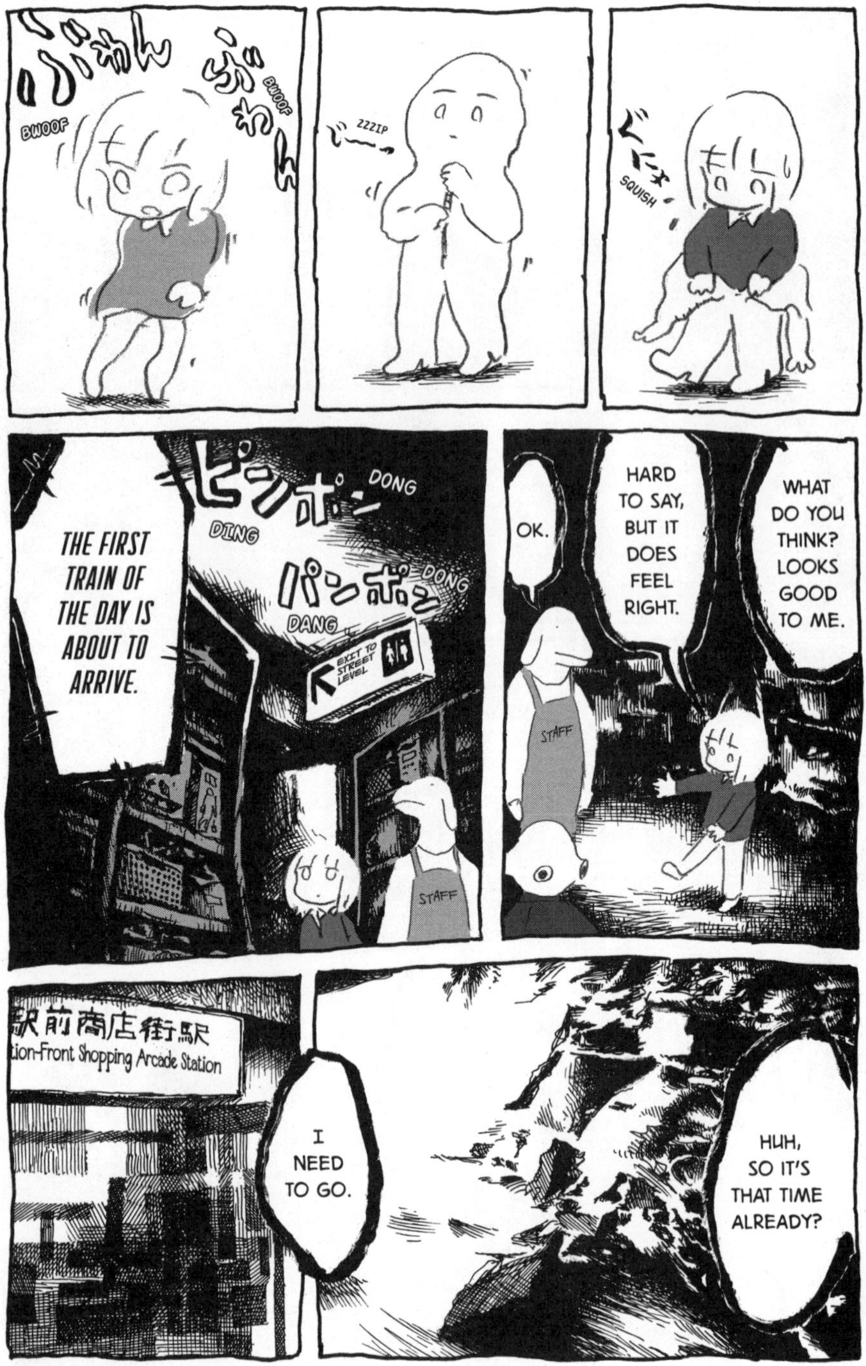
ぐにゃ
SQUISH
じー
ZZZIP
ぶわん
BWOOF
ぶわん
BWOOF
WHAT DO YOU THINK? LOOKS GOOD TO ME.
HARD TO SAY, BUT IT DOES FEEL RIGHT.
OK.
ピンポン
DING
DONG
パンポン
DANG
DONG
EXIT TO STREET LEVEL
THE FIRST TRAIN OF THE DAY IS ABOUT TO ARRIVE.
HUH, SO IT'S THAT TIME ALREADY?
I NEED TO GO.
駅前商店街駅
tion-Front Shopping Arcade Station

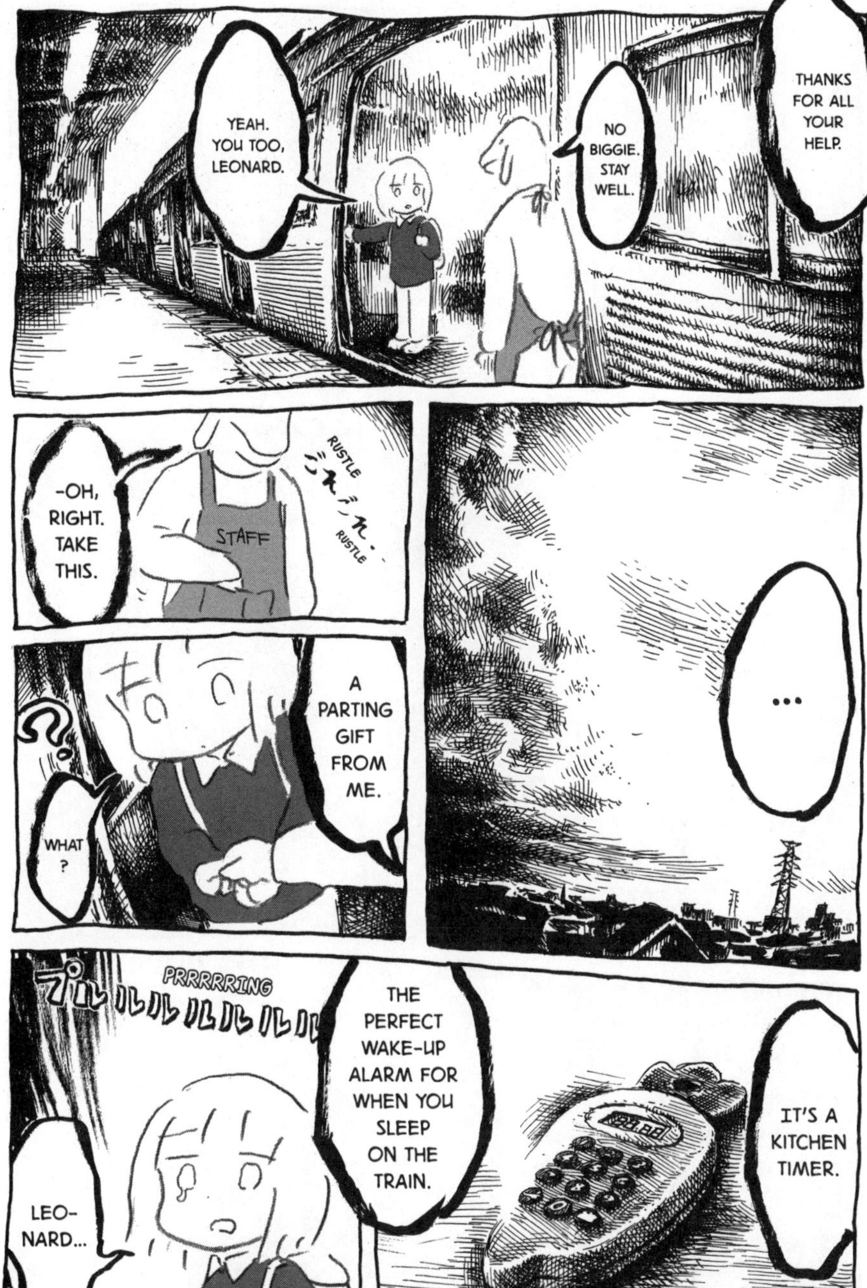
THANKS FOR ALL YOUR HELP.
NO BIGGIE. STAY WELL.
YEAH. YOU TOO, LEONARD.
...
-OH, RIGHT. TAKE THIS.
RUSTLE
ごそごそ
RUSTLE
STAFF
A PARTING GIFT FROM ME.
WHAT?
IT'S A KITCHEN TIMER.
THE PERFECT WAKE-UP ALARM FOR WHEN YOU SLEEP ON THE TRAIN.
PRRRRRING
LEO-NARD...

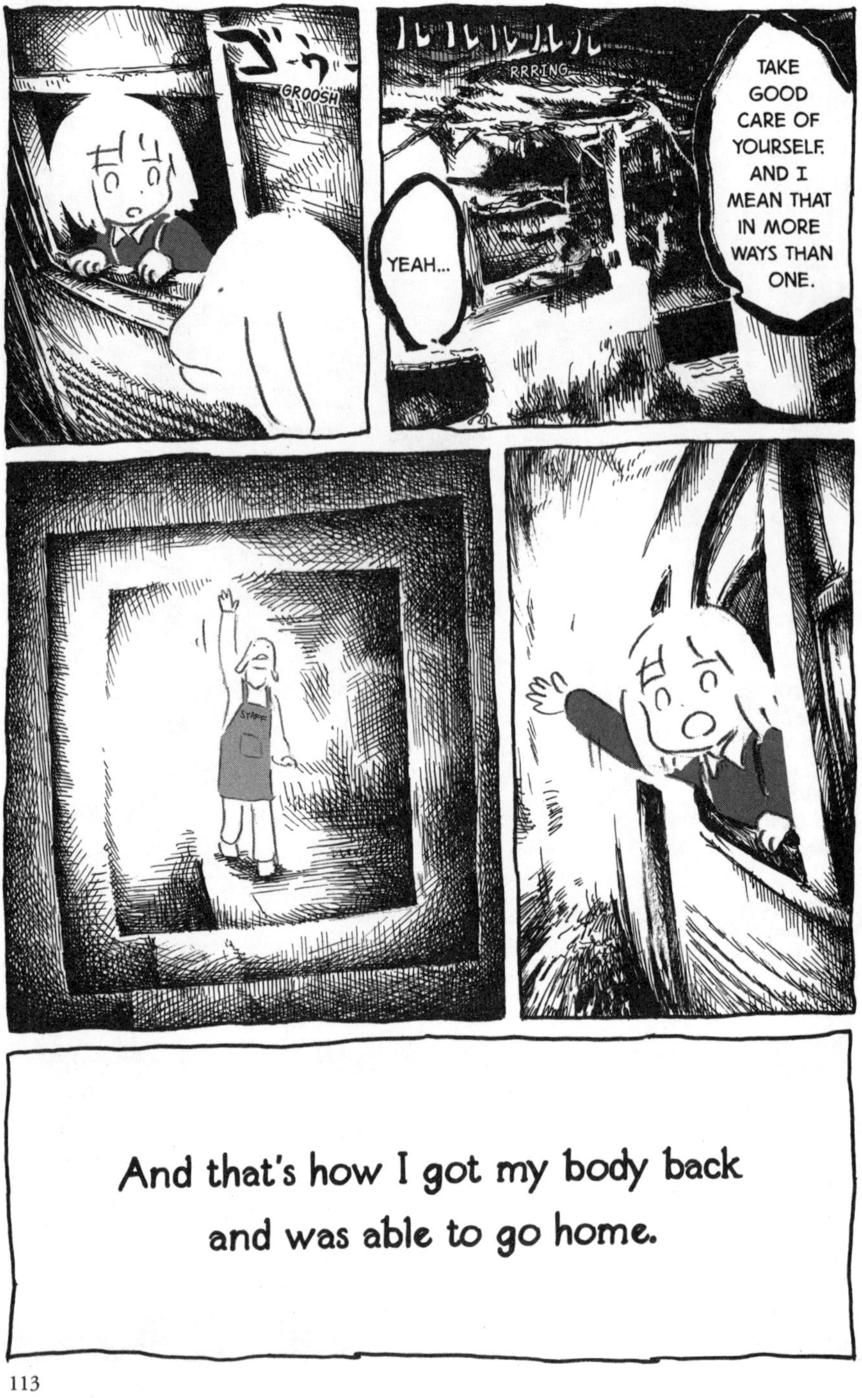
TAKE GOOD CARE OF YOURSELF. AND I MEAN THAT IN MORE WAYS THAN ONE.
RRRING
YEAH...
GROOSH
STAFF

And that's how I got my body back and was able to go home.

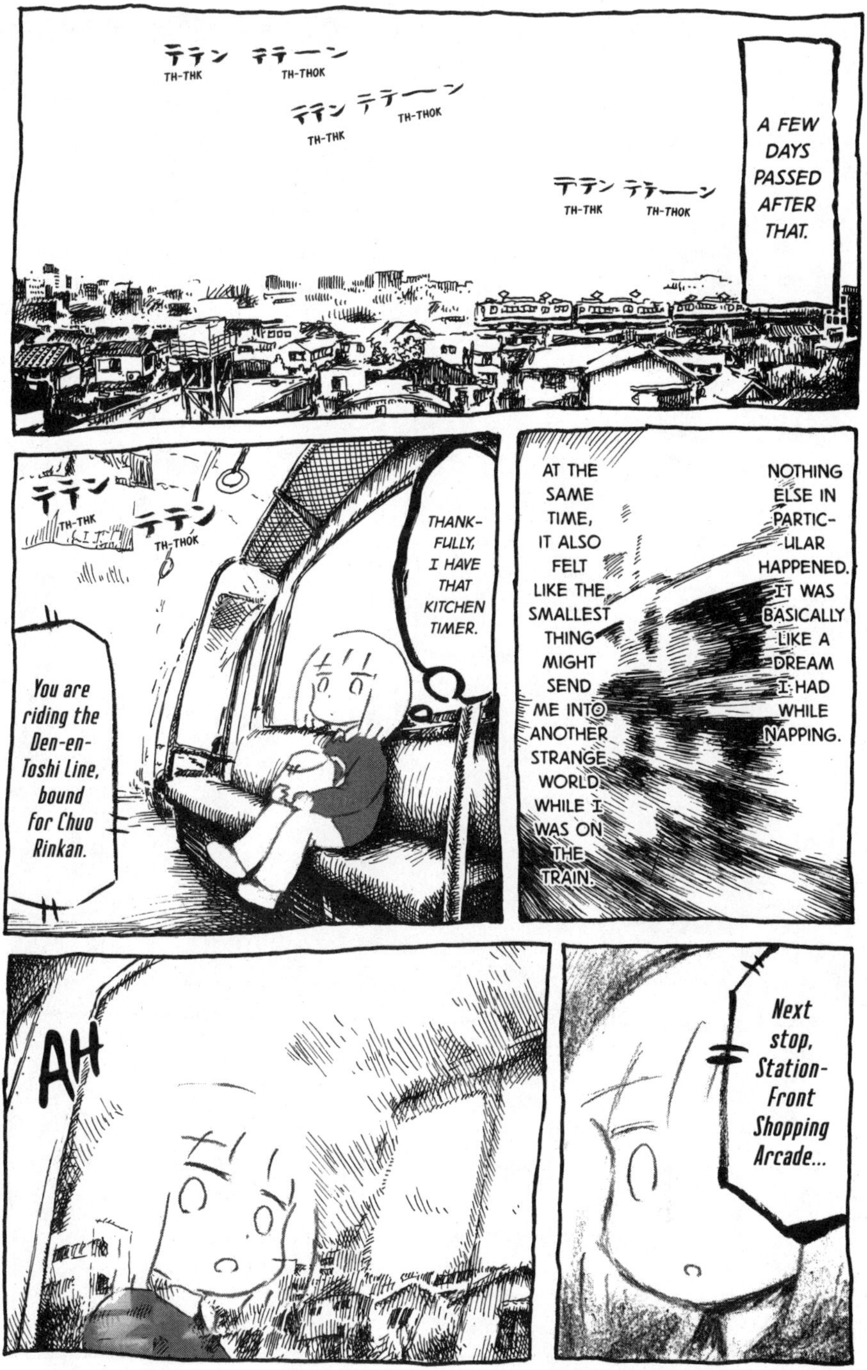
A FEW DAYS PASSED AFTER THAT.
テテン テテーン
TH-THK TH-THOK
テテン テテーン
TH-THK TH-THOK
テテン テテーン
TH-THK TH-THOK
NOTHING ELSE IN PARTIC-ULAR HAPPENED. IT WAS BASICALLY LIKE A DREAM I HAD WHILE NAPPING.
AT THE SAME TIME, IT ALSO FELT LIKE THE SMALLEST THING MIGHT SEND ME INTO ANOTHER STRANGE WORLD WHILE I WAS ON THE TRAIN.
THANK-FULLY, I HAVE THAT KITCHEN TIMER.
テテン
TH-THK
テテン
TH-THOK
You are riding the Den-en-Toshi Line, bound for Chuo Rinkan.
Next stop, Station-Front Shopping Arcade...
AH

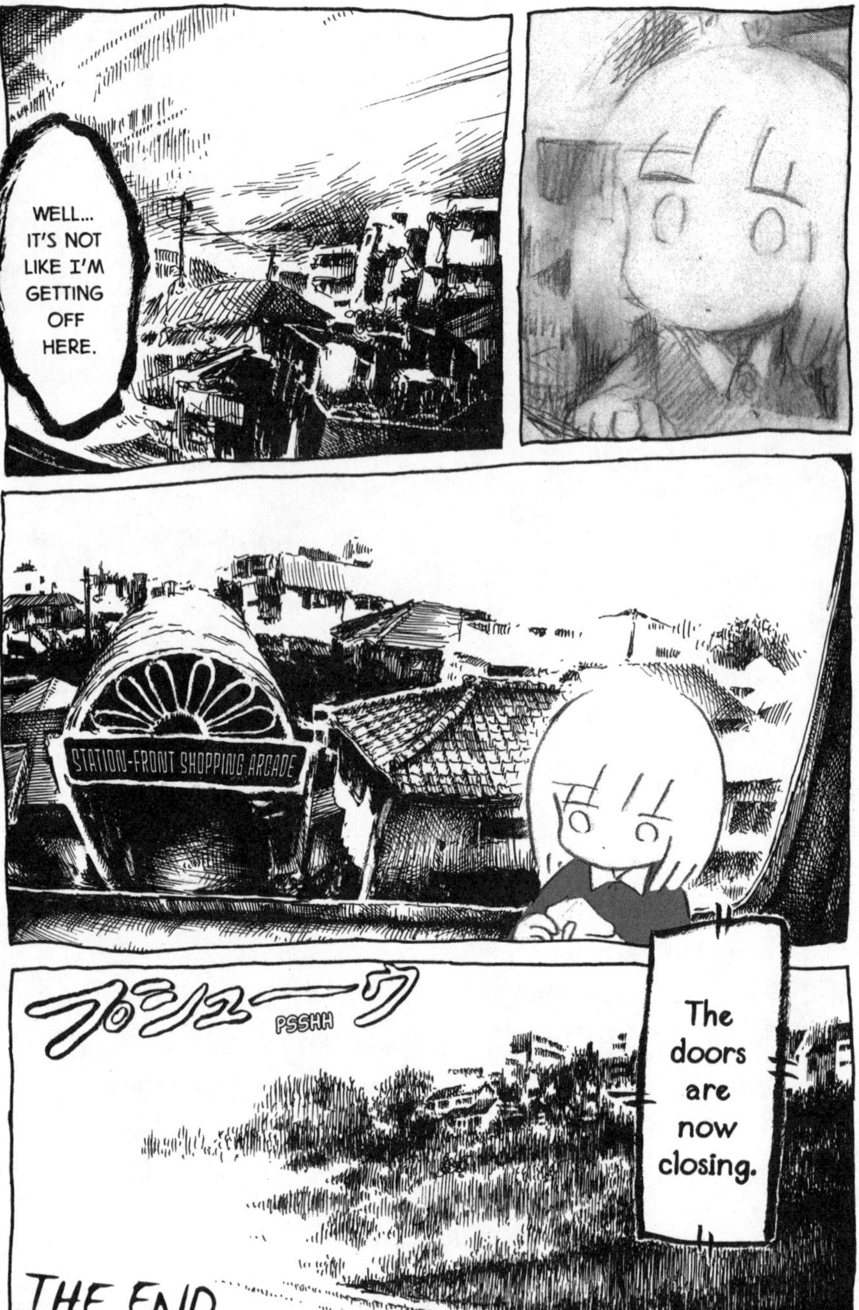
WELL... IT'S NOT LIKE I'M GETTING OFF HERE.
STATION-FRONT SHOPPING ARCADE
The doors are now closing.
PSSHH
THE END

The Case of the Giant Salamander

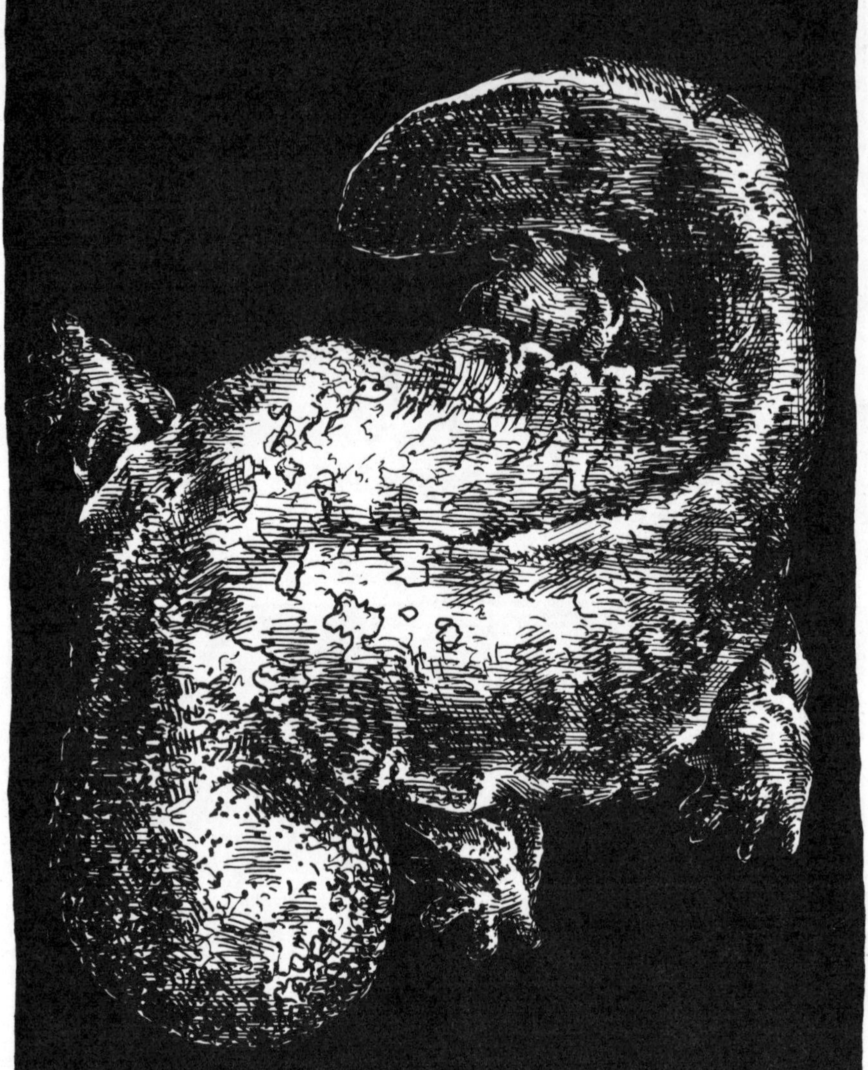

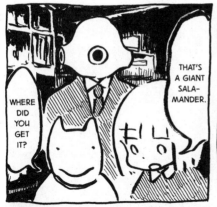

WHOA!
THAT'S A GIANT SALA-MANDER.
WHERE DID YOU GET IT?
YEAH, THEY'RE VERY EASY TO CATCH IN THE AMAZON RIVER. I ASKED SOME LOCALS TO GET ME ONE AND HAD THEM SEND IT HERE.
HUH, I NEVER KNEW THAT.
ASK THEM TO SEND US ONE, TOO.
SURE, I COULD DO THAT.
ACTUALLY, THEY'LL BE SENDING ME ANOTHER ONE SOON. I DON'T MIND IF YOU TAKE THIS ONE.
WHAT, REALLY? HOO-RAY!

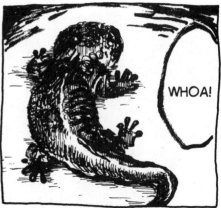

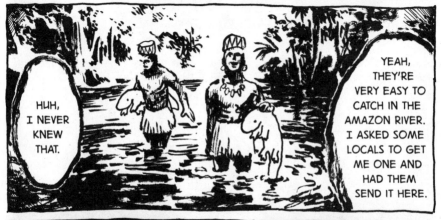

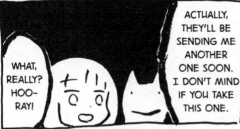

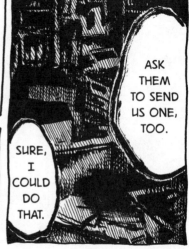

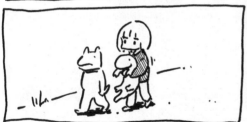

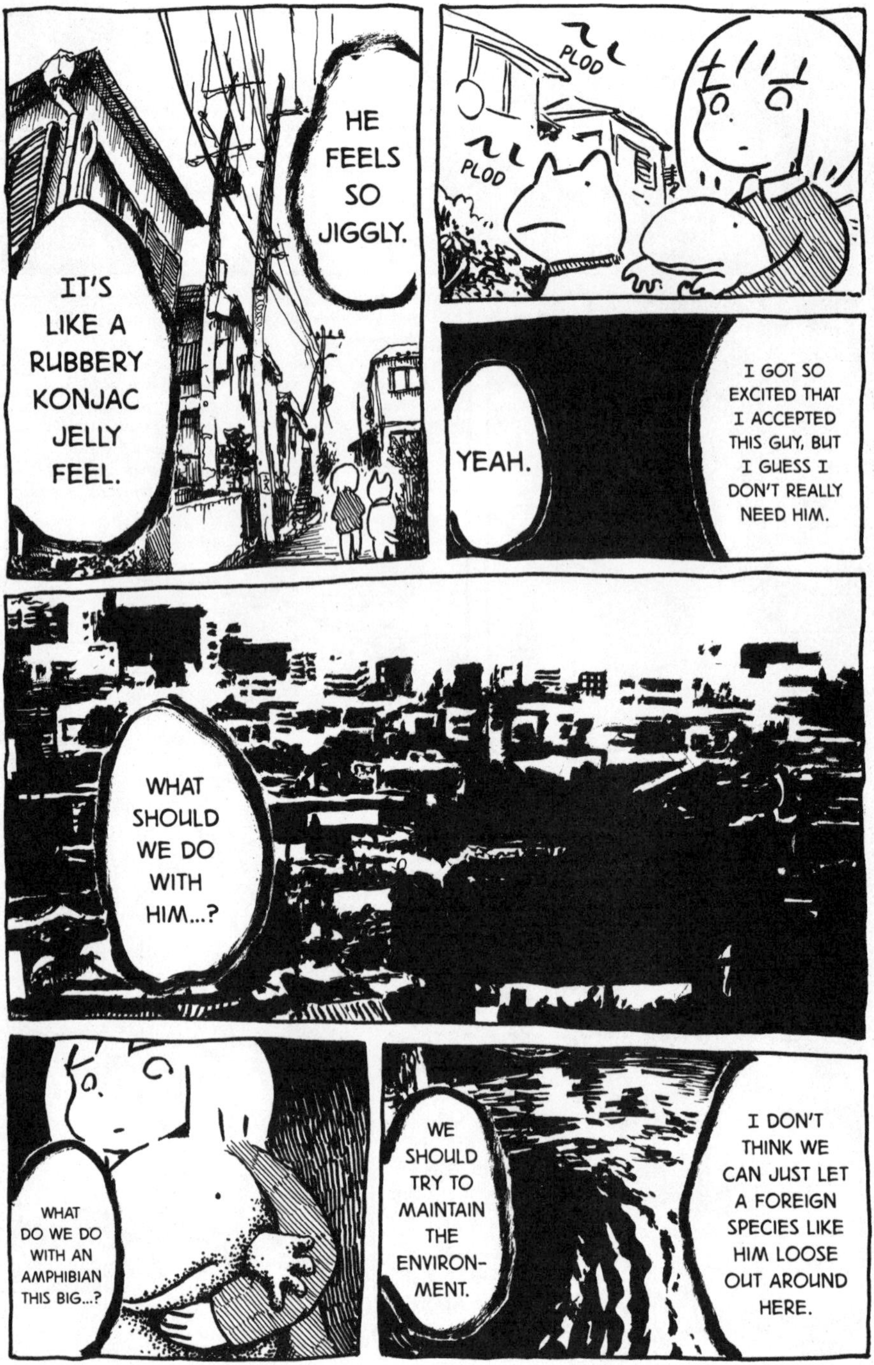
PLOD
PLOD
I GOT SO EXCITED THAT I ACCEPTED THIS GUY, BUT I GUESS I DON'T REALLY NEED HIM.
YEAH.
HE FEELS SO JIGGLY.
IT'S LIKE A RUBBERY KONJAC JELLY FEEL.
WHAT SHOULD WE DO WITH HIM...?
I DON'T THINK WE CAN JUST LET A FOREIGN SPECIES LIKE HIM LOOSE OUT AROUND HERE.
WE SHOULD TRY TO MAINTAIN THE ENVIRON-MENT.
WHAT DO WE DO WITH AN AMPHIBIAN THIS BIG...?

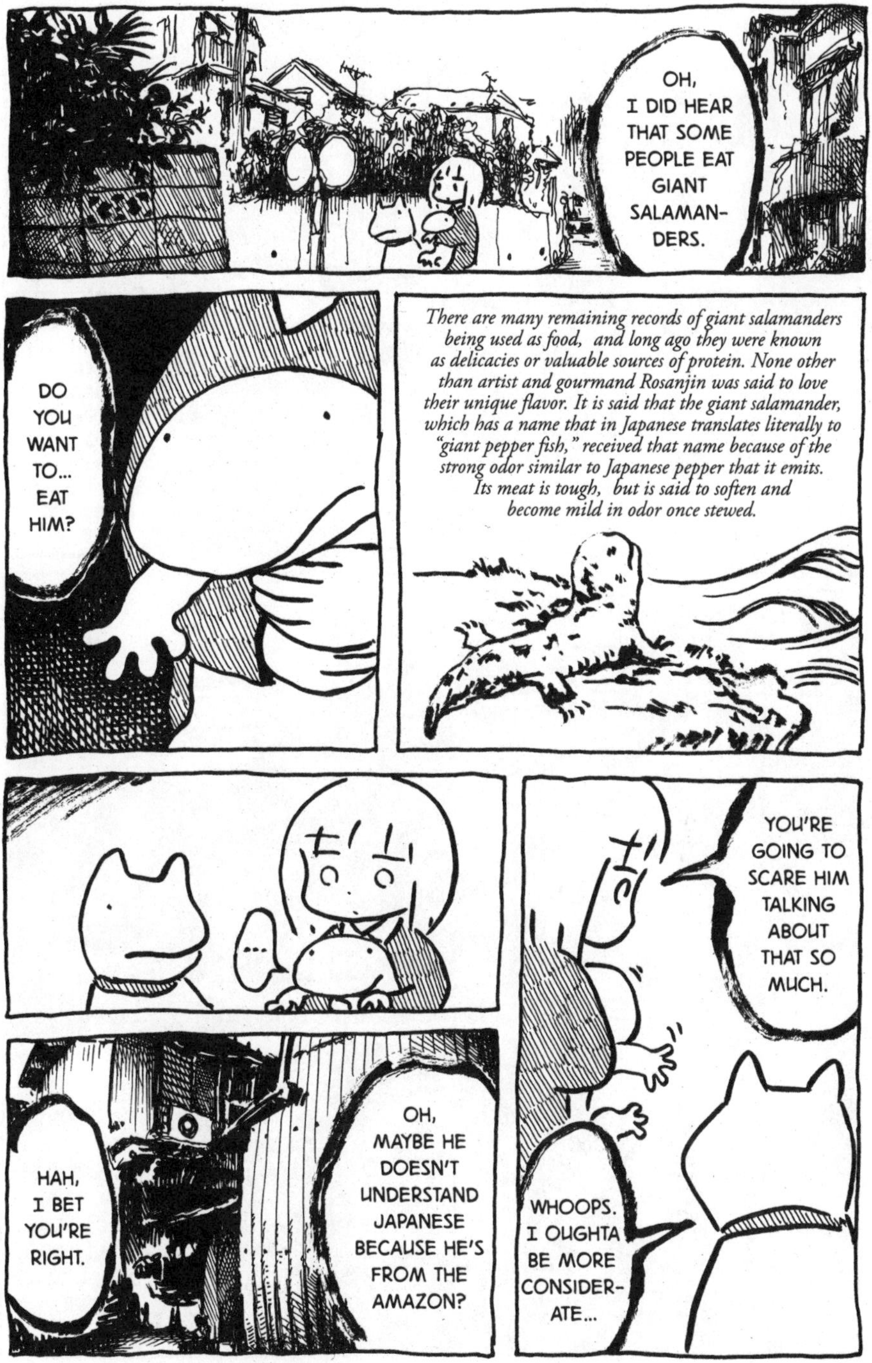
OH, I DID HEAR THAT SOME PEOPLE EAT GIANT SALAMANDERS.
There are many remaining records of giant salamanders being used as food, and long ago they were known as delicacies or valuable sources of protein. None other than artist and gourmand Rosanjin was said to love their unique flavor. It is said that the giant salamander, which has a name that in Japanese translates literally to "giant pepper fish," received that name because of the strong odor similar to Japanese pepper that it emits. Its meat is tough, but is said to soften and become mild in odor once stewed.
DO YOU WANT TO... EAT HIM?
YOU'RE GOING TO SCARE HIM TALKING ABOUT THAT SO MUCH.
WHOOPS. I OUGHTA BE MORE CONSIDER-ATE...
...
OH, MAYBE HE DOESN'T UNDERSTAND JAPANESE BECAUSE HE'S FROM THE AMAZON?
HAH, I BET YOU'RE RIGHT.

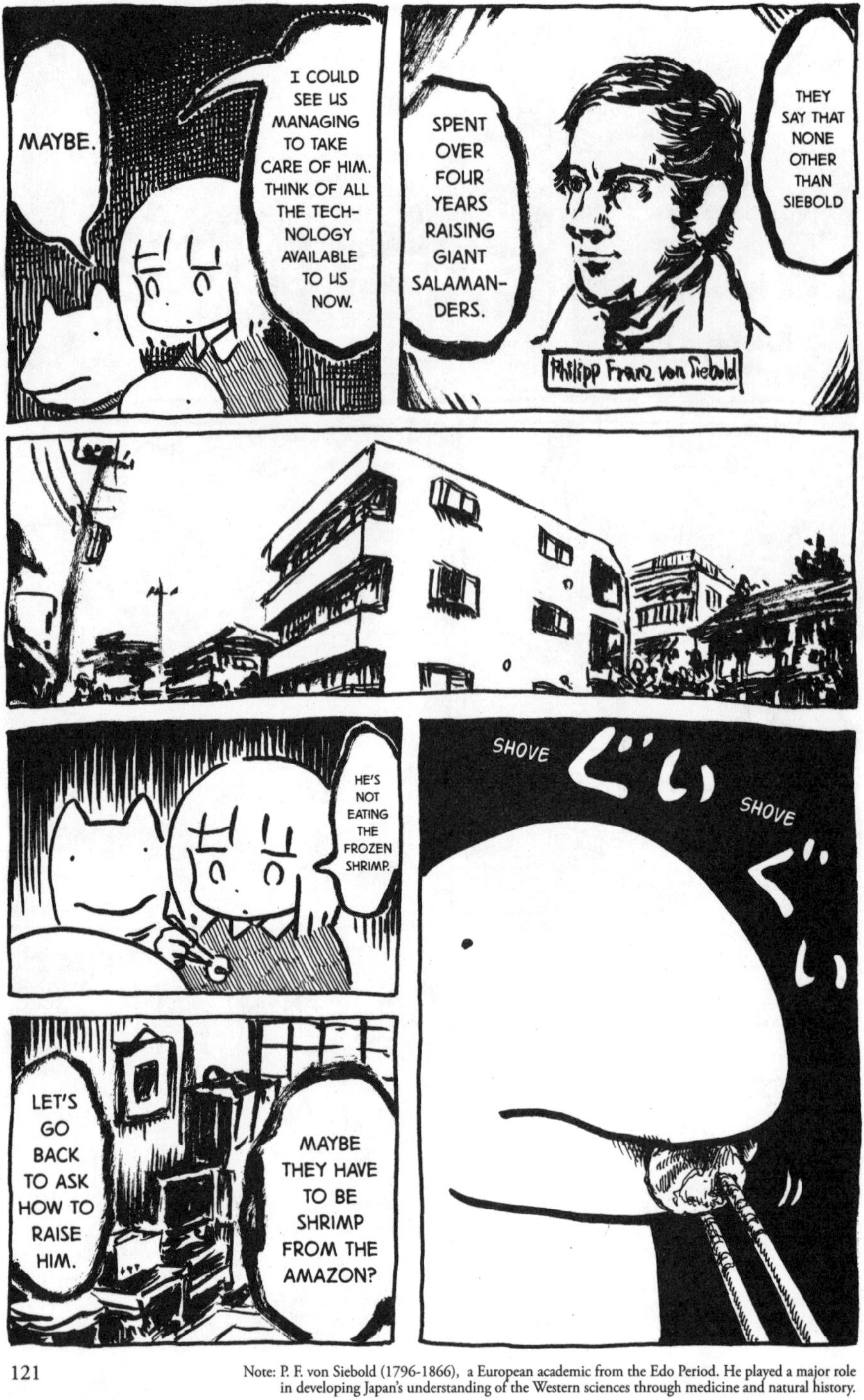
THEY SAY THAT NONE OTHER THAN SIEBOLD
SPENT OVER FOUR YEARS RAISING GIANT SALAMANDERS.
Philipp Franz von Siebold
I COULD SEE US MANAGING TO TAKE CARE OF HIM. THINK OF ALL THE TECH-NOLOGY AVAILABLE TO US NOW.
MAYBE.
SHOVE
ぐい
SHOVE
ぐい
HE'S NOT EATING THE FROZEN SHRIMP.
MAYBE THEY HAVE TO BE SHRIMP FROM THE AMAZON?
LET'S GO BACK TO ASK HOW TO RAISE HIM.

Note: P. F. von Siebold (1796-1866), a European academic from the Edo Period. He played a major role in developing Japan's understanding of the Western sciences through medicine and natural history.

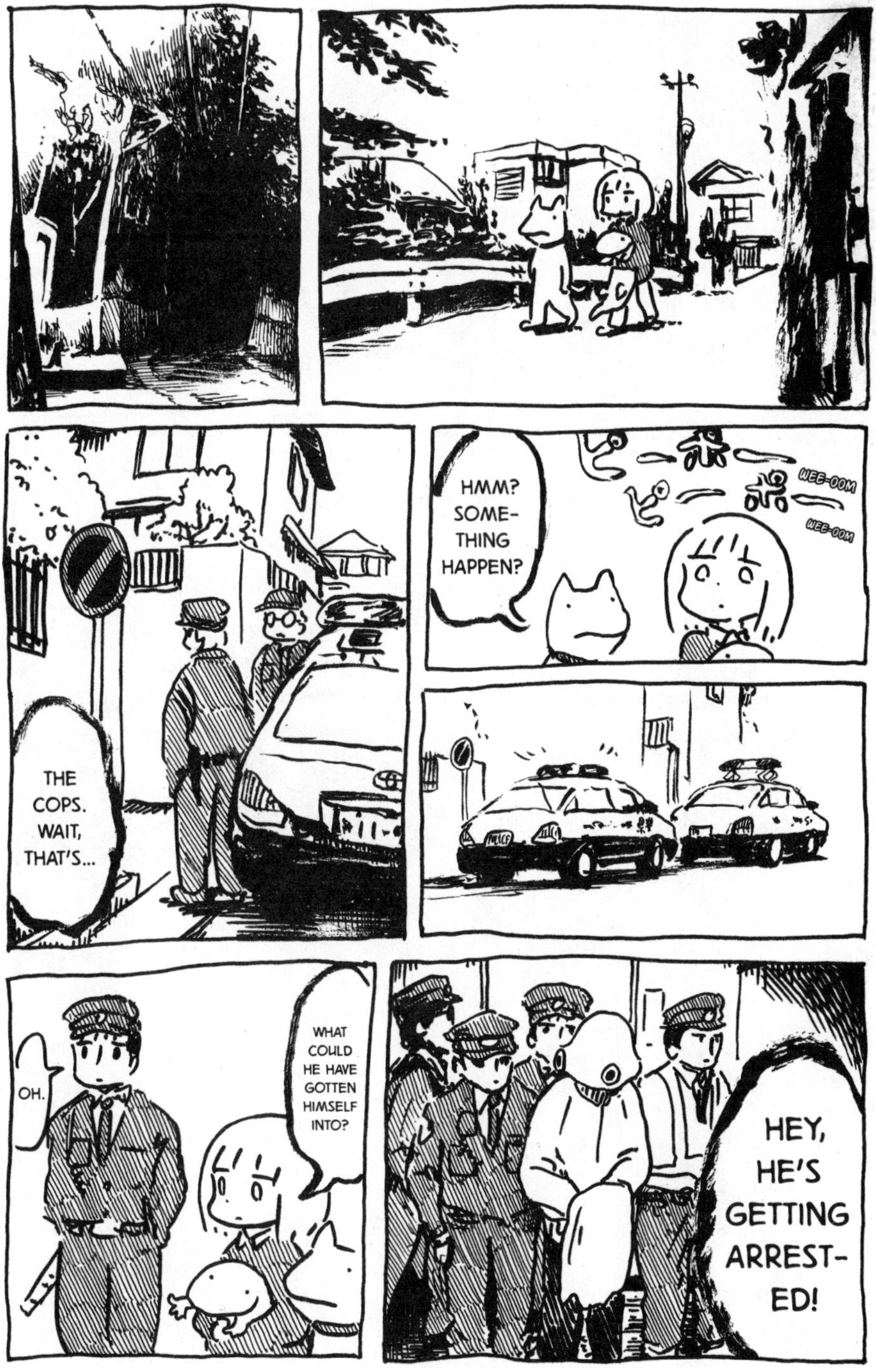
HMM? SOME-THING HAPPEN?
ピーポー ピーポー
WEE-OOM
WEE-OOM
THE COPS. WAIT, THAT'S...
HEY, HE'S GETTING ARREST-ED!
WHAT COULD HE HAVE GOTTEN HIMSELF INTO?
OH.

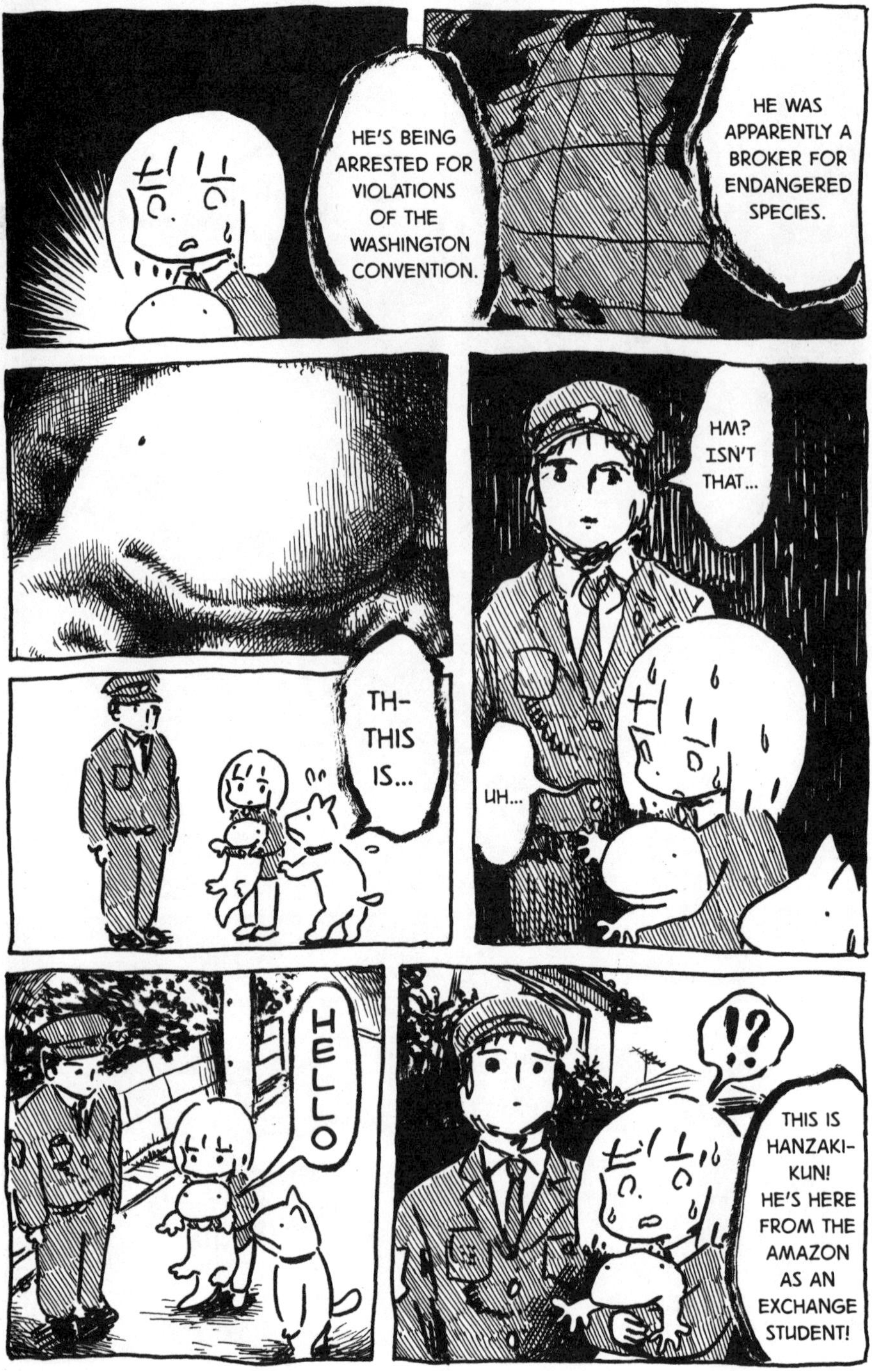
HE WAS APPARENTLY A BROKER FOR ENDANGERED SPECIES.
HE'S BEING ARRESTED FOR VIOLATIONS OF THE WASHINGTON CONVENTION.
HM? ISN'T THAT...
UH...
TH- THIS IS...
!?
THIS IS HANZAKI-KUN! HE'S HERE FROM THE AMAZON AS AN EXCHANGE STUDENT!
HELLO

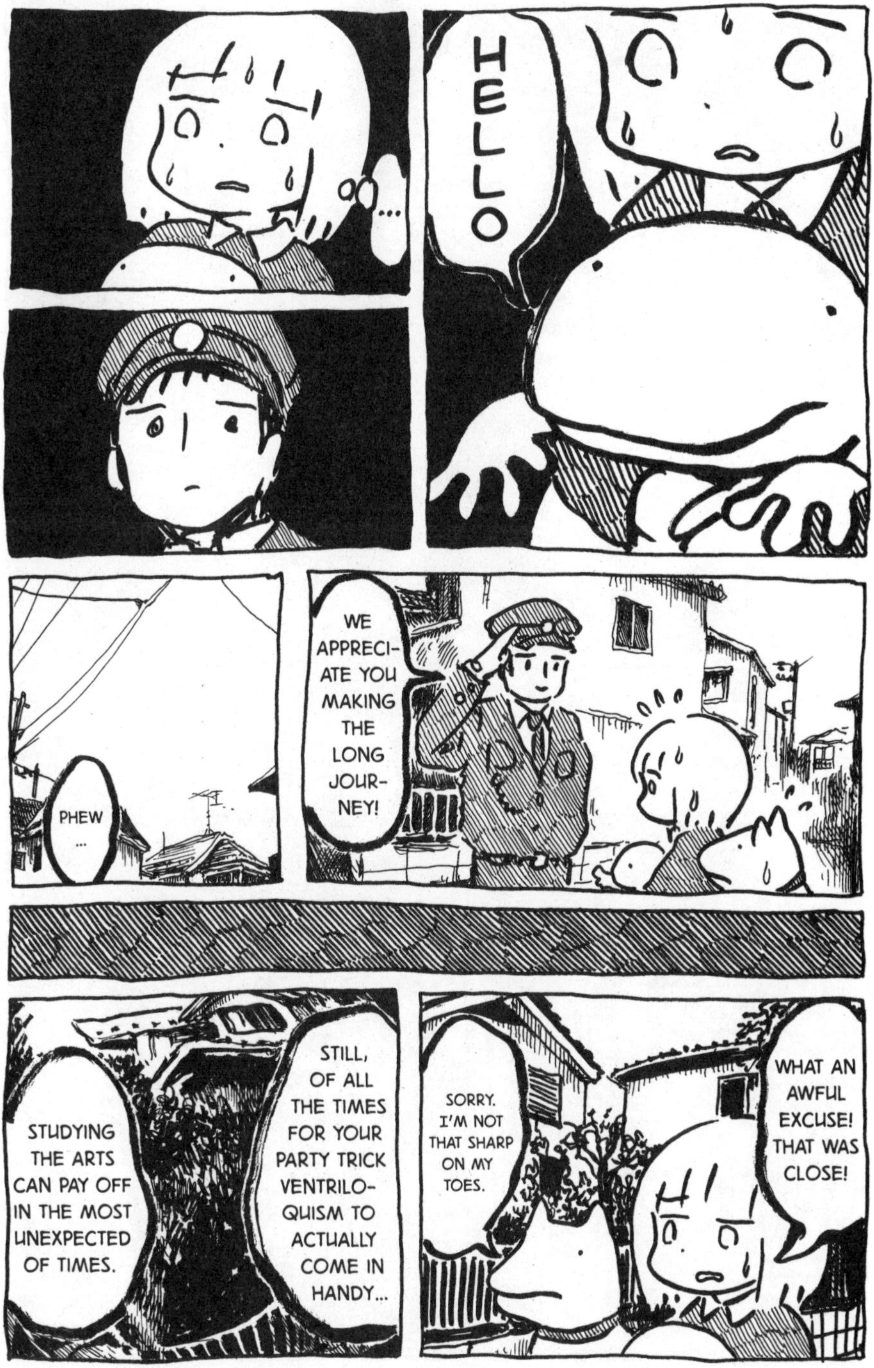
HELLO
...
WE APPRECIATE YOU MAKING THE LONG JOURNEY!
PHEW ...
WHAT AN AWFUL EXCUSE! THAT WAS CLOSE!
SORRY. I'M NOT THAT SHARP ON MY TOES.
STILL, OF ALL THE TIMES FOR YOUR PARTY TRICK VENTRILOQUISM TO ACTUALLY COME IN HANDY...
STUDYING THE ARTS CAN PAY OFF IN THE MOST UNEXPECTED OF TIMES.

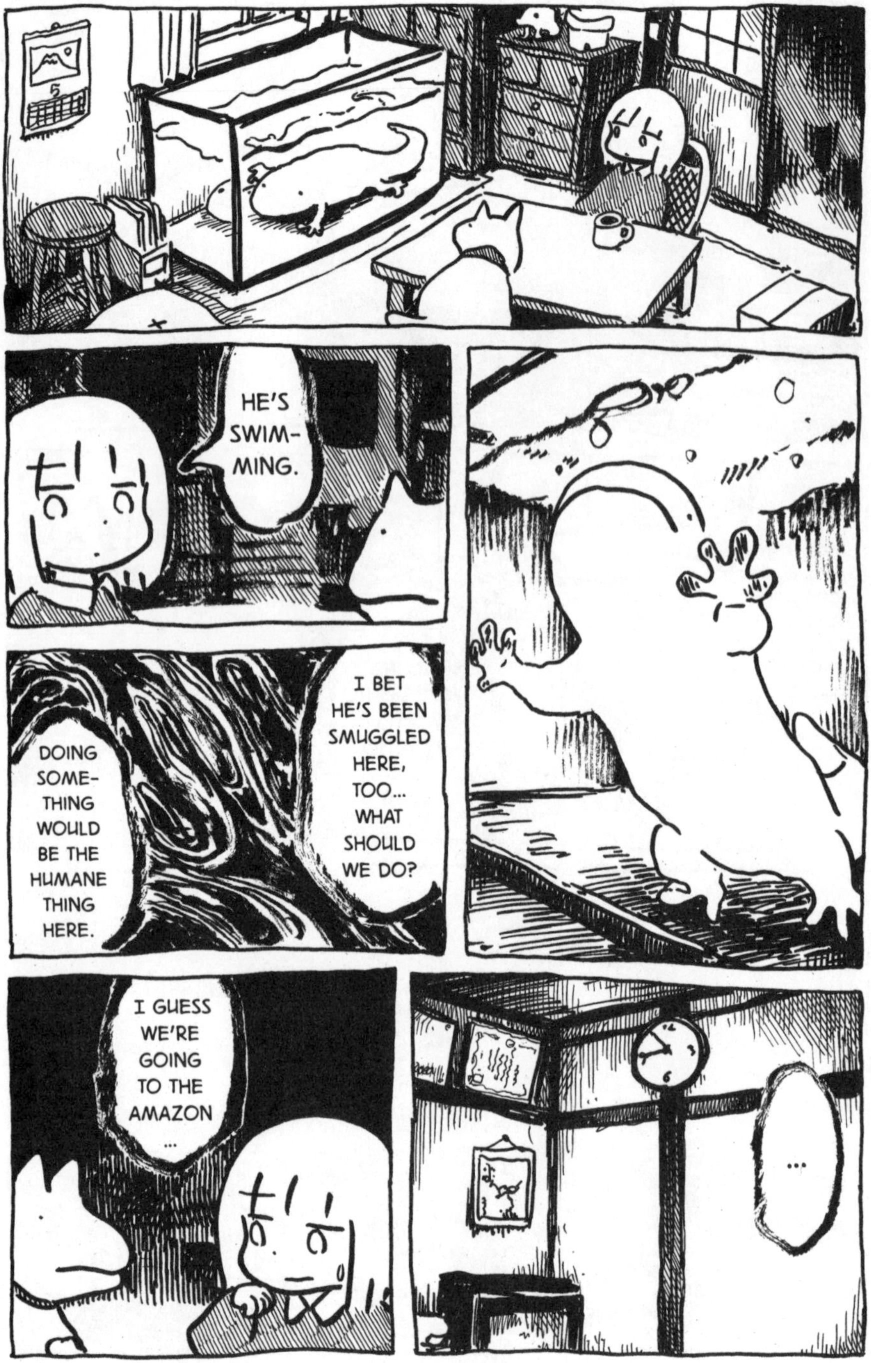
HE'S SWIMMING.
I BET HE'S BEEN SMUGGLED HERE, TOO... WHAT SHOULD WE DO?
DOING SOMETHING WOULD BE THE HUMANE THING HERE.
...
I GUESS WE'RE GOING TO THE AMAZON ...

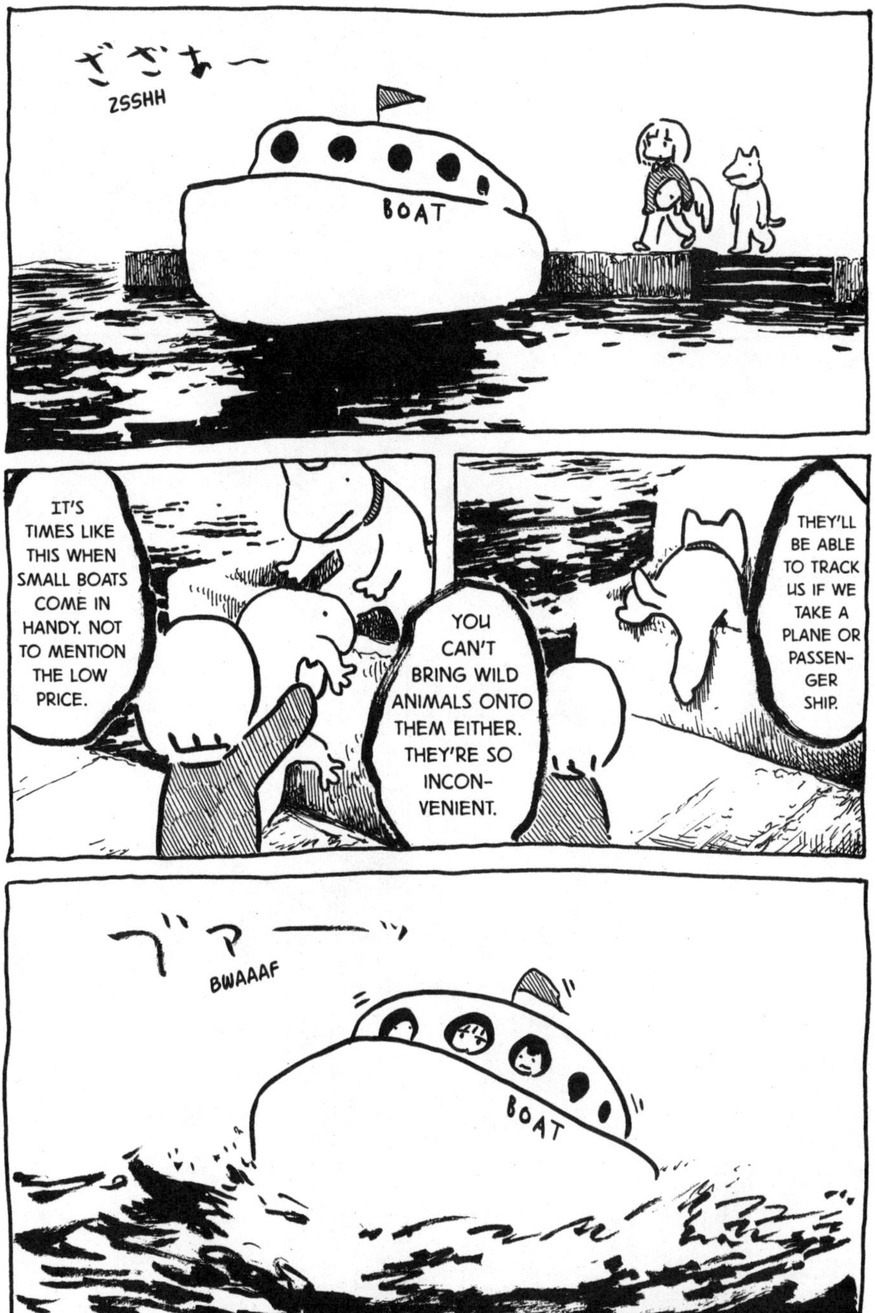
ざざあ〜
ZSSHH
BOAT
THEY'LL BE ABLE TO TRACK US IF WE TAKE A PLANE OR PASSENGER SHIP.
YOU CAN'T BRING WILD ANIMALS ONTO THEM EITHER. THEY'RE SO INCONVENIENT.
IT'S TIMES LIKE THIS WHEN SMALL BOATS COME IN HANDY. NOT TO MENTION THE LOW PRICE.
ブァーッ
BWAAAF
BOAT

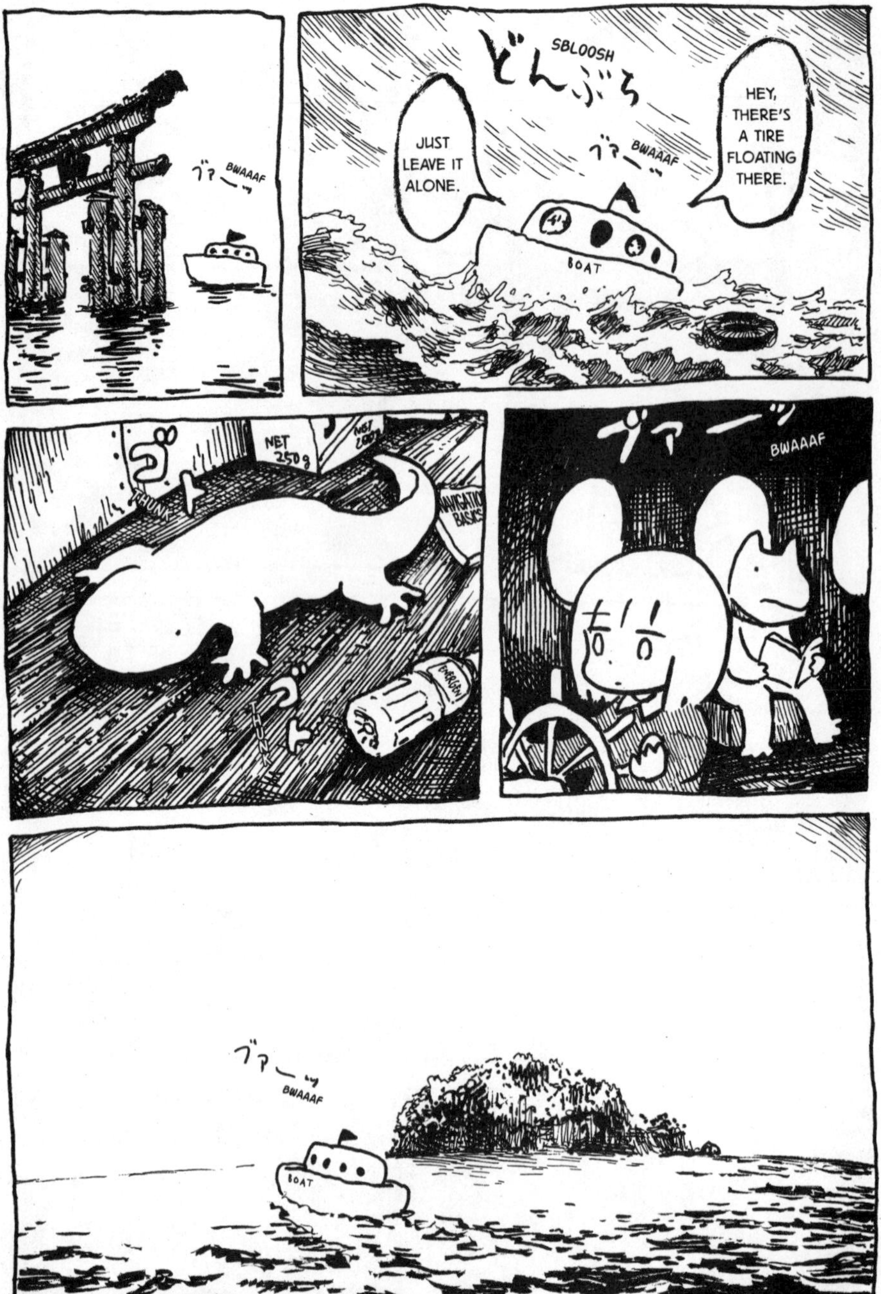
SBLOOSH
HEY, THERE'S A TIRE FLOATING THERE.
BWAAAF
JUST LEAVE IT ALONE.
BOAT
BWAAAF
BWAAAF
NET 250g
THUNK
NAVIGATION BASICS
THUNK
BWAAAF
BOAT

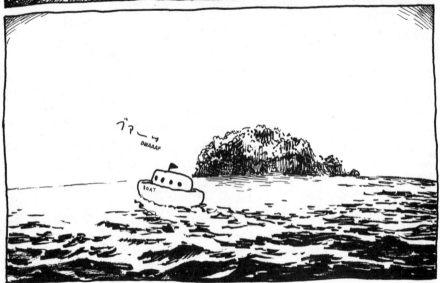

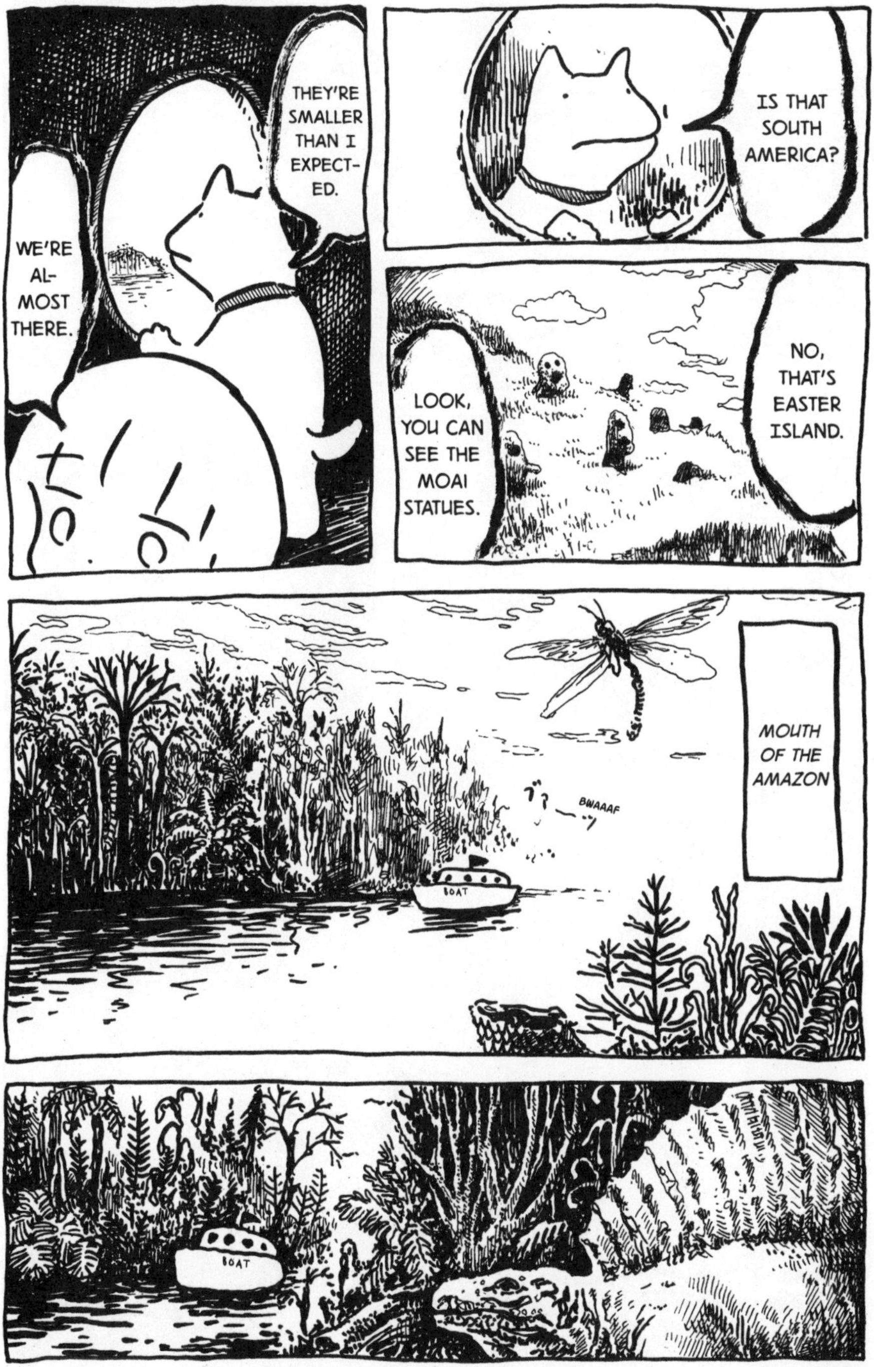
IS THAT SOUTH AMERICA?
NO, THAT'S EASTER ISLAND.
LOOK, YOU CAN SEE THE MOAI STATUES.
THEY'RE SMALLER THAN I EXPECT-ED.
WE'RE AL-MOST THERE.
MOUTH OF THE AMAZON
BWAAAF
BOAT
BOAT

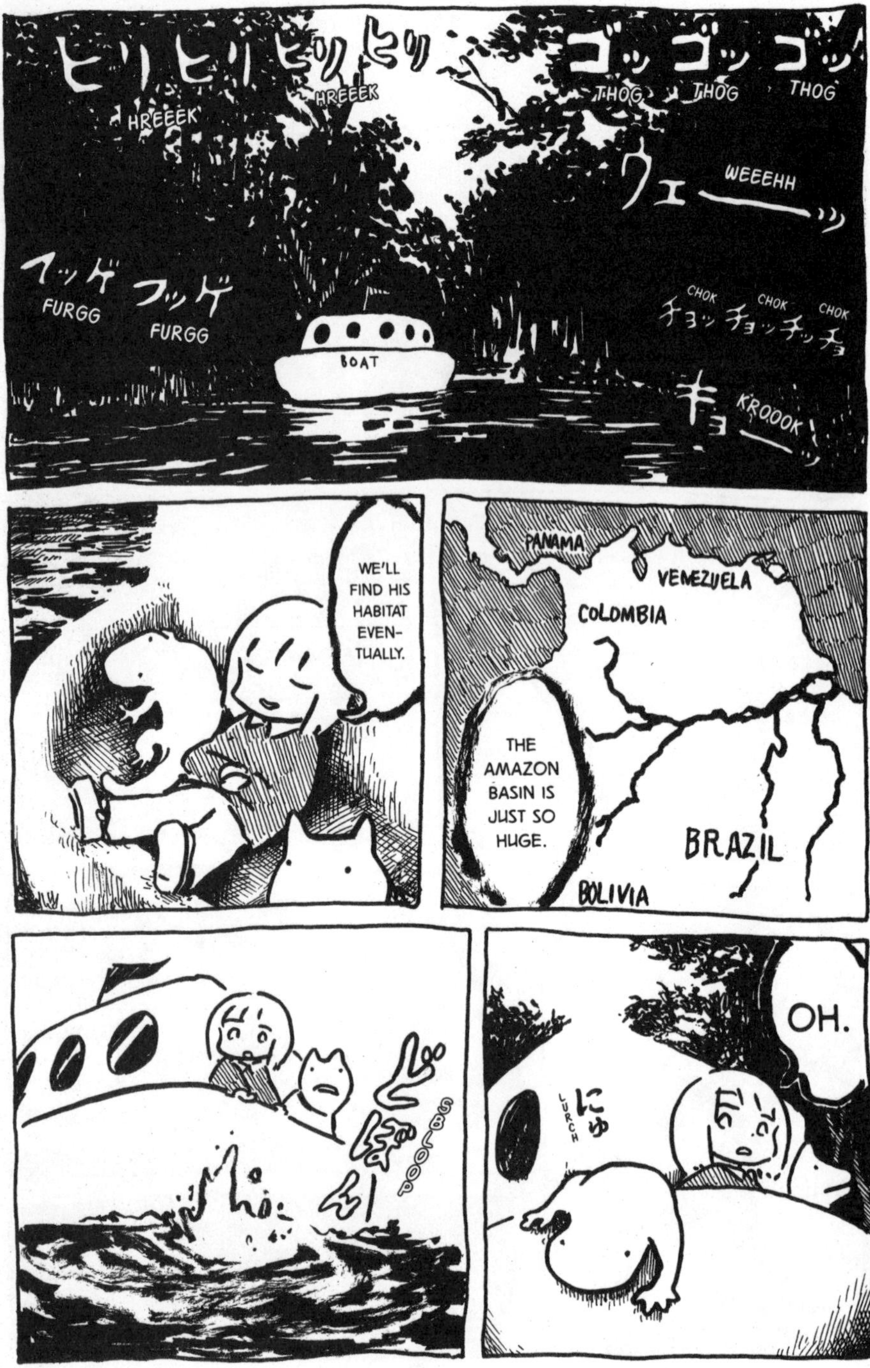
ゴッゴッゴッ
THOG THOG THOG
ヒリヒリヒリヒリ
HREEEK
HREEEK
ウェーーッ
WEEEHH
チョッチョッチッチョ
CHOK CHOK CHOK
フッゲフッゲ
FURGG FURGG
BOAT
キョーーッ
KROOOK
PANAMA
VENEZUELA
COLOMBIA
THE AMAZON BASIN IS JUST SO HUGE.
BRAZIL
BOLIVIA
WE'LL FIND HIS HABITAT EVENTUALLY.
OH.
にゅ
LURCH
どぼん
SBLOOP

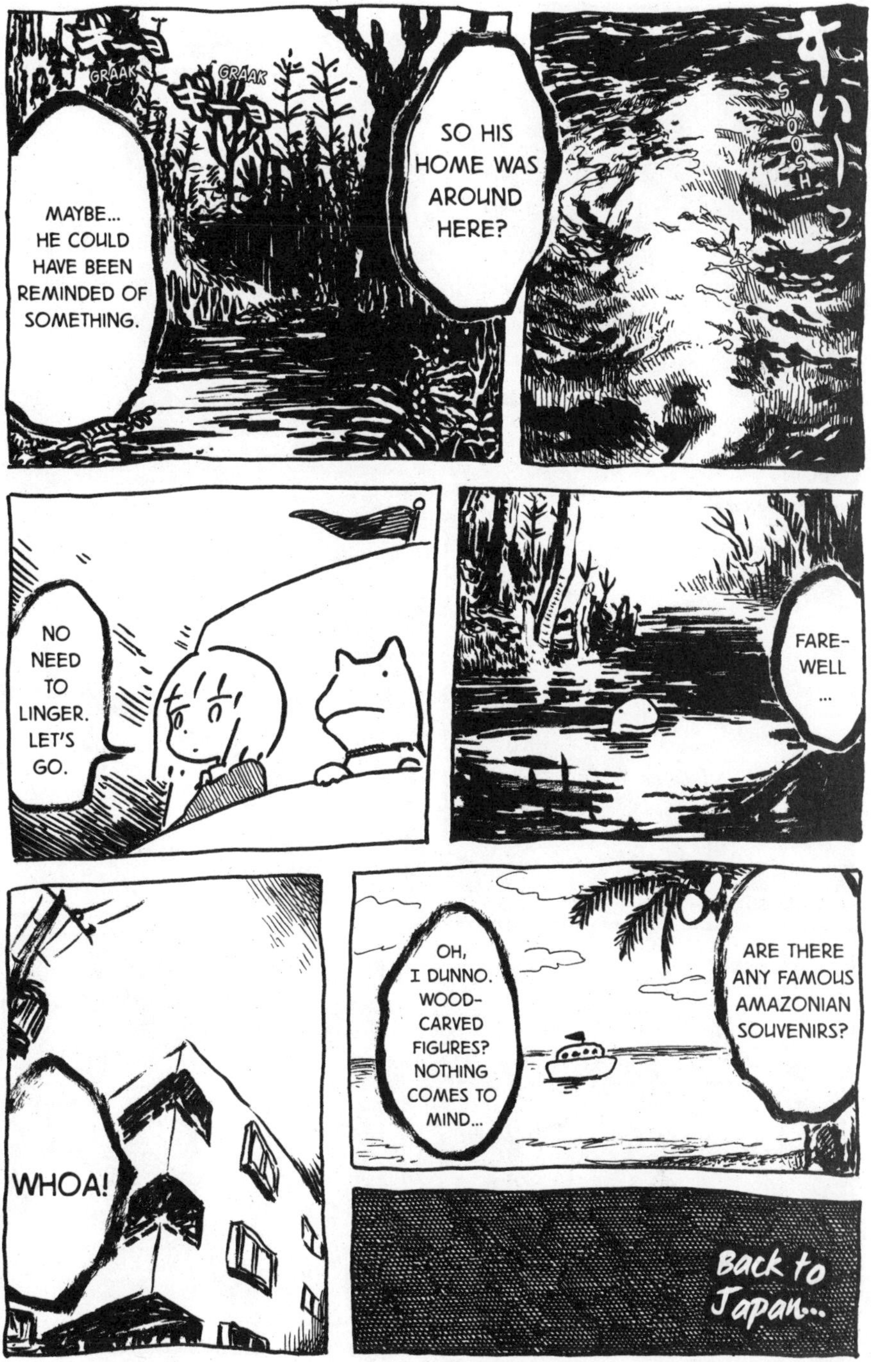
SWOOSH
SO HIS HOME WAS AROUND HERE?
GRAAK
GRAAK
MAYBE... HE COULD HAVE BEEN REMINDED OF SOMETHING.
FARE-WELL ...
NO NEED TO LINGER. LET'S GO.
ARE THERE ANY FAMOUS AMAZONIAN SOUVENIRS?
OH, I DUNNO. WOOD-CARVED FIGURES? NOTHING COMES TO MIND...
Back to Japan...
WHOA!

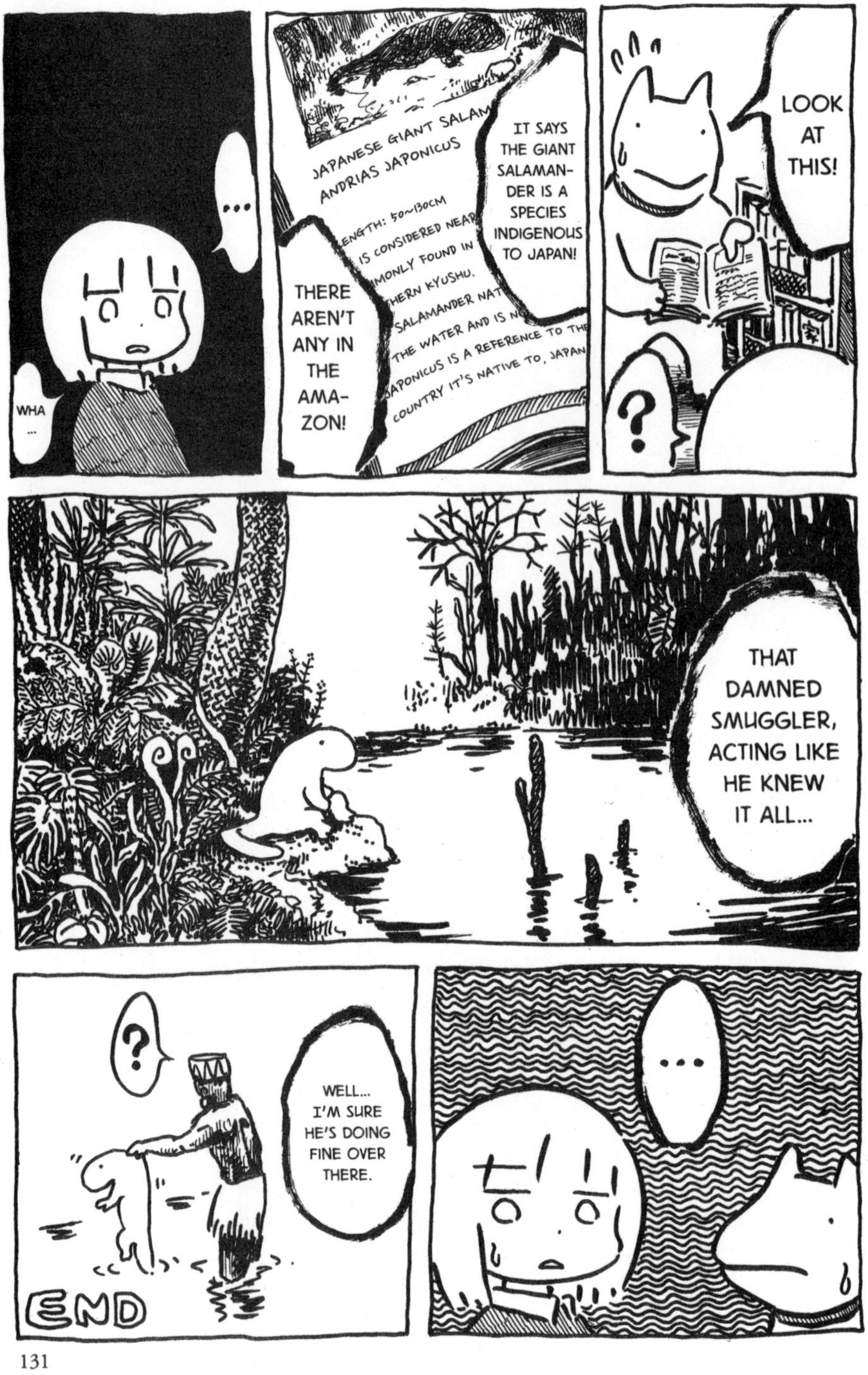
LOOK AT THIS!
?
JAPANESE GIANT SALAM
ANDRIAS JAPONICUS
LENGTH: 50~130CM
IS CONSIDERED NEAR
MONLY FOUND IN
THERN KYUSHU.
SALAMANDER NAT
THE WATER AND IS N
JAPONICUS IS A REFERENCE TO THE
COUNTRY IT'S NATIVE TO, JAPAN
IT SAYS THE GIANT SALAMANDER IS A SPECIES INDIGENOUS TO JAPAN!
THERE AREN'T ANY IN THE AMAZON!
...
WHA ...
THAT DAMNED SMUGGLER, ACTING LIKE HE KNEW IT ALL...
...
?
WELL... I'M SURE HE'S DOING FINE OVER THERE.
END

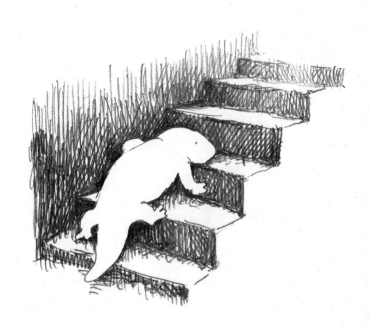

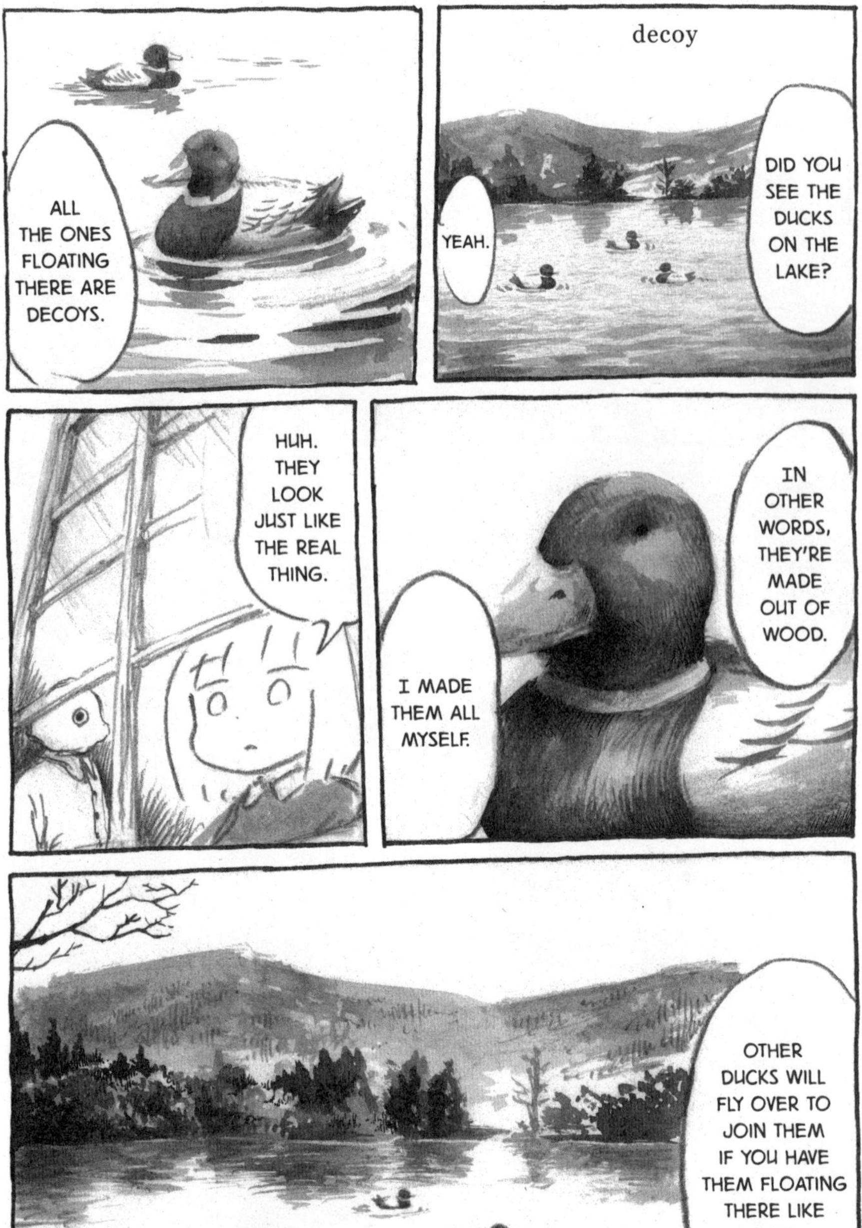
decoy
DID YOU SEE THE DUCKS ON THE LAKE?
YEAH.
ALL THE ONES FLOATING THERE ARE DECOYS.
IN OTHER WORDS, THEY'RE MADE OUT OF WOOD.
I MADE THEM ALL MYSELF.
HUH. THEY LOOK JUST LIKE THE REAL THING.
OTHER DUCKS WILL FLY OVER TO JOIN THEM IF YOU HAVE THEM FLOATING THERE LIKE THAT.

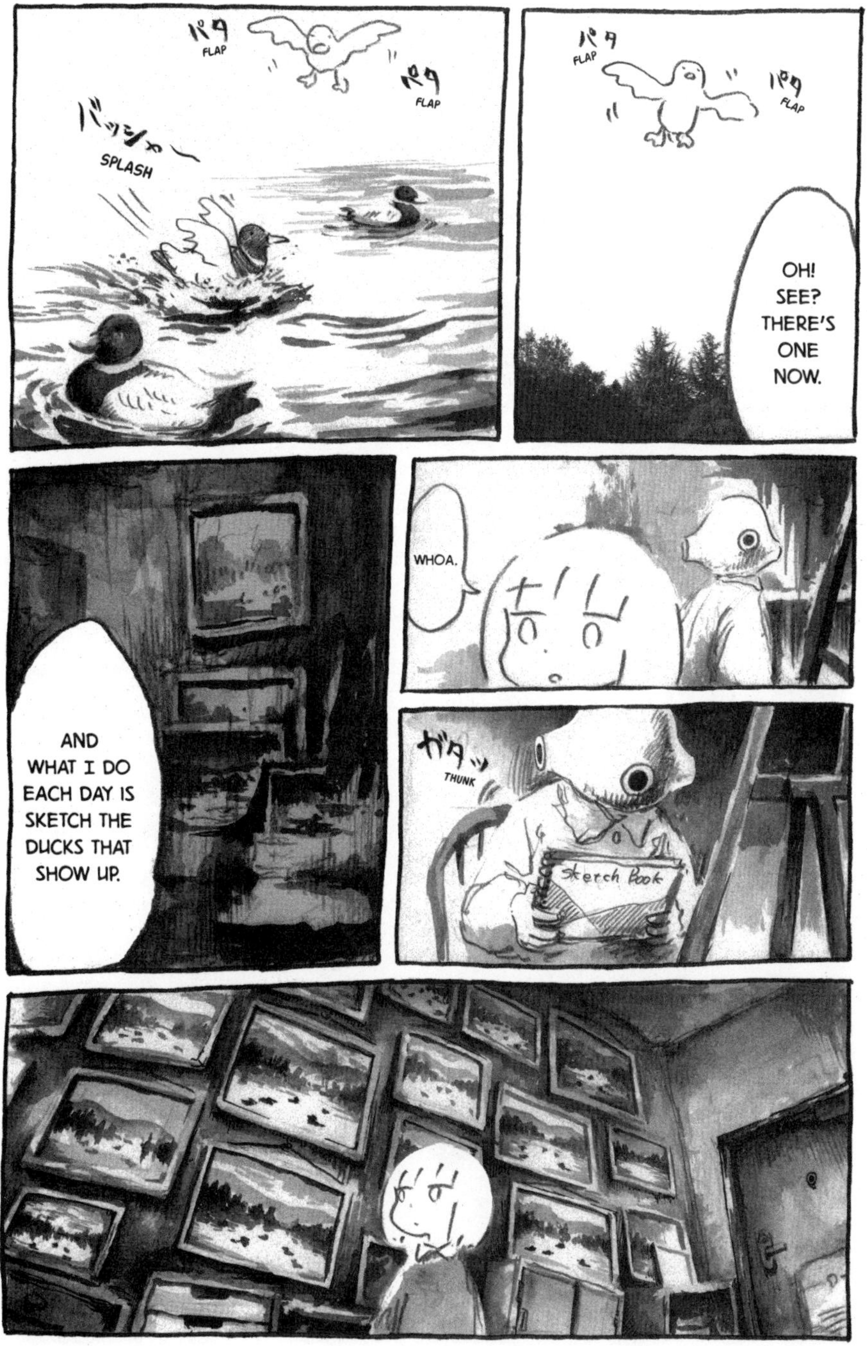
パタ
FLAP
パタ
FLAP
OH! SEE? THERE'S ONE NOW.
パタ
FLAP
パタ
FLAP
バッシャ〜
SPLASH
WHOA.
ガタッ
THUNK
Sketch Book
AND WHAT I DO EACH DAY IS SKETCH THE DUCKS THAT SHOW UP.

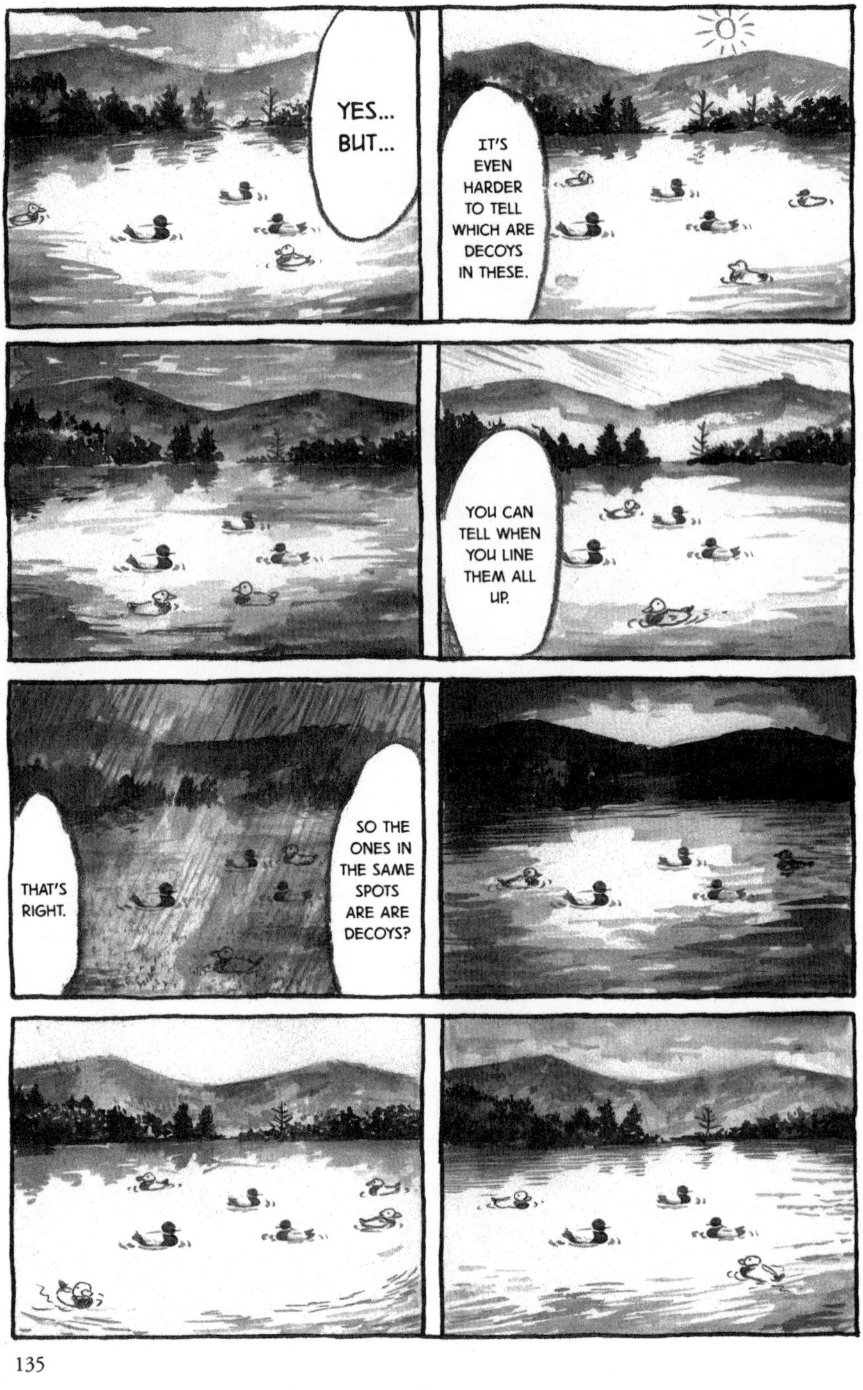
IT'S EVEN HARDER TO TELL WHICH ARE DECOYS IN THESE.
YES... BUT...
YOU CAN TELL WHEN YOU LINE THEM ALL UP.
SO THE ONES IN THE SAME SPOTS ARE ARE DECOYS?
THAT'S RIGHT.

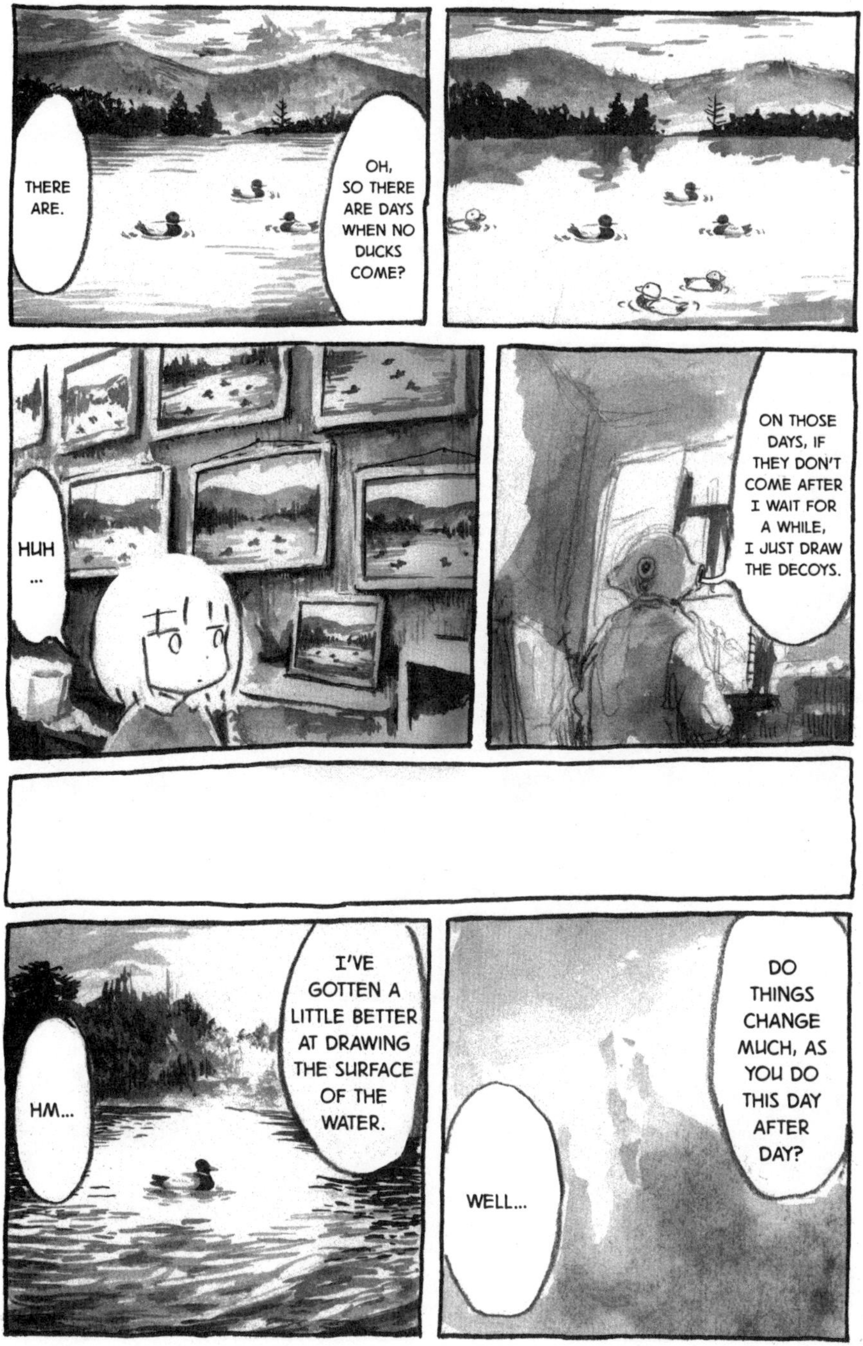
OH, SO THERE ARE DAYS WHEN NO DUCKS COME?
THERE ARE.
ON THOSE DAYS, IF THEY DON'T COME AFTER I WAIT FOR A WHILE, I JUST DRAW THE DECOYS.
HUH ...
DO THINGS CHANGE MUCH, AS YOU DO THIS DAY AFTER DAY?
WELL...
I'VE GOTTEN A LITTLE BETTER AT DRAWING THE SURFACE OF THE WATER.
HM...

Blinking

While it's been hot again these past few days, it's been windy and cool this evening with the sound of thunder coming from somewhere in the distance. It seems like it's rained a little, too.

We, of course, describe rain as falling in dots and drops from the sky. Yet, we normally see rain with our eyes as lines; straight lines pouring from above.

At times, when there are things that move too fast for our eyes to keep up with, we see them as lines. It reminds me of how I can see the individual blades of this fan I'm running when it's stopped, but once it gets fast enough, it simply looks like a semi-transparent circle that wind comes out of. In other words, we only perceive the afterimage of something once it breaks a speed that's comprehensible to our eyes.

I'm not sure about light from fluorescent bulbs, either. I've heard that they blink as well. Because of how electrical frequencies work, electricity's direction changes 50 or 60 times a second, which means that fluorescent bulbs also flicker at an ultra-high speed. You can even see the way that they blink if you look at a fluorescent light through a digital camera's screen. I guess we can see this because the maximum speed at which the human eye can react is different from the maximum processing speed of a digital camera. Human eyes aren't normally too bothered by the blinking of a fluorescent light. I guess human eyes are just something that are dully made.

If we were to think of fluorescent lights and raindrops at the same time, something blinking at a high speed would look like a completely normal straight ray of light to us.

There's also the case of flipbook animation. They seem to move in a choppy way when you go through their pages slowly, but once you go past a certain speed, they look smooth. You could say it's this speed that is the point at which raindrops start to look like lines.

Imagine animation where there are a thousand different drawings shown in a single second. I wonder what it would look like. What does it look like when something moves that far beyond the limits of human observation? Would it look like any other moving picture? I do feel like it would have some kind of magical power to it, though.

September 1, 2013

SENSATION

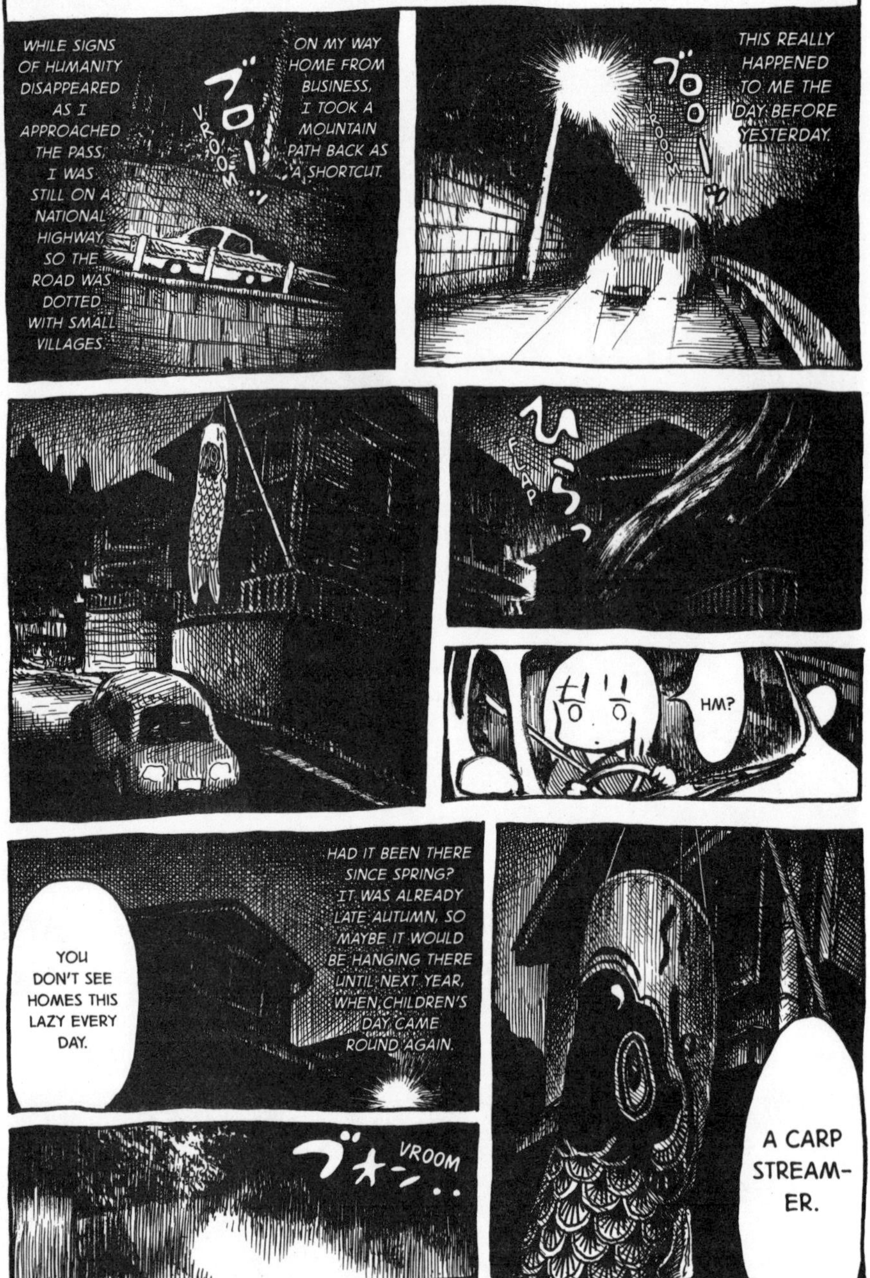
THIS REALLY HAPPENED TO ME THE DAY BEFORE YESTERDAY.
ブロロー
VROOOOM
ON MY WAY HOME FROM BUSINESS, I TOOK A MOUNTAIN PATH BACK AS A SHORTCUT.
WHILE SIGNS OF HUMANITY DISAPPEARED AS I APPROACHED THE PASS, I WAS STILL ON A NATIONAL HIGHWAY, SO THE ROAD WAS DOTTED WITH SMALL VILLAGES.
ブロロー
VROOM
ひらっ
FLAP
HM?
A CARP STREAMER.
HAD IT BEEN THERE SINCE SPRING? IT WAS ALREADY LATE AUTUMN, SO MAYBE IT WOULD BE HANGING THERE UNTIL NEXT YEAR, WHEN CHILDREN'S DAY CAME ROUND AGAIN.
YOU DON'T SEE HOMES THIS LAZY EVERY DAY.
ブォーン
VROOM

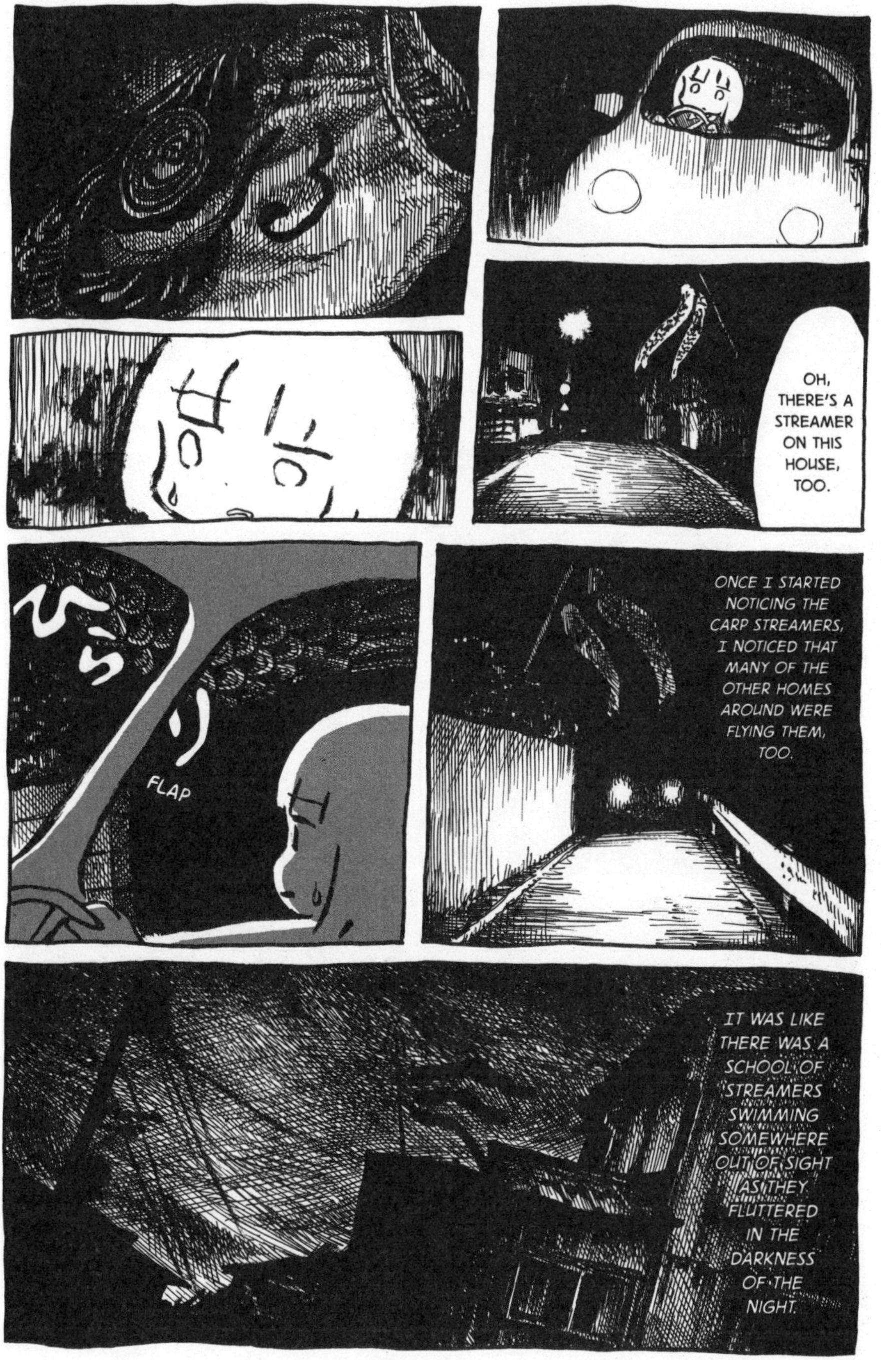
OH, THERE'S A STREAMER ON THIS HOUSE, TOO.
ONCE I STARTED NOTICING THE CARP STREAMERS, I NOTICED THAT MANY OF THE OTHER HOMES AROUND WERE FLYING THEM, TOO.
ひらり
FLAP
IT WAS LIKE THERE WAS A SCHOOL OF STREAMERS SWIMMING SOMEWHERE OUT OF SIGHT AS THEY FLUTTERED IN THE DARKNESS OF THE NIGHT.

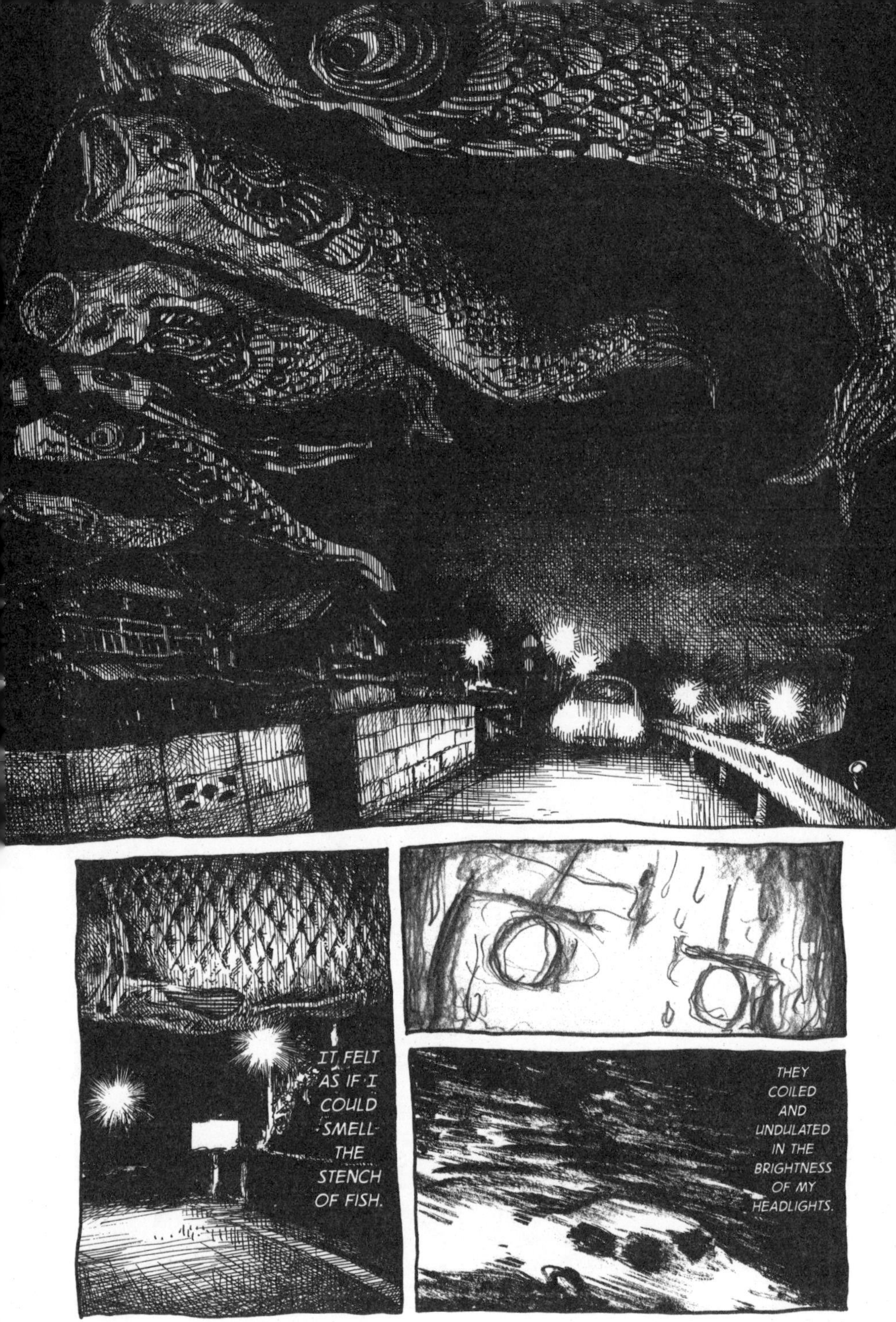
THEY COILED AND UNDULATED IN THE BRIGHTNESS OF MY HEADLIGHTS.
IT FELT AS IF I COULD SMELL THE STENCH OF FISH.

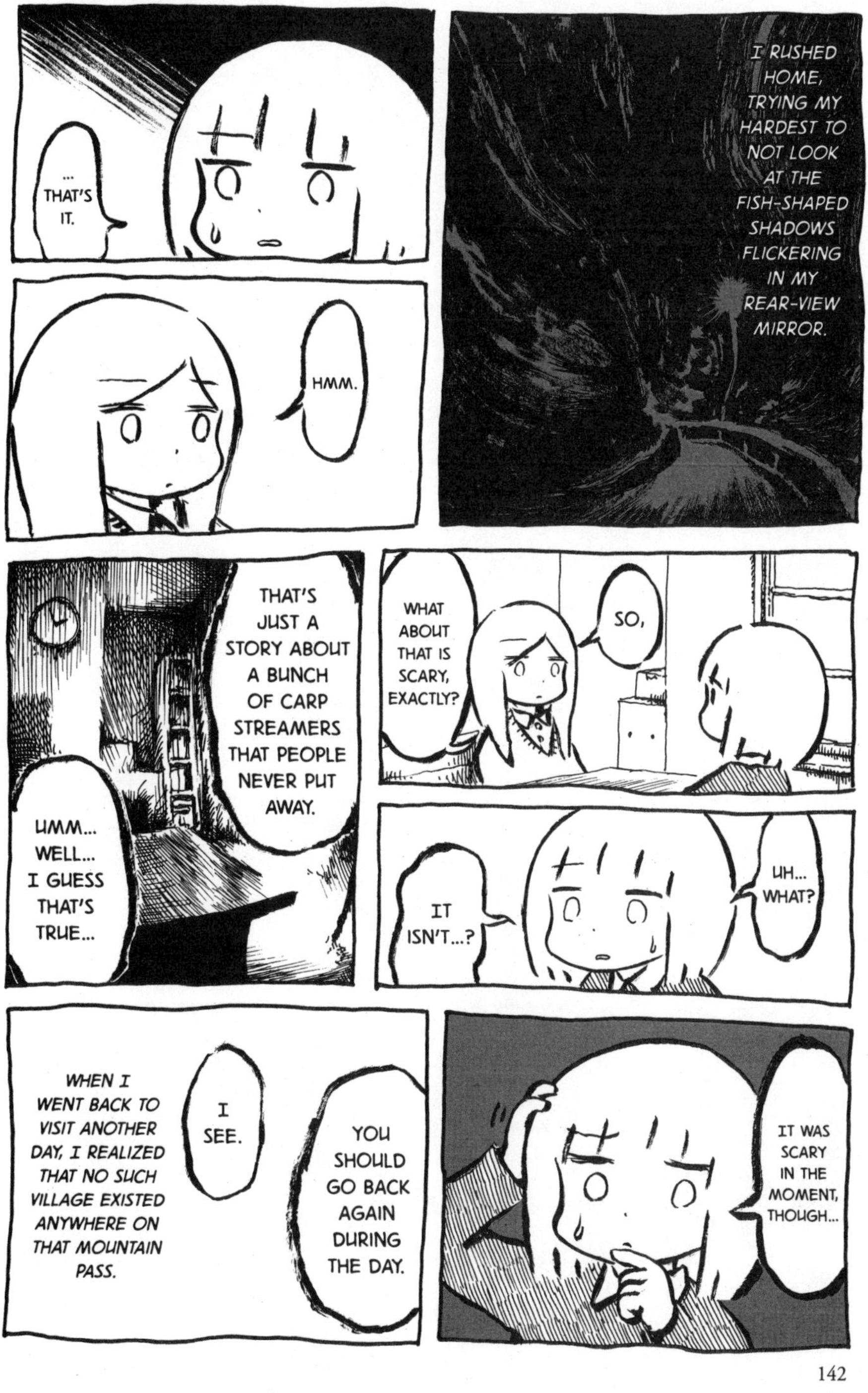
I RUSHED HOME, TRYING MY HARDEST TO NOT LOOK AT THE FISH-SHAPED SHADOWS FLICKERING IN MY REAR-VIEW MIRROR.
... THAT'S IT.
HMM.
SO,
WHAT ABOUT THAT IS SCARY, EXACTLY?
UH... WHAT?
IT ISN'T...?
THAT'S JUST A STORY ABOUT A BUNCH OF CARP STREAMERS THAT PEOPLE NEVER PUT AWAY.
UMM... WELL... I GUESS THAT'S TRUE...
IT WAS SCARY IN THE MOMENT, THOUGH...
I SEE.
YOU SHOULD GO BACK AGAIN DURING THE DAY.
WHEN I WENT BACK TO VISIT ANOTHER DAY, I REALIZED THAT NO SUCH VILLAGE EXISTED ANYWHERE ON THAT MOUNTAIN PASS.

Brightness

If you walk down streets that aren't part of commercial districts at night, there are times when without any lights around it gets completely dark. When you see shadows at times like these, they're blackness inside of blackness. Those shadows make you wonder if something that dark could really exist. But if you close your eyes tight in one of these seemingly pitch-dark places, you find yourself in another type of darkness from the one in the outside world. I actually feel like it's brighter than when I have my eyes open, but maybe it's just me. Could it just be me?

You would normally think that you're shutting out more light by having your eyes closed, so things might get darker. It seems impossible for it to get brighter, but strangely enough, it's as if there's a weak light being generated inside of your eyelids.

While the darkness outside is pitch black, the darkness you see with closed eyes is somewhere between red and green, or almost like you're seeing red and green at the same time. Either that or it's like you're able to see a kind of fluorescent darkness together with a random assortment of colored lines. This is what seems brighter than the darkness you see with open eyes. Thinking back on it, this is something I've seen since I was a child. I've previously thought that maybe I was getting a small glimpse at the back of my eyelids, since they were pink, but that still wouldn't be a reason for it to look brighter than the outside world if you're in complete darkness.

When I looked it up, it said that eyes work in a way where they sense physical stimulation as light. In other words, they think that the pressure from when you close your eyelids puts a force onto your eyeballs, which is sensed as a vague visual signal. Hmm, I see...

What makes me uncomfortable about that is how I had always assumed that everything I sensed as light coming into my eyeballs was really just that, but in reality, I had been seeing other forces on my eyelids as light as well. Knowing I've been "seeing" other things on a daily basis makes me feel strange, even if it is something natural.

October 1, 2013

TAKUAN DREAM

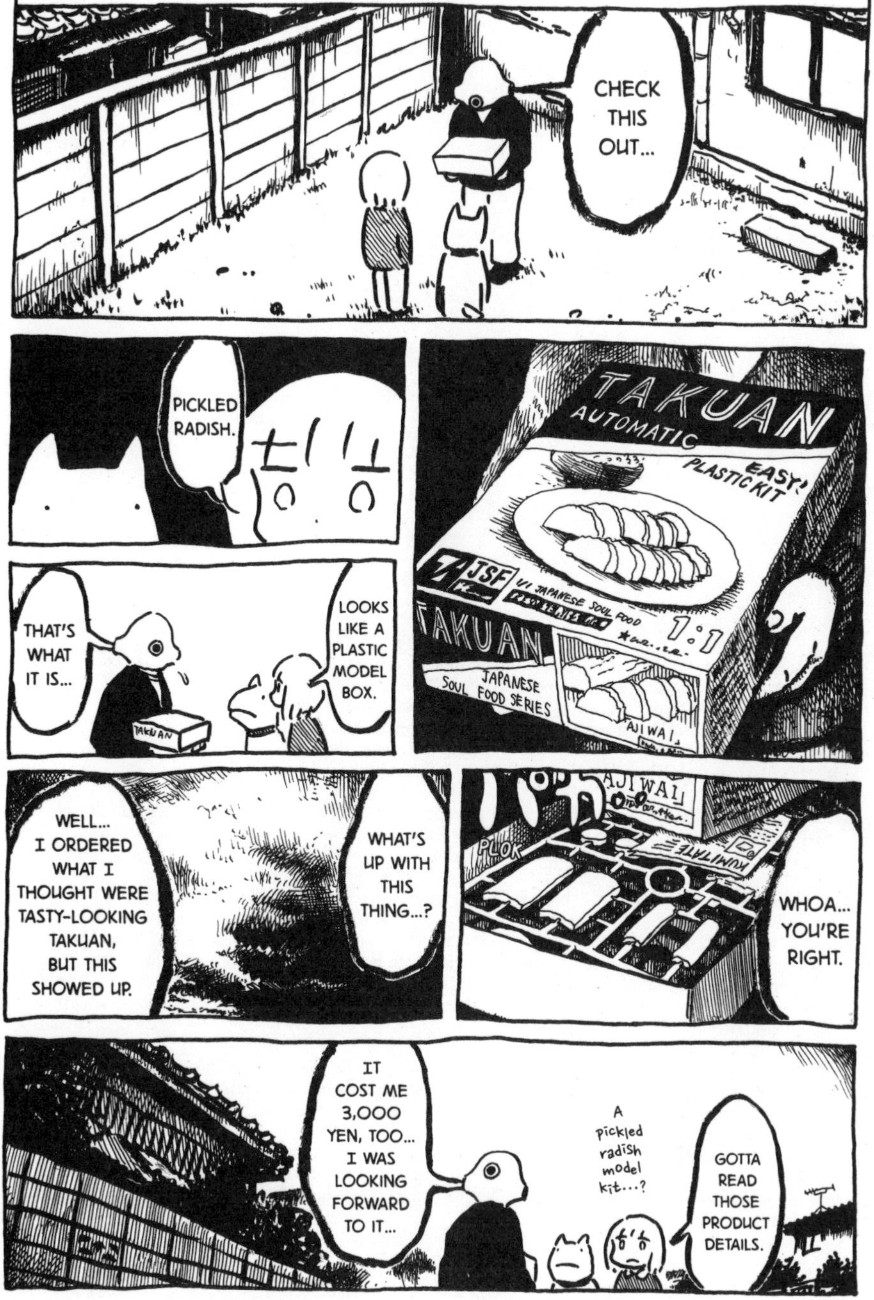
CHECK THIS OUT...
TAKUAN
AUTOMATIC
EASY! PLASTIC KIT
JSF
JAPANESE SOUL FOOD
1:1
TAKUAN
JAPANESE SOUL FOOD SERIES
AJIWAI
PICKLED RADISH.
LOOKS LIKE A PLASTIC MODEL BOX.
THAT'S WHAT IT IS...
TAKUAN
パカ
PLOK
AJIWAI
KUMITATE
WHOA... YOU'RE RIGHT.
WHAT'S UP WITH THIS THING...?
WELL... I ORDERED WHAT I THOUGHT WERE TASTY-LOOKING TAKUAN, BUT THIS SHOWED UP.
GOTTA READ THOSE PRODUCT DETAILS.
A pickled radish model kit...?
IT COST ME 3,000 YEN, TOO... I WAS LOOKING FORWARD TO IT...

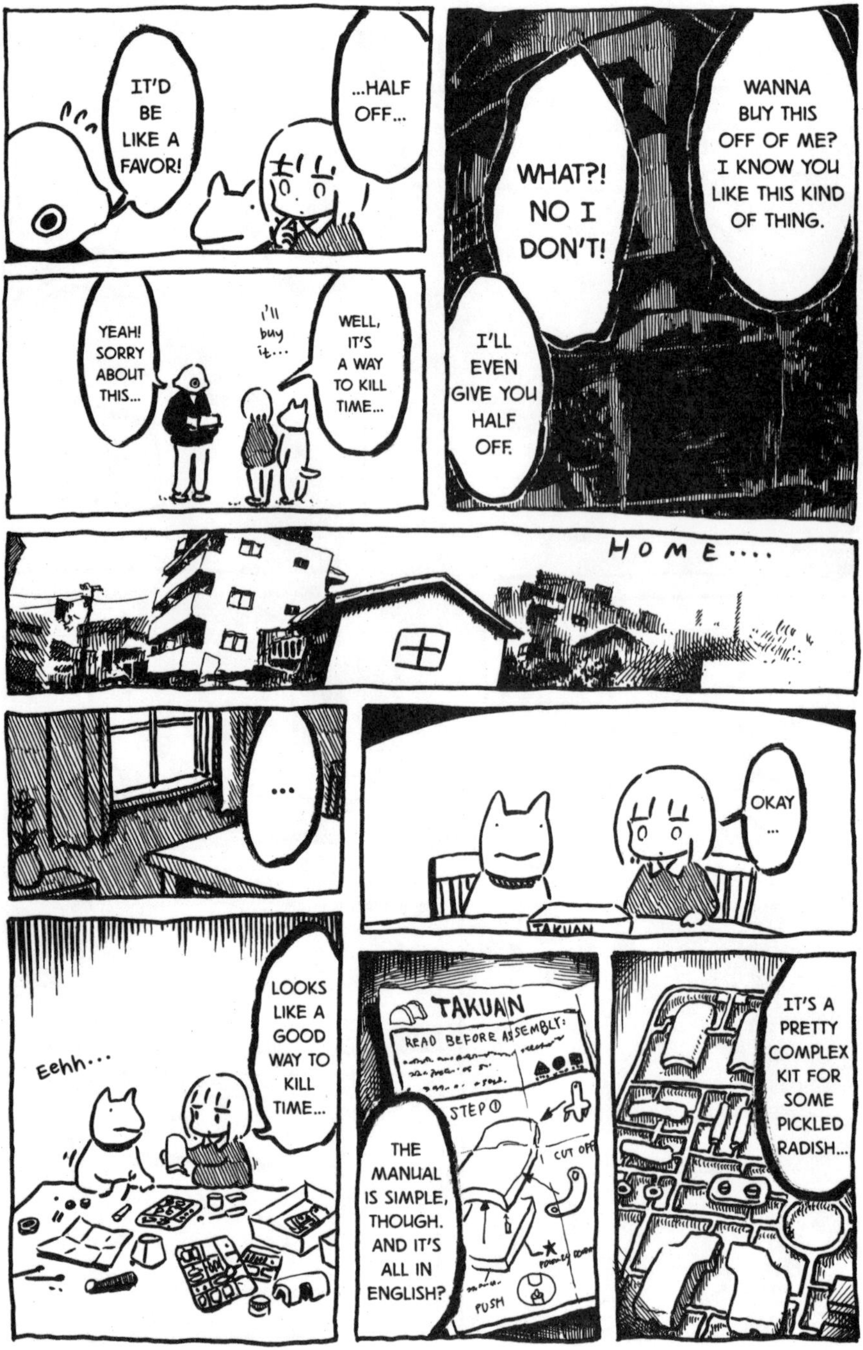
WANNA BUY THIS OFF OF ME? I KNOW YOU LIKE THIS KIND OF THING.
WHAT?! NO I DON'T!
I'LL EVEN GIVE YOU HALF OFF.
...HALF OFF...
IT'D BE LIKE A FAVOR!
WELL, IT'S A WAY TO KILL TIME...
I'll buy it...
YEAH! SORRY ABOUT THIS...
HOME....
OKAY ...
TAKUAN
...
IT'S A PRETTY COMPLEX KIT FOR SOME PICKLED RADISH...
TAKUAN
READ BEFORE ASSEMBLY:
STEP ①
CUT OFF
PUSH
THE MANUAL IS SIMPLE, THOUGH. AND IT'S ALL IN ENGLISH?
LOOKS LIKE A GOOD WAY TO KILL TIME...
Eehh...

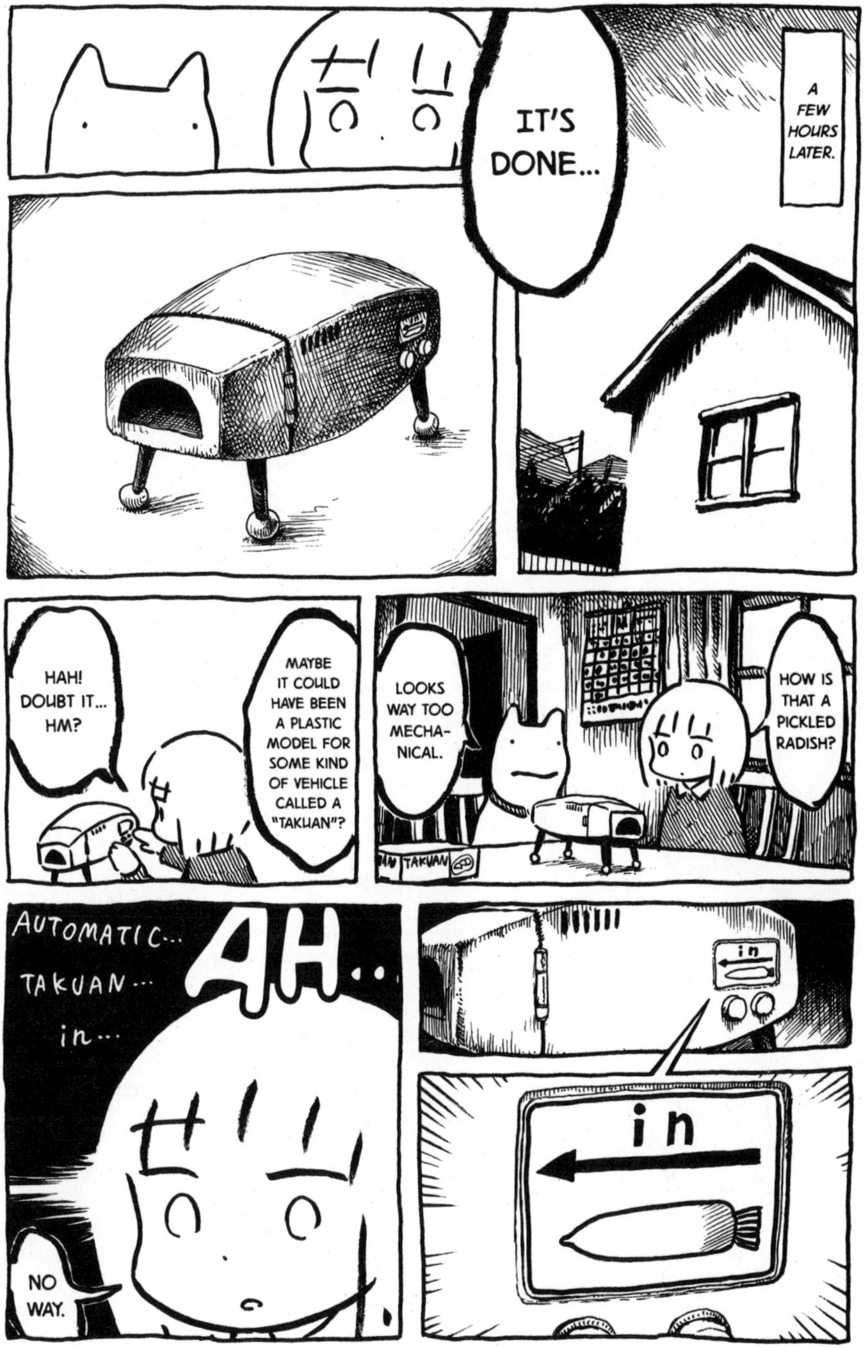
A FEW HOURS LATER.
IT'S DONE...
HOW IS THAT A PICKLED RADISH?
LOOKS WAY TOO MECHA-NICAL.
MAYBE IT COULD HAVE BEEN A PLASTIC MODEL FOR SOME KIND OF VEHICLE CALLED A "TAKUAN"?
HAH! DOUBT IT... HM?
in
in
AUTOMATIC... TAKUAN... in...
AH..
NO WAY.

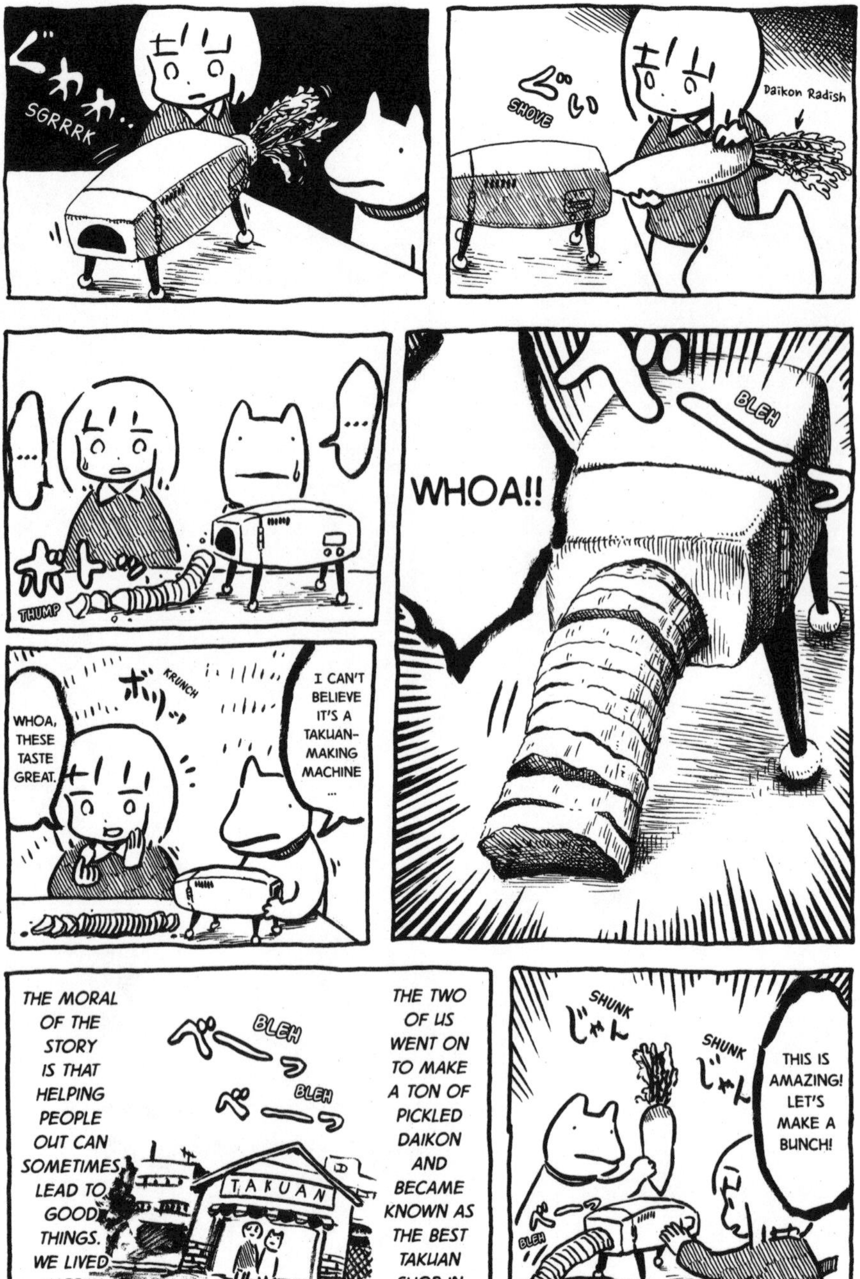
Daikon Radish
ぐい
SHOVE
ぐわわ‥
SGRRRK
BLEH
WHOA!!
...
...
ボトッ
THUMP
I CAN'T BELIEVE IT'S A TAKUAN-MAKING MACHINE ...
ポリッ
KRUNCH
WHOA, THESE TASTE GREAT.
THIS IS AMAZING! LET'S MAKE A BUNCH!
じゃん
SHUNK
じゃん
SHUNK
ぺーっ
BLEH
THE TWO OF US WENT ON TO MAKE A TON OF PICKLED DAIKON AND BECAME KNOWN AS THE BEST TAKUAN SHOP IN THE AREA.
ぺーっ
BLEH
ぺーっ
BLEH
TAKUAN
THE MORAL OF THE STORY IS THAT HELPING PEOPLE OUT CAN SOMETIMES LEAD TO GOOD THINGS. WE LIVED HAPPILY EVER AFTER.

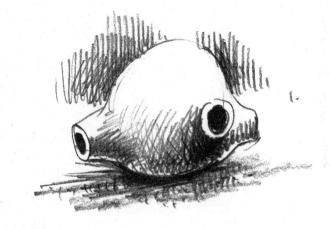

A Dream from January 31, 2014

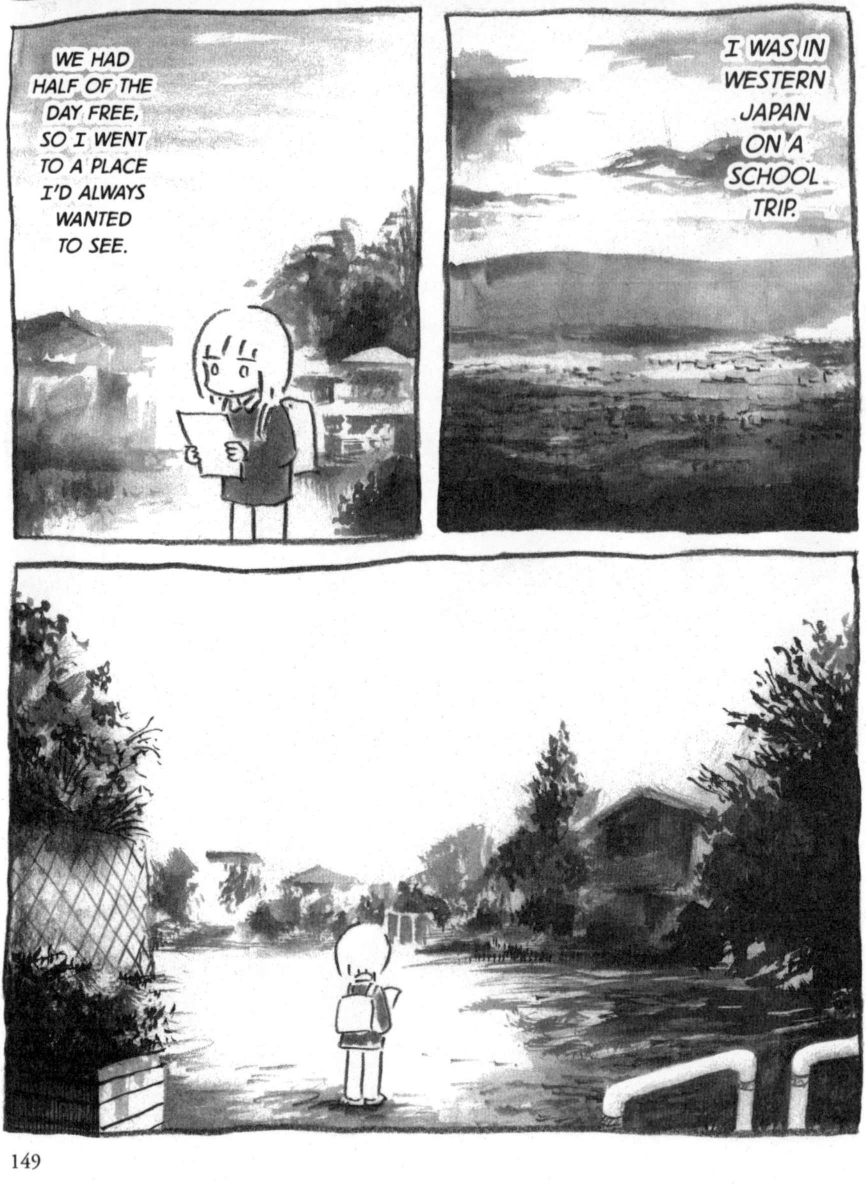
I WAS IN WESTERN JAPAN ON A SCHOOL TRIP.
WE HAD HALF OF THE DAY FREE, SO I WENT TO A PLACE I'D ALWAYS WANTED TO SEE.

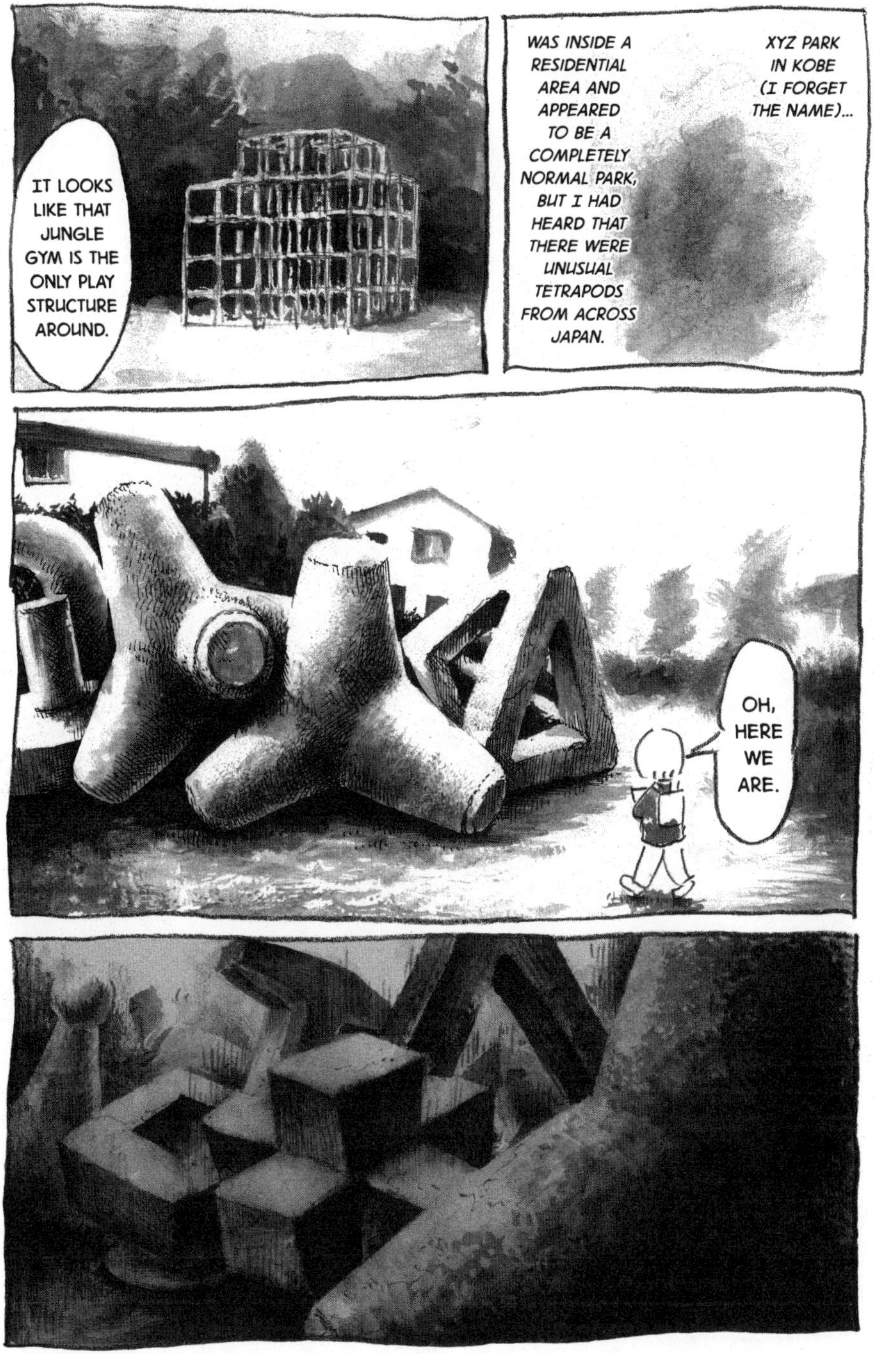
XYZ PARK IN KOBE (I FORGET THE NAME)...
WAS INSIDE A RESIDENTIAL AREA AND APPEARED TO BE A COMPLETELY NORMAL PARK, BUT I HAD HEARD THAT THERE WERE UNUSUAL TETRAPODS FROM ACROSS JAPAN.
IT LOOKS LIKE THAT JUNGLE GYM IS THE ONLY PLAY STRUCTURE AROUND.
OH, HERE WE ARE.

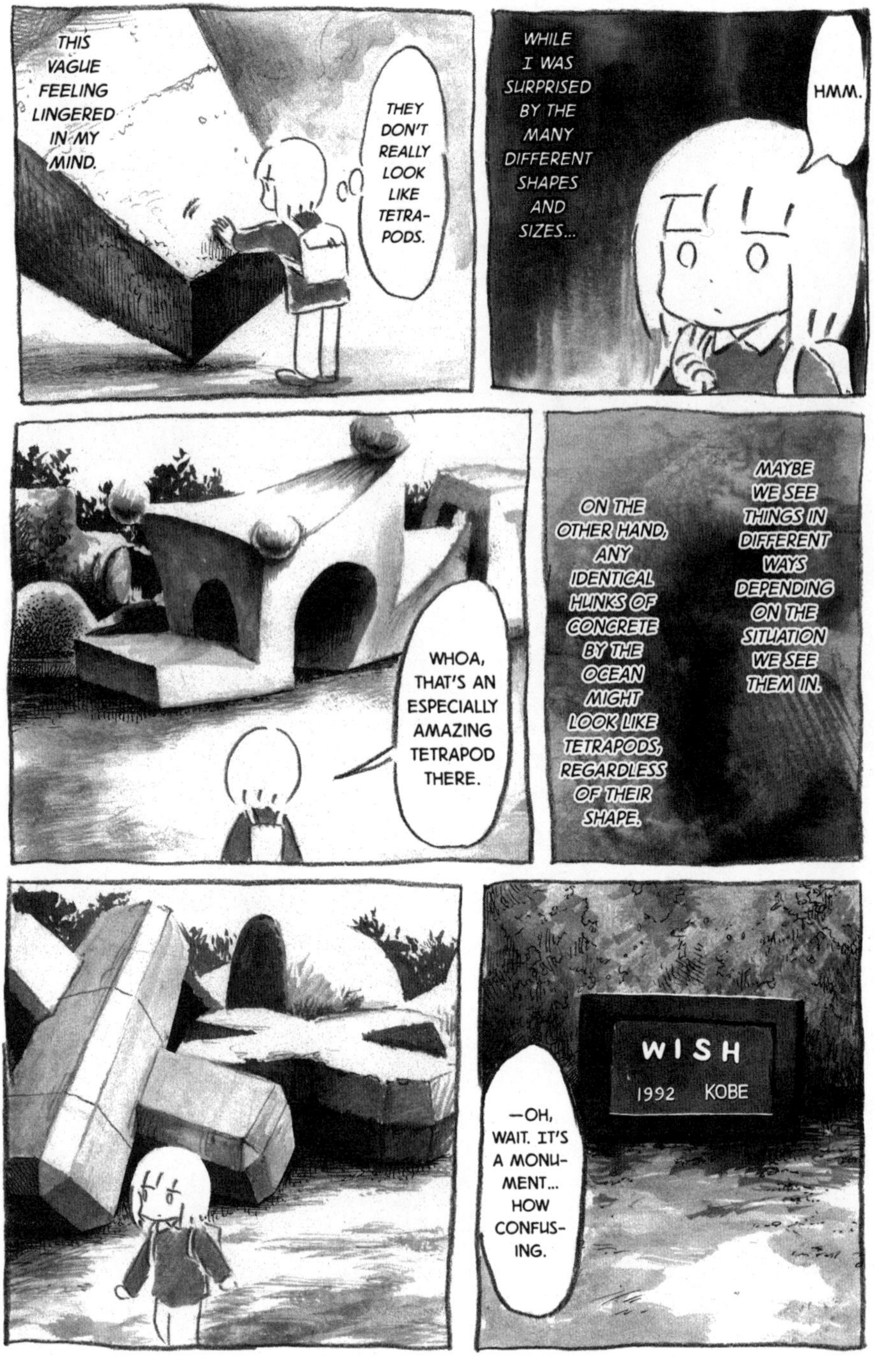
HMM.
WHILE I WAS SURPRISED BY THE MANY DIFFERENT SHAPES AND SIZES...
THIS VAGUE FEELING LINGERED IN MY MIND.
THEY DON'T REALLY LOOK LIKE TETRA-PODS.
MAYBE WE SEE THINGS IN DIFFERENT WAYS DEPENDING ON THE SITUATION WE SEE THEM IN.
ON THE OTHER HAND, ANY IDENTICAL HUNKS OF CONCRETE BY THE OCEAN MIGHT LOOK LIKE TETRAPODS, REGARDLESS OF THEIR SHAPE.
WHOA, THAT'S AN ESPECIALLY AMAZING TETRAPOD THERE.
WISH
1992 KOBE
—OH, WAIT. IT'S A MONU-MENT... HOW CONFUS-ING.

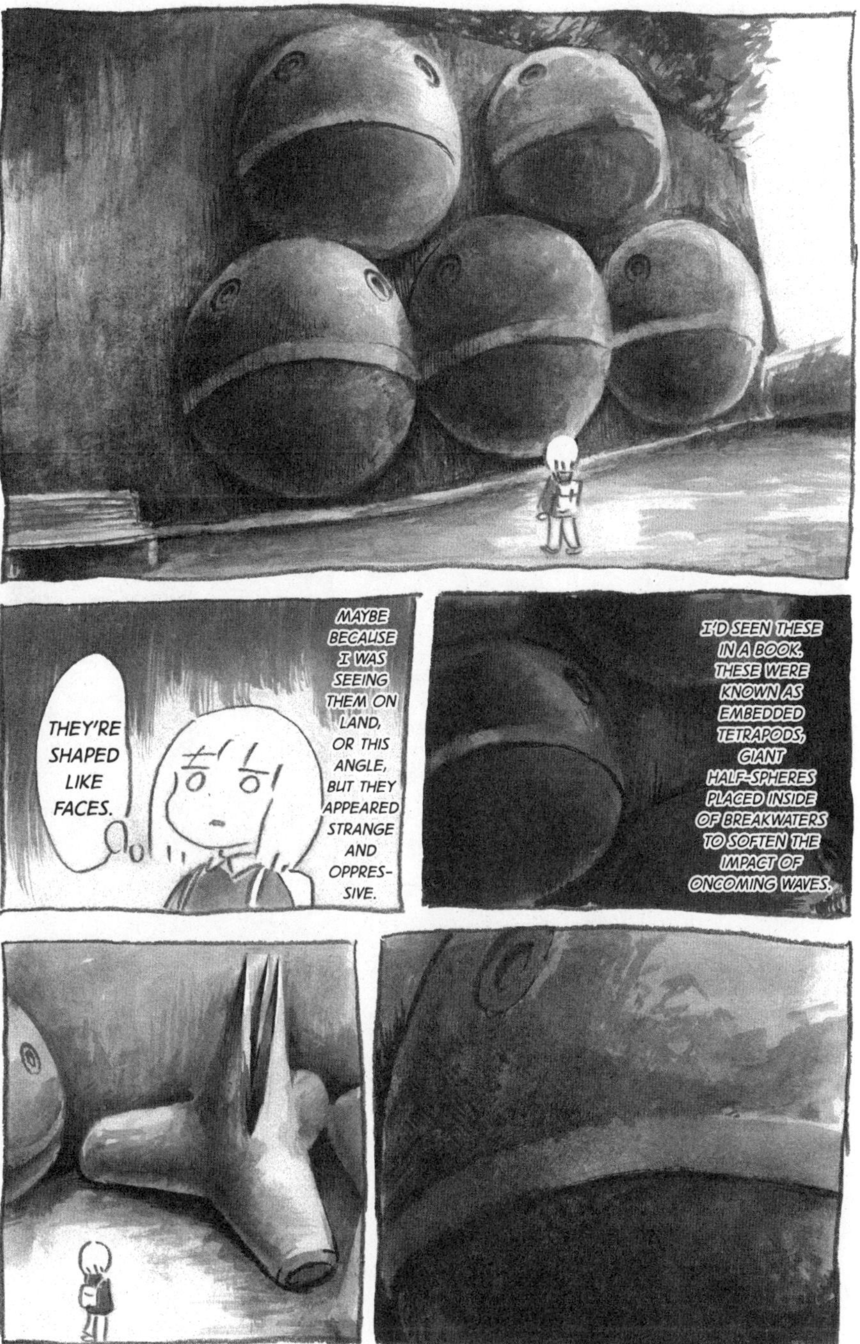
I'D SEEN THESE IN A BOOK. THESE WERE KNOWN AS EMBEDDED TETRAPODS, GIANT HALF-SPHERES PLACED INSIDE OF BREAKWATERS TO SOFTEN THE IMPACT OF ONCOMING WAVES.
MAYBE BECAUSE I WAS SEEING THEM ON LAND, OR THIS ANGLE, BUT THEY APPEARED STRANGE AND OPPRES-SIVE.
THEY'RE SHAPED LIKE FACES.

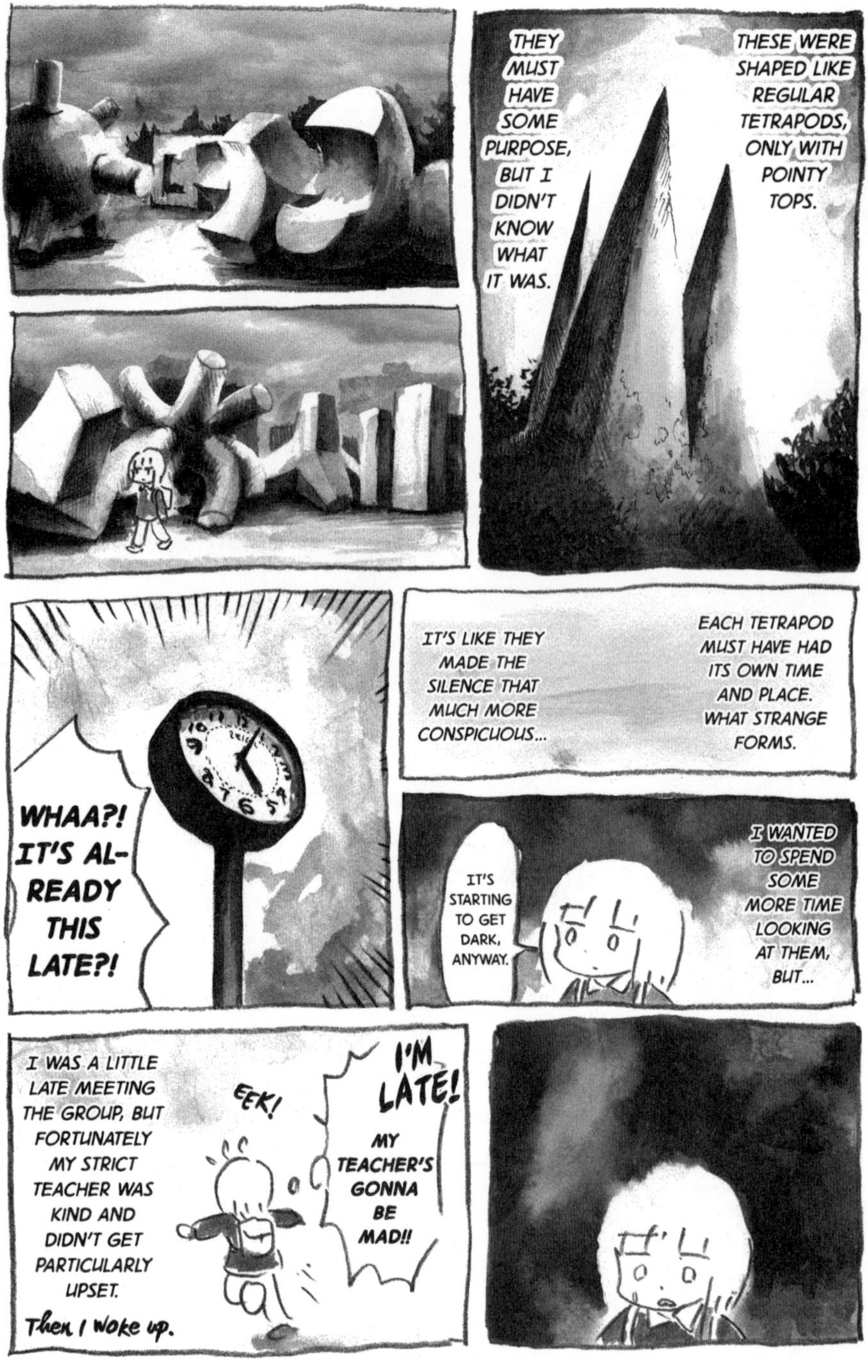
THESE WERE SHAPED LIKE REGULAR TETRAPODS, ONLY WITH POINTY TOPS.
THEY MUST HAVE SOME PURPOSE, BUT I DIDN'T KNOW WHAT IT WAS.
EACH TETRAPOD MUST HAVE HAD ITS OWN TIME AND PLACE. WHAT STRANGE FORMS.
IT'S LIKE THEY MADE THE SILENCE THAT MUCH MORE CONSPICUOUS...
I WANTED TO SPEND SOME MORE TIME LOOKING AT THEM, BUT...
IT'S STARTING TO GET DARK, ANYWAY.
WHAA?! IT'S AL-READY THIS LATE?!
I'M LATE!
MY TEACHER'S GONNA BE MAD!!
EEK!
I WAS A LITTLE LATE MEETING THE GROUP, BUT FORTUNATELY MY STRICT TEACHER WAS KIND AND DIDN'T GET PARTICULARLY UPSET.
Then I woke up.

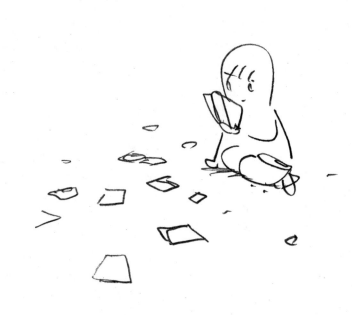

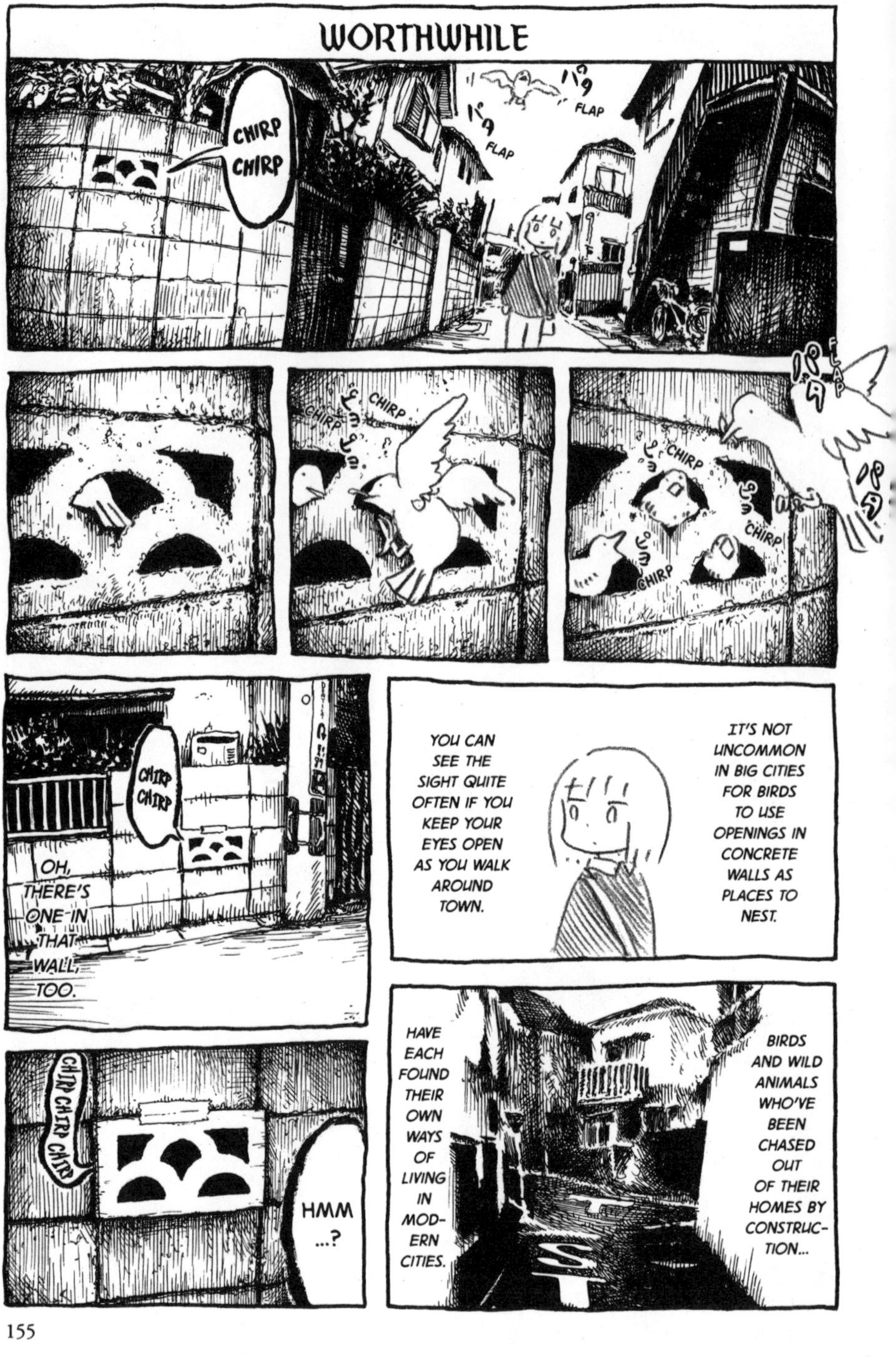
WORTHWHILE
CHIRP CHIRP
FLAP
FLAP
FLAP
CHIRP
CHIRP
CHIRP
CHIRP
CHIRP
IT'S NOT UNCOMMON IN BIG CITIES FOR BIRDS TO USE OPENINGS IN CONCRETE WALLS AS PLACES TO NEST.
YOU CAN SEE THE SIGHT QUITE OFTEN IF YOU KEEP YOUR EYES OPEN AS YOU WALK AROUND TOWN.
CHIRP CHIRP
OH, THERE'S ONE IN THAT WALL, TOO.
BIRDS AND WILD ANIMALS WHO'VE BEEN CHASED OUT OF THEIR HOMES BY CONSTRUC-TION...
HAVE EACH FOUND THEIR OWN WAYS OF LIVING IN MOD-ERN CITIES.
HMM ...?
CHIRP CHIRP CHIRP

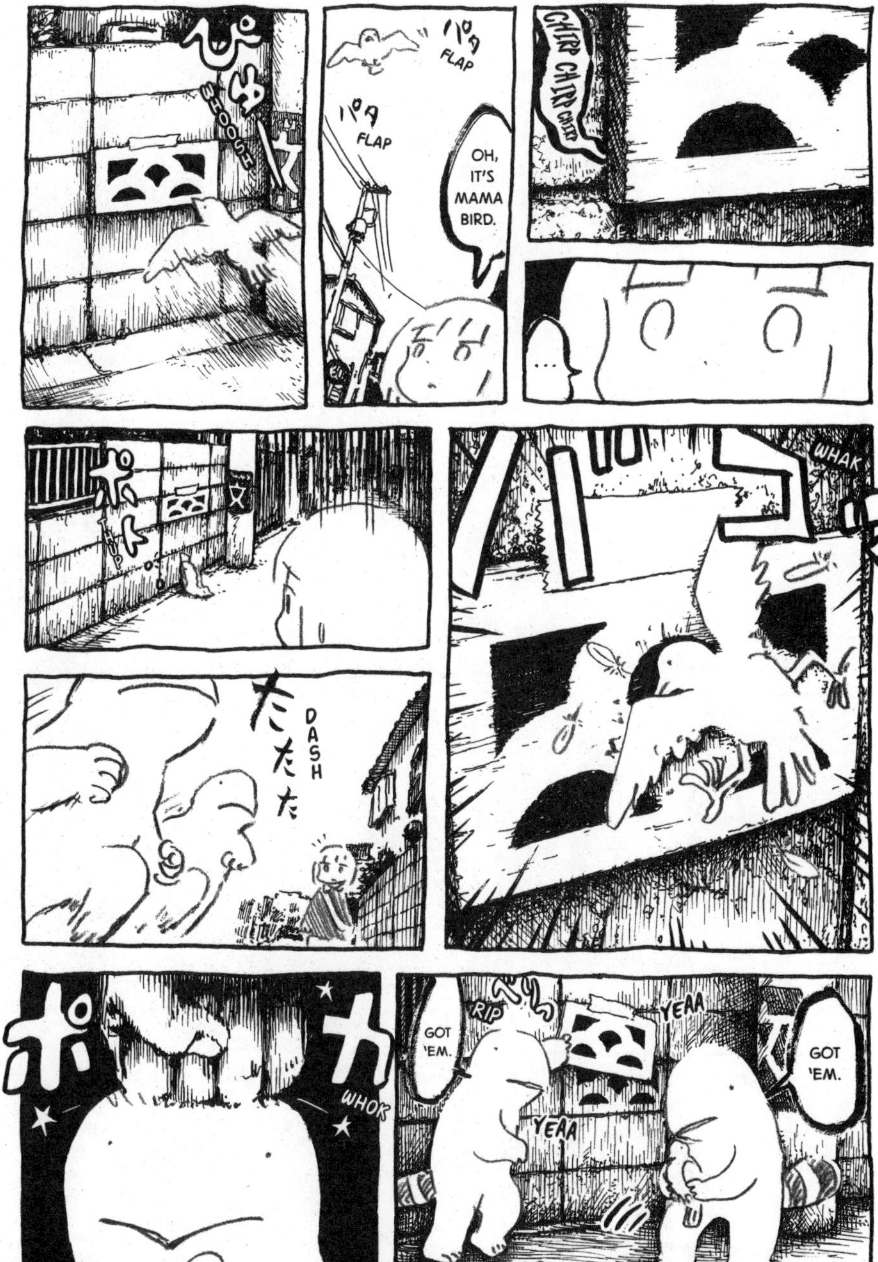
CHIRP CHIRP CHIRP
...
パタ
FLAP
パタ
FLAP
OH, IT'S MAMA BIRD.
ぴゅ
WHOOSH
文
WHAK
ポト
THUP
文
たたた
DASH
GOT 'EM.
YEAA
べり
RIP
GOT 'EM.
YEAA
ポカ
WHOK
AH

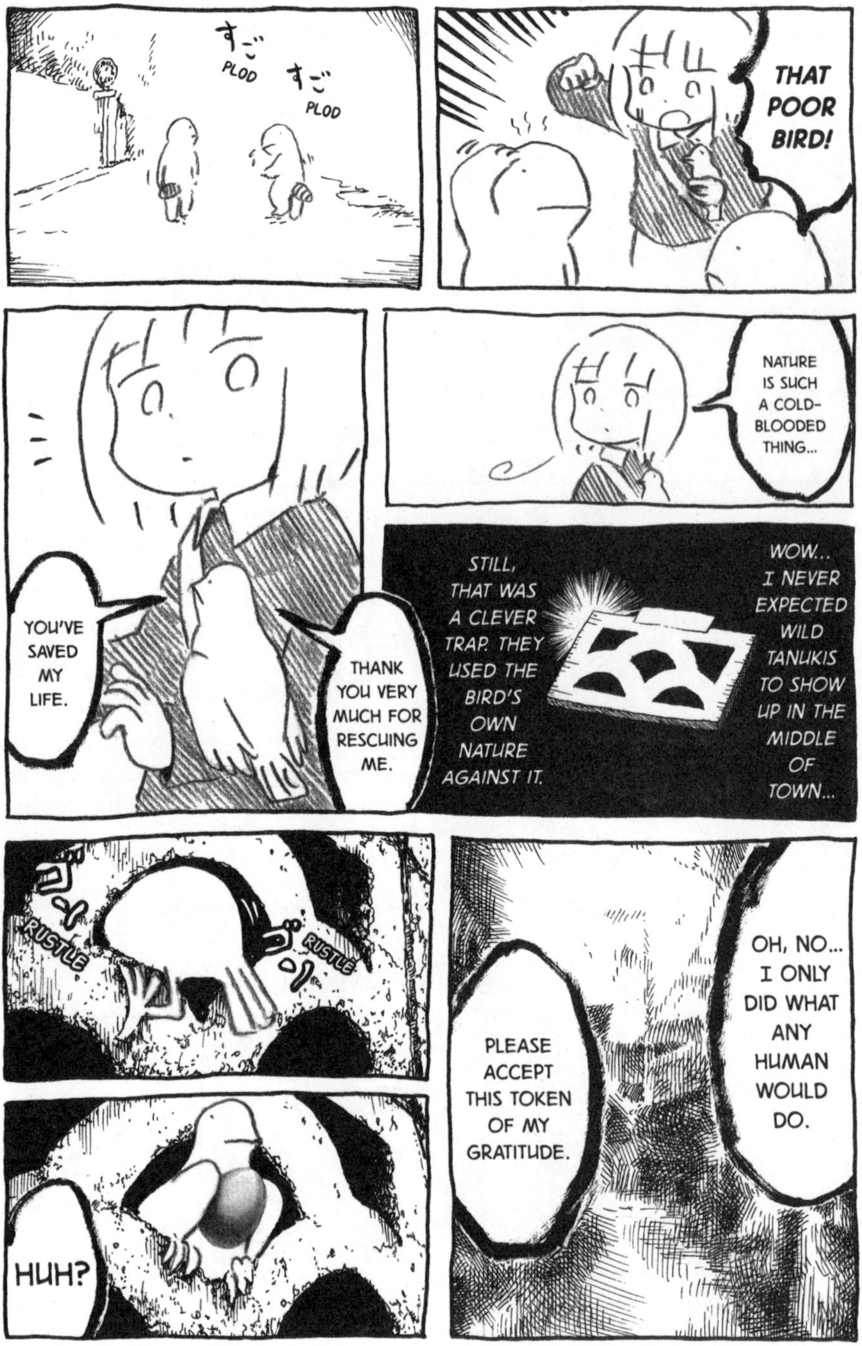
THAT POOR BIRD!
すご PLOD
すご PLOD
NATURE IS SUCH A COLD-BLOODED THING...
WOW... I NEVER EXPECTED WILD TANUKIS TO SHOW UP IN THE MIDDLE OF TOWN...
STILL, THAT WAS A CLEVER TRAP. THEY USED THE BIRD'S OWN NATURE AGAINST IT.
THANK YOU VERY MUCH FOR RESCUING ME.
YOU'VE SAVED MY LIFE.
OH, NO... I ONLY DID WHAT ANY HUMAN WOULD DO.
PLEASE ACCEPT THIS TOKEN OF MY GRATITUDE.
RUSTLE
RUSTLE
HUH?

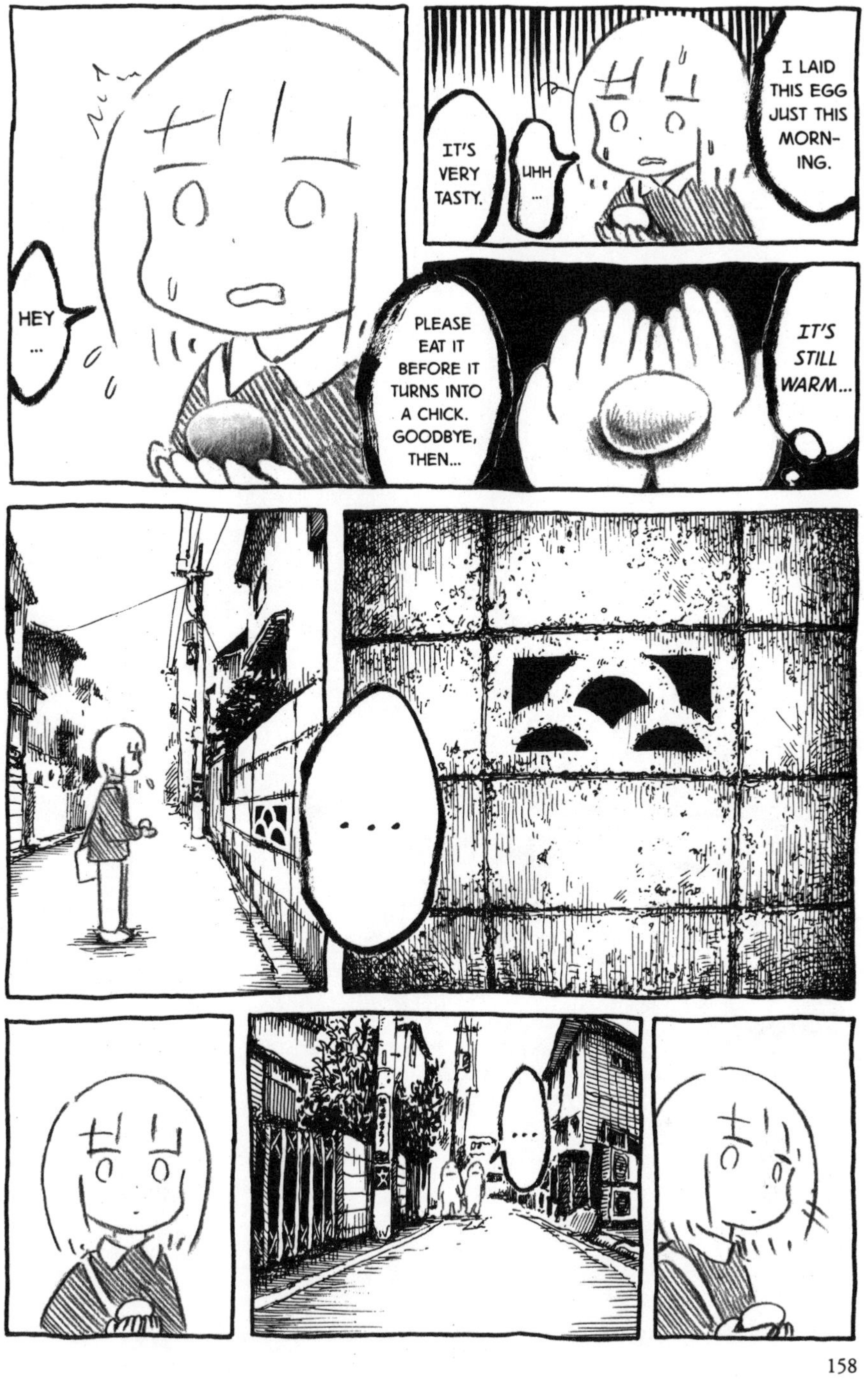

I LAID THIS EGG JUST THIS MORNING.
UHH ...
IT'S VERY TASTY.
IT'S STILL WARM...
PLEASE EAT IT BEFORE IT TURNS INTO A CHICK. GOODBYE, THEN...
HEY ...
...
...

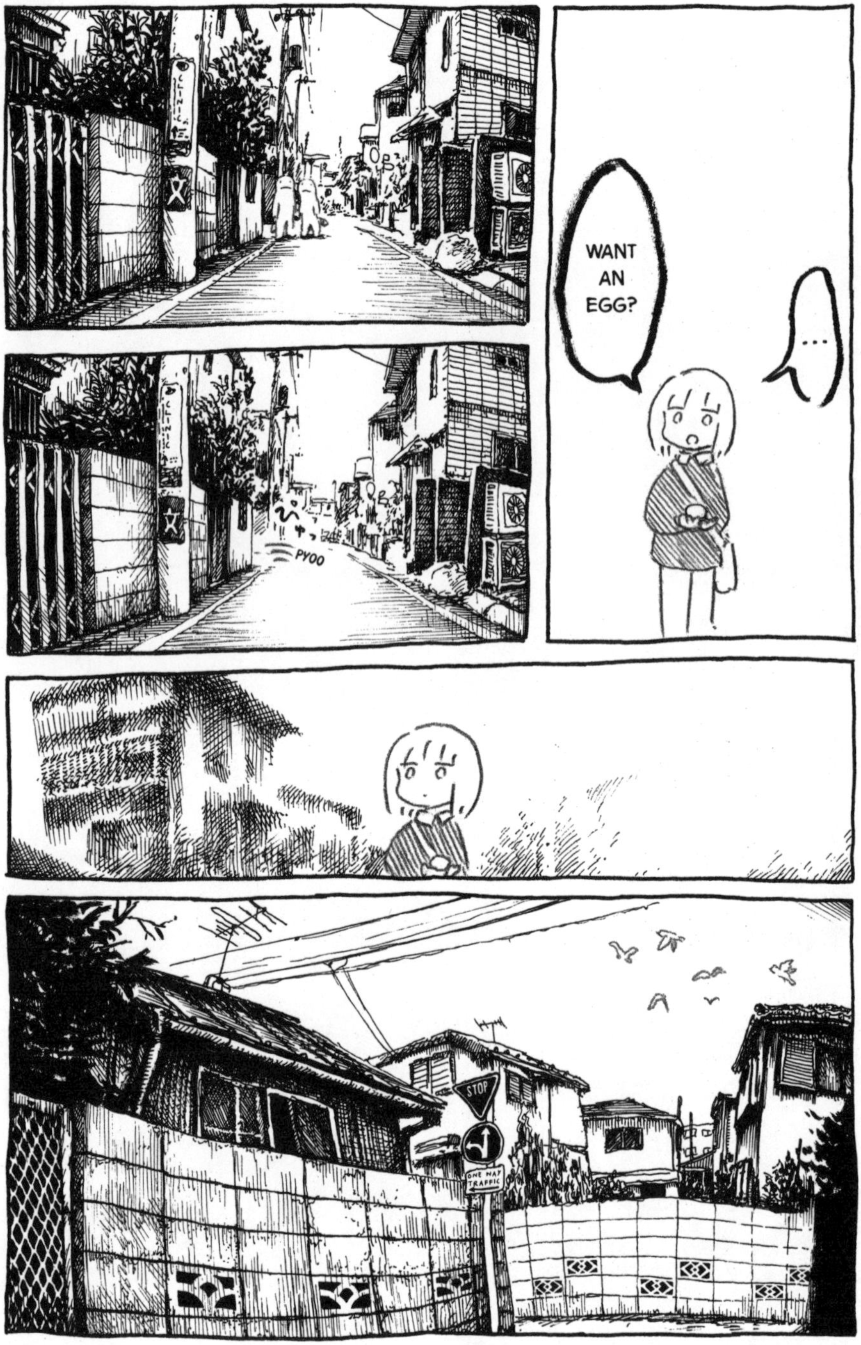
WANT AN EGG?
...
CLINIC
CLINIC
ぴゅっ
PYOO
STOP
ONE WAY TRAFFIC

A RESTLESS DAY

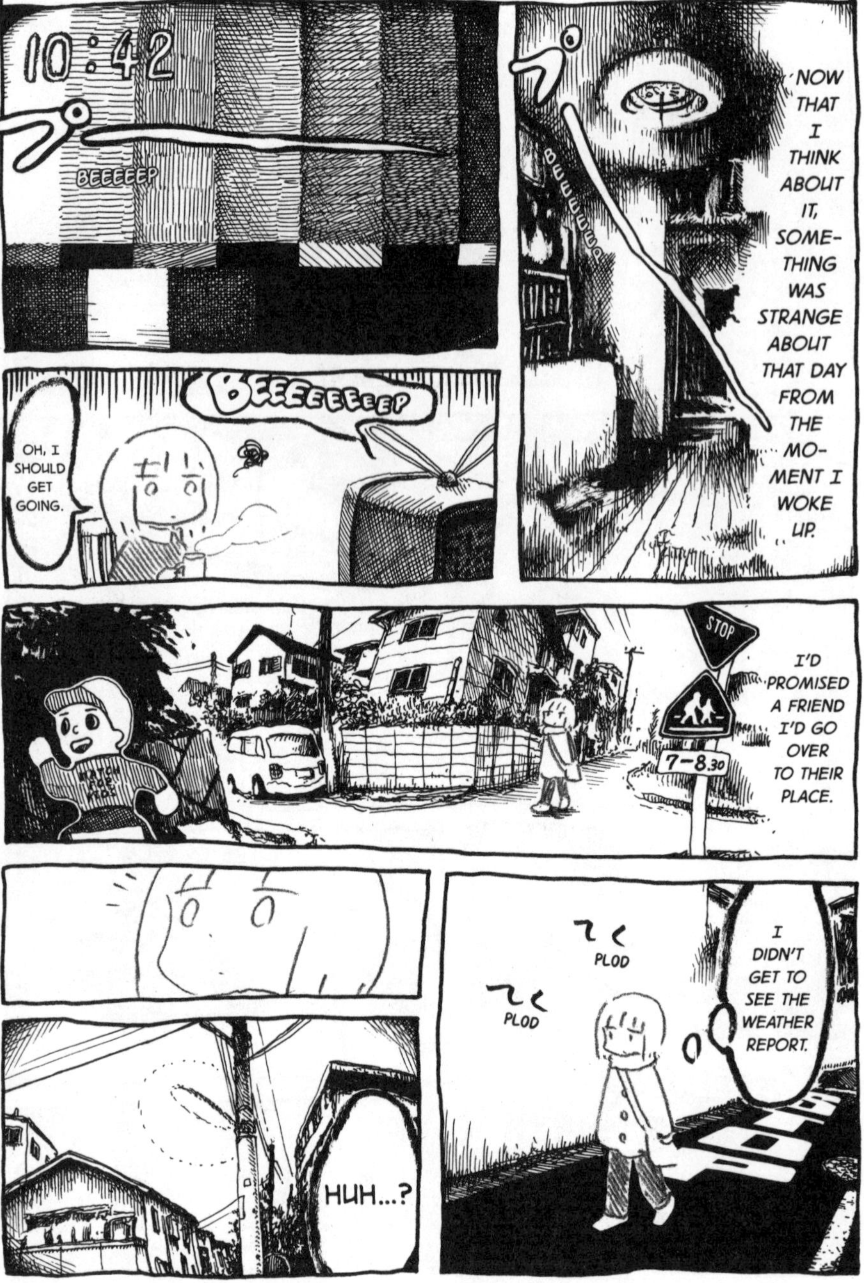

ピ
NOW THAT I THINK ABOUT IT, SOMETHING WAS STRANGE ABOUT THAT DAY FROM THE MOMENT I WOKE UP.
10:42
ピ
BEEEEEP
BEEEEEEEEEP
OH, I SHOULD GET GOING.
STOP
I'D PROMISED A FRIEND I'D GO OVER TO THEIR PLACE.
7-8.30
てく PLOD
てく PLOD
I DIDN'T GET TO SEE THE WEATHER REPORT.
HUH...?

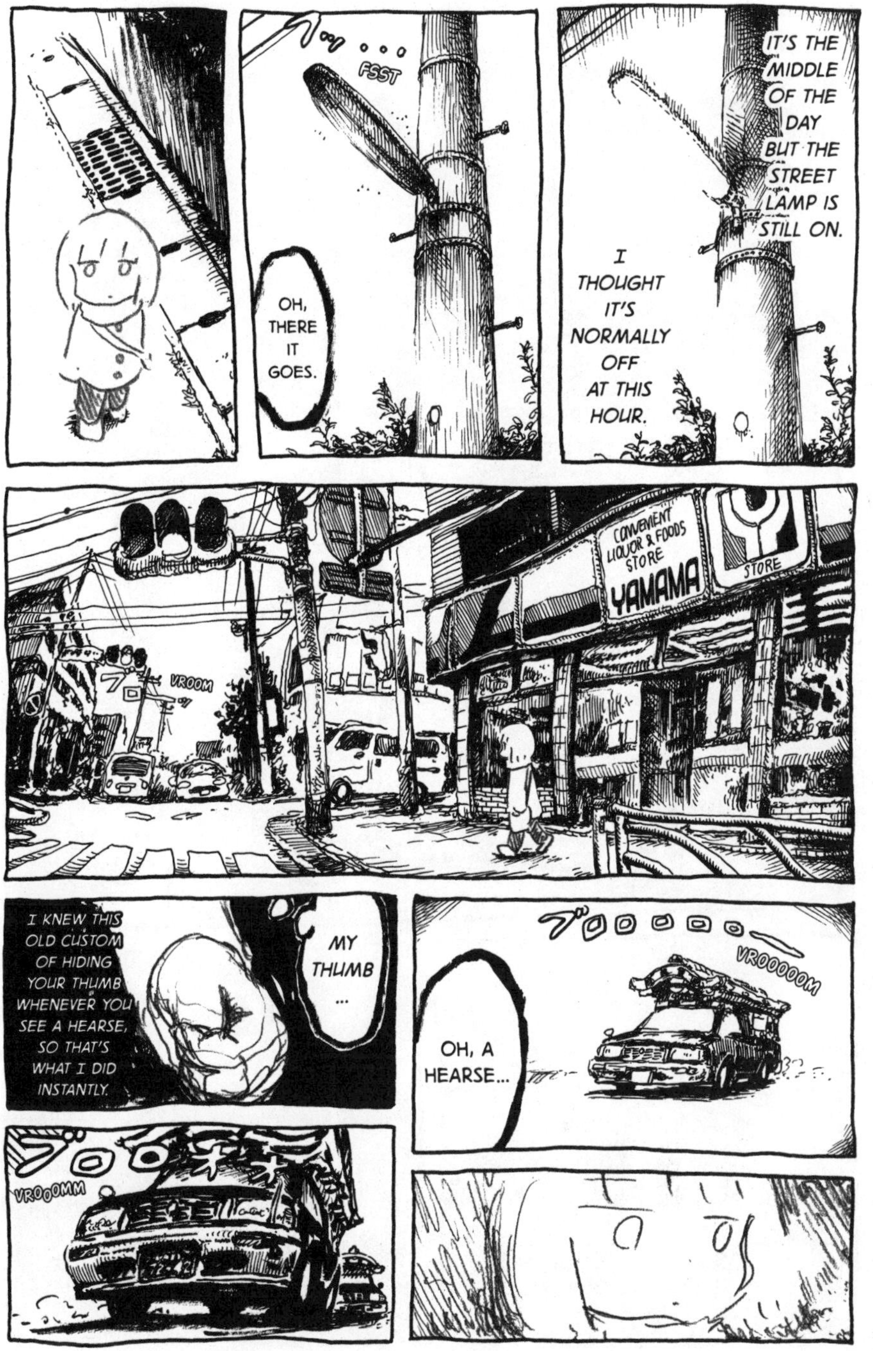
IT'S THE MIDDLE OF THE DAY BUT THE STREET LAMP IS STILL ON.
I THOUGHT IT'S NORMALLY OFF AT THIS HOUR.
FSST
OH, THERE IT GOES.
CONVENIENT LIQUOR & FOODS STORE
YAMAMA
STORE
VROOM
VROOOOOOM
OH, A HEARSE...
MY THUMB ...
I KNEW THIS OLD CUSTOM OF HIDING YOUR THUMB WHENEVER YOU SEE A HEARSE, SO THAT'S WHAT I DID INSTANTLY.
VROOOMM

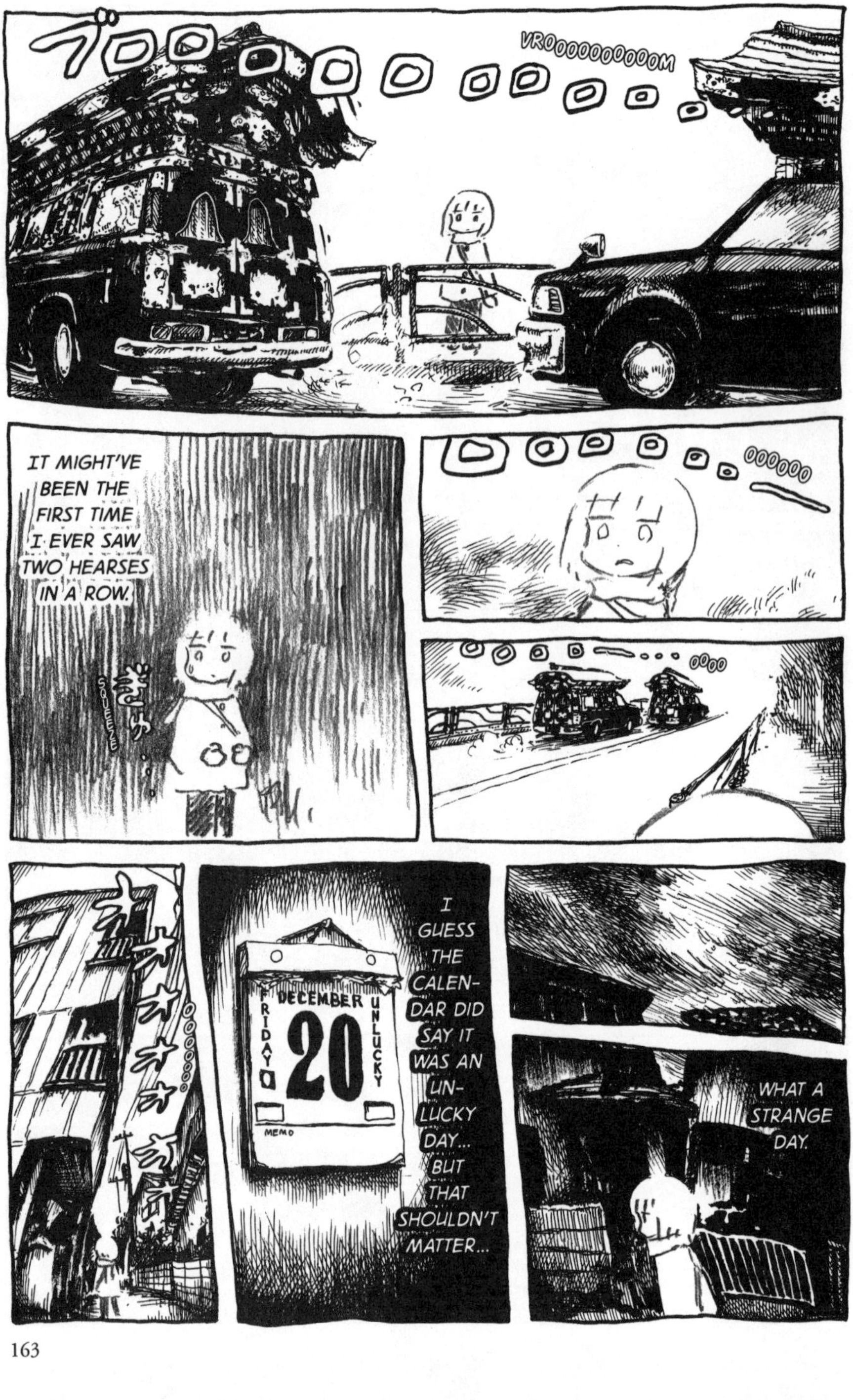
VROOOOOOOOOOM
OOOOOO
OOOO
IT MIGHT'VE BEEN THE FIRST TIME I EVER SAW TWO HEARSES IN A ROW.
SQUEEZE
WHAT A STRANGE DAY.
I GUESS THE CALEN-DAR DID SAY IT WAS AN UN-LUCKY DAY... BUT THAT SHOULDN'T MATTER...
DECEMBER
FRIDAY
20
UNLUCKY
MEMO
OOOOOOO

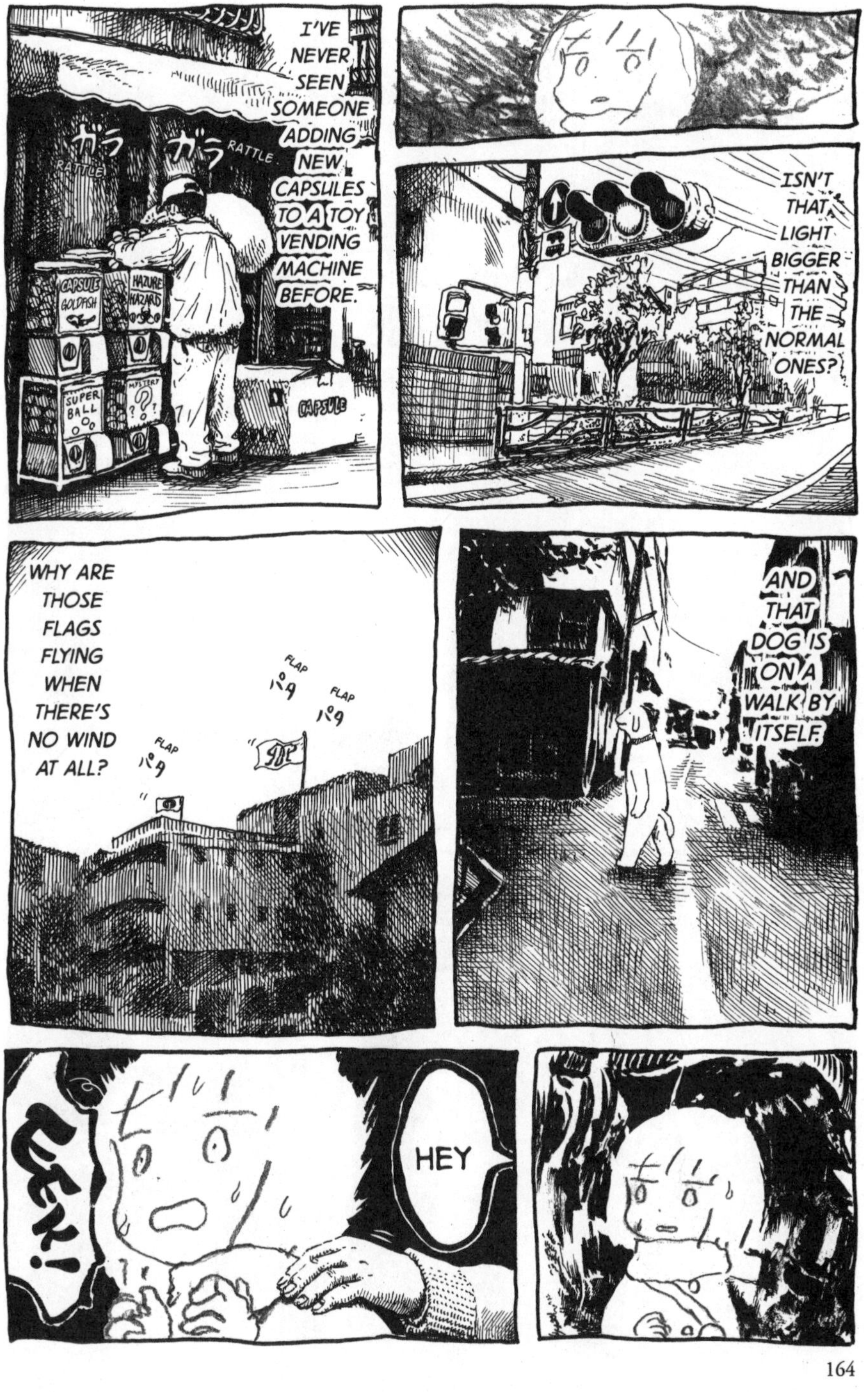
ISN'T THAT LIGHT BIGGER THAN THE NORMAL ONES?
I'VE NEVER SEEN SOMEONE ADDING NEW CAPSULES TO A TOY VENDING MACHINE BEFORE.
ガラ RATTLE
ガラ RATTLE
HAZURE HAZARDS
CAPSULE GOLDFISH
MYSTERY ?
SUPER BALL
CAPSULE
AND THAT DOG IS ON A WALK BY ITSELF.
WHY ARE THOSE FLAGS FLYING WHEN THERE'S NO WIND AT ALL?
パタ FLAP
パタ FLAP
パタ FLAP
HEY
EEK!

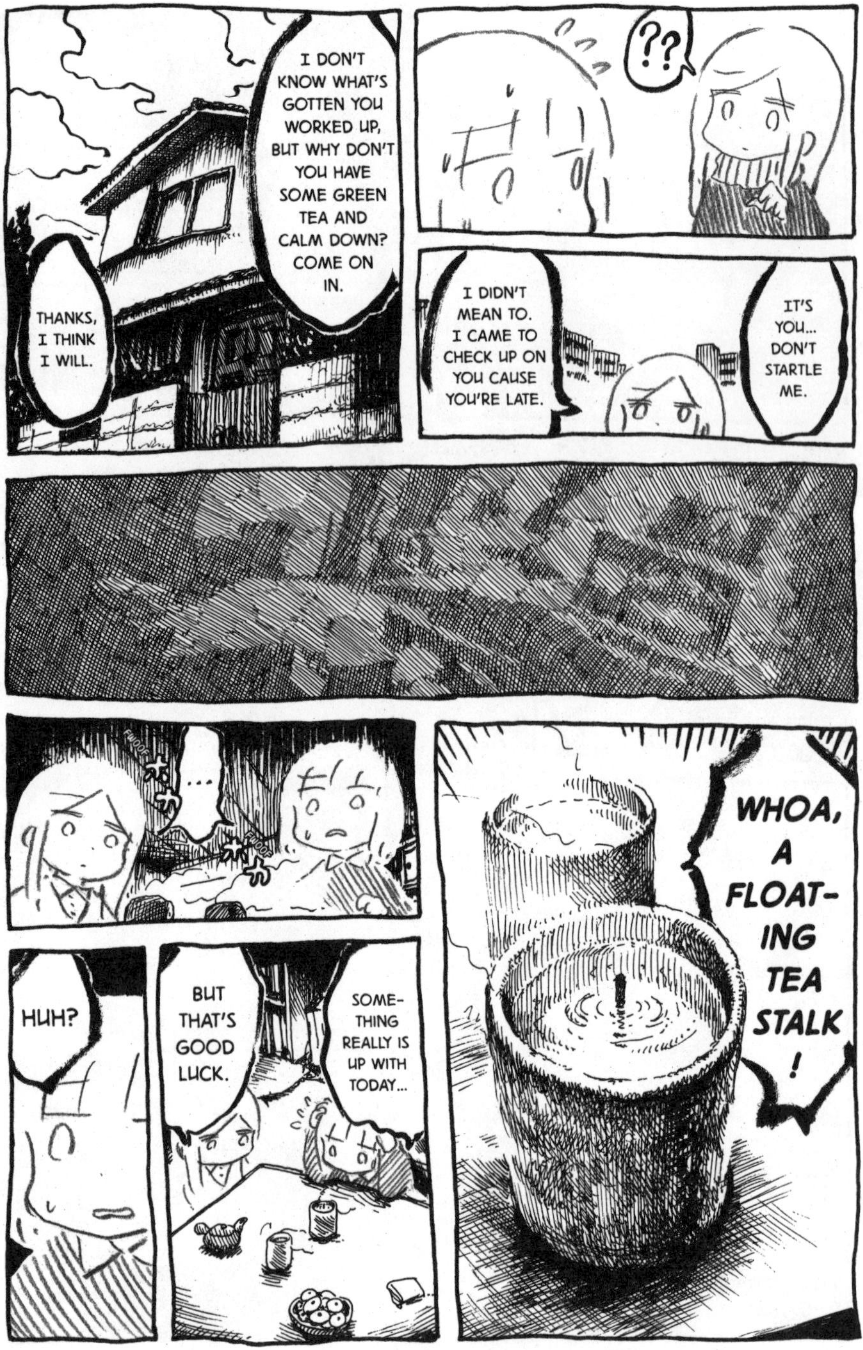
??
IT'S YOU... DON'T STARTLE ME.
I DIDN'T MEAN TO. I CAME TO CHECK UP ON YOU CAUSE YOU'RE LATE.
I DON'T KNOW WHAT'S GOTTEN YOU WORKED UP, BUT WHY DON'T YOU HAVE SOME GREEN TEA AND CALM DOWN? COME ON IN.
THANKS, I THINK I WILL.
WHOA, A FLOATING TEA STALK!
...
FWOOF
FWOOF
SOMETHING REALLY IS UP WITH TODAY...
BUT THAT'S GOOD LUCK.
HUH?

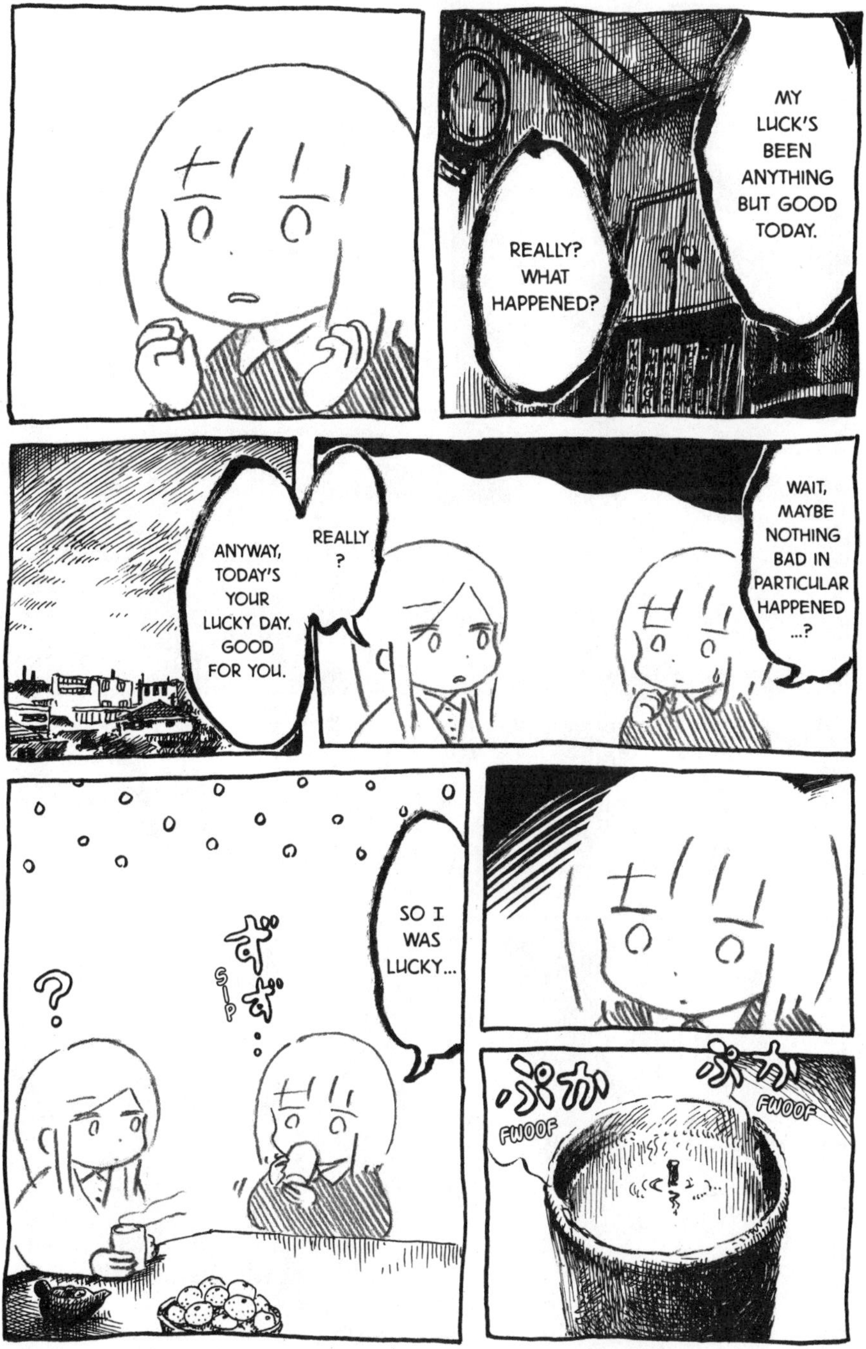
MY LUCK'S BEEN ANYTHING BUT GOOD TODAY.
REALLY? WHAT HAPPENED?
WAIT, MAYBE NOTHING BAD IN PARTICULAR HAPPENED ...?
REALLY ?
ANYWAY, TODAY'S YOUR LUCKY DAY. GOOD FOR YOU.
ぷか
FWOOF
ぷか
FWOOF
SO I WAS LUCKY...
ずず
SIP
?

No Details

Just about any object in this world has tiny details to it. Something that may look smooth will have small scratches or a kind of texture to it. And if you use a microscope, you'd be able to see that they're made up of molecules and atoms.

Go out onto the street corner to take a careful look and you'll find details everywhere. Structures have individual screws on them. You can trace the wood grain on a plank of wood with your hand or your finger. Where there's electricity, there are electrical lines. Follow the cables and you can figure out where the switches that use that electricity are. For all I know, every drop of rain could be unique.

We're able to naturally ignore details despite them being there. So, we generally ignore them when we don't have any use for the minutia, but there are a countless number of things we could trace with our eyes at a glance. All that matters for us is to understand things on the level that we have a personal use for.

I've been thinking about things free of details. Like animation, right? Trees in the background won't sway in the wind, and people who aren't talking don't move an inch. The only parts that are moving all around are the areas that the viewers' eyes are focused on. I don't mean to generalize, there are some detailed works of animation, but, at some point, they all stop having details. They're able to exist because they limit what is being drawn.

I think there's something within details. I can't help but think about how we ignore them if they are mundane. It's possible that we're ignoring some incredibly important things. There could be a ghost on the street corner, but we'd ignore it if it was indistinguishable from a human (though I'm sure we'd notice if someone we needed to interact with was a ghost).

Still, it's not as if we can keep track of every detail we come across as we live our lives. Like how there might be a new species of winged insect in a room we enter, or how the number of specks of dust on a desk add up to a lucky number.

We live our lives while ignoring even details that we can't believe when we first see them. We live in an animation-esque world.

December 5, 2012

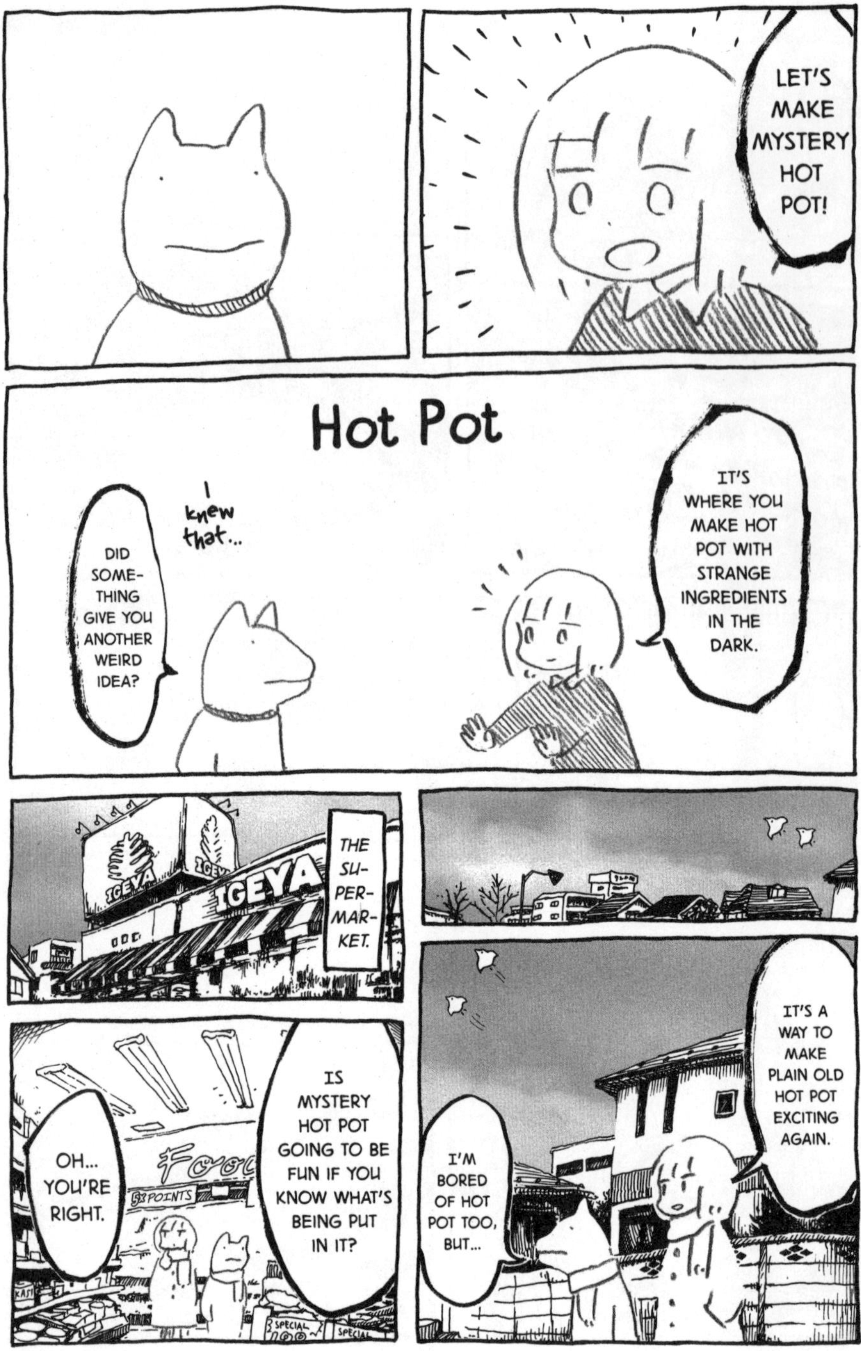
LET'S MAKE MYSTERY HOT POT!
Hot Pot
IT'S WHERE YOU MAKE HOT POT WITH STRANGE INGREDIENTS IN THE DARK.
I knew that...
DID SOME-THING GIVE YOU ANOTHER WEIRD IDEA?
IGEYA
IGEYA
IGEYA
THE SU-PER-MAR-KET.
IT'S A WAY TO MAKE PLAIN OLD HOT POT EXCITING AGAIN.
I'M BORED OF HOT POT TOO, BUT...
IS MYSTERY HOT POT GOING TO BE FUN IF YOU KNOW WHAT'S BEING PUT IN IT?
OH... YOU'RE RIGHT.
SPECIAL
SPECIAL

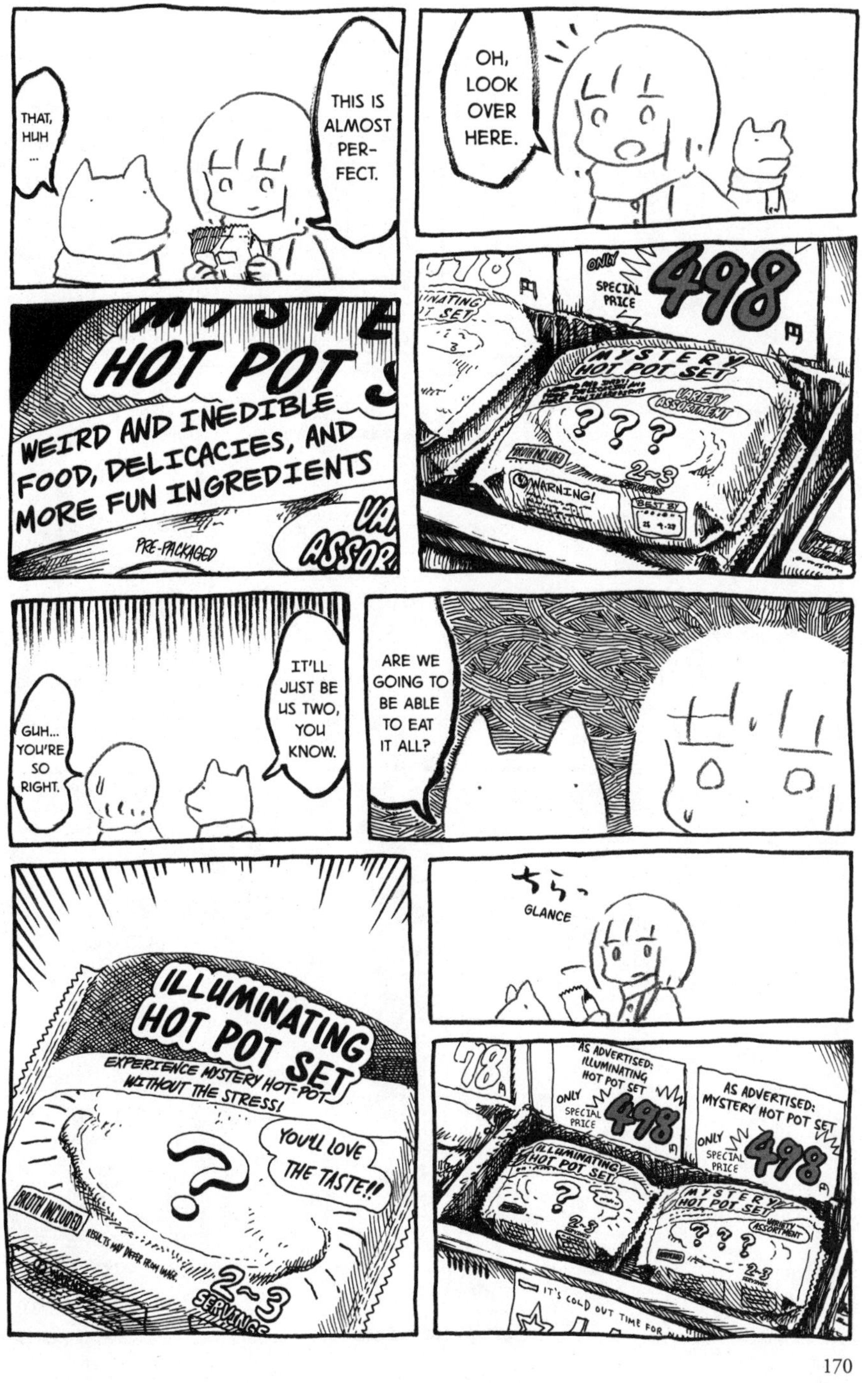
OH, LOOK OVER HERE.
THIS IS ALMOST PERFECT.
THAT, HUH ...
ONLY SPECIAL PRICE 498 円
MYSTERY HOT POT SET
VARIETY ASSORTMENT
???
BROTH INCLUDED
2~3
WARNING!
BEST BY
HOT POT S
WEIRD AND INEDIBLE FOOD, DELICACIES, AND MORE FUN INGREDIENTS
PRE-PACKAGED
ARE WE GOING TO BE ABLE TO EAT IT ALL?
IT'LL JUST BE US TWO, YOU KNOW.
GUH... YOU'RE SO RIGHT.
ちらっ
GLANCE
AS ADVERTISED: ILLUMINATING HOT POT SET
ONLY SPECIAL PRICE 498 円
AS ADVERTISED: MYSTERY HOT POT SET
ONLY SPECIAL PRICE 498 円
IT'S COLD OUT TIME FOR
ILLUMINATING HOT POT SET
EXPERIENCE MYSTERY HOT-POT WITHOUT THE STRESS!
?
YOU'LL LOVE THE TASTE!!
BROTH INCLUDED
RESULTS MAY DIFFER FROM IMAGE.
2~3 SERVINGS

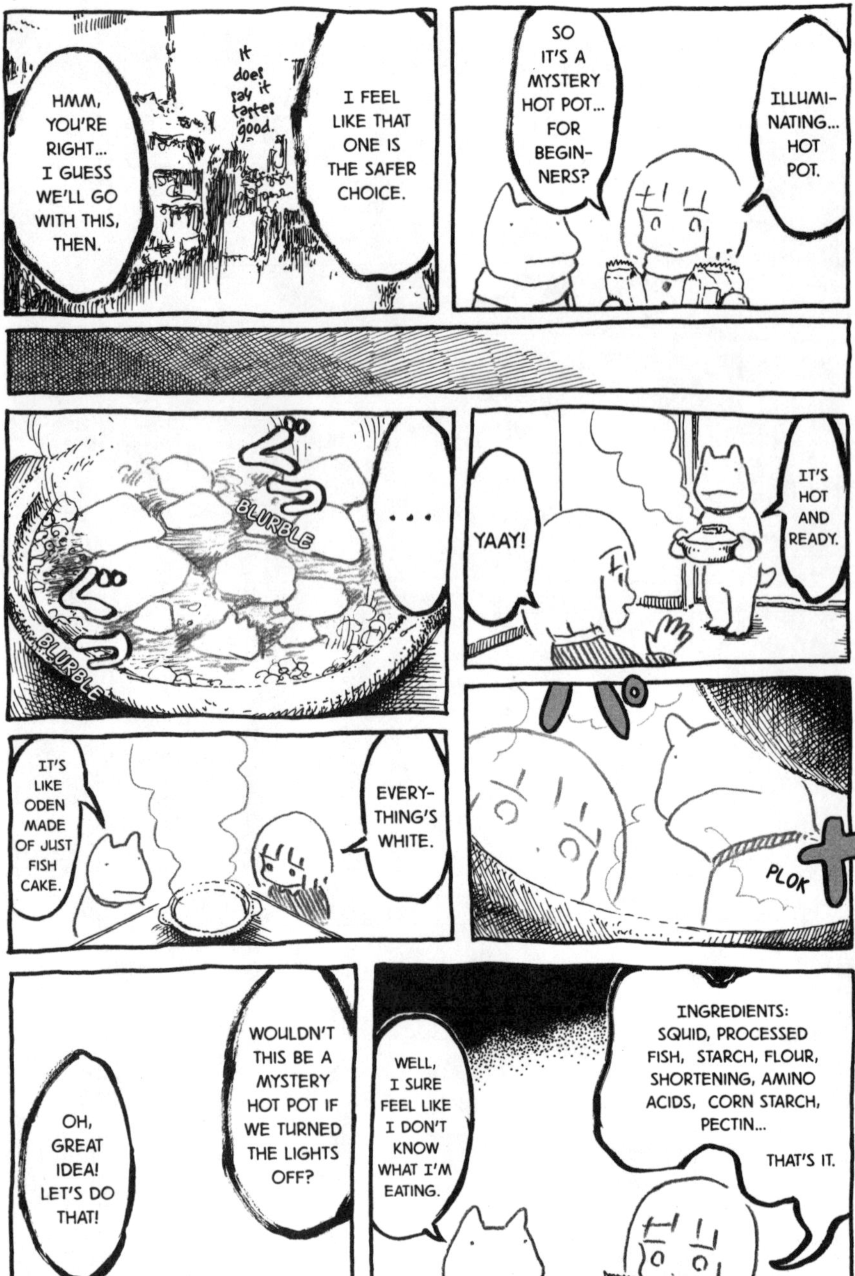
ILLUMINATING... HOT POT.
SO IT'S A MYSTERY HOT POT... FOR BEGINNERS?
I FEEL LIKE THAT ONE IS THE SAFER CHOICE.
It does say it tastes good.
HMM, YOU'RE RIGHT... I GUESS WE'LL GO WITH THIS, THEN.
IT'S HOT AND READY.
YAAY!
...
BLURBLE
BLURBLE
PLOK
EVERYTHING'S WHITE.
IT'S LIKE ODEN MADE OF JUST FISH CAKE.
INGREDIENTS: SQUID, PROCESSED FISH, STARCH, FLOUR, SHORTENING, AMINO ACIDS, CORN STARCH, PECTIN...
THAT'S IT.
WELL, I SURE FEEL LIKE I DON'T KNOW WHAT I'M EATING.
WOULDN'T THIS BE A MYSTERY HOT POT IF WE TURNED THE LIGHTS OFF?
OH, GREAT IDEA! LET'S DO THAT!

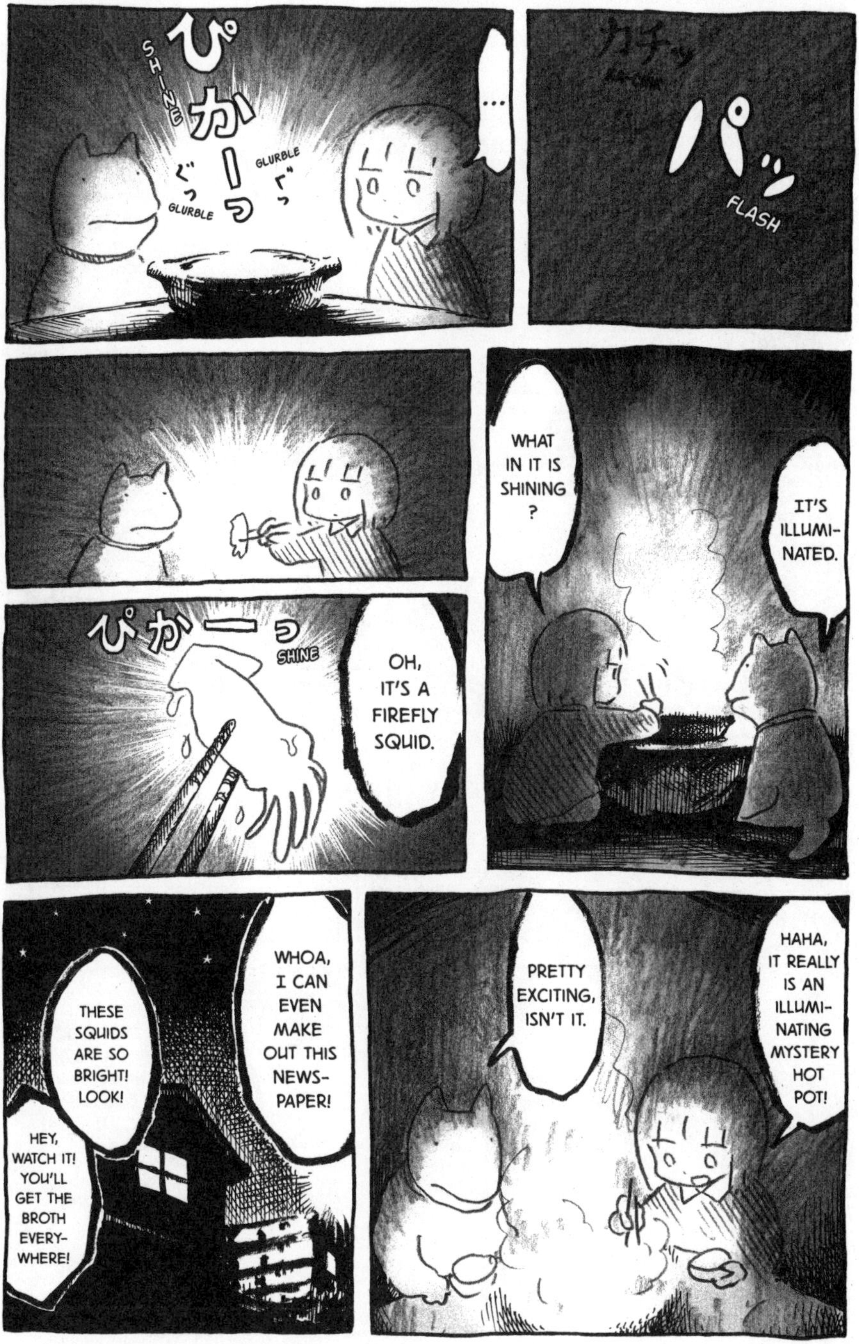
カチッ
パッ
FLASH
ぴかーっ
SHINE
ぐっ
GLURBLE
ぐっ
GLURBLE
...
WHAT IN IT IS SHINING?
IT'S ILLUMINATED.
ぴかーっ
SHINE
OH, IT'S A FIREFLY SQUID.
HAHA, IT REALLY IS AN ILLUMINATING MYSTERY HOT POT!
PRETTY EXCITING, ISN'T IT.
WHOA, I CAN EVEN MAKE OUT THIS NEWSPAPER!
THESE SQUIDS ARE SO BRIGHT! LOOK!
HEY, WATCH IT! YOU'LL GET THE BROTH EVERYWHERE!

THE PERFECT SUNDAY

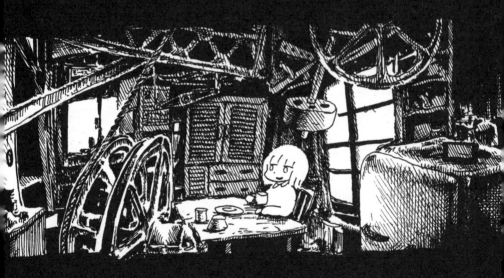

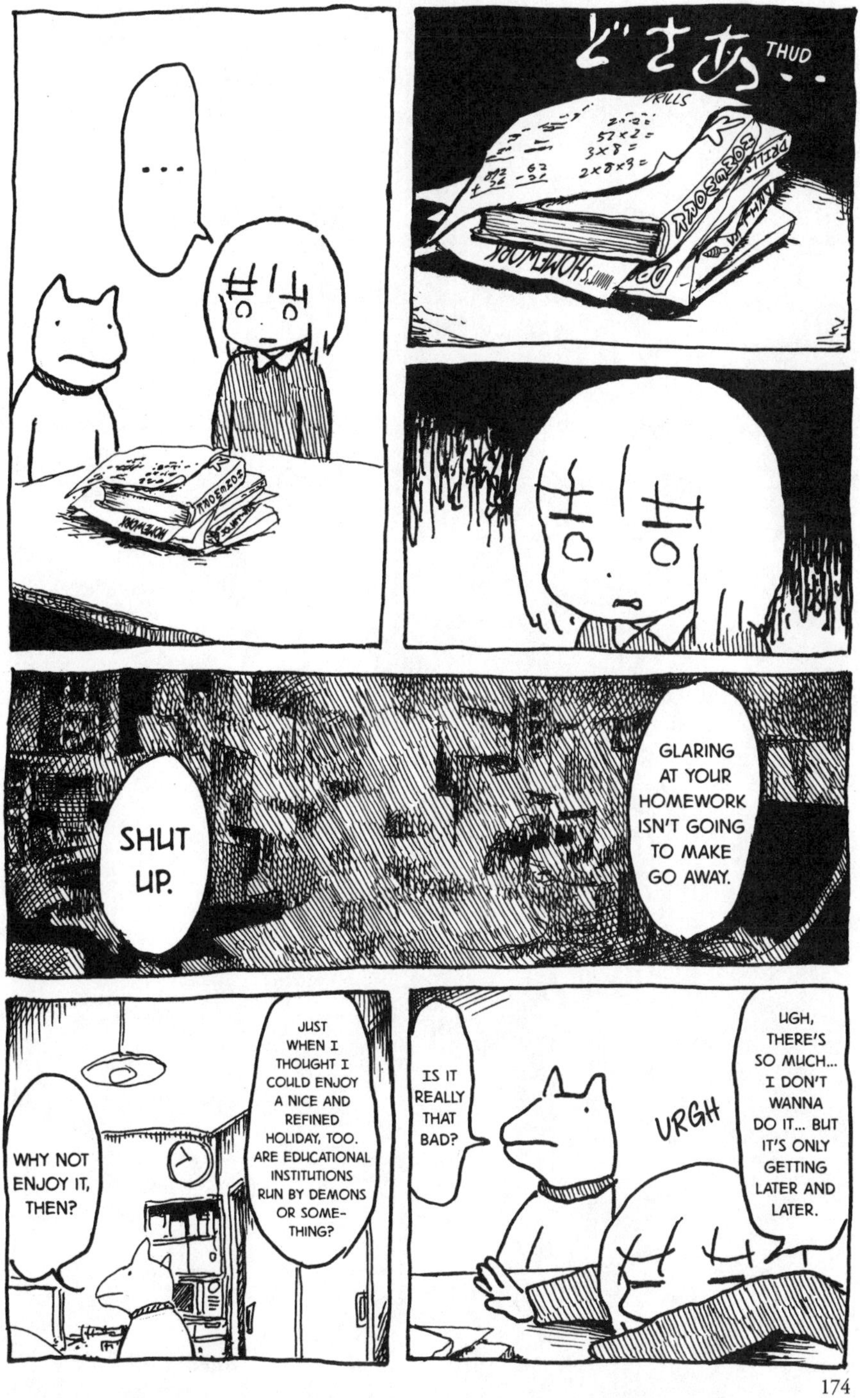
どさあ
THUD
DRILLS
52×2 =
3×8 =
2×8×3 =
HOMEWORK
...
GLARING AT YOUR HOMEWORK ISN'T GOING TO MAKE GO AWAY.
SHUT UP.
UGH, THERE'S SO MUCH... I DON'T WANNA DO IT... BUT IT'S ONLY GETTING LATER AND LATER.
URGH
IS IT REALLY THAT BAD?
JUST WHEN I THOUGHT I COULD ENJOY A NICE AND REFINED HOLIDAY, TOO. ARE EDUCATIONAL INSTITUTIONS RUN BY DEMONS OR SOME-THING?
WHY NOT ENJOY IT, THEN?

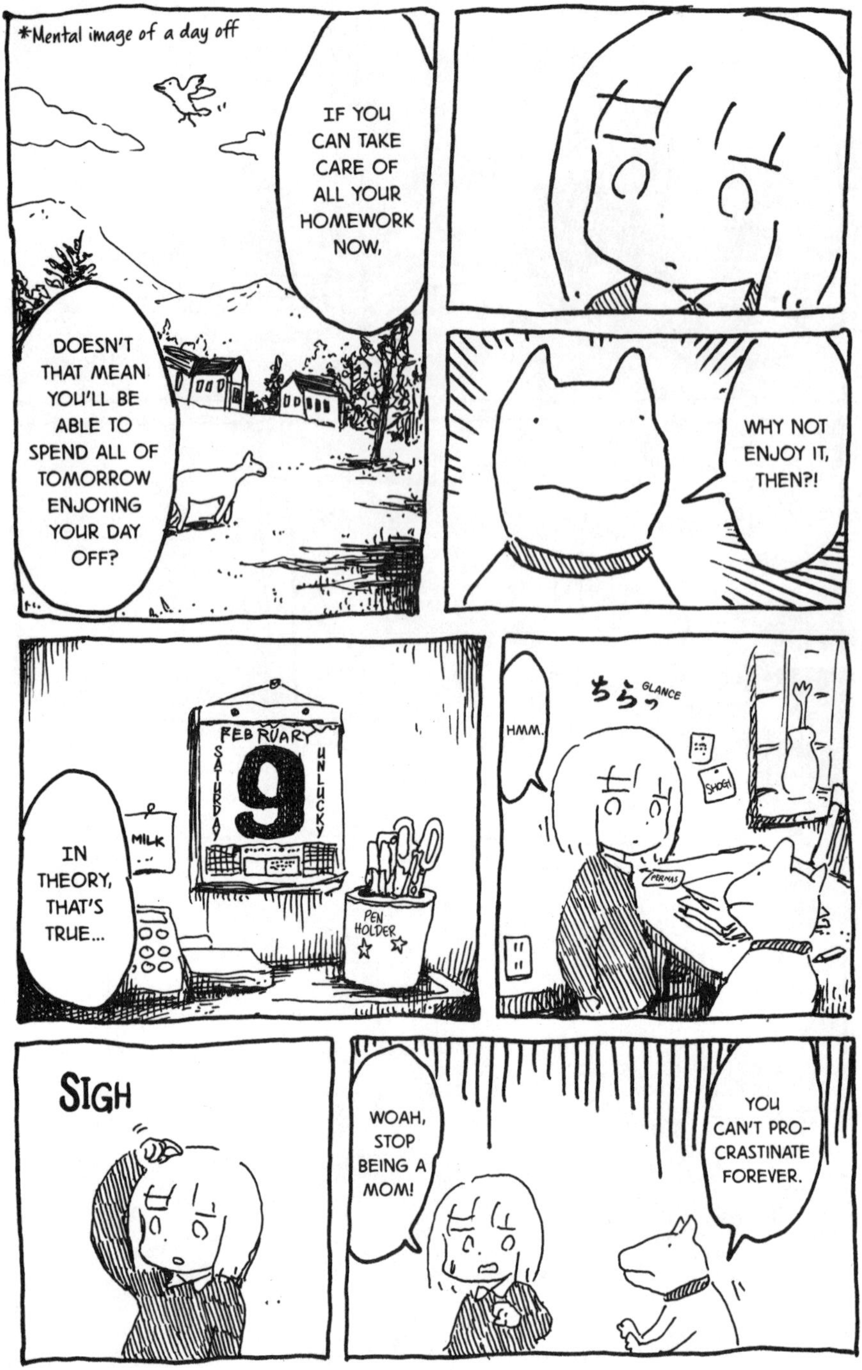

WHY NOT ENJOY IT, THEN?!
*Mental image of a day off
IF YOU CAN TAKE CARE OF ALL YOUR HOMEWORK NOW,
DOESN'T THAT MEAN YOU'LL BE ABLE TO SPEND ALL OF TOMORROW ENJOYING YOUR DAY OFF?
ちらっ GLANCE
SHOGI
HMM.
FEBRUARY
SATURDAY
9
UNLUCKY
MILK
PEN HOLDER
IN THEORY, THAT'S TRUE...
YOU CAN'T PRO-CRASTINATE FOREVER.
WOAH, STOP BEING A MOM!
SIGH

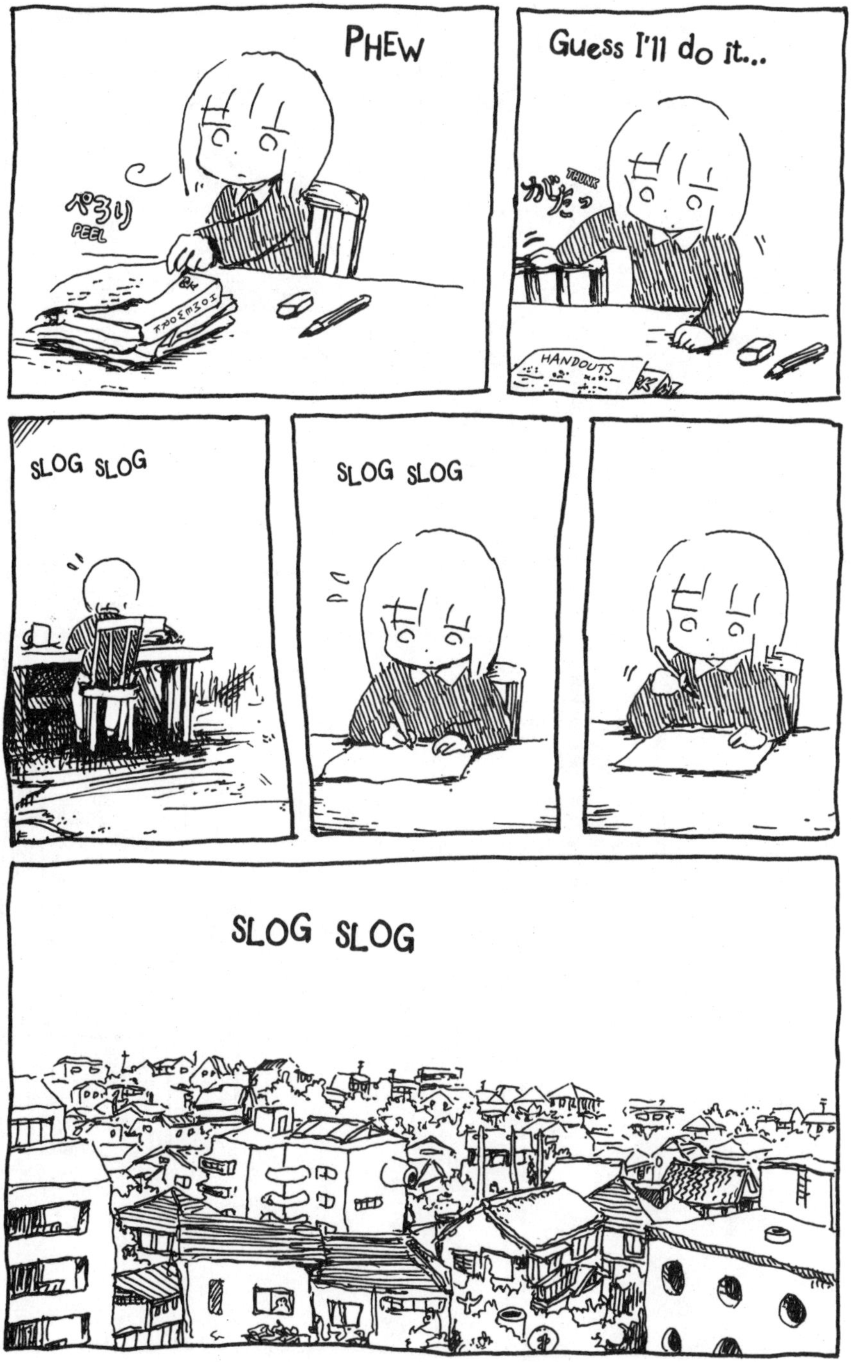
Guess I'll do it...
がたっ
THUNK
HANDOUTS
PHEW
ぺろり
PEEL
SLOG SLOG
SLOG SLOG
SLOG SLOG

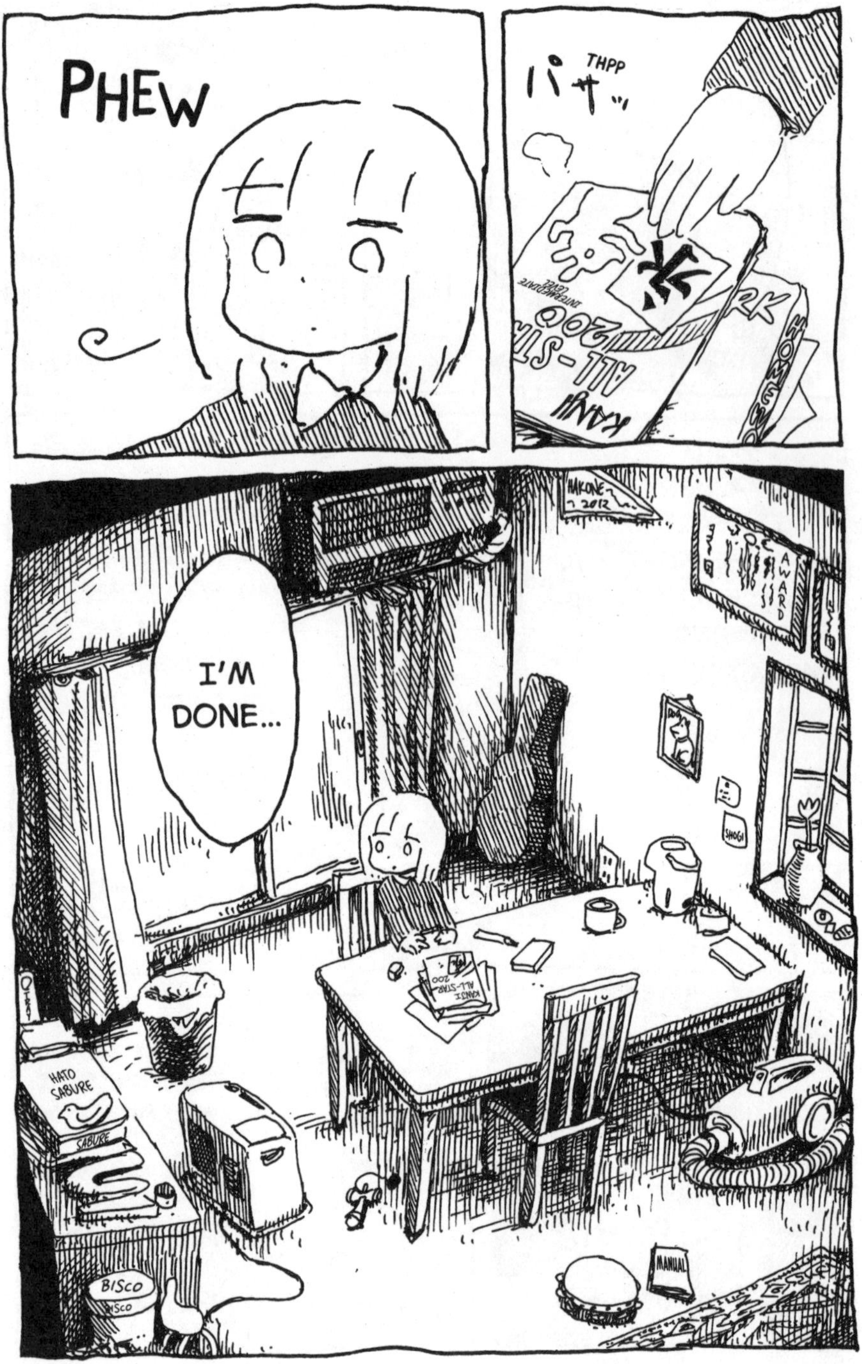

THPP
パサッ
KANJI ALL-STAR 200
INTERMEDIATE LEVEL
PHEW
I'M DONE...
HAKONE 2012
AWARD
SHOGI
HATO SABURE
SABURE
KANJI ALL-STAR 200
BISCO
BISCO
MANUAL

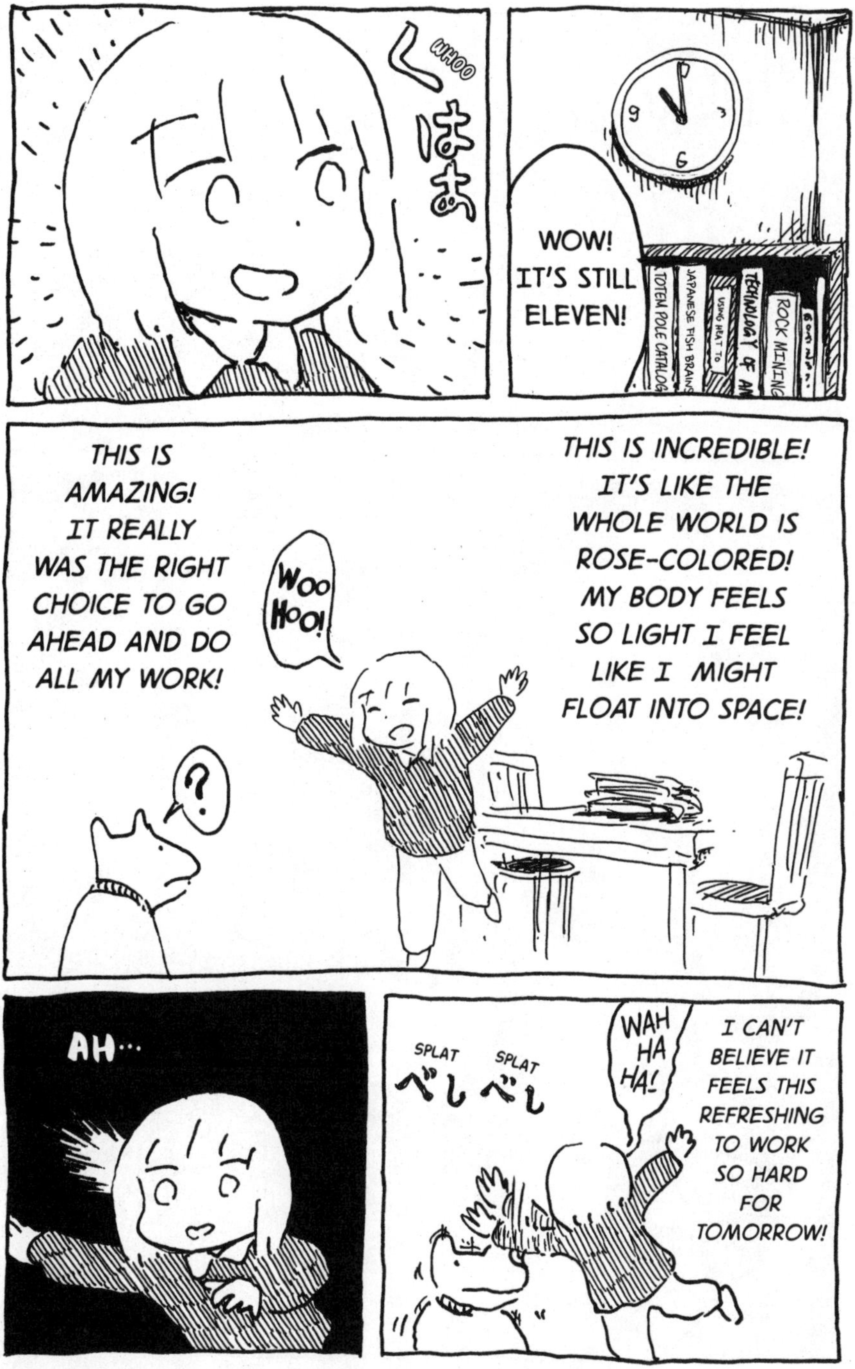
ROCK MINING
USING HEAT TO
JAPANESE FISH BRAINS
TOTEM POLE CATALOG
WOW! IT'S STILL ELEVEN!
WHOO
くはぁ
THIS IS INCREDIBLE! IT'S LIKE THE WHOLE WORLD IS ROSE-COLORED! MY BODY FEELS SO LIGHT I FEEL LIKE I MIGHT FLOAT INTO SPACE!
WOO HOO!
THIS IS AMAZING! IT REALLY WAS THE RIGHT CHOICE TO GO AHEAD AND DO ALL MY WORK!
?
I CAN'T BELIEVE IT FEELS THIS REFRESHING TO WORK SO HARD FOR TOMORROW!
WAH HA HA!
SPLAT SPLAT
べしべし
AH...

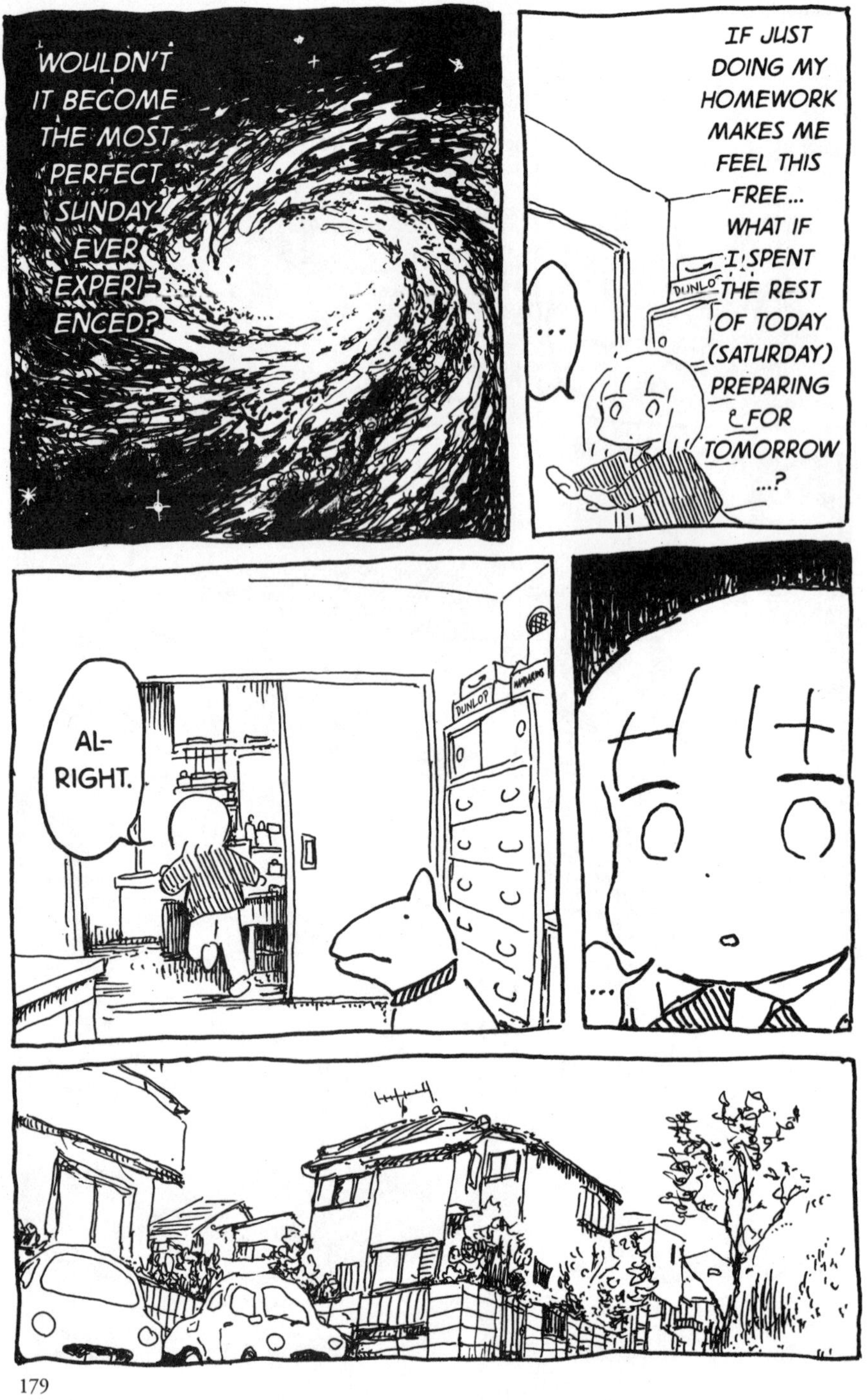
IF JUST DOING MY HOMEWORK MAKES ME FEEL THIS FREE... WHAT IF I SPENT THE REST OF TODAY (SATURDAY) PREPARING FOR TOMORROW ...?
...
WOULDN'T IT BECOME THE MOST PERFECT SUNDAY EVER EXPERI-ENCED?
...
AL-RIGHT.

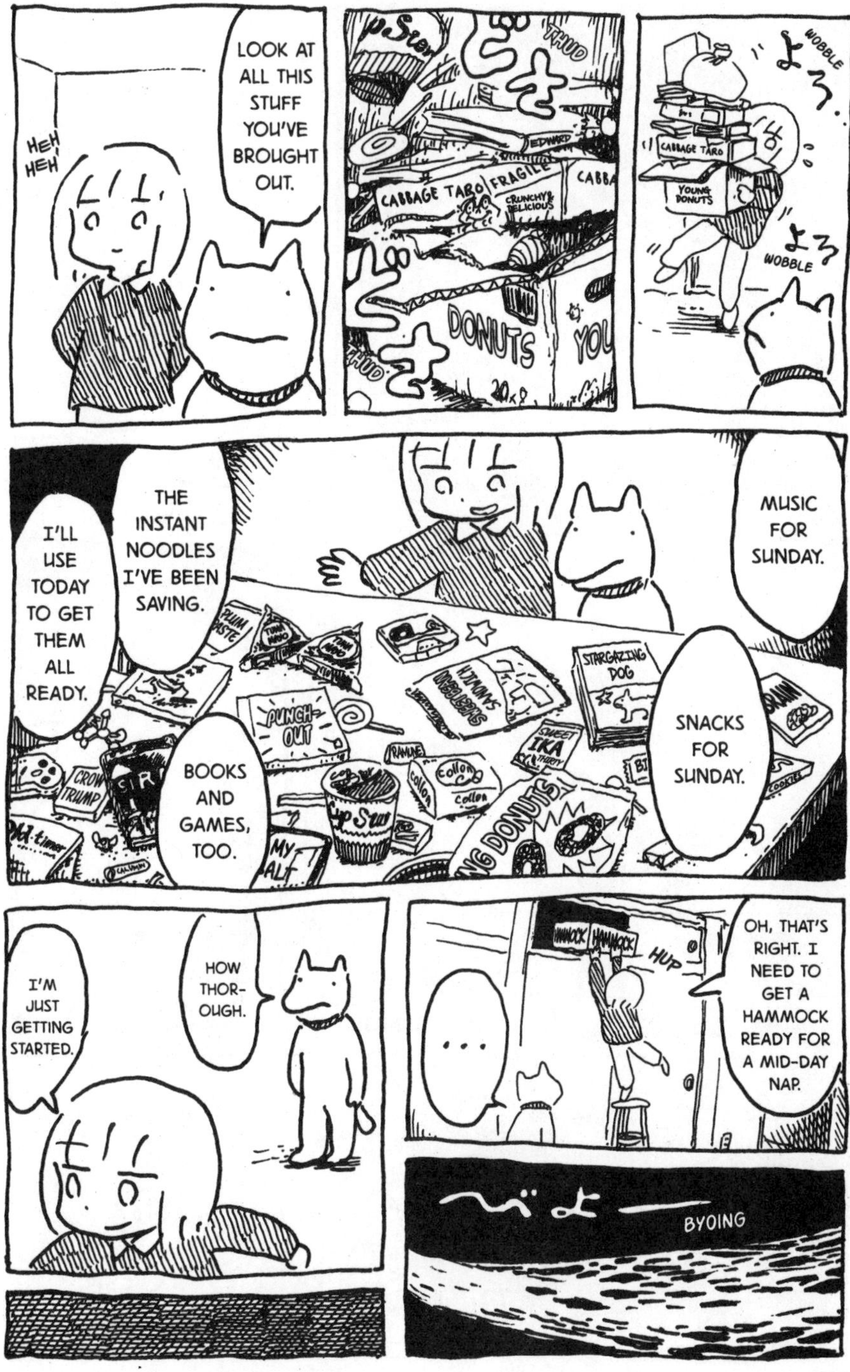
よろ
WOBBLE
CABBAGE TARO
YOUNG DONUTS
よろ
WOBBLE
どさ
THUD
CABBAGE TARO
FRAGILE
CRUNCHY & DELICIOUS
DONUTS
どさ
THUD
LOOK AT ALL THIS STUFF YOU'VE BROUGHT OUT.
HEH HEH
MUSIC FOR SUNDAY.
THE INSTANT NOODLES I'VE BEEN SAVING.
I'LL USE TODAY TO GET THEM ALL READY.
STARGAZING DOG
PUNCH-OUT
SWEET IKA
SNACKS FOR SUNDAY.
CROW TRUMP
BOOKS AND GAMES, TOO.
OH, THAT'S RIGHT. I NEED TO GET A HAMMOCK READY FOR A MID-DAY NAP.
HAMMOCK
HAMMOCK
HUP
...
びよー
BYOING
HOW THOROUGH.
I'M JUST GETTING STARTED.

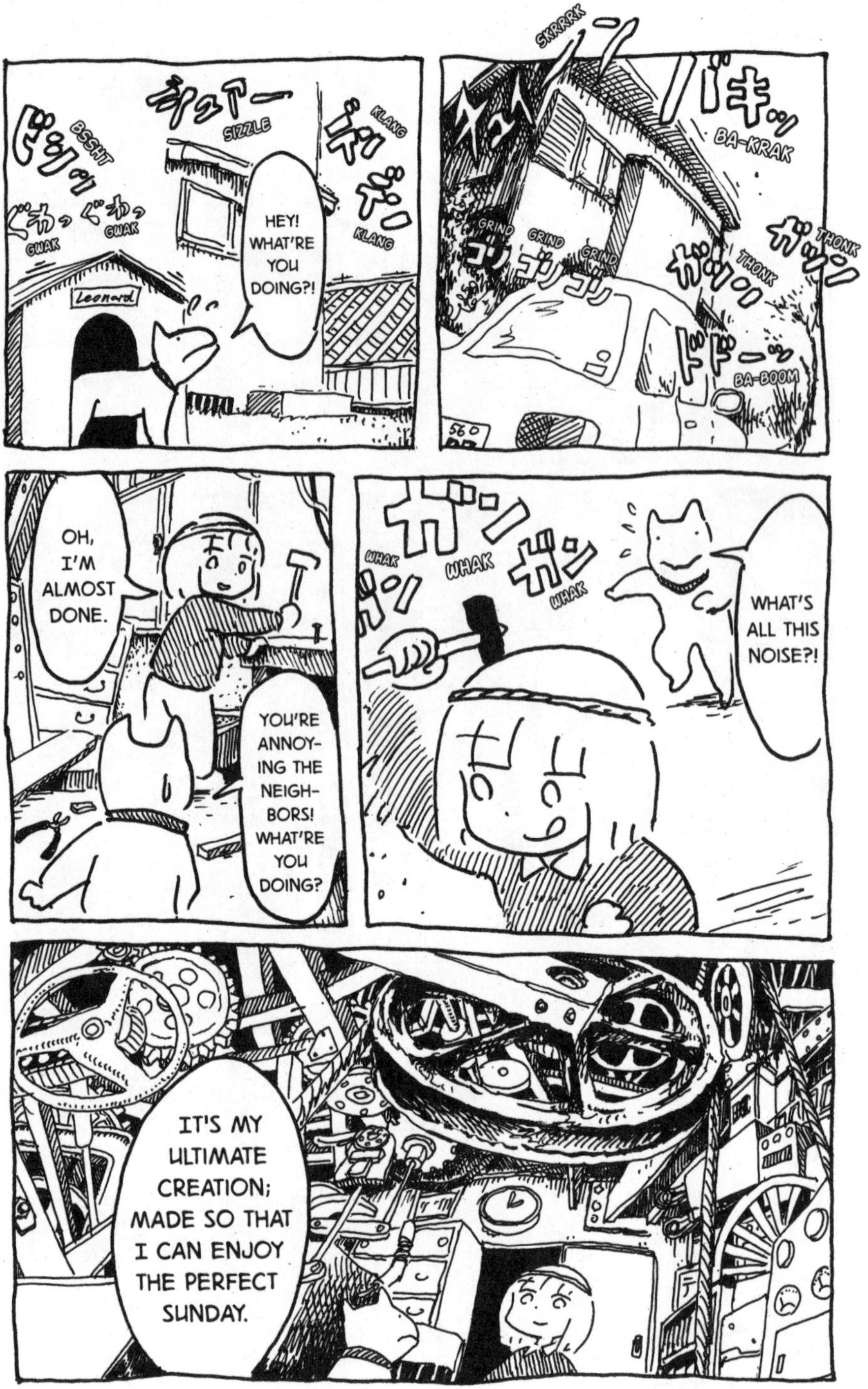
SKRRRK
BA-KRAK
GRIND
GRIND
GRIND
THONK
THONK
BA-BOOM
SIZZLE
KLANG
BSSHT
HEY! WHAT'RE YOU DOING?!
KLANG
GWAK
GWAK
WHAK
WHAT'S ALL THIS NOISE?!
WHAK
WHAK
OH, I'M ALMOST DONE.
YOU'RE ANNOY-ING THE NEIGH-BORS! WHAT'RE YOU DOING?
IT'S MY ULTIMATE CREATION; MADE SO THAT I CAN ENJOY THE PERFECT SUNDAY.

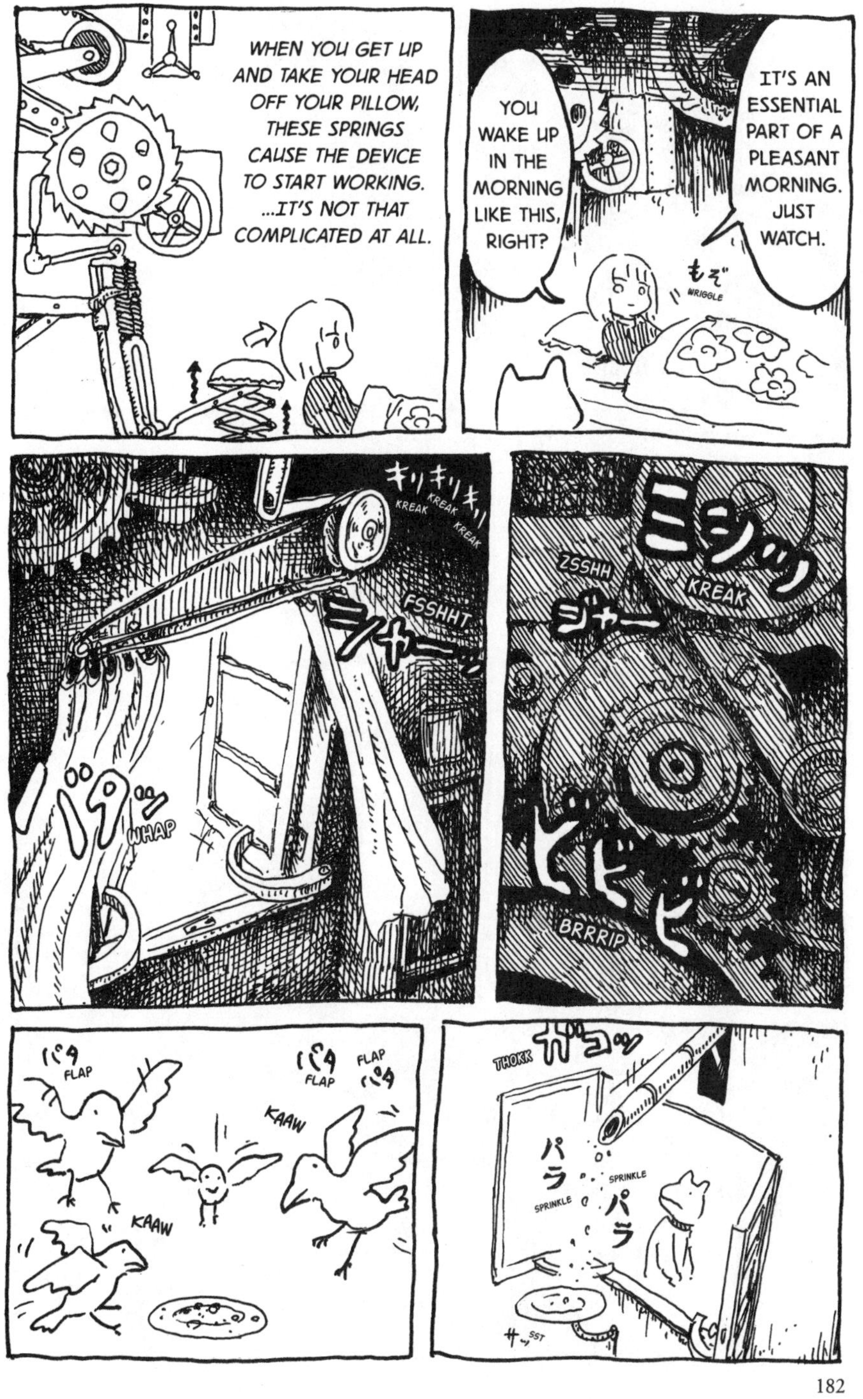
IT'S AN ESSENTIAL PART OF A PLEASANT MORNING. JUST WATCH.
YOU WAKE UP IN THE MORNING LIKE THIS, RIGHT?
もぞ WRIGGLE
WHEN YOU GET UP AND TAKE YOUR HEAD OFF YOUR PILLOW, THESE SPRINGS CAUSE THE DEVICE TO START WORKING. ...IT'S NOT THAT COMPLICATED AT ALL.
ミシッ KREAK
ZSSHH ジャー
ビビビ
BRRRIP
キリキリキリ KREAK KREAK KREAK
FSSHHT シャー
パタッ WHAP
THOKK ガコッ
パラ SPRINKLE
パラ SPRINKLE
サッ SST
パタ FLAP
パタ FLAP
FLAP パタ
KAAW
KAAW

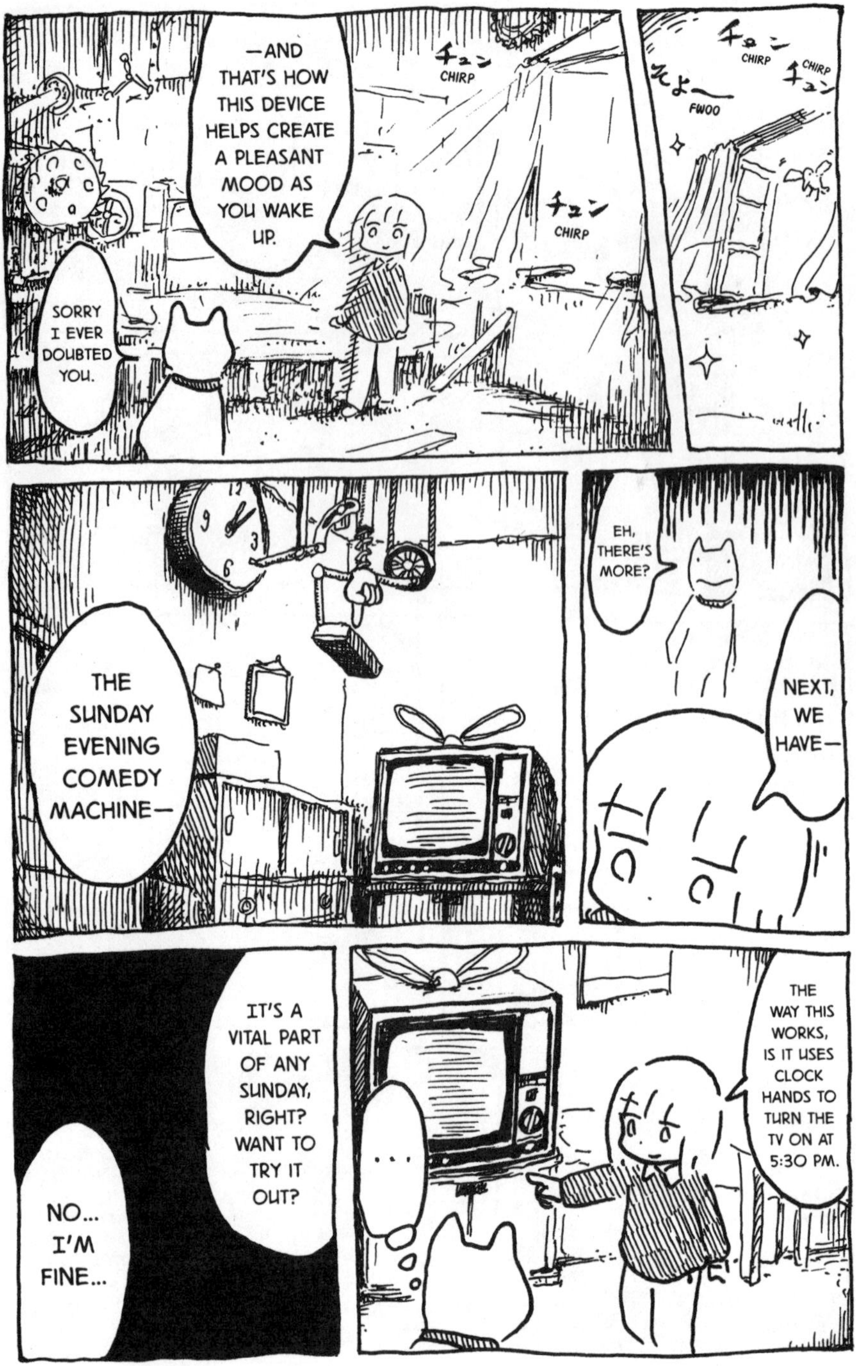
チュン
CHIRP
チュン
CHIRP
そよ〜
FWOO
チュン
CHIRP
—AND THAT'S HOW THIS DEVICE HELPS CREATE A PLEASANT MOOD AS YOU WAKE UP.
チュン
CHIRP
SORRY I EVER DOUBTED YOU.
EH, THERE'S MORE?
NEXT, WE HAVE—
THE SUNDAY EVENING COMEDY MACHINE—
THE WAY THIS WORKS, IS IT USES CLOCK HANDS TO TURN THE TV ON AT 5:30 PM.
. . .
IT'S A VITAL PART OF ANY SUNDAY, RIGHT? WANT TO TRY IT OUT?
NO... I'M FINE...

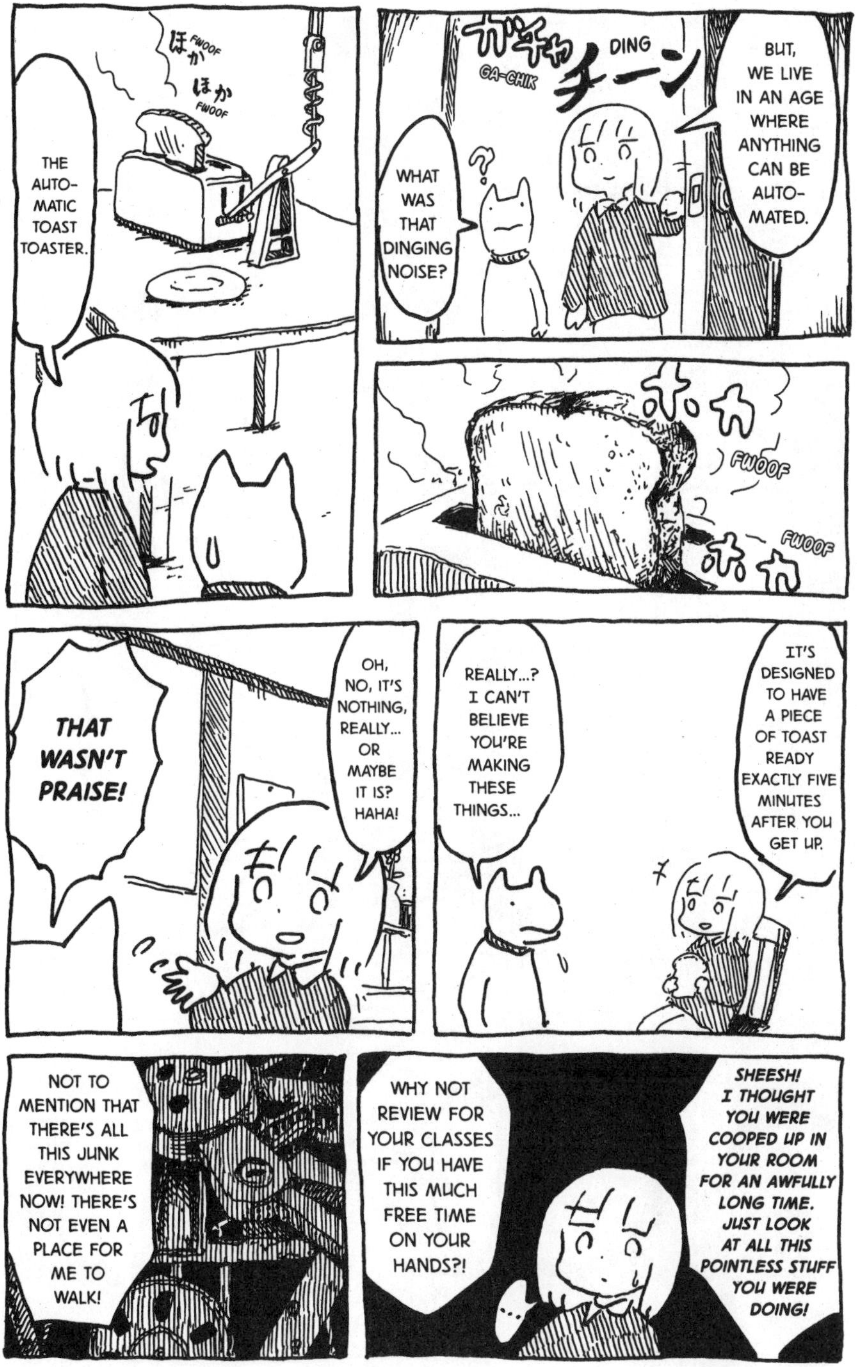
ガチャ
GA-CHIK
チーン
DING
BUT, WE LIVE IN AN AGE WHERE ANYTHING CAN BE AUTO-MATED.
WHAT WAS THAT DINGING NOISE?
ホカ
FWOOF
ホカ
FWOOF
ほか
FWOOF
ほか
FWOOF
THE AUTO-MATIC TOAST TOASTER.
IT'S DESIGNED TO HAVE A PIECE OF TOAST READY EXACTLY FIVE MINUTES AFTER YOU GET UP.
REALLY...? I CAN'T BELIEVE YOU'RE MAKING THESE THINGS...
OH, NO, IT'S NOTHING, REALLY... OR MAYBE IT IS? HAHA!
THAT WASN'T PRAISE!
SHEESH! I THOUGHT YOU WERE COOPED UP IN YOUR ROOM FOR AN AWFULLY LONG TIME. JUST LOOK AT ALL THIS POINTLESS STUFF YOU WERE DOING!
WHY NOT REVIEW FOR YOUR CLASSES IF YOU HAVE THIS MUCH FREE TIME ON YOUR HANDS?!
...
NOT TO MENTION THAT THERE'S ALL THIS JUNK EVERYWHERE NOW! THERE'S NOT EVEN A PLACE FOR ME TO WALK!

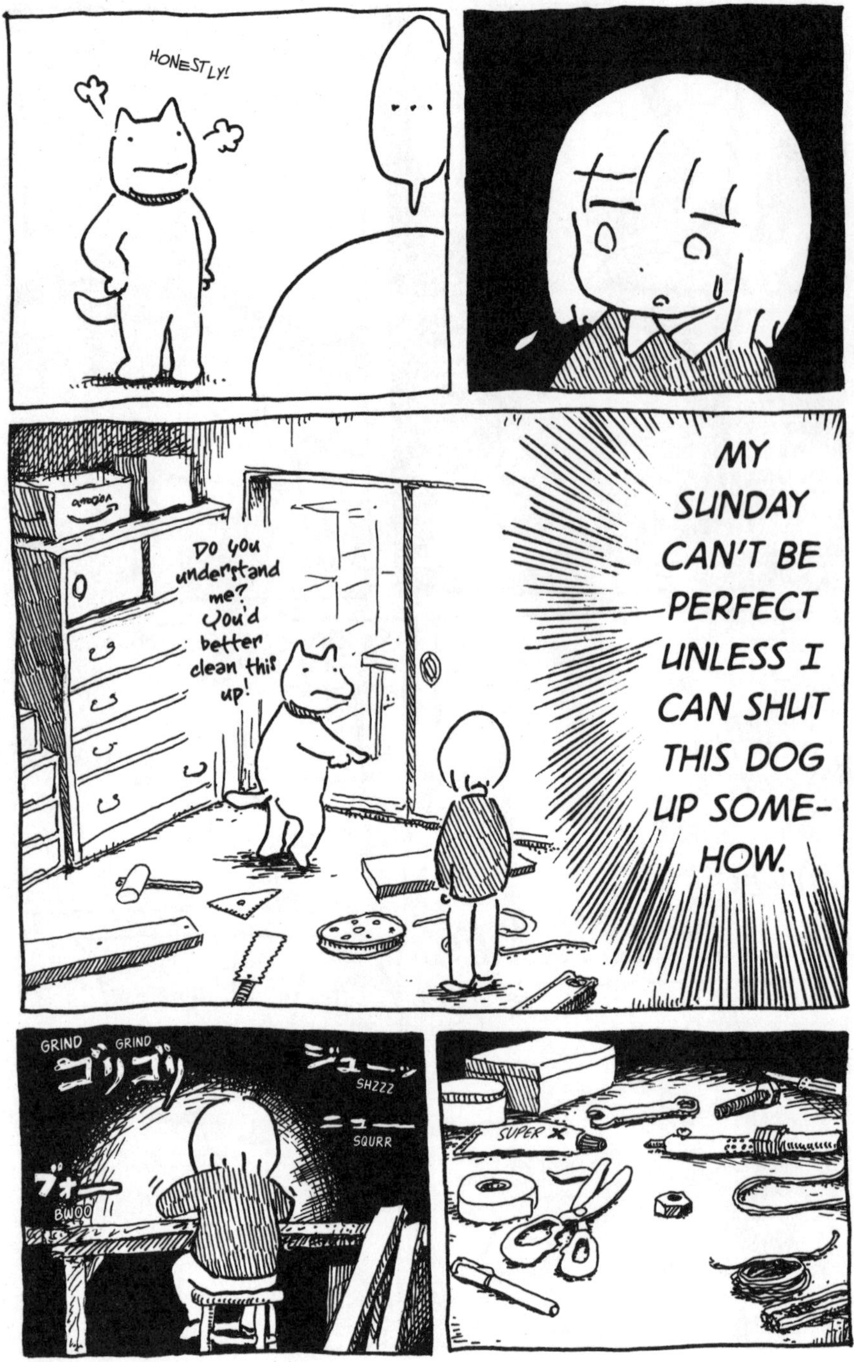
HONESTLY!
...
MY SUNDAY CAN'T BE PERFECT UNLESS I CAN SHUT THIS DOG UP SOMEHOW.
Do you understand me? You'd better clean this up!
ジューッ
SHZZZ
GRIND GRIND
ゴリゴリ
ニュー
SQURR
ブォー
BWOO
SUPER X

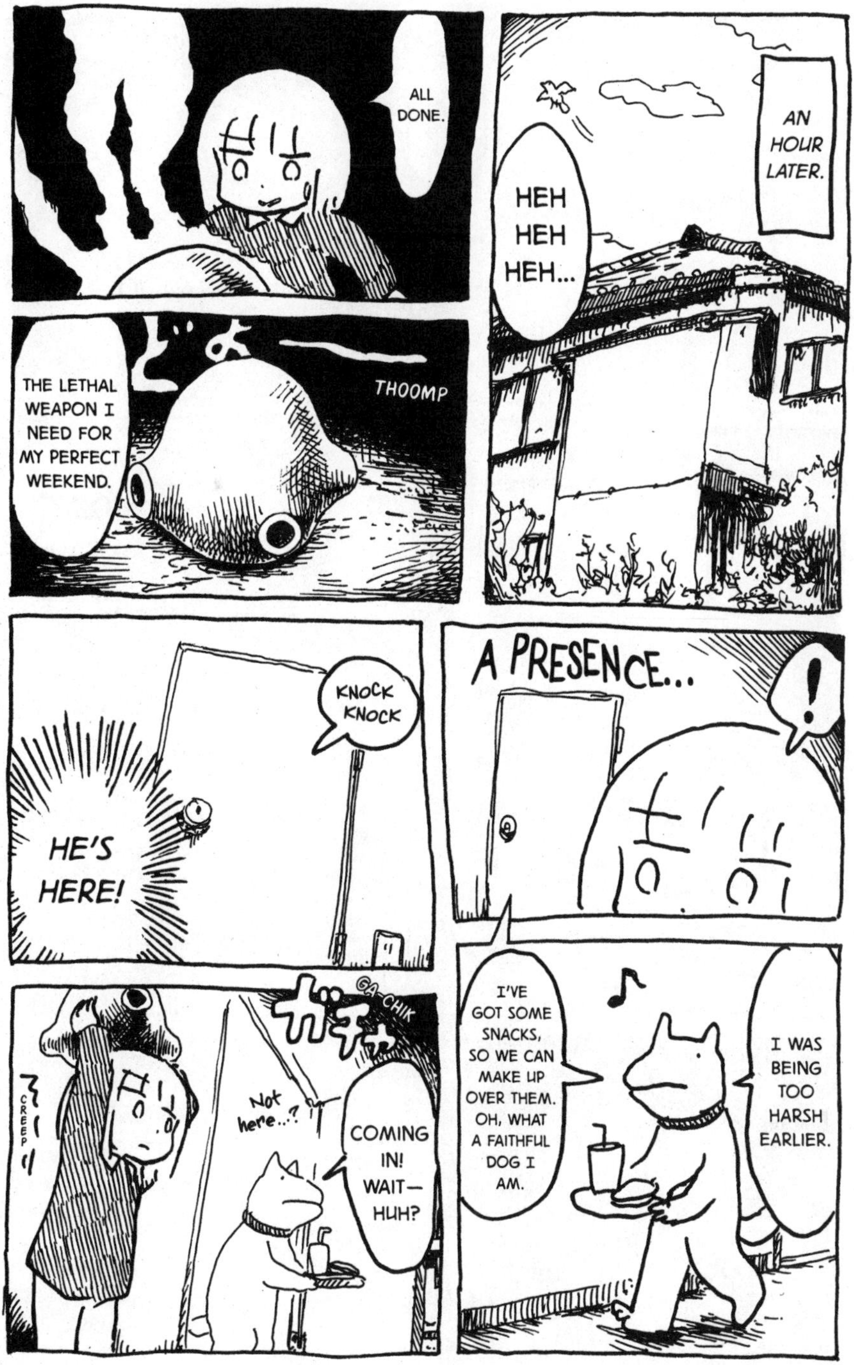
AN HOUR LATER.
HEH HEH HEH...
ALL DONE.
THE LETHAL WEAPON I NEED FOR MY PERFECT WEEKEND.
THOOMP
A PRESENCE...
!
KNOCK KNOCK
HE'S HERE!
I WAS BEING TOO HARSH EARLIER.
I'VE GOT SOME SNACKS, SO WE CAN MAKE UP OVER THEM. OH, WHAT A FAITHFUL DOG I AM.
ガチャ
GA-CHIK
COMING IN! WAIT— HUH?
Not here...?
CREEP

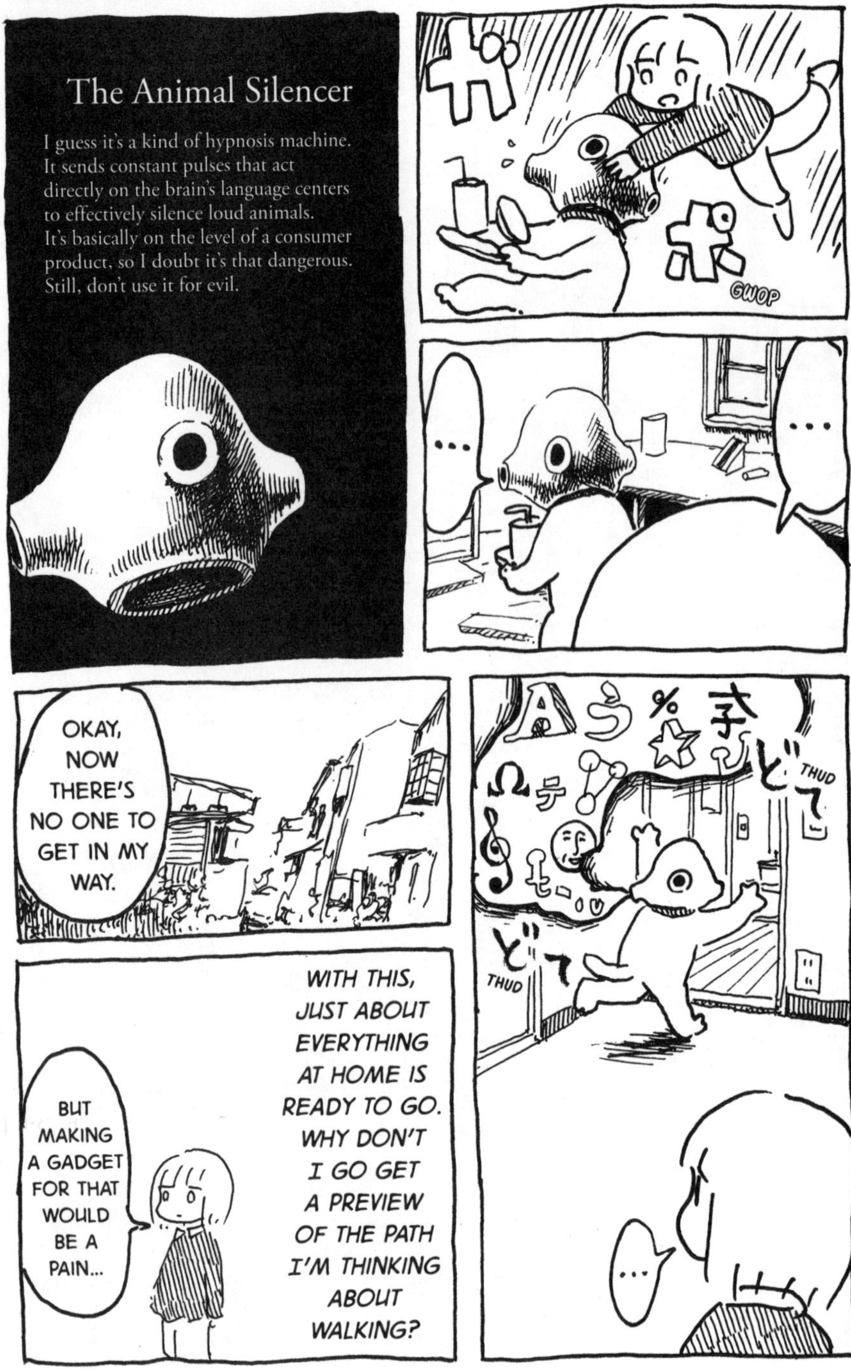
ガ ポ
GWOP
...
...
The Animal Silencer
I guess it's a kind of hypnosis machine. It sends constant pulses that act directly on the brain's language centers to effectively silence loud animals. It's basically on the level of a consumer product, so I doubt it's that dangerous. Still, don't use it for evil.
どて
THUD
どて
THUD
...
OKAY, NOW THERE'S NO ONE TO GET IN MY WAY.
WITH THIS, JUST ABOUT EVERYTHING AT HOME IS READY TO GO. WHY DON'T I GO GET A PREVIEW OF THE PATH I'M THINKING ABOUT WALKING?
BUT MAKING A GADGET FOR THAT WOULD BE A PAIN...

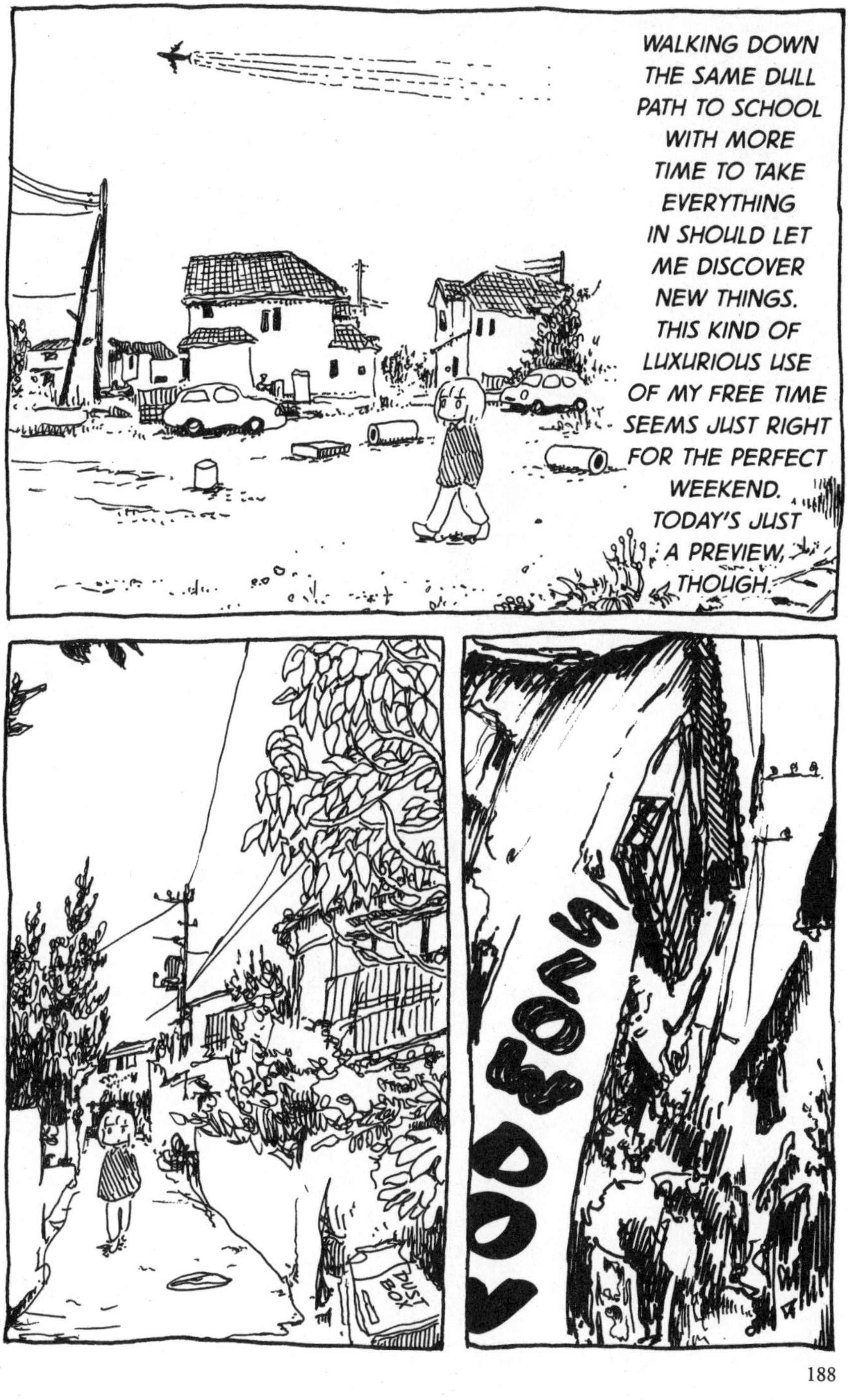
WALKING DOWN THE SAME DULL PATH TO SCHOOL WITH MORE TIME TO TAKE EVERYTHING IN SHOULD LET ME DISCOVER NEW THINGS. THIS KIND OF LUXURIOUS USE OF MY FREE TIME SEEMS JUST RIGHT FOR THE PERFECT WEEKEND. TODAY'S JUST A PREVIEW, THOUGH.
DUST BOX

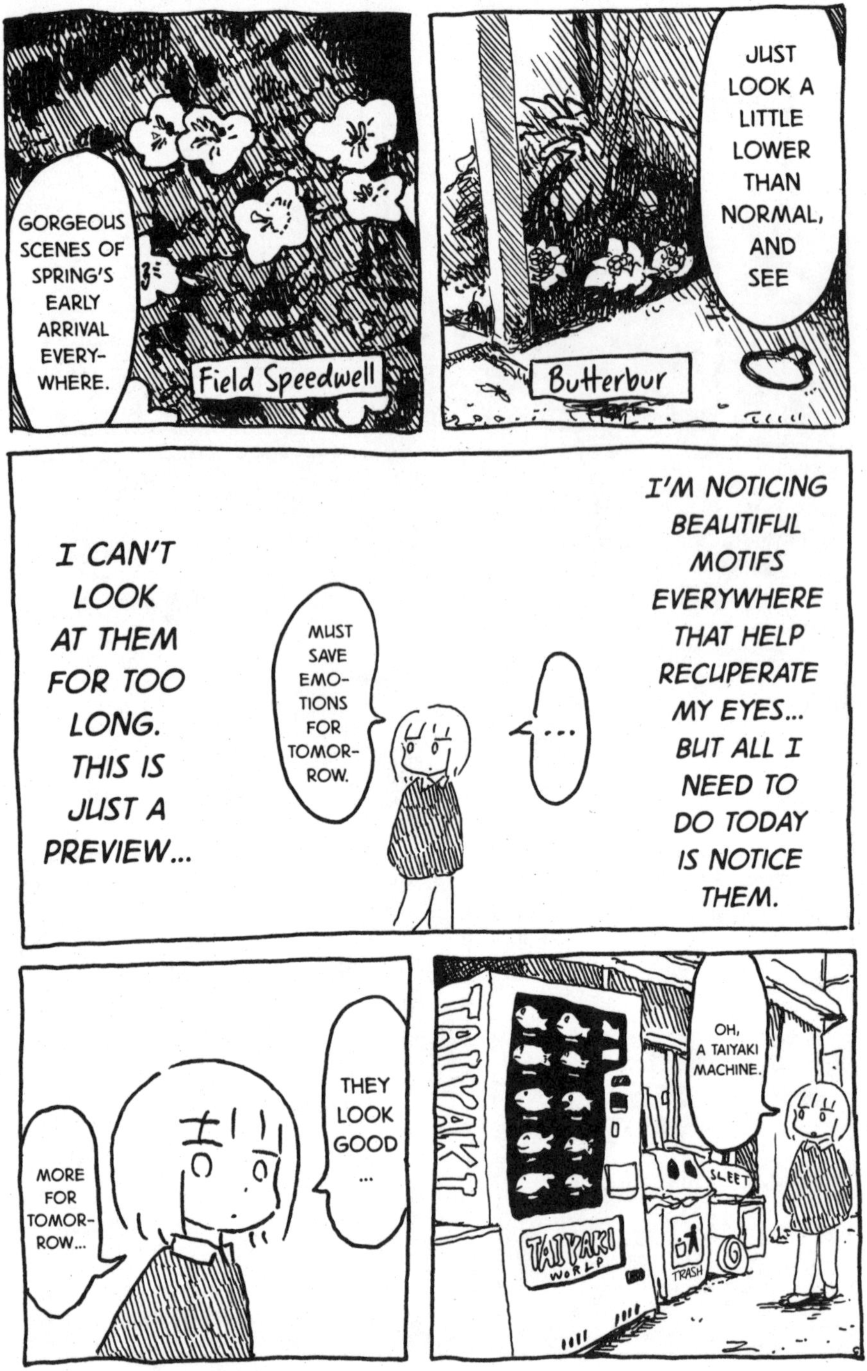
JUST LOOK A LITTLE LOWER THAN NORMAL, AND SEE
Butterbur
GORGEOUS SCENES OF SPRING'S EARLY ARRIVAL EVERY-WHERE.
Field Speedwell
I'M NOTICING BEAUTIFUL MOTIFS EVERYWHERE THAT HELP RECUPERATE MY EYES... BUT ALL I NEED TO DO TODAY IS NOTICE THEM.
...
MUST SAVE EMO-TIONS FOR TOMOR-ROW.
I CAN'T LOOK AT THEM FOR TOO LONG. THIS IS JUST A PREVIEW...
OH, A TAIYAKI MACHINE.
TAIYAKI
TAIYAKI WORLD
SLEET
TRASH
THEY LOOK GOOD ...
MORE FOR TOMOR-ROW...

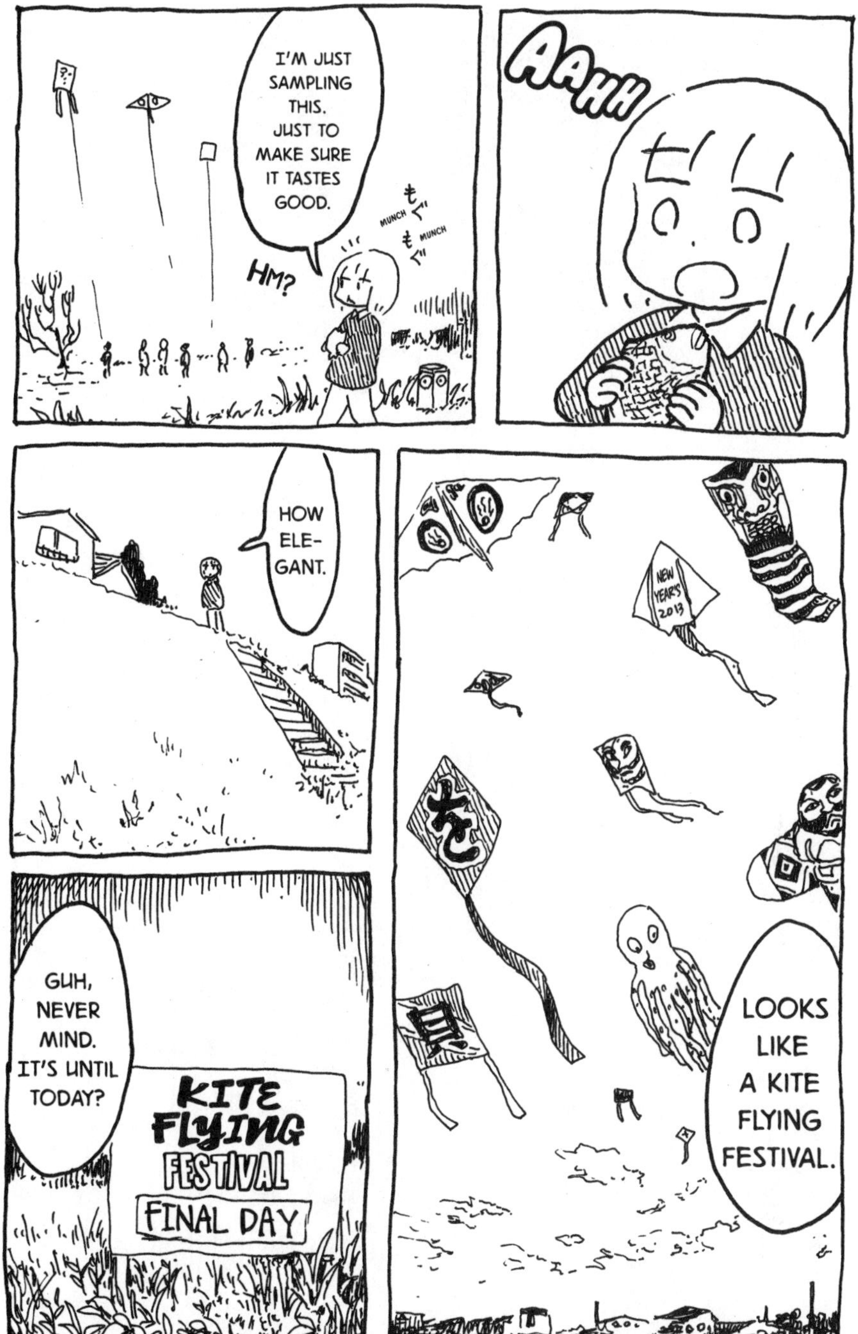
AAHH
I'M JUST SAMPLING THIS. JUST TO MAKE SURE IT TASTES GOOD.
もぐ MUNCH
もぐ MUNCH
HM?
NEW YEAR'S 2013
LOOKS LIKE A KITE FLYING FESTIVAL.
HOW ELE-GANT.
KITE FLYING FESTIVAL FINAL DAY
GUH, NEVER MIND. IT'S UNTIL TODAY?

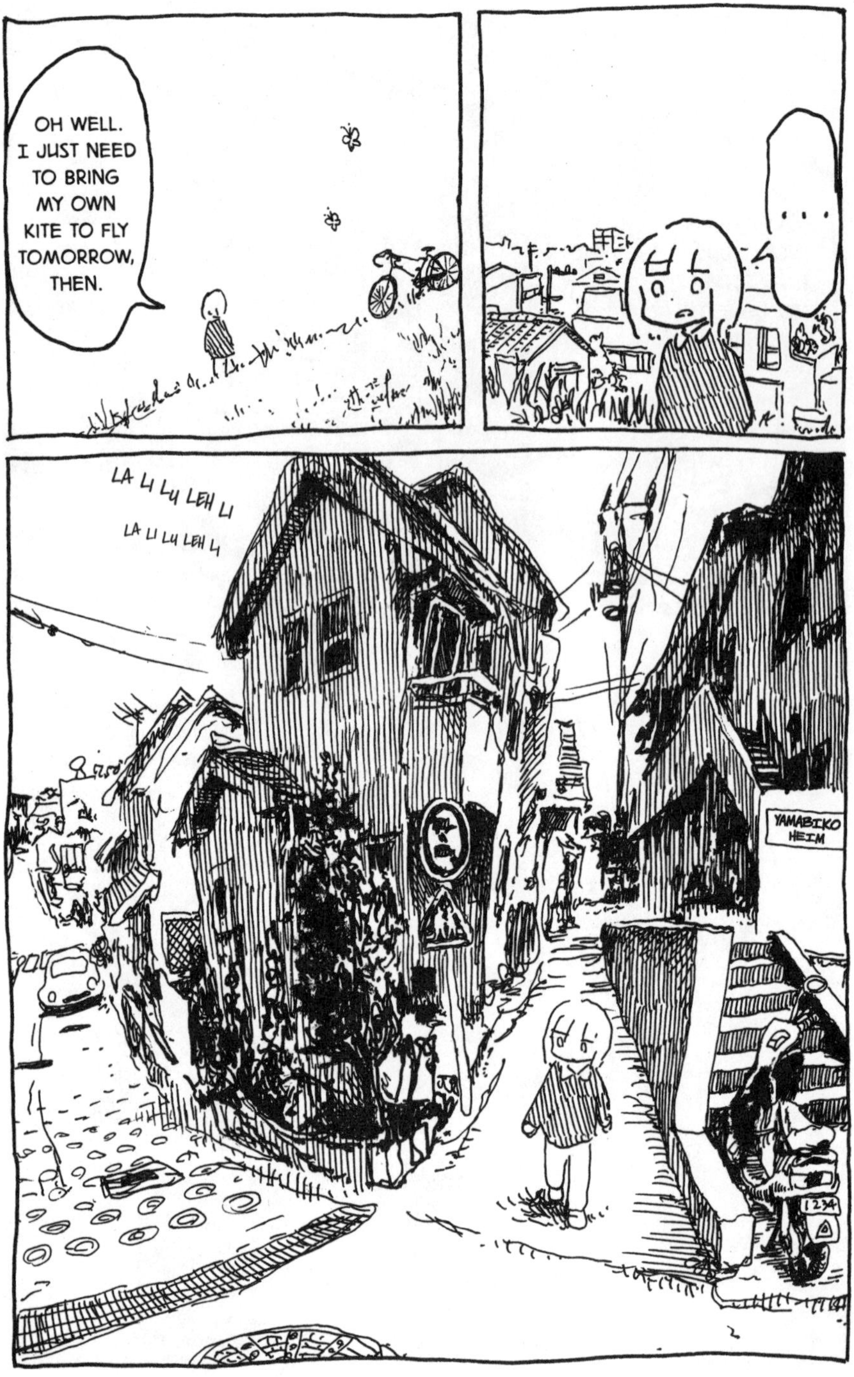
...
OH WELL. I JUST NEED TO BRING MY OWN KITE TO FLY TOMORROW, THEN.
LA LI LU LEH LI
LA LI LU LEH LI
YAMABIKO HEIM
1234

NOW THAT I'M OUT HERE, I'LL TRY TAKING A PATH I DON'T NORMALLY USE.
DENTIST
THIS WAY
SCHOOL ZONE
文
THAT'LL MAKE THIS PREVIEW MORE WORTHWHILE. IF IT'S A BORING PATH, THEN I JUST DON'T HAVE TO TAKE IT TOMORROW.
NOT SCHOOL ZONE
SHORTCUT
HYDRANT
OH, THERE'S A PATH I DON'T USE ON MY WAY TO SCHOOL.

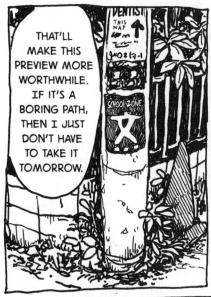

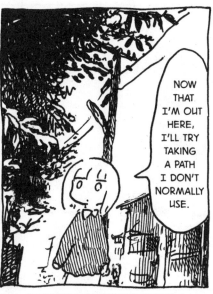

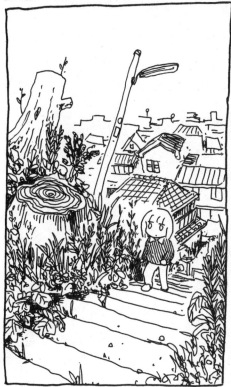

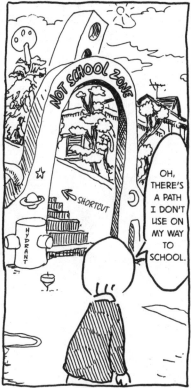

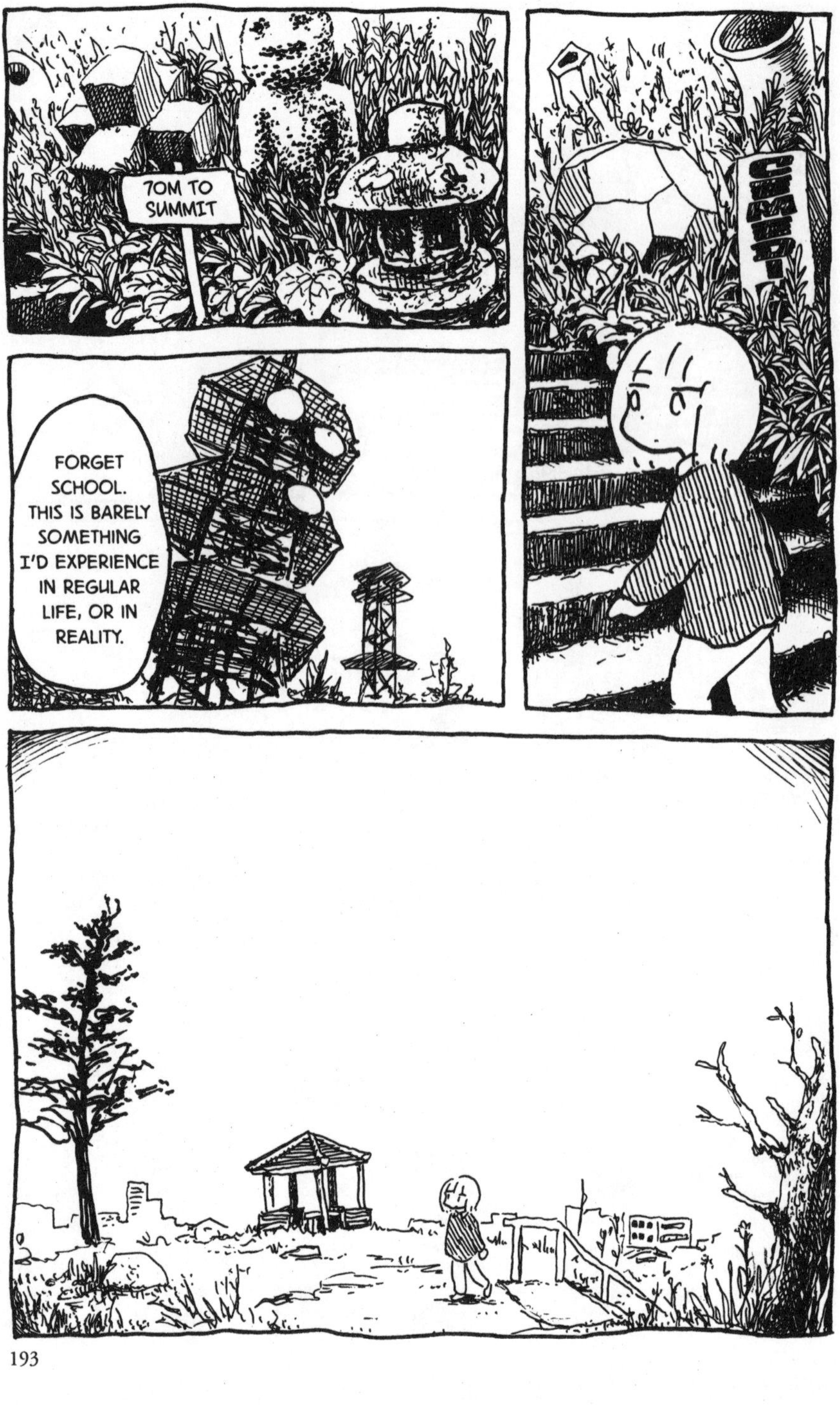
70M TO SUMMIT
FORGET SCHOOL. THIS IS BARELY SOMETHING I'D EXPERIENCE IN REGULAR LIFE, OR IN REALITY.

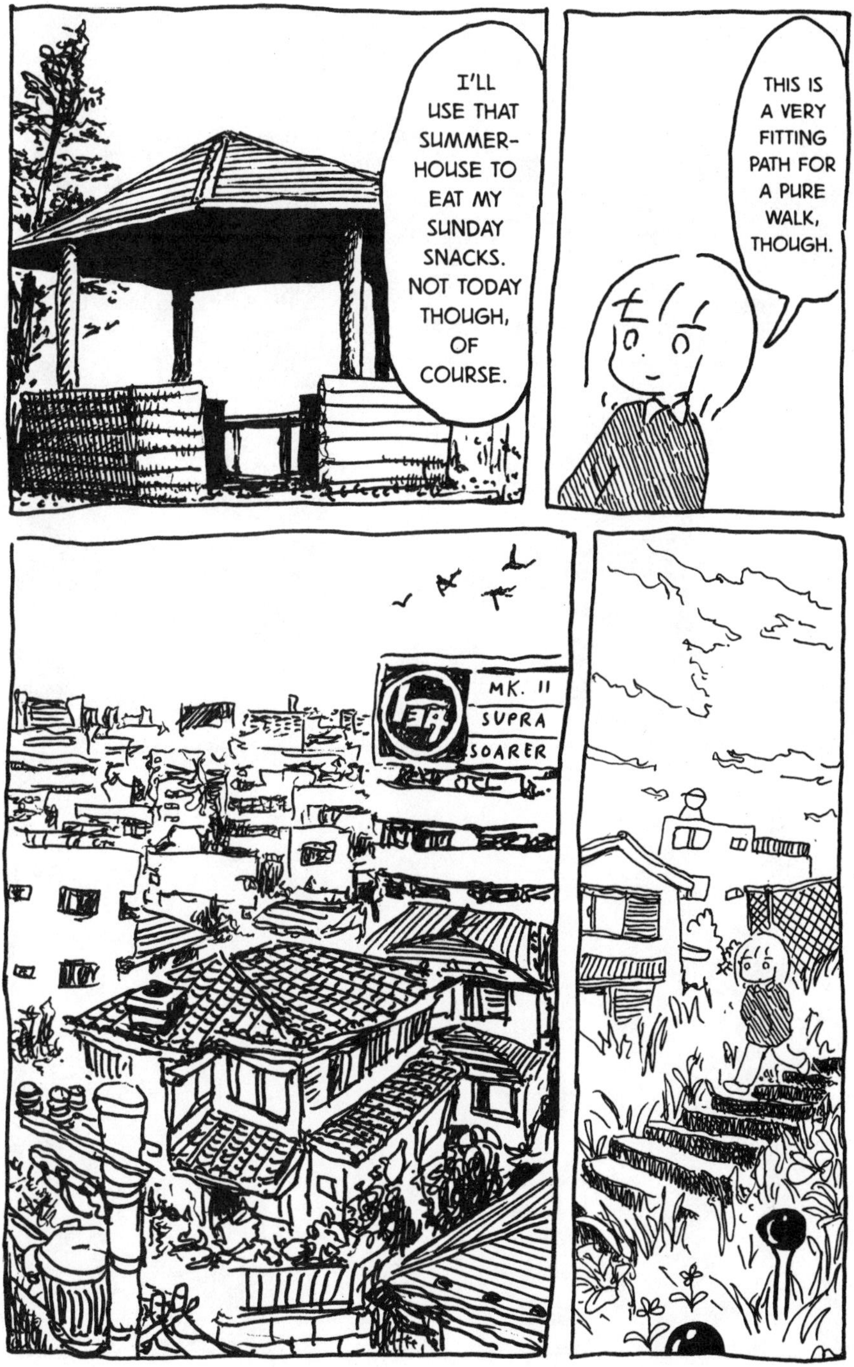
THIS IS A VERY FITTING PATH FOR A PURE WALK, THOUGH.
I'LL USE THAT SUMMER-HOUSE TO EAT MY SUNDAY SNACKS. NOT TODAY THOUGH, OF COURSE.
MK. II
SUPRA
SOARER

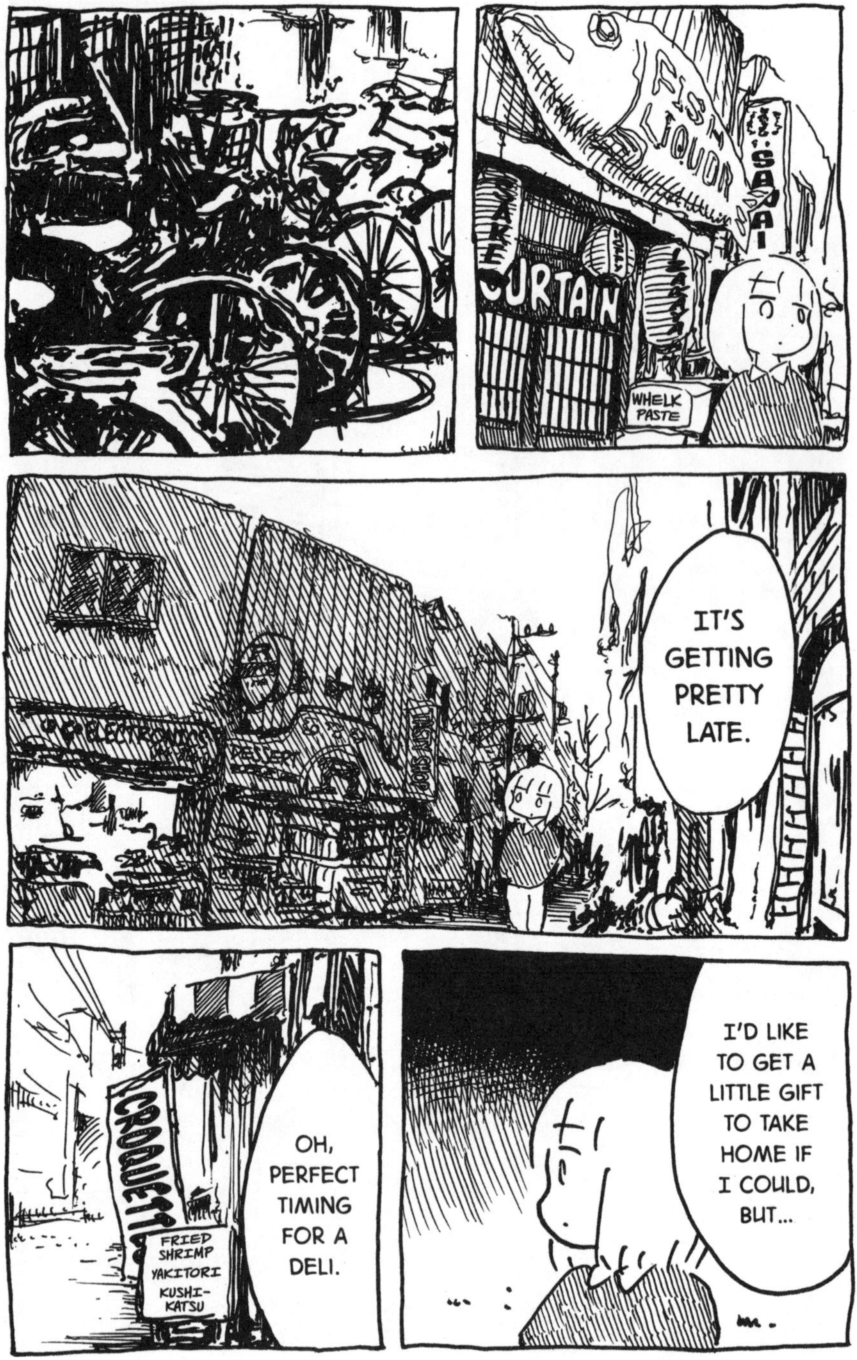

FISH
LIQUOR
SAKE
CURTAIN
WHELK PASTE
IT'S GETTING PRETTY LATE.
I'D LIKE TO GET A LITTLE GIFT TO TAKE HOME IF I COULD, BUT...
OH, PERFECT TIMING FOR A DELI.
FRIED SHRIMP
YAKITORI
KUSHI-KATSU

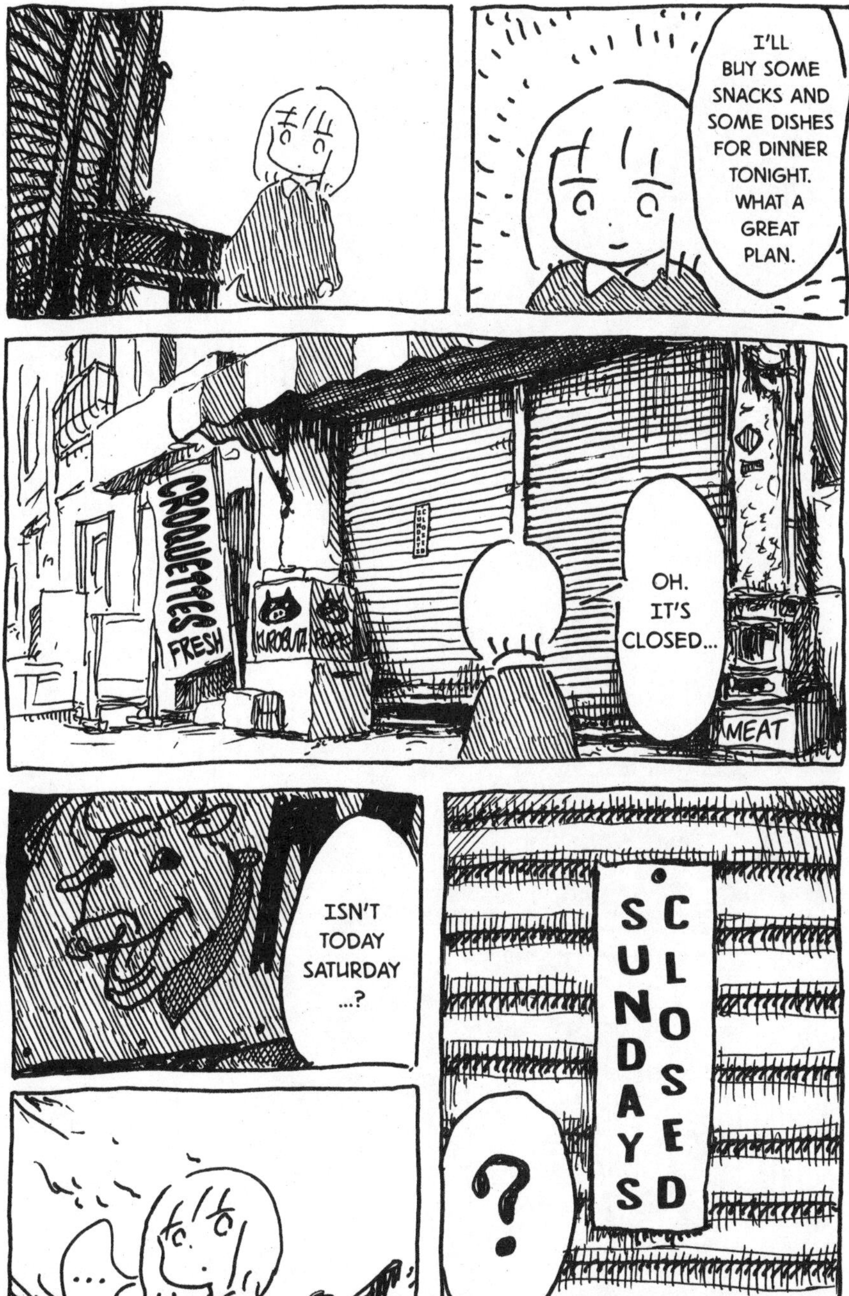
I'LL BUY SOME SNACKS AND SOME DISHES FOR DINNER TONIGHT. WHAT A GREAT PLAN.
OH. IT'S CLOSED...
MEAT
PORK
KUROBUTA
CROQUETTES FRESH
CLOSED SUNDAYS
?
ISN'T TODAY SATURDAY ...?
...

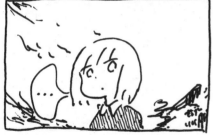

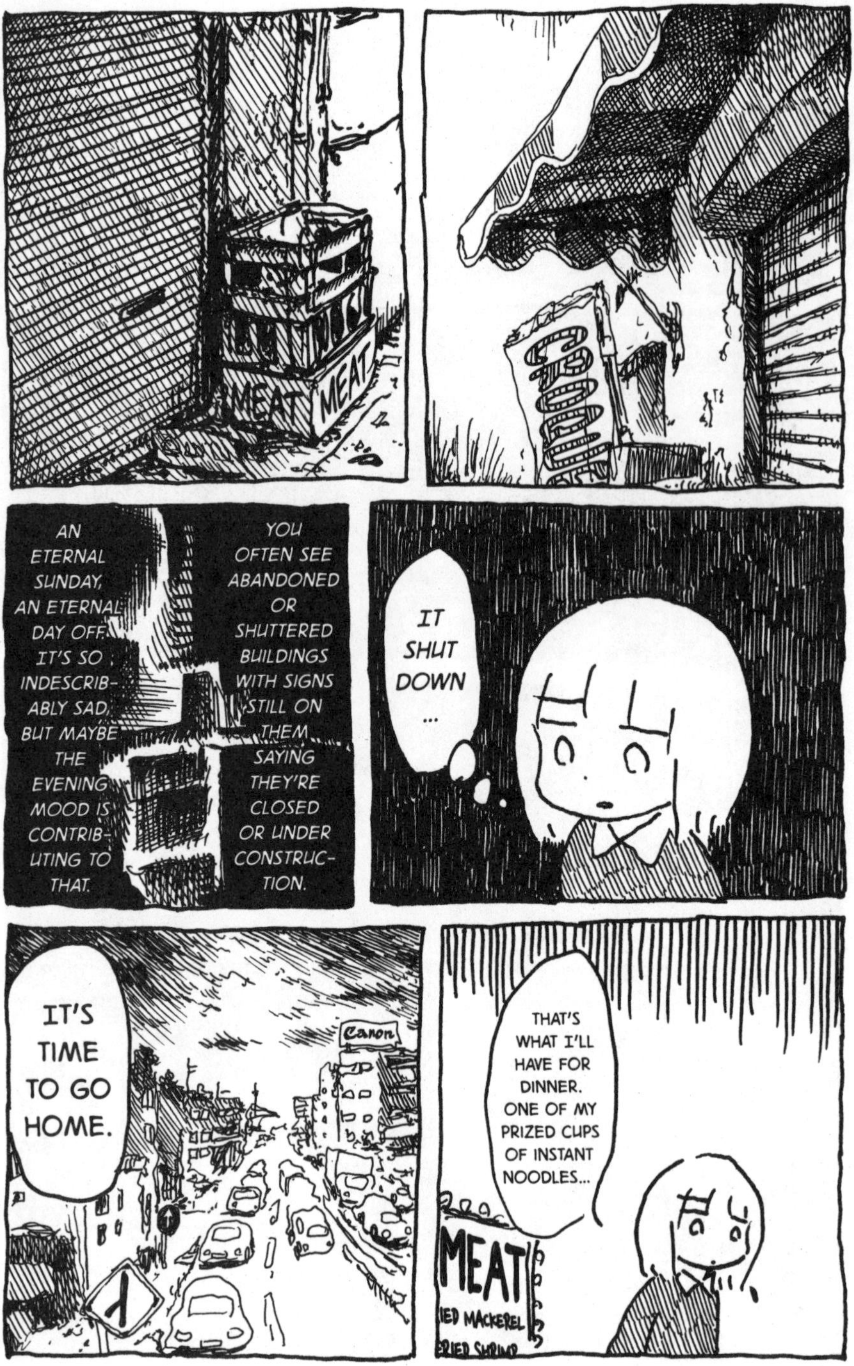
MEAT
MEAT
IT SHUT DOWN ...
YOU OFTEN SEE ABANDONED OR SHUTTERED BUILDINGS WITH SIGNS STILL ON THEM SAYING THEY'RE CLOSED OR UNDER CONSTRUCTION.
AN ETERNAL SUNDAY, AN ETERNAL DAY OFF. IT'S SO INDESCRIBABLY SAD, BUT MAYBE THE EVENING MOOD IS CONTRIBUTING TO THAT.
THAT'S WHAT I'LL HAVE FOR DINNER. ONE OF MY PRIZED CUPS OF INSTANT NOODLES...
MEAT
IT'S TIME TO GO HOME.
Canon

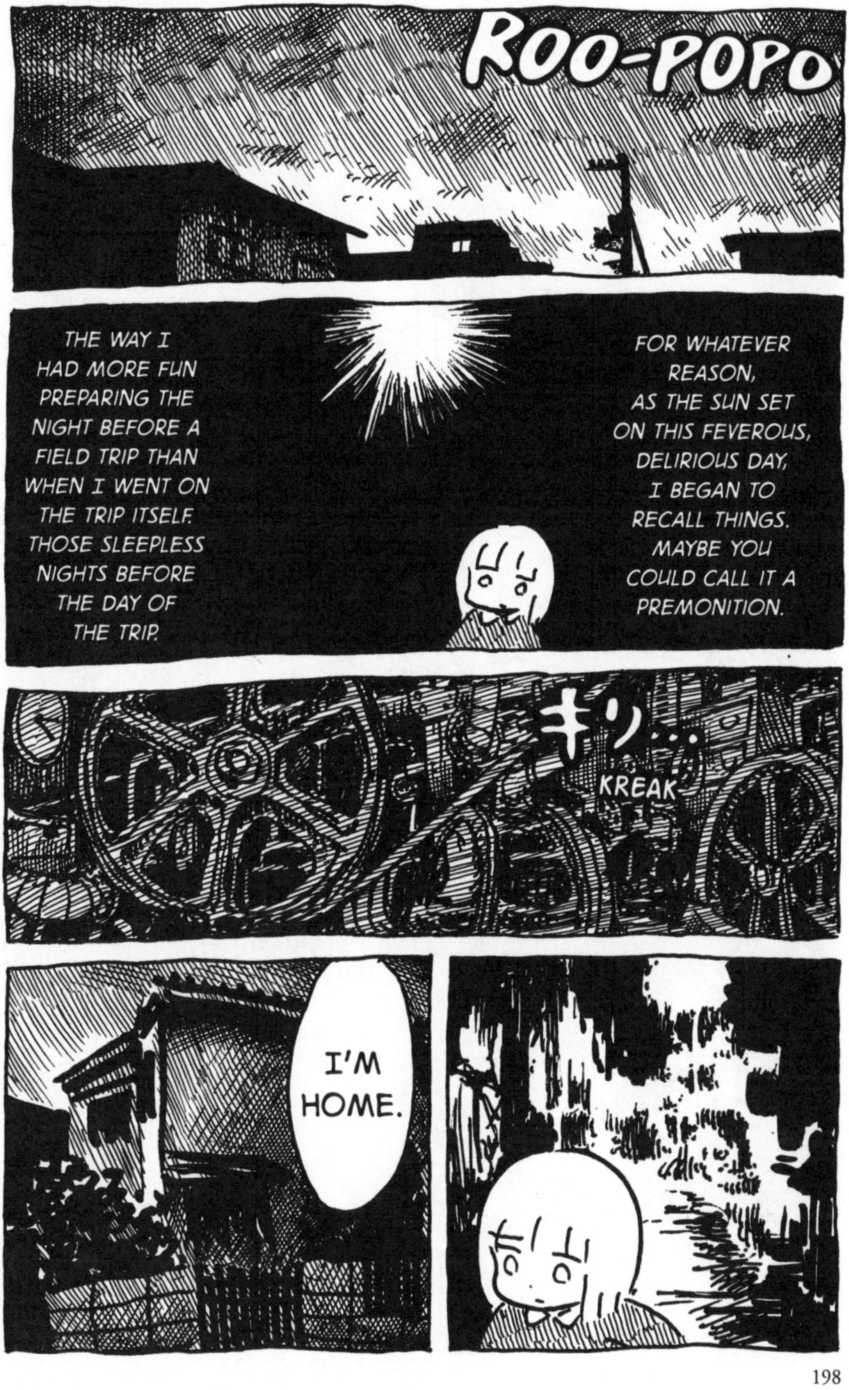
ROO-POPO
FOR WHATEVER REASON, AS THE SUN SET ON THIS FEVEROUS, DELIRIOUS DAY, I BEGAN TO RECALL THINGS. MAYBE YOU COULD CALL IT A PREMONITION.
THE WAY I HAD MORE FUN PREPARING THE NIGHT BEFORE A FIELD TRIP THAN WHEN I WENT ON THE TRIP ITSELF. THOSE SLEEPLESS NIGHTS BEFORE THE DAY OF THE TRIP.
キリ…
KREAK
I'M HOME.

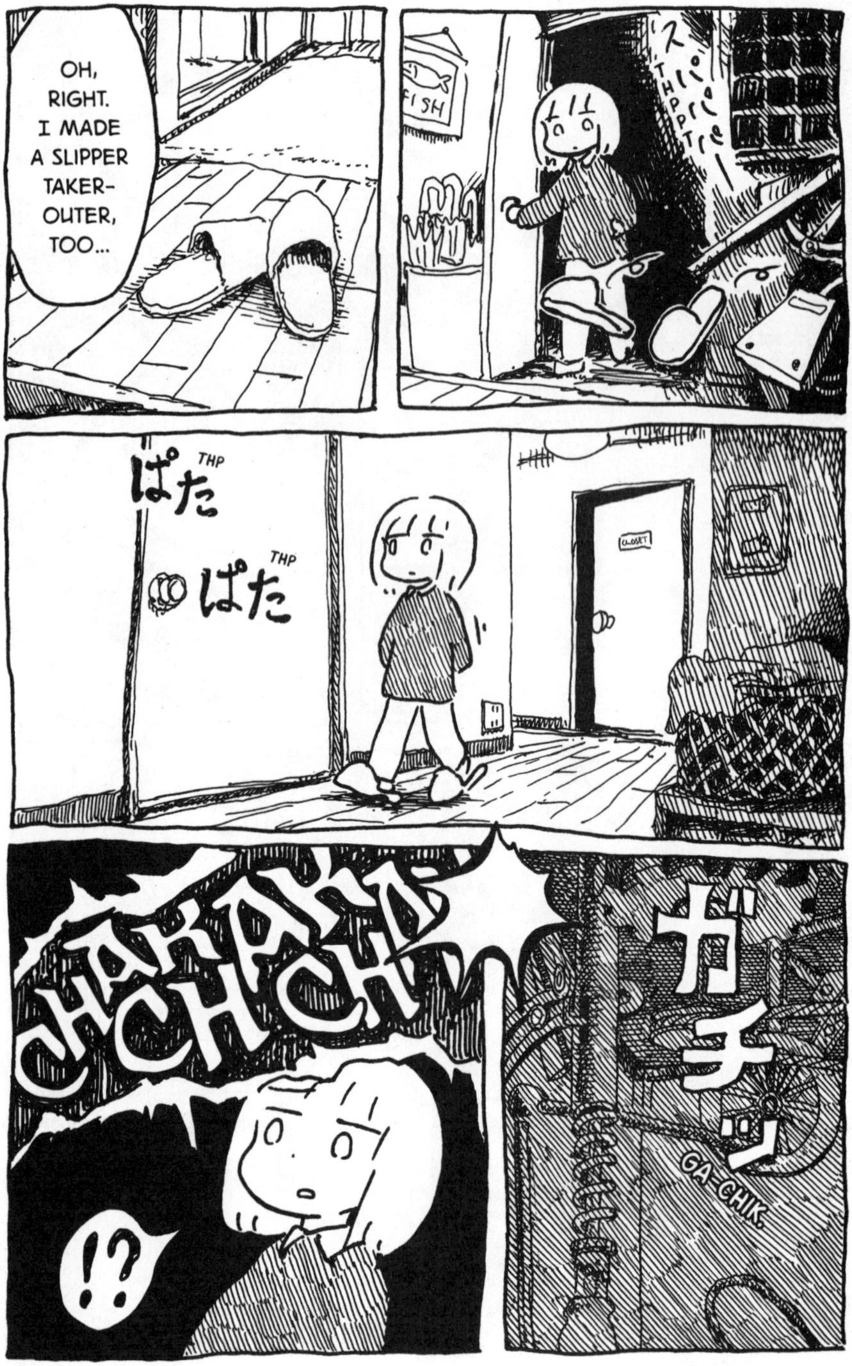
スパパパー
THPPT
OH, RIGHT. I MADE A SLIPPER TAKER-OUTER, TOO...
ぱた
THP
ぱた
THP
ガチッ
GA-CHIK
CHAKA CHCH
!?

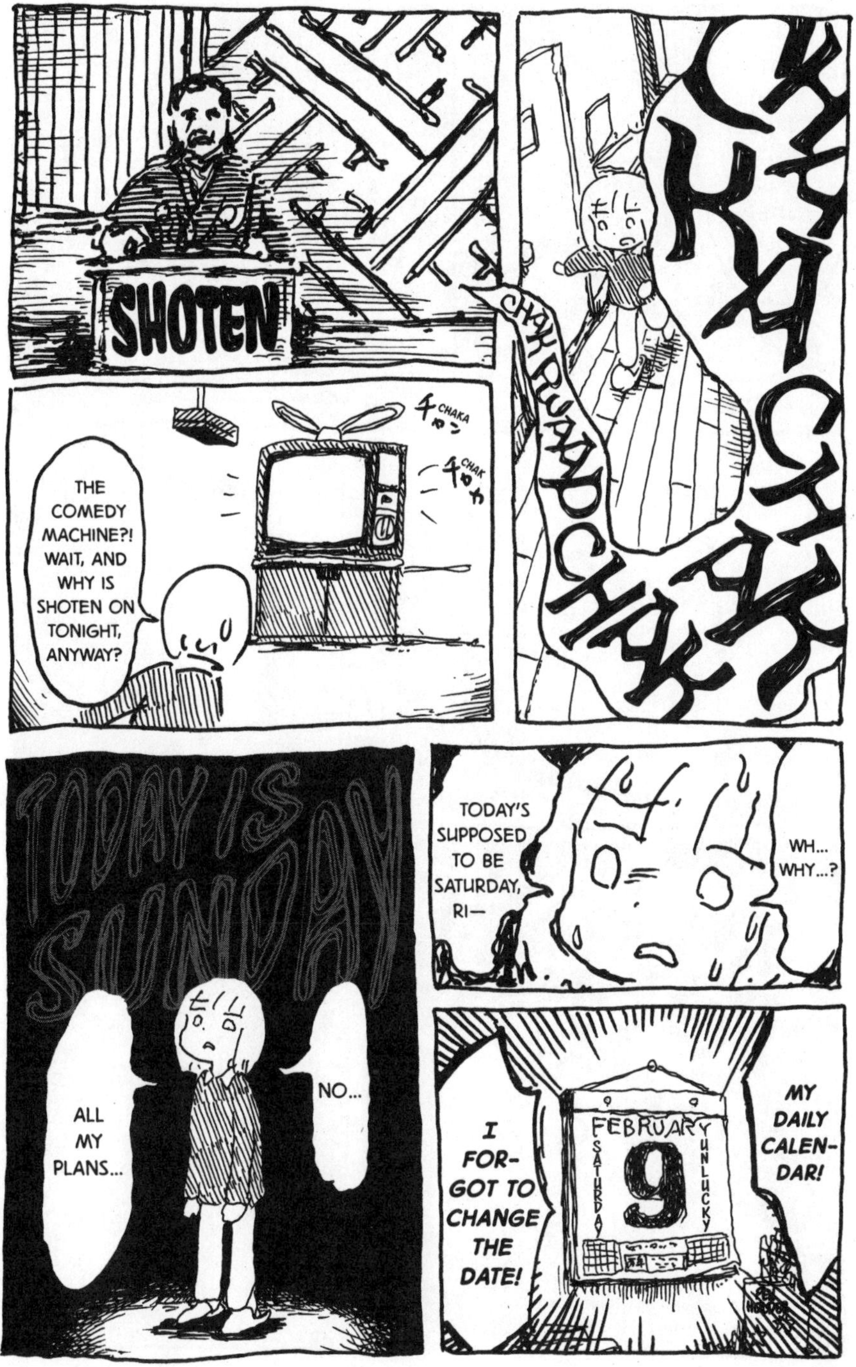
CHAKA CHAKA
CHAK PUAAAD CHAK
SHOTEN
CHAKA
CHAK
THE COMEDY MACHINE?! WAIT, AND WHY IS SHOTEN ON TONIGHT, ANYWAY?
WH... WHY...?
TODAY'S SUPPOSED TO BE SATURDAY, RI—
MY DAILY CALEN-DAR!
FEBRUARY 9 SATURDAY UNLUCKY
I FOR-GOT TO CHANGE THE DATE!
TODAY IS SUNDAY
NO...
ALL MY PLANS...

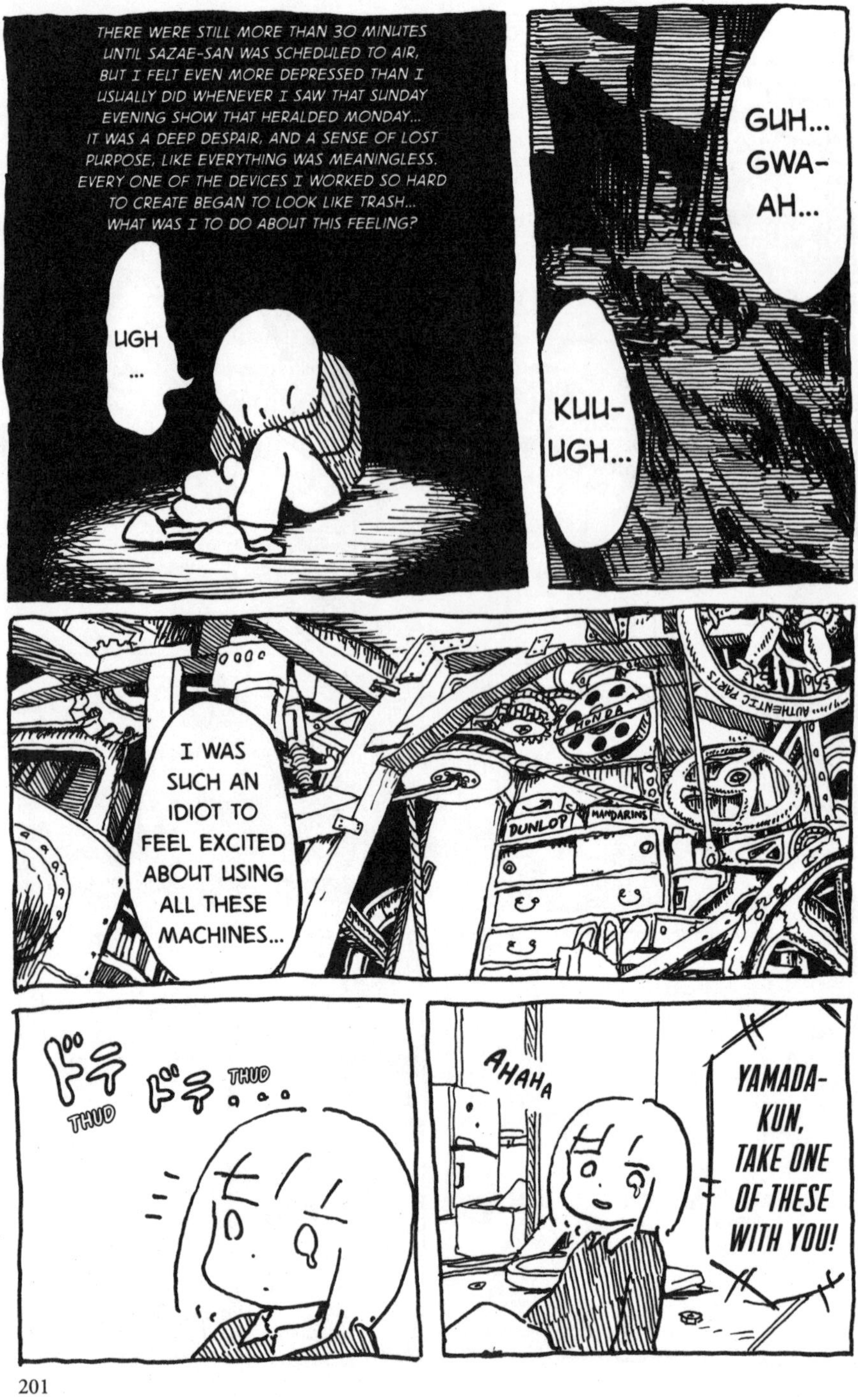
GUH... GWA-AH...
KUU-UGH...
THERE WERE STILL MORE THAN 30 MINUTES UNTIL SAZAE-SAN WAS SCHEDULED TO AIR, BUT I FELT EVEN MORE DEPRESSED THAN I USUALLY DID WHENEVER I SAW THAT SUNDAY EVENING SHOW THAT HERALDED MONDAY... IT WAS A DEEP DESPAIR, AND A SENSE OF LOST PURPOSE, LIKE EVERYTHING WAS MEANINGLESS. EVERY ONE OF THE DEVICES I WORKED SO HARD TO CREATE BEGAN TO LOOK LIKE TRASH... WHAT WAS I TO DO ABOUT THIS FEELING?
UGH ...
I WAS SUCH AN IDIOT TO FEEL EXCITED ABOUT USING ALL THESE MACHINES...
AUTHENTIC PARTS
HONDA
DUNLOP
MANDARINS
AHAHA
YAMADA-KUN, TAKE ONE OF THESE WITH YOU!
ドテ
THUD
ドテ
THUD

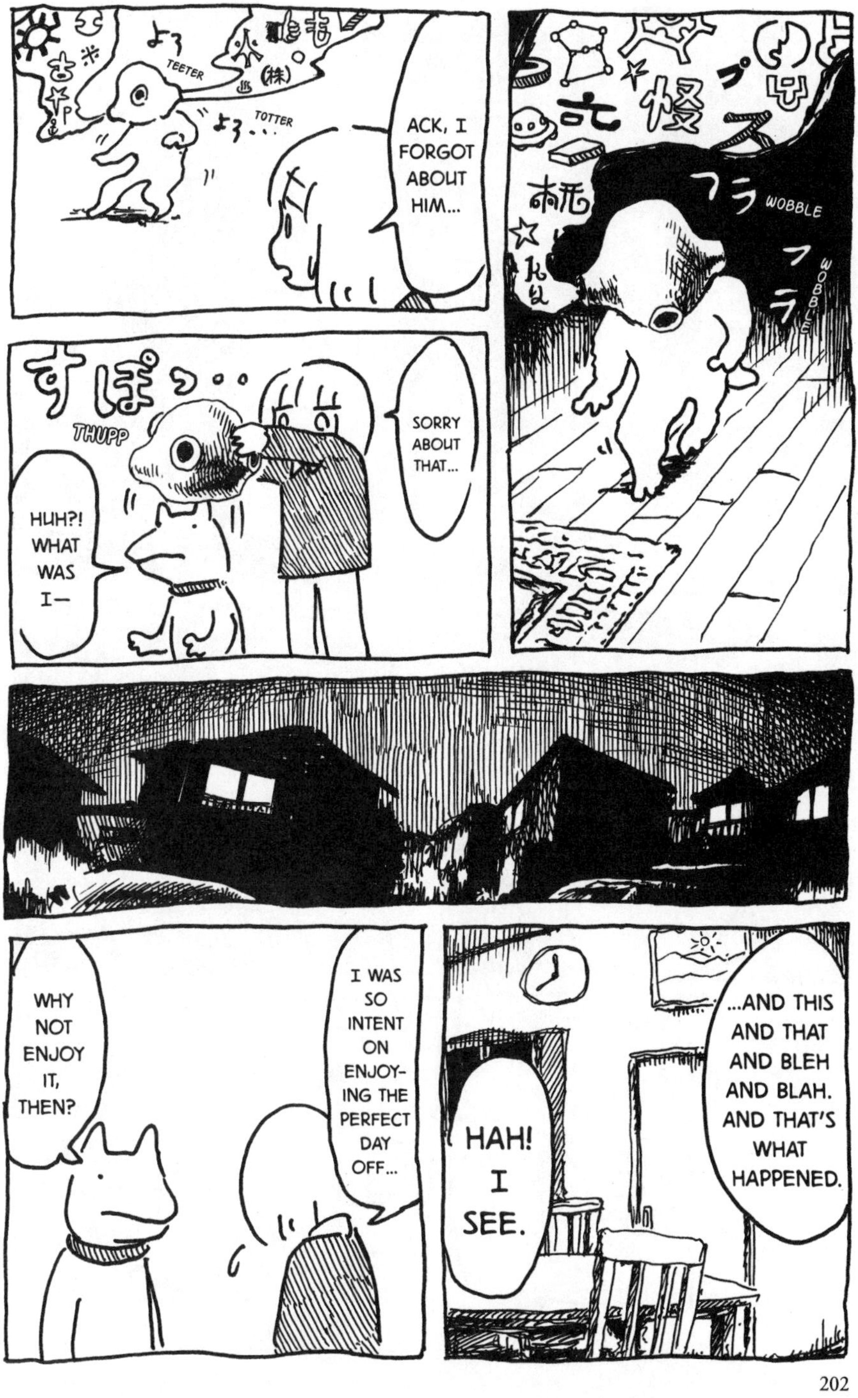
フラ
WOBBLE
フラフラ
WOBBLE
よろ
TEETER
よろ…
TOTTER
ACK, I FORGOT ABOUT HIM...
SORRY ABOUT THAT...
すぽっ…
THUPP
HUH?! WHAT WAS I—
...AND THIS AND THAT AND BLEH AND BLAH. AND THAT'S WHAT HAPPENED.
HAH! I SEE.
I WAS SO INTENT ON ENJOY-ING THE PERFECT DAY OFF...
WHY NOT ENJOY IT, THEN?

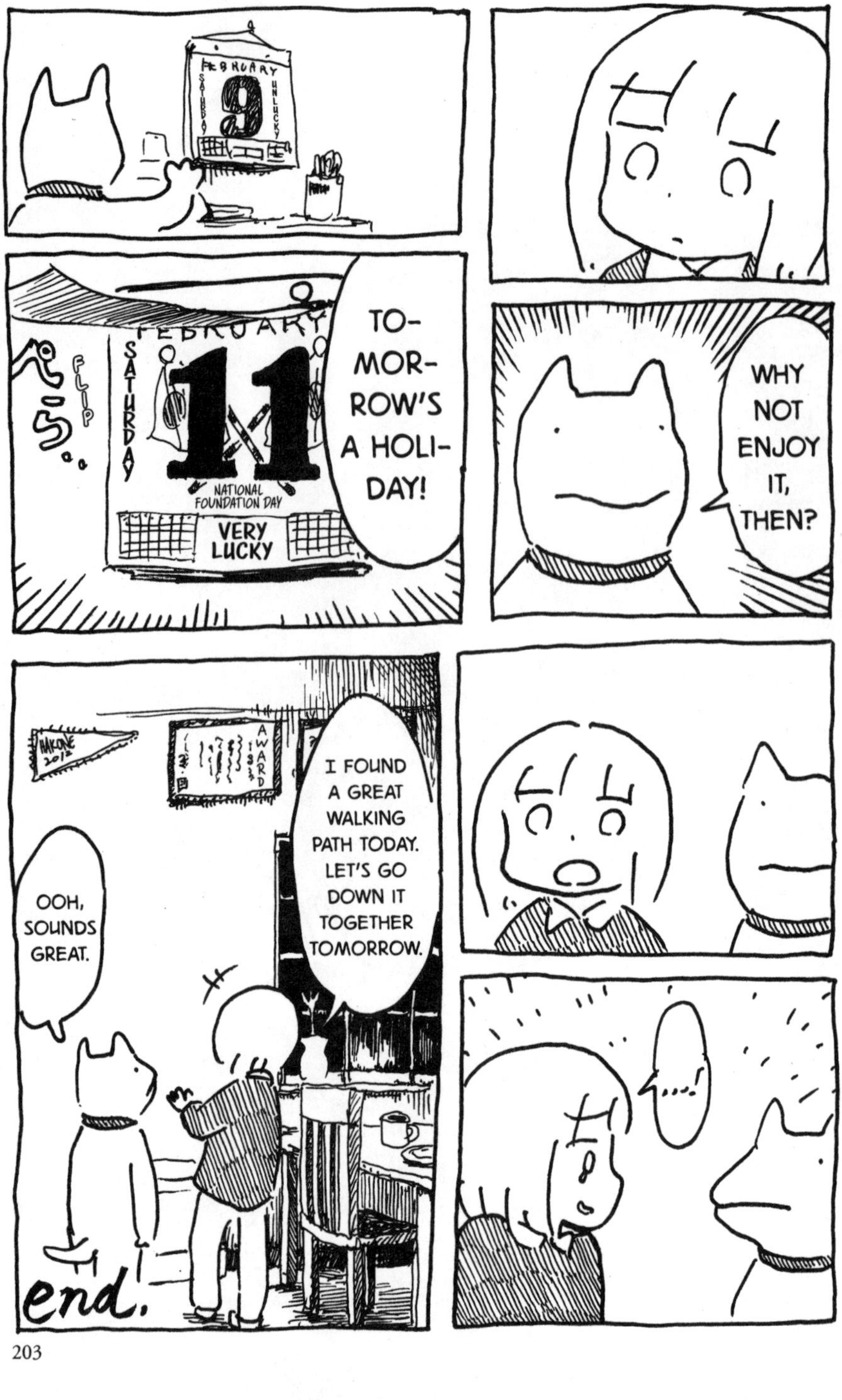
FEBRUARY
SATURDAY
9
UNLUCKY
WHY NOT ENJOY IT, THEN?
TO-MORROW'S A HOLIDAY!
FEBRUARY
SATURDAY
11
NATIONAL FOUNDATION DAY
VERY LUCKY
FLIP
....!
I FOUND A GREAT WALKING PATH TODAY. LET'S GO DOWN IT TOGETHER TOMORROW.
AWARD
HAKONE 2012
OOH, SOUNDS GREAT.
end.

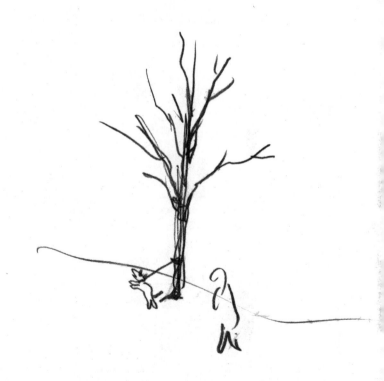

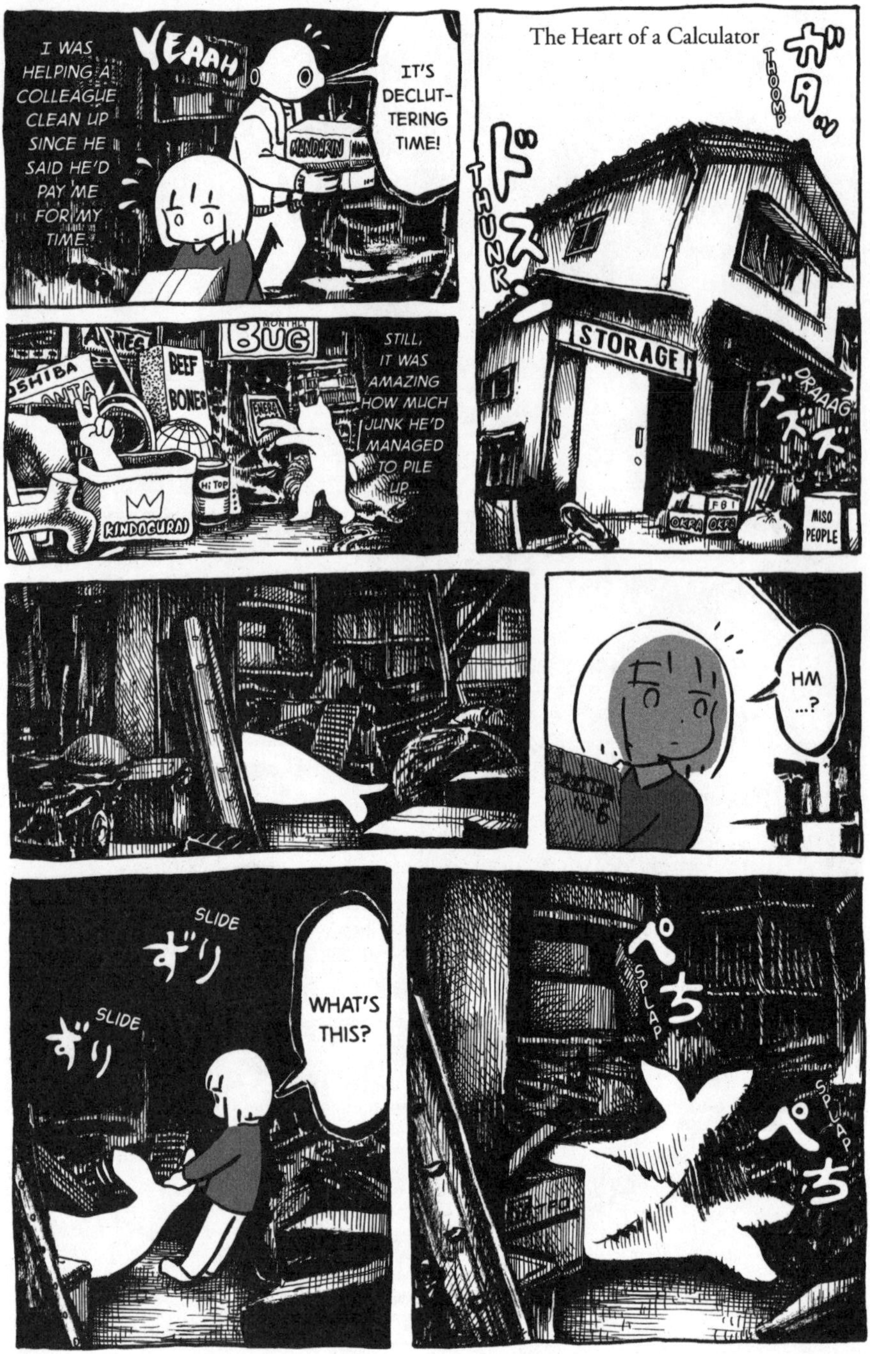
The Heart of a Calculator
ガタッ
THOOMP
ドス
THUNK
STORAGE
ズズズ
DRAAAG
FBI
OKRA
OKRA
MISO PEOPLE
IT'S DECLUTTERING TIME!
YEAAH
I WAS HELPING A COLLEAGUE CLEAN UP SINCE HE SAID HE'D PAY ME FOR MY TIME.
MANDARIN
STILL, IT WAS AMAZING HOW MUCH JUNK HE'D MANAGED TO PILE UP...
MONTHLY BUG
BEEF BONES
OSHIBA
Hi Top
KINDOGURAI
HM ...?
ぺち
SPLAP
ぺち
SPLAP
WHAT'S THIS?
ずり
SLIDE
ずり
SLIDE

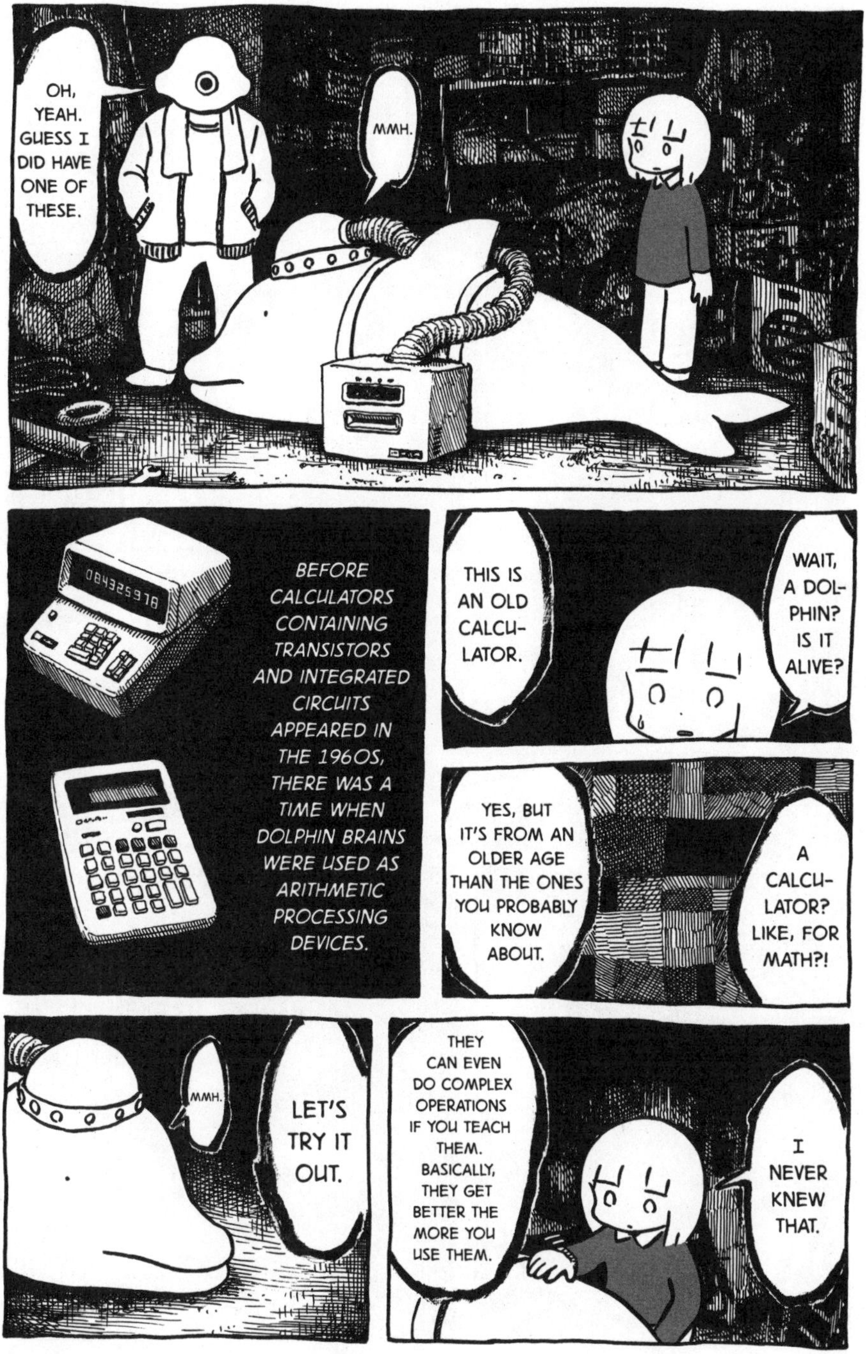
MMH.
OH, YEAH. GUESS I DID HAVE ONE OF THESE.
WAIT, A DOL-PHIN? IS IT ALIVE?
THIS IS AN OLD CALCU-LATOR.
A CALCU-LATOR? LIKE, FOR MATH?!
YES, BUT IT'S FROM AN OLDER AGE THAN THE ONES YOU PROBABLY KNOW ABOUT.
BEFORE CALCULATORS CONTAINING TRANSISTORS AND INTEGRATED CIRCUITS APPEARED IN THE 1960S, THERE WAS A TIME WHEN DOLPHIN BRAINS WERE USED AS ARITHMETIC PROCESSING DEVICES.
084325978
I NEVER KNEW THAT.
THEY CAN EVEN DO COMPLEX OPERATIONS IF YOU TEACH THEM. BASICALLY, THEY GET BETTER THE MORE YOU USE THEM.
LET'S TRY IT OUT.
MMH.

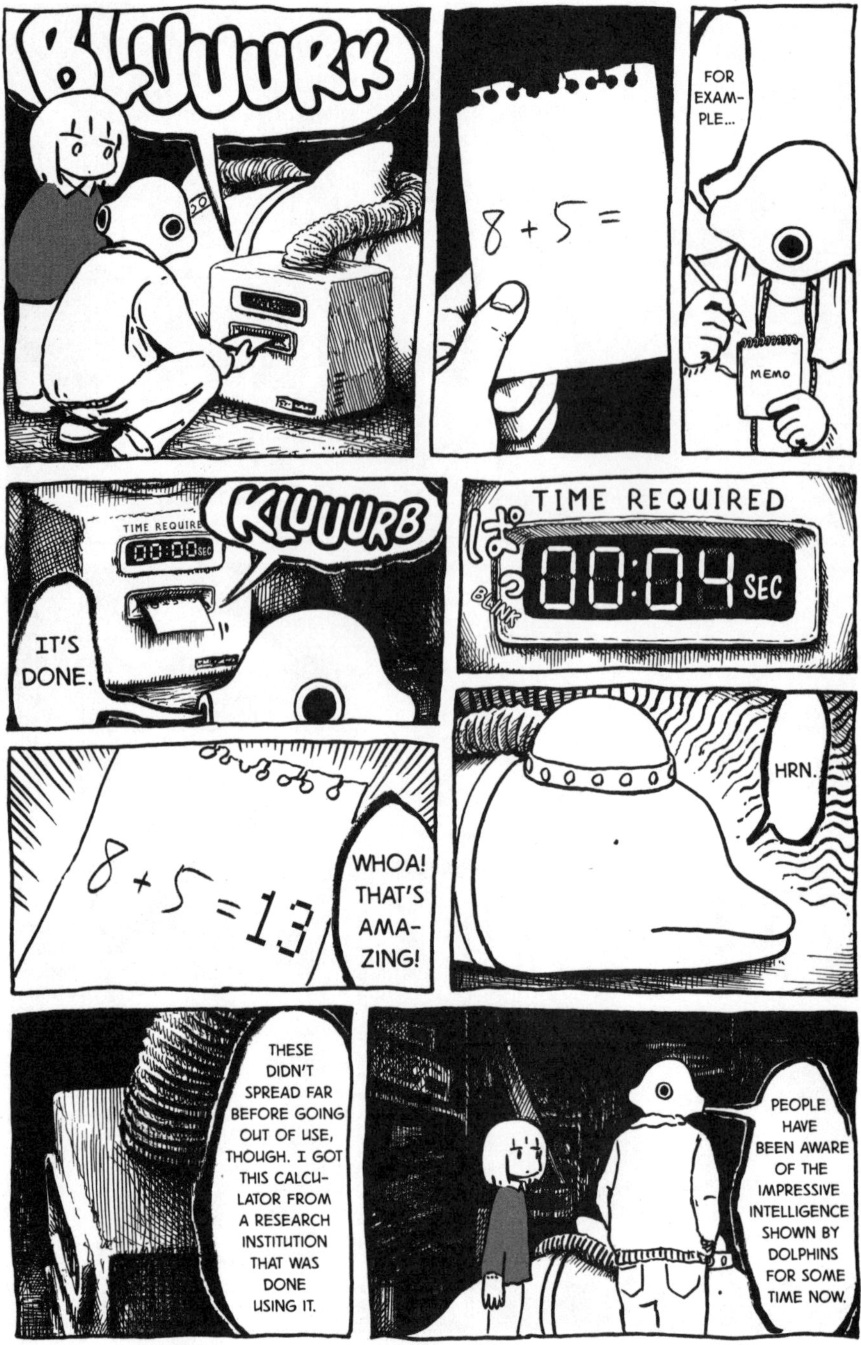
FOR EXAM-PLE...
MEMO
8 + 5 =
BLUUURK
TIME REQUIRED
ぱっ
BLINK
00:04 SEC
KLUUURB
TIME REQUIRE
00:00 SEC
IT'S DONE.
HRN.
WHOA! THAT'S AMA-ZING!
8 + 5 = 13
PEOPLE HAVE BEEN AWARE OF THE IMPRESSIVE INTELLIGENCE SHOWN BY DOLPHINS FOR SOME TIME NOW.
THESE DIDN'T SPREAD FAR BEFORE GOING OUT OF USE, THOUGH. I GOT THIS CALCU-LATOR FROM A RESEARCH INSTITUTION THAT WAS DONE USING IT.

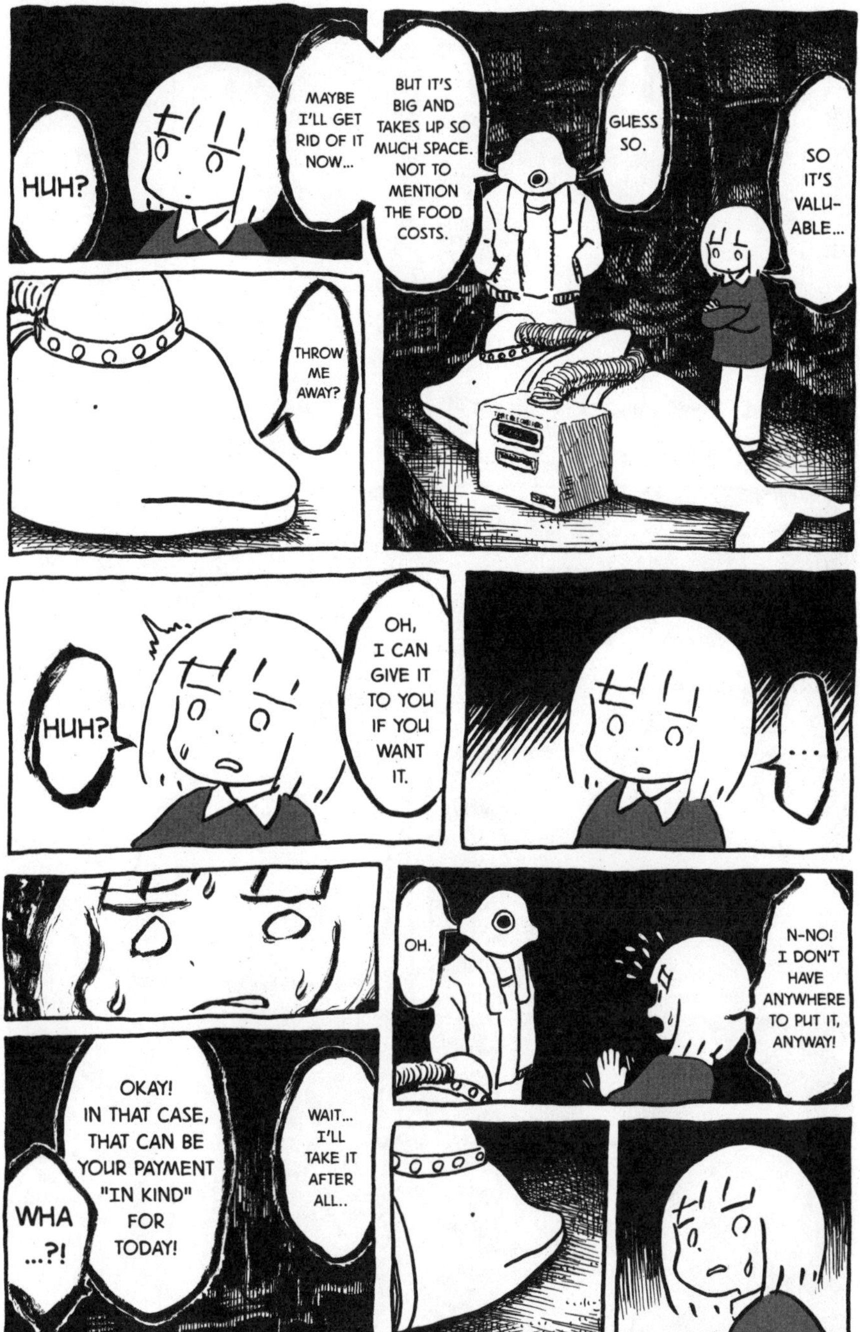
SO IT'S VALUABLE...
GUESS SO.
BUT IT'S BIG AND TAKES UP SO MUCH SPACE. NOT TO MENTION THE FOOD COSTS.
MAYBE I'LL GET RID OF IT NOW...
HUH?
THROW ME AWAY?
...
OH, I CAN GIVE IT TO YOU IF YOU WANT IT.
HUH?
N-NO! I DON'T HAVE ANYWHERE TO PUT IT, ANYWAY!
OH.
WAIT... I'LL TAKE IT AFTER ALL..
OKAY! IN THAT CASE, THAT CAN BE YOUR PAYMENT "IN KIND" FOR TODAY!
WHA ...?!

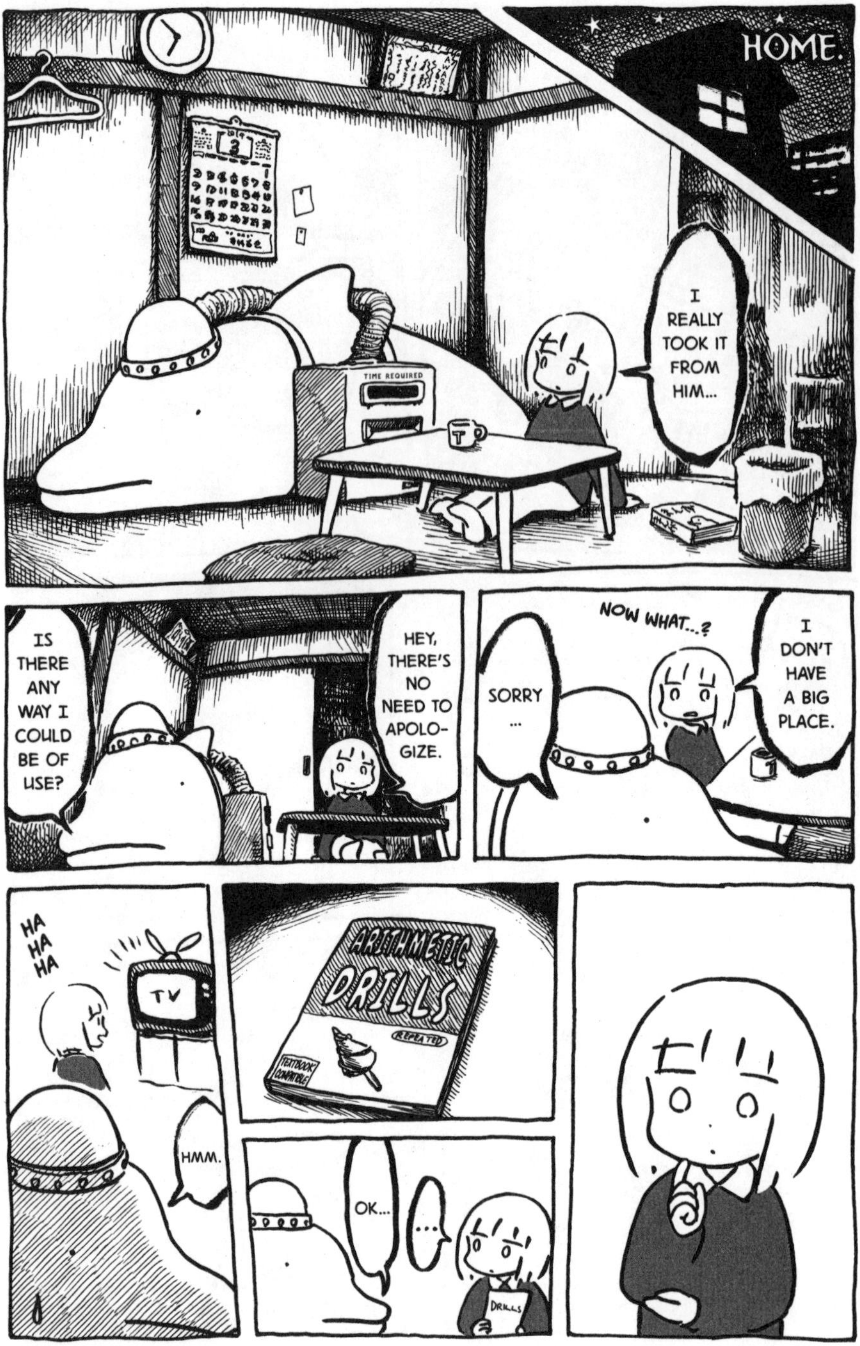
HOME.
TIME REQUIRED
I REALLY TOOK IT FROM HIM...
I DON'T HAVE A BIG PLACE.
NOW WHAT...?
SORRY ...
HEY, THERE'S NO NEED TO APOLO-GIZE.
IS THERE ANY WAY I COULD BE OF USE?
ARITHMETIC DRILLS
REPEATED
TEXTBOOK COMPATIBLE
OK...
...
DRILLS
HA HA HA
TV
HMM.

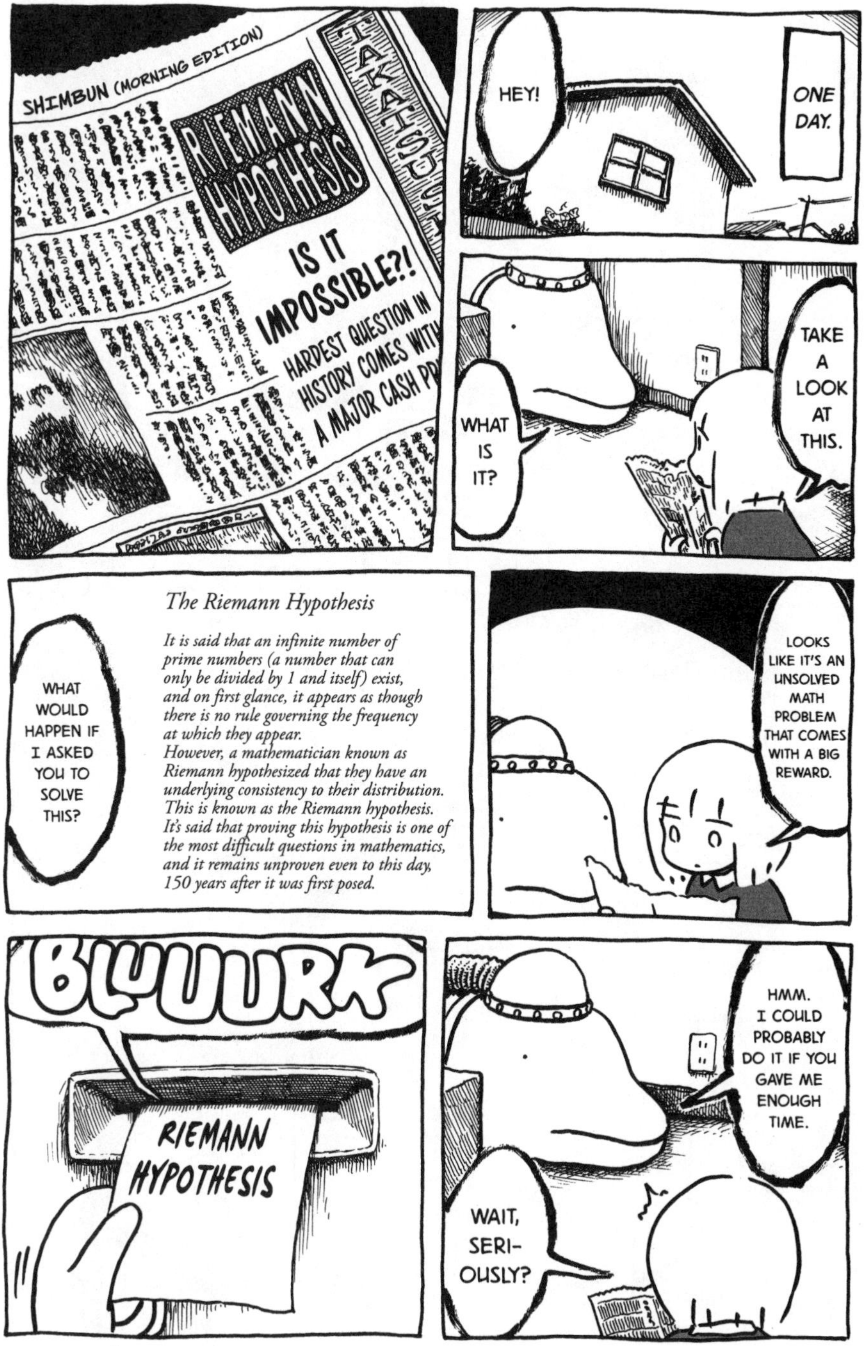
ONE DAY.
HEY!
TAKE A LOOK AT THIS.
WHAT IS IT?
SHIMBUN (MORNING EDITION)
RIEMANN HYPOTHESIS
IS IT IMPOSSIBLE?!
HARDEST QUESTION IN HISTORY COMES WITH A MAJOR CASH PR
LOOKS LIKE IT'S AN UNSOLVED MATH PROBLEM THAT COMES WITH A BIG REWARD.
The Riemann Hypothesis
It is said that an infinite number of prime numbers (a number that can only be divided by 1 and itself) exist, and on first glance, it appears as though there is no rule governing the frequency at which they appear.
However, a mathematician known as Riemann hypothesized that they have an underlying consistency to their distribution. This is known as the Riemann hypothesis.
It's said that proving this hypothesis is one of the most difficult questions in mathematics, and it remains unproven even to this day, 150 years after it was first posed.
WHAT WOULD HAPPEN IF I ASKED YOU TO SOLVE THIS?
HMM. I COULD PROBABLY DO IT IF YOU GAVE ME ENOUGH TIME.
WAIT, SERI-OUSLY?
BLUUURK
RIEMANN HYPOTHESIS

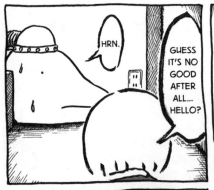

TIME REQUIRED
YR
GUESS IT'S NO GOOD AFTER ALL... HELLO?
HRN.
HRN.
HEY ...?
HRN.
...
HRN.
IT SEEMED AS THOUGH THERE WAS NO WAY TO CANCEL A PROBLEM ONCE IT STARTED ON ONE.

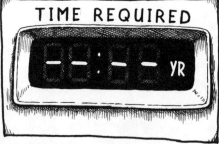

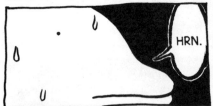

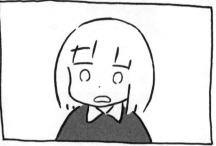

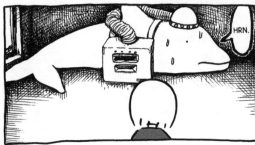

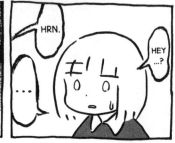

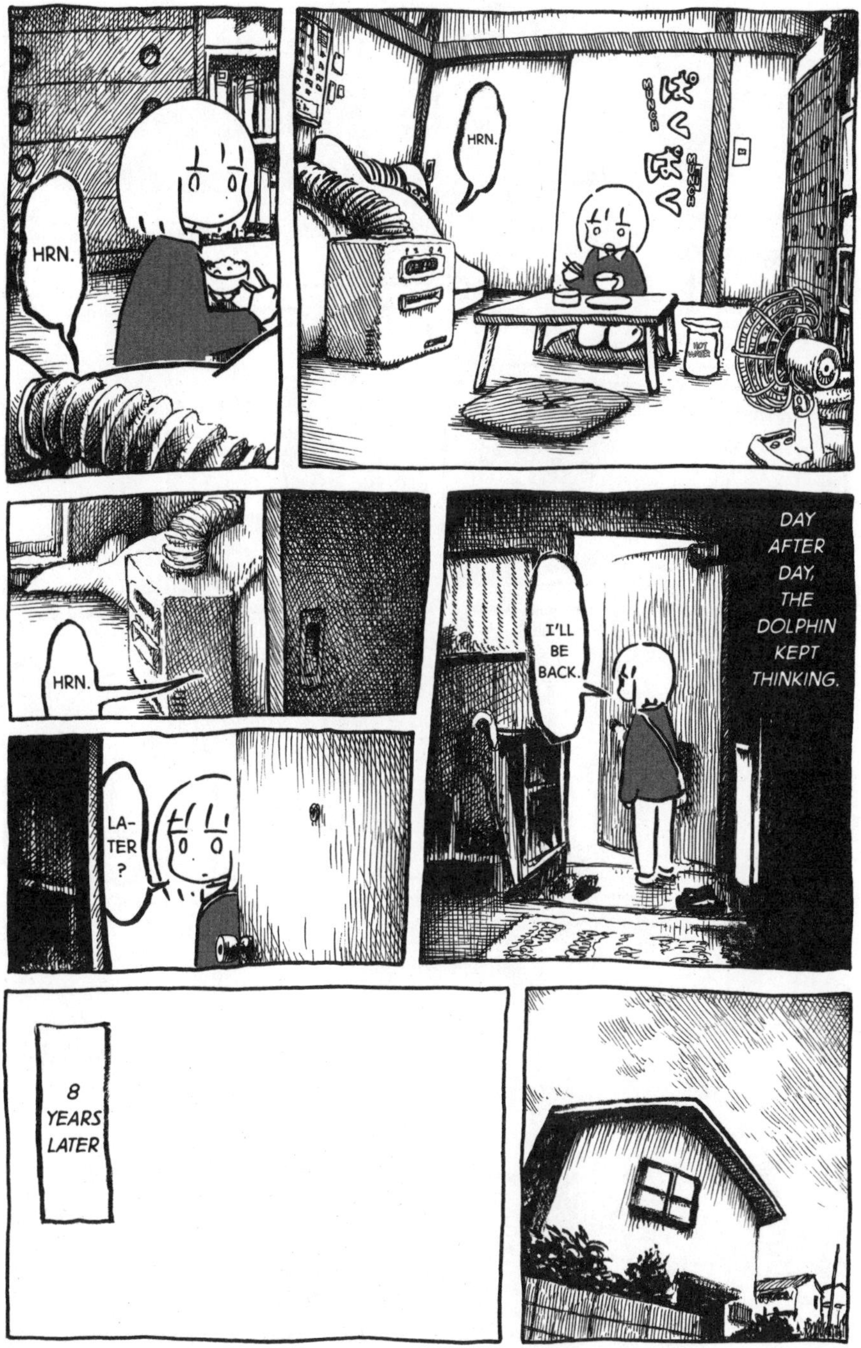
HRN.
ぱくぱく
MUNCH MUNCH
HOT WATER
HRN.
DAY AFTER DAY, THE DOLPHIN KEPT THINKING.
I'LL BE BACK.
HRN.
LA-TER?
8 YEARS LATER

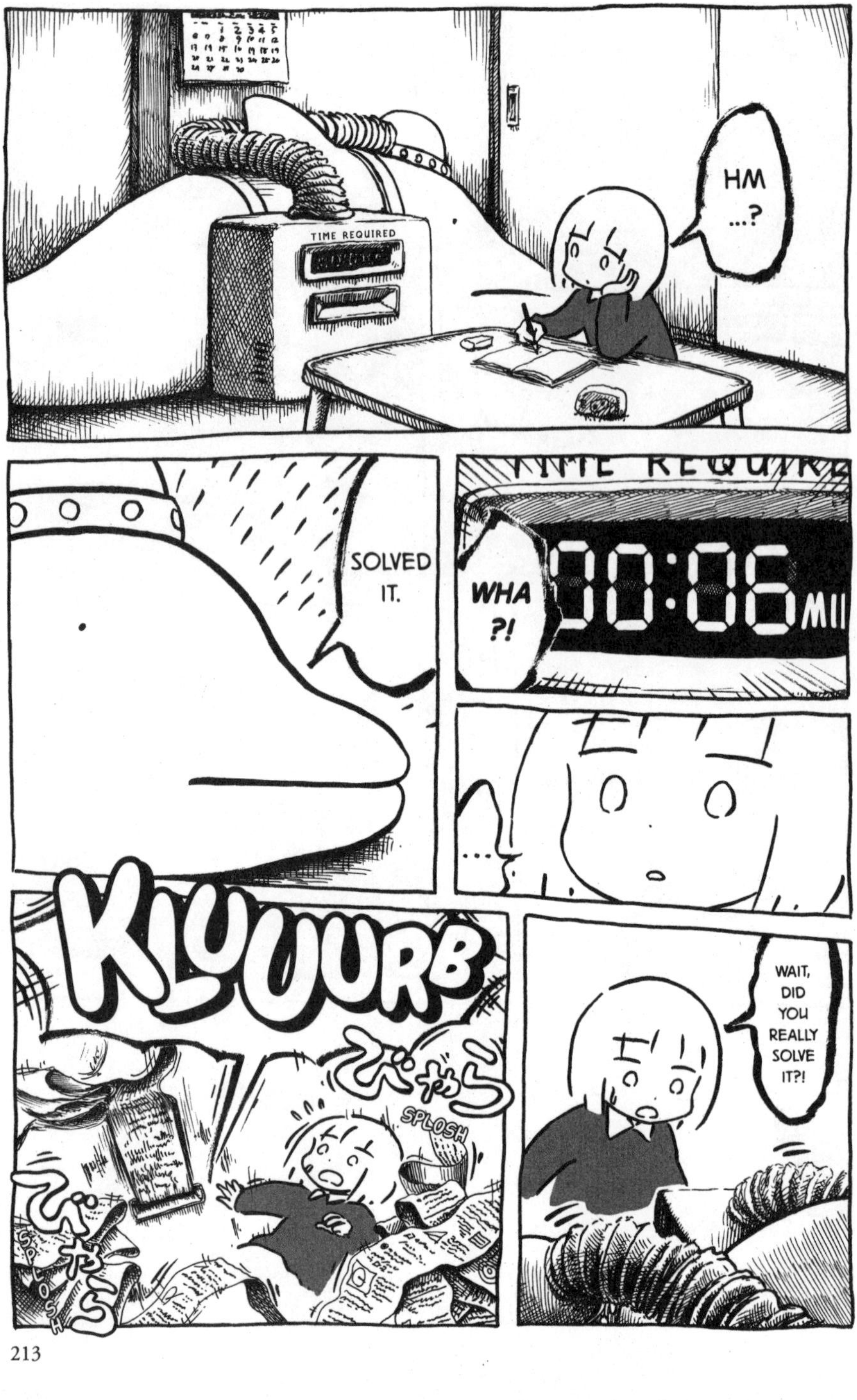
TIME REQUIRED
HM ...?
TIME REQUIRE
WHA ?!
00:06 MI
....
SOLVED IT.
WAIT, DID YOU REALLY SOLVE IT?!
KLUUURB
SPLOSH
SPLOSH

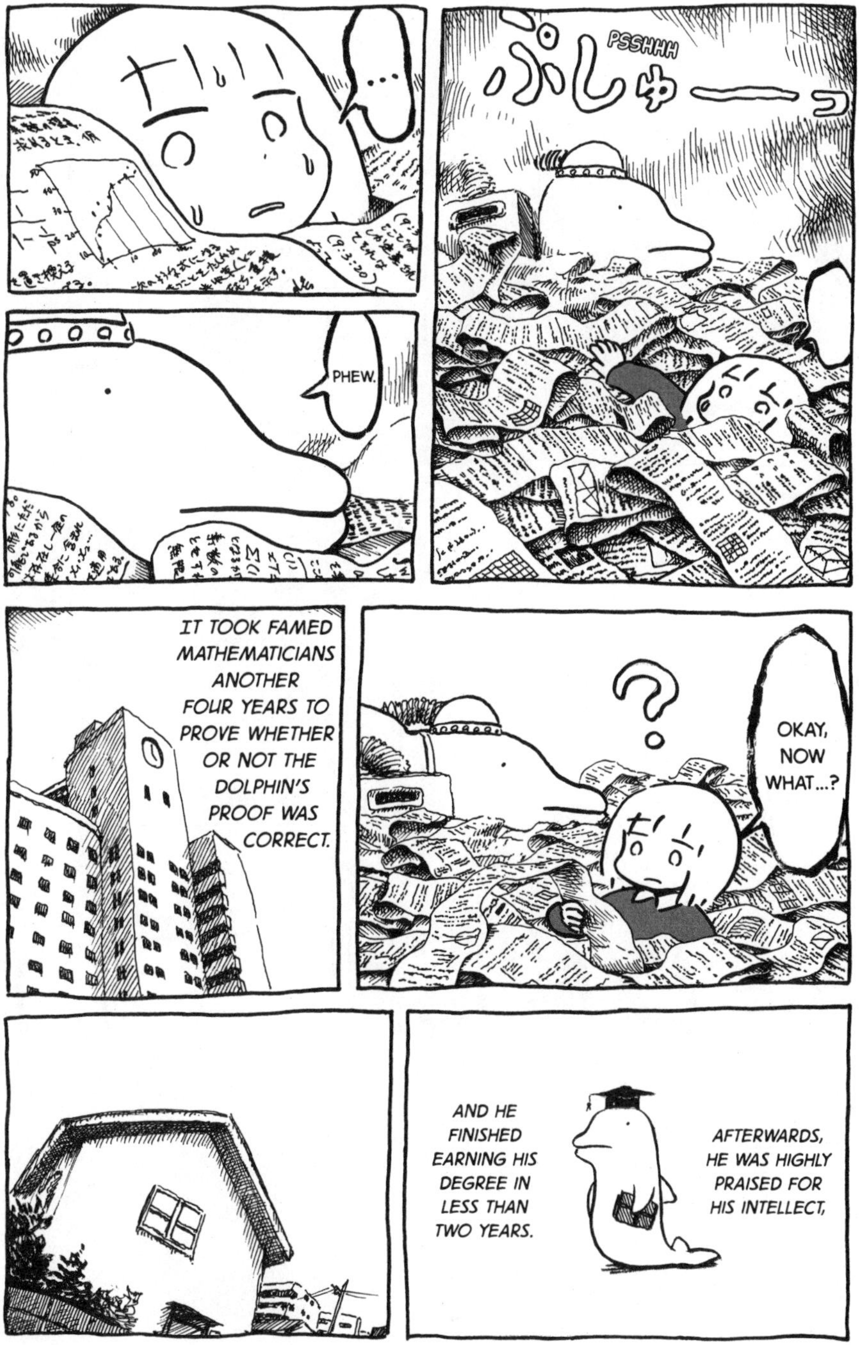

PSSHHH
ぷしゅーーっ
...
PHEW.
?
OKAY, NOW WHAT...?
IT TOOK FAMED MATHEMATICIANS ANOTHER FOUR YEARS TO PROVE WHETHER OR NOT THE DOLPHIN'S PROOF WAS CORRECT.
AFTERWARDS, HE WAS HIGHLY PRAISED FOR HIS INTELLECT,
AND HE FINISHED EARNING HIS DEGREE IN LESS THAN TWO YEARS.

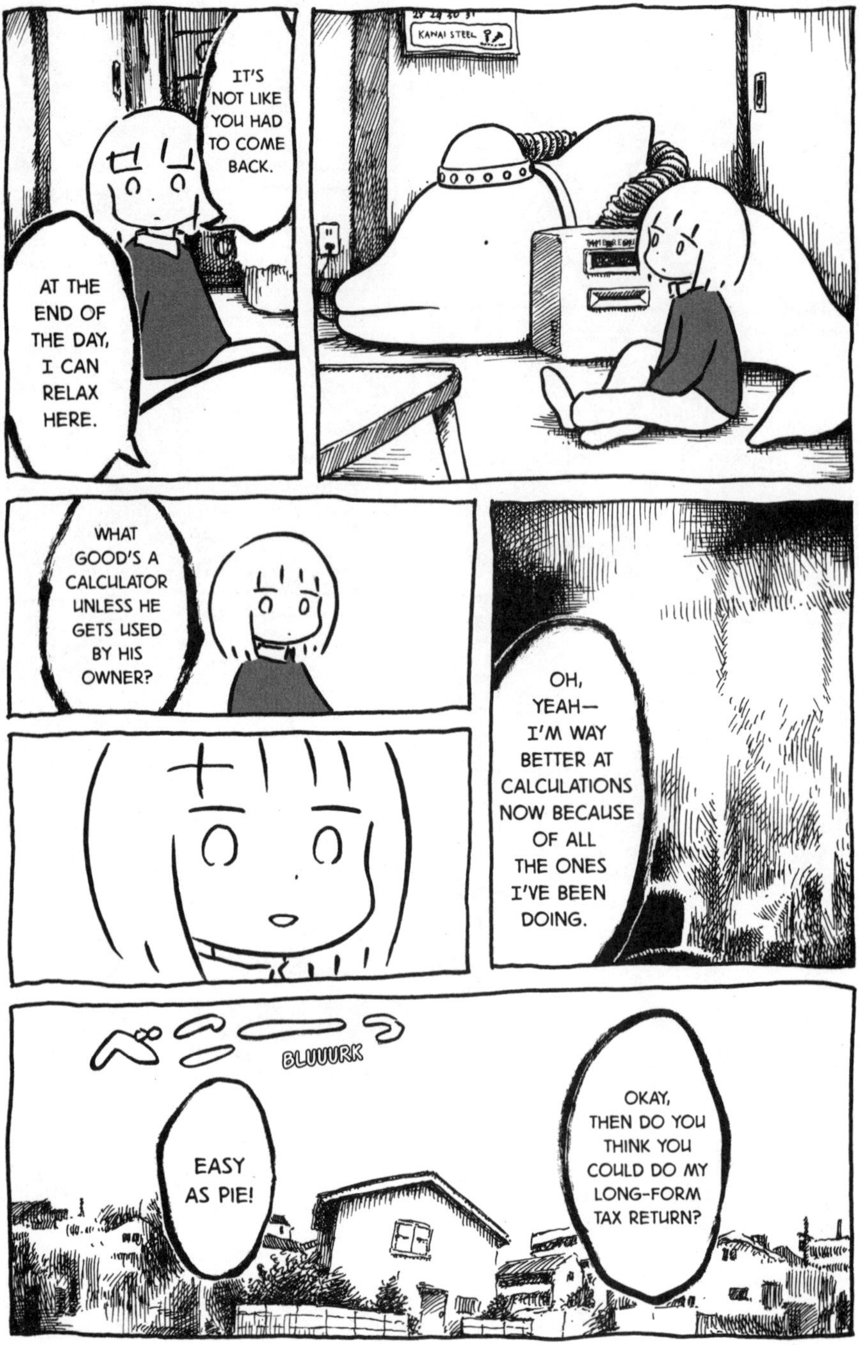
KANAI STEEL
IT'S NOT LIKE YOU HAD TO COME BACK.
AT THE END OF THE DAY, I CAN RELAX HERE.
OH, YEAH— I'M WAY BETTER AT CALCULATIONS NOW BECAUSE OF ALL THE ONES I'VE BEEN DOING.
WHAT GOOD'S A CALCULATOR UNLESS HE GETS USED BY HIS OWNER?
BLUUURK
OKAY, THEN DO YOU THINK YOU COULD DO MY LONG-FORM TAX RETURN?
EASY AS PIE!

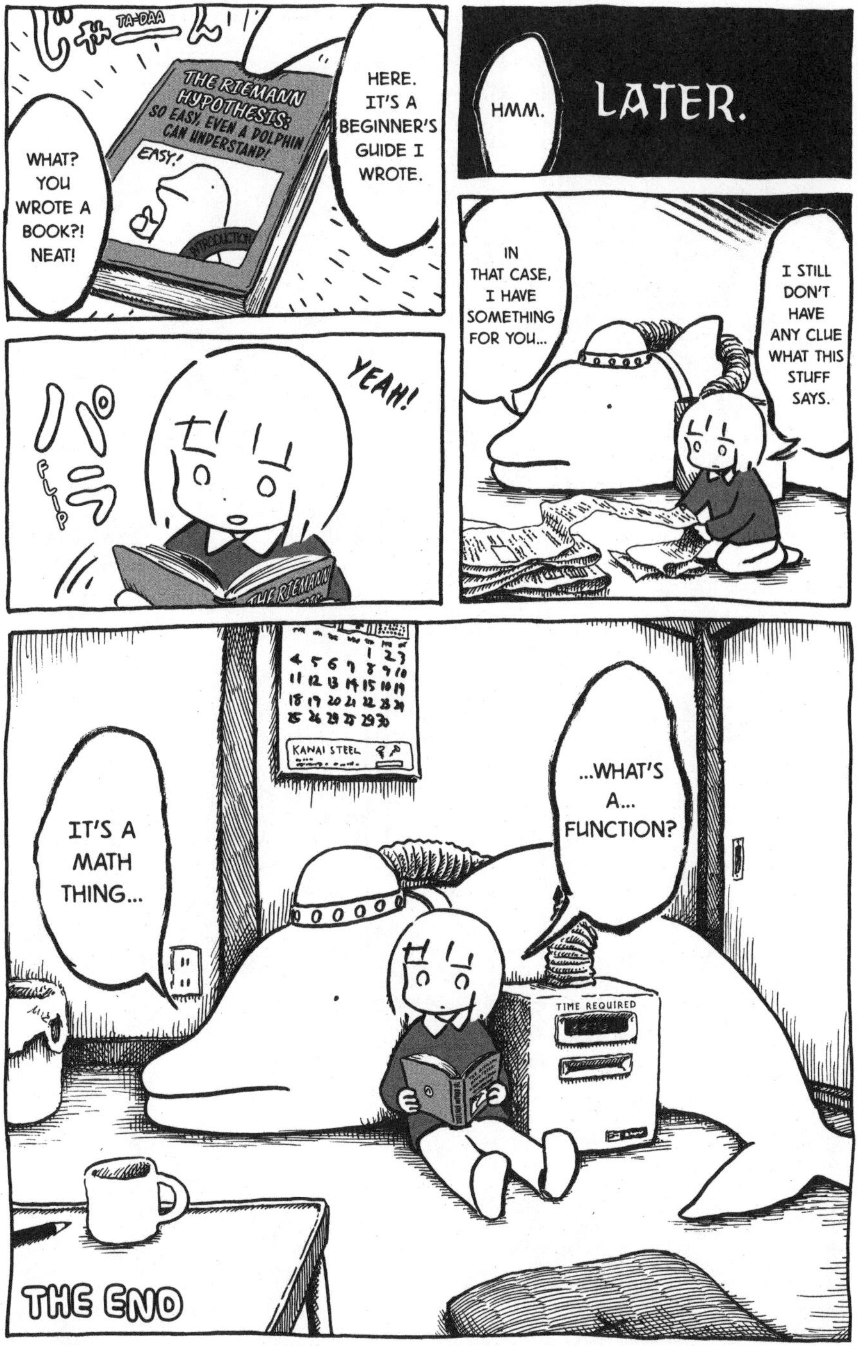
LATER.
HMM.
I STILL DON'T HAVE ANY CLUE WHAT THIS STUFF SAYS.
IN THAT CASE, I HAVE SOMETHING FOR YOU...
じゃーん
TA-DAA
THE RIEMANN HYPOTHESIS: SO EASY, EVEN A DOLPHIN CAN UNDERSTAND!
EASY!
INTRODUCTION
HERE. IT'S A BEGINNER'S GUIDE I WROTE.
WHAT? YOU WROTE A BOOK?! NEAT!
YEAH!
パラ
FLIP
THE RIEMANN
KANAI STEEL
TIME REQUIRED
...WHAT'S A... FUNCTION?
IT'S A MATH THING...
THE END

Strange Things Exist

There's no such thing as something that exists without a reason or a cause. Structures or products were created by someone somewhere, and living creatures were all born and raised in some location themselves.

A wild animal that appears out of seemingly nowhere.
An electronic product that you wonder who would ever buy.
A ramp on the side of the road that seems to have been placed there for no reason.
An untraceable rumor.
A ghost.
A pointless seeming disclaimer.
A dog that howls every week, but only on Mondays…

No matter how strange something may be, it's being produced by someone or something. Whether it's someone's intentions, their failures, or just coincidence, it's possible to explain their true form in one way or another.

Other times, when you're thinking about things, the thought of something strange, whose reason or cause or origin seems unclear, might suddenly pop into your head. You might go to sleep and dream up an incoherent dream. While we might call these flashes of inspiration when they're positive, they don't mean anything for the most part.

Whatever the case, they often don't have much to do directly with our real life (you can generally understand the reason for something if it has something to do with you directly), so they end up kind of fading away as they leave you not fully satisfied.

Lately, I've started to feel like this is kind of a waste. I think about how I can make sense of these thoughts before forgetting them. I think about the true form of every strange thing I encounter now, but it only seems to make them harder to understand as new, unclear ideas spring into my mind. Even so, I feel like part of me enjoys these vague and pointless thoughts.

April 25, 2014

El-Go

Gr-Ko

INDEX

Aa-Ca

Ca-Eg

Sn-Te

Te-Zz

INDEX

La-Po

Po-Sn

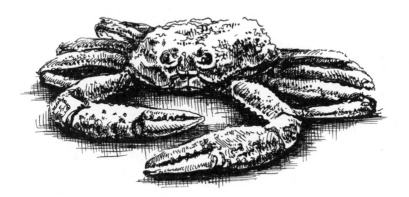

*promotional book cover

CRAB

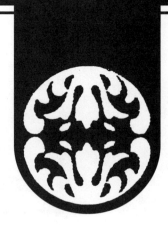

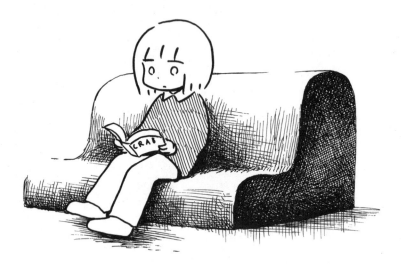

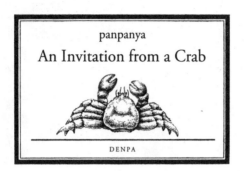

panpanya

An Invitation from a Crab

DENPA

Translator: Ko Ransom
Production: Nicole Dochych

KANI NI SASOWARETE by panpanya
© panpanya 2014
All rights reserved.
First published in Japan in 2014 by HAKUSENSHA, INC., Tokyo.
English language translation rights arranged with HAKUSENSHA, INC.
through Tuttle-Mori Agency, Inc., Tokyo.
Published in English by Denpa, LLC., Portland, Oregon, 2018.

Originally published in Japanese as *Kani ni Sasowarete* by HAKUSENSHA, Inc., 2014.
An Invitation from a Crab partially serialized in *Rakuen*, HAKUSENSHA, Inc., 2013-2014.

This is a work of fiction.

ISBN-13: 978-1-63442-920-7

Printed in the USA

First Edition

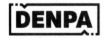

Denpa, LLC.
625 NW 17th Ave
Portland, OR 97209
www.denpa.pub